Prey Upon the Lambs

THE WOLVES OF KALININ BOOK 1

JACK FINN

ANUCI PRESS

First paperback edition 2025

Anuci Press edition 2025

www.anuci-press.com

CoverDesign by Ruth Anna Evans

ruthannaevans.com (google.com)

ISBN 979-8-9926529-0-1 (paperback)

ISBN 979-8-9926529-1-8 (eBook)

Prey Upon the Lambs

The Wolves of Kalinin

Book 1

Jack Finn

For Roxana, my inspiration for all things great and small.

"*All stories are about wolves. All worth repeating, that is. Anything else is sentimental drivel....Think about it. There's escaping from the wolves, fighting the wolves, capturing the wolves, taming the wolves. Being thrown to the wolves, or throwing others to the wolves so the wolves will eat them instead of you. Running with the wolf pack. Turning into a wolf. Best of all, turning into the head wolf. No other decent stories exist.*"

  • *Margaret Atwood*

"*If you are afraid of wolves...stay out of the forest.*"
- *Russian Proverb.*

Chapter 1

The Farmer

The farmer awoke suddenly as the violent spasms of his lungs devolved into a hacking cough. He rolled onto his side, one arm pressed against his chest as if trying to hold the shattered remnants of a glass figurine together, a hand bringing the stained rag to his lips to catch the flecks of greenish mucus and blood. With eyes clenched shut and teeth gritted against the pain, the farmer rode out the convulsing of his lungs until the needling pain subsided.

Wiping the red-green spittle from his lips, the man slowly gasped. As the dank air of the room gradually found its way into his tattered lungs, he reached a calloused hand out to feel the empty place beside him on the bed. The thin, coarse sheet covering the bed was cold; his wife had been up for some time as he slumbered. A pang of guilt twinged his heart; the ravages of the wasting illness had been even less kind to his wife.

The farmer rolled onto his back and stared up at the cottage's thatched roof. He had slept in his clothes again, a futile attempt to chase away the chills accompanying the cold sweats that plagued him ceaselessly now. The light streaming through the cracked bedroom shutters was bright enough for him to know he had slept well into the morning. His hand ran over his dark beard in frustration; he should have been up with the dawn preparing food for his wife, letting his love sleep and conserve what little energy the illness afforded her.

He stood on unsteady legs, fighting the swooning feeling as his illness-ravaged body sputtered into motion. The handful of steps from the bed to the door threatened to launch a new fit of coughing, but he managed to stifle it back as he walked into the cottage's main room.

The fragrant scent of herbs and vegetables filled his nostrils as he entered the room. The cottage was simple, even by the village's humble standards, and little changed from the days of the old widow he had purchased it from a decade ago. Animal woodcarvings sat growing dusty on shelves, carved in happier times. The rough-hewn wooden table where he would place a fresh bouquet from the field every Sunday now sat empty and bare.

Sadness pinched his heart at the sight of the bare table. He and his wife had laughed for hours seated at that table before the illness came. His eyes drifted to the figure hunched over the stew pot cooking over the hearth fire. The woman's once delicate fingers, now boney and branch-like, sprinkled a dried green herb into the stew.

"Good morning," the farmer hated the raspy sound of his voice but tried to fill it with as much cheer as he could muster.

The woman turned from her ministrations, a weak smile spreading across her face, creasing the skin around her dark, sunken eyes. Her soft white skin had sallowed with illness, and a sheen of sweat prickled her forehead. She self-consciously tried to fix her hair as he crossed the room to her.

The farmer smiled warmly at her, brushing a wayward strand of dark hair from her face and tucking it behind her ear.

"I must look a fright," she looked away from him and back toward the pot of steaming stew.

"You look beautiful, Ana," he gently turned her to face him and, kissing her tenderly on her lips, pulled her into a close embrace. "You should have stayed in bed with me; the roosters have barely been awake."

"This is why my father said you would make a terrible farmer," she giggled softly into his chest. "You enjoy your sleep too much; the roosters have been up for hours!"

"With such a pretty wife," the farmer nuzzled his chin against the top of her head, "what man would want to spring out of bed in the morning?"

"You're going to make me burn the giveche," she patted him lightly on the chest and turned back to stir the boiling pot of vegetables.

"Giveche, so late in the year?" the farmer raised an eyebrow in surprise.

"Yes, I took some of the tomatoes and peppers we stored for the winter," she refused to meet his gaze.

The farmer bit his lip to hold back the wave of despair that rose inside him. The thought left unspoken between them. The illness would take them both long before the dark days of winter could.

"It smells delicious," the farmer wrapped an arm around her waist and kissed her cheek. "I'll be right back."

"Are you off to tend to those chickens again?" she shot him a glance. "The last time, you coughed yourself unconscious..."

"No, the chickens can tend to themselves today," he winked at her as he shuffled to the door. "I saw some crocus poking up by the barn the other day, and I thought I would pick a bouquet for the table."

The farmer slipped out the door into the sunlight before she could protest further. The autumn air felt brisk against his skin as the farmer raised his face to the sky, letting the sun's warmth chase the coolness away. He loved the smell of fall as the winds blew down from the mountains and carried the scent of the change of seasons into the lowlands.

The farmer breathed in deeply, filling his lungs with the cool air and his nostrils with the fragrance of wet leaves and dried branches. It was a moment of resplendent joy, far removed from the odor of sickness that hung about him these days. However, the moment quickly slipped away as the air filled the tattered ruin of his lungs, causing his chest to heave in violent spasms. He wrapped his arms around his ribs in a futile effort to ward off the searing corset of pain that squeezed his body with every hacking cough.

His eyes blurred with tears as he fell to his knees, gasping desperately for air as the rolling tide of coughs continued unabated. Spittle shot forth from his mouth, spraying the dark earth with droplets of blood and gobs of phlegm. The farmer saw darkness creeping around the corners of his vision, and he struggled to remain conscious.

Stupid, stupid, stupid, the farmer silently chastised himself for attempting such a deep breath. Just needed to take it slow, pick the flowers, and get back to Ana.

He tried clenching his teeth to hold back the coughing, but the foul air pushed through his teeth and out his nose, leaving long strings of mucus swinging from his upper lip and the metallic taste of blood filling his mouth. The farmer toppled to the ground and rolled onto his side, curling into a fetal position until the barrage of coughing subsided.

His body wanted to gasp in mouthfuls of air, however, the farmer fought back the urge for fear of bringing on another coughing fit. The little air that slipped into his chest felt like burning coals in his frayed lungs. The farmer lay as still as possible until his breathing normalized, then slowly sat up. He brushed the leaves and dirt from his hair and beard with shaking hands.

The farmer slowly got to his feet, half walking and shuffling toward the small purple patch of crocus flowers poking up alongside the barn. He pulled his sheepskin coat close across the chest, warding off the cold as ragged white clouds of breath puffed from his mouth, threatening a new round of hacking.

He stared at the bright lavender flowers growing low to the ground beside the barn. It was early for crocus to bloom; they were typically a late winter to early spring flower, where they could provide early food for bees. The farmer smiled sadly at the three delicate flowers. They were Ana's favorite. He knew neither of them would live long enough to see the spring blooms, so these three tiny miracle blossoms were a cherished gift.

The farmer bent gingerly down and plucked the three flowers with great care not to jostle loose any of the lavender petals. He cradled them protectively against his chest as he headed back to the house, thoughts of Ana's joy at seeing the crocus warming the chill from his body.

Was that like that before? The farmer's eye caught a glimpse of the barn door slightly ajar. *I could have sworn that was closed when I passed a moment ago.*

With a sigh at the thought of deviating from his path, the farmer slowly shuffled toward the barn. This time of year, predators would come down from the mountains hungry and looking for an easy meal. With the barn door open, his meager flock of chickens would make a tasty morsel for an adventurous fox or wandering bear.

The farmer stopped and peered into the darkness of the barn. Were his eyes playing tricks on him, or had he just seen something large moving within, concealed within the darkness of the doorway? He squinted as he slowly moved forward, trying to catch the outline of the dark shape again.

As the farmer neared the door, a person-sized shadow retreated quickly into the barn's shadows. A startled gasp escaped his lips, coming so suddenly that it nearly brought a renewed barrage of coughing.

"Who's there?" the farmer rasped as he fought back his body's urge to cough.

He could hear something moving within the barn, causing the chickens to cluck noisily at the disturbance.

"Come now, who's in there?" the farmer placed a shaky hand upon the barn door and swung it wide.

Sunlight streamed into the barn, illuminating the darkness as a dozen chickens eagerly rushed out to forage in the daylight. The farmer frowned as a lavender crocus petal fell free of the flower and glided slowly to the ground. A skinny brown hen pecked at the delicate leaf as soon as it touched the ground.

The farmer shuffled forward into the barn, annoyed that this interloper had caused such a desecration to one of the flowers. His eyes scanned the empty stalls and meager stack of grain stores for the intruder.

"I have no time for games," the farmer wheezed, failing to keep the anger from his voice. "Who's in here?"

"I mean you no trouble, friend," a strangely accented voice called from a darkened stall to the farmer's left.

"Who are you?" the farmer stared into the blackened stall and could detect the faintest outline of the man standing within.

"I am just a traveler passing through," the man stepped forward so that a band of sunshine coming through one of the barn shutters cast a slash of light across his eyes and face. "I sought a room in the village last night, but all turned me away. It was very late when I reached your farm; I was cold and merely sought shelter in your barn for the night. I assure you I have caused no damage or theft."

"Yes. The people around here, they... well, they can be less than hospitable to strangers," the farmer gave a mirthless laugh that triggered a wracking cough that doubled him over.

"Sir, are you okay?" the stranger stepped forward but halted as the farmer raised a warning hand.

"Stay back," the farmer coughed a bloody wad onto the floor and braced himself against the doorway when the coughing mercifully subsided. "I am not well. My wife and I have consumption."

"I am sorry. Is there anything I can do for you?" the stranger's blue eyes studied the farmer with genuine concern.

The farmer overturned an empty bucket and sat down on it with a sigh. "No, there is nothing..." he paused as sudden emotion flared up and tightened his throat.

A silence passed between the two men as the farmer stared quietly at the floor, lost in thoughts of his mortality.

"My good man, were you a soldier?" the stranger gestured to an old rifle hanging covered in dust and cobwebs beside the barn entrance.

"Once, long ago," the farmer glanced at the rifle and smiled faintly. "Ana cannot stand the sight of the thing, so I have kept it out here all these years."

"I was a soldier myself," the stranger crossed his arms and leaned against the stall wall, still concealed by the shadows. "Where did you serve?"

"I fought with Prince Vlad and King Carol against the Turks at the Battle of Pleven," the farmer straightened up and squared his shoulders with pride. "The Russians broke and ran, but we pushed the Turks back and took the city. It was a bloody day; we fought them hand to hand all across that red field and through the gates of that cursed city. We lost some good boys that day—some real goddamn good boys.

"I spent the coin I earned there to buy this farm about ten years back. I cannot say I ever amounted to much of a farmer, but we had a good life here."

The farmer brought his hand to his mouth, grimacing as he stifled a cough. The stranger stepped from the darkness and squatted across from the farmer. The man was tall and dressed in a dyed green wool shirt and brown leather trousers common to foresters. He stroked his trimmed blonde beard and studied the farmer with pale, blue intense eyes.

"You should keep your distance," the farmer spat a wad of phlegm that the stranger could see was flecked with blood. "This cursed plague is contagious."

"I have a rather strong constitution," the stranger flashed a half-smile of bright white teeth. "How long have you had it?"

"Ana came down with it first; caught it in the village, I think," the farmer looked long at the house. "I got the cough a few weeks later. We're close to the end of it now."

"Those for her?" the stranger smiled and gestured toward the crocus.

The farmer chuckled as he looked at the lavender flowers, "Yes, they are her favorite. I almost forgot I was holding them."

"Where I am from, that flower grows white petals with dark purple stripes," the stranger smiled in a way that made his face look warm and welcoming.

"And where exactly is that?" the farmer wheezed out the words, the conversation taxing his frail lungs. "I can tell from your accent you are not from these parts."

"I am from Ireland, though it has been a long time since I set foot on her blessed shores," the stranger leaned his head back against the wall and stared at the farmer through slitted eyes. "I came with the Eighty-Ninth Regiment of Foot, Princess Victoria's Regiment, to fight the Russians in the Crimea. We landed with nearly seven hundred men in December of fifty-four; the winter was so harsh that we lost almost a hundred men to the cold and sickness before we even attacked Sebastopol.

"When the fighting came our way, the Russians poured into our trenches. We fired our weapons point-blank into their faces, but still, they came at us. We stabbed at them with our bayonets; the trench was so thick with Russians that I would slide my bayonet out of one and dash the brains out of another with the butt of my rifle. Some men dropped their rifles and fought the bastards with their fists. It was a bloody affair."

The two men sat silently for a moment, both lost in the thoughts of their violent past.

"Do you know what I remember most?" the stranger gave the farmer a wry smile. "The coffee."

"The coffee?" the farmer's eyebrows shot up in surprise, and his outburst nearly brought on a coughing fit.

"Yes, the coffee," the stranger said, picking up a strand of hay and twisting it in his fingers as he spoke. "They would give us these green coffee beans, and we would pour them onto a trench shovel and roast them over the campfire."

"We would pound those roasted beans up real well," the stranger made a pounding motion with his fist, "then throw them in boiling water and drink it with our biscuits."

"Was it any good?" the farmer stared intently at the stranger.

"It tasted like donkey piss," the stranger broke into a barking laugh.

The farmer found the stranger's laugh infectious and joined in the laughter, careful not to elicit a fresh round of coughing. Then, the laughter died on his lips, and the farmer gave the stranger a severe look.

"Something wrong, friend?" the stranger's grin only lessened slightly at the sight of the farmer's harsh stare.

"The battle of Sebastopol was over thirty years ago," the farmer squinted his eyes at the stranger. "You look barely a few years older than me."

"I will take that as a compliment," the stranger grinned broadly and winked. "I reach my sixty-fifth year this winter. I told you, I have a robust constitution."

I guess it's possible, the farmer thought as he eyed the stranger, noting the creases around the man's eyes and the gray flecks in his blonde beard. All the men he met who lived into their sixties had lived hard lives, and it showed on their faces. This man looked very well-kept and had soft, nimble fingers, not the coarse, calloused digits of a man accustomed to hard work and rough living.

"You have been very hospitable to me, and I am dreadfully sorry to have given you a scare, holding up here unannounced in your barn," the stranger reached into the pouch at his waist and produced a shiny silver coin. "I would like to pay you for my night's stay."

"That's not necessary," the farmer waved the offered coin away. "I am afraid my wife and I no longer have much need of coin. But let me ask you, where are you headed from here?"

"I am headed west to France," the stranger shrugged. "If the winds prevail, I may head back to Ireland; see if any of my kin remain."

"The road to France will be long, and the winter weather will be quickly upon you," the farmer's voice was a low wheeze. "I will make you an offer."

"Oh, what's that?" the stranger raised an eyebrow and flicked away the twisted strand of hay.

"You can winter here in my barn. There will be plenty of fresh eggs from the chickens, and I have stores of vegetables and dried meats in the loft," the farmer pointed toward the ladder going to the barn's loft. "We have a well with fresh water, and I have a cow out in the pasture that will give you good warm milk. Come spring, you can trade her for a mule to get you to France faster than walking on your two feet."

"Sir," the stranger held his hand over his heart and gave the farmer a look of disbelief, "you would show such kindness to a stranger? We do not even know each other's names."

"I told you it was an offer," the farmer raised a finger, then pointed at the stranger. "I want something from you in return."

The stranger met the farmer's gaze. "I would give you anything in my possession."

"Each morning, I want you to bring two eggs from the chickens and leave them on our doorstep," the farmer's eyes were sad and serious. "We're too ill to come to the barn any longer."

"I will do this for you, my friend," the stranger nodded enthusiastically.

"However, a day will come when we do not collect the eggs," the farmer bit his lip to hold back the emotion. "When seven days have passed that we have not taken the eggs, I want you to set the house on fire."

The stranger began to protest, but the farmer cut him off.

"Ana and I do not want to be buried in the cold ground, food for worms and crawly things. We want our bodies burned to drift together as smoke on the wind until the end of time. I need you to promise you will do this thing for me."

The stranger nodded again, "I will do this for you."

"Good," the farmer nodded and slowly rose to his feet. "What is your name, friend?"

"My name is Nobody. My father and mother, all my other friends, they call me Nobody," the stranger punctuated the sentence with a theatrical flourishing wave of his hand.

"What?" The farmer's face screwed into a look of bewilderment.

"I am just jesting with you," the stranger chuckled. "It was a line from a play I once saw in England. It was the Greek warrior's response to a monster when the creature asked his name."

"Oh," the farmer thought on it for a moment. "What did the monster do?"

"It threatened to eat the warrior," the stranger winked and gave the farmer a broad grin. "Based upon the nature of our arrangement, I will call you my friend in the house, and I will be your friend in the barn.

The farmer shrugged his shoulders, "Then it is time for me to get these flowers inside before Ana starts to worry."

"You are a very kind and generous man," the stranger rose to his feet and bowed slightly to the farmer. "I wish life had been kinder than to bestow this fate upon you."

"Thank you," the farmer smiled and nodded as he shuffled toward the house, leaving the stranger in the barn doorway. "I do as well."

The farmer glanced down at the three flowers as he walked, smiling as he imagined his wife's joy. The morning encounter with the stranger had tired him more than he wanted to admit, and his breath had slipped into furtive gasps by the time he was halfway to the house and stopped for a moment.

He could smell the aroma of the giveche wafting up from the hearth fire, and his stomach rumbled loudly. The farmer let out a breath and willed his legs to continue the rest of the way to the house. He glanced over his shoulder; the stranger had retired into the barn, leaving the sun above as the solitary witness to his trek back to the house.

As his foot crunched down upon the soft earth, something large and powerful crashed into his back, driving him to the ground. The air fled his lungs in a whoosh, and he immediately descended into a violent spasm of coughs as his mind raced to understand what had happened.

A strong, musky smell assailed his nostrils as the weight of something heavy pressed down upon his back. A thickly muscled, dark-furred leg stepped beside his face; the huge paw bore long, tapered fingers tipped with black claws. The human-like appendage looked unnatural, sprouting from the end of the lupine leg. The farmer felt the creature's hot breath upon his neck as his body continued to betray him with deep, wracking coughs. Through eyes blurry with tears, the farmer looked over his shoulder, and a strangled cry escaped his blood and phlegm-covered lips.

An immense black wolf, his muzzle reared back in a snarl that revealed a mountain range of sharp teeth, glared down at him with coal-black eyes. The farmer struggled against the beast's imposing weight, but his illness-ravaged body could not muster the strength to dislodge the wolf.

Saliva dripped from the wolf's mouth and landed warmly on the farmer's cheek. The crushing weight of the beast on his back compressed his chest so that even a cough could no longer escape. He lay there, gasping, his body trembling with fear and his eyes filling with tears as the wolf lowered its head close to his neck.

The farmer's eyes were momentarily distracted by a splash of bright color as they fell upon the crushed form of the three flowers, stems broken and petals scattered.

Ana is going to be so disappointed, the thought felt distant in his mind as the wolf's jaws clamped down on the soft flesh between his shoulder and neck.

***

The farmer's eyes fluttered open. A warm stickiness felt slick upon his face. He felt distant and detached from the world, a throbbing pain pulsing from the wolf's savage bite on his shoulder. Moving slowly to avoid attracting the beast's attention if it was still near, he glanced down at his shoulder. His sheepskin jacket had torn away, exposing his pale skin to the autumn air. Deep, circular punctures in his skin oozed thick, dark rivers of blood and marked the outline of the wolf's massive jaws. The farmer was surprised that his skin was not torn and ravaged by the beast; the bite mark was deep but clean.

Through the haze enshrouding his mind, the strangeness of the attack seeped through. He had never heard of a wolf biting someone and running away like a stray dog. Wolves tore flesh from bone and feasted upon their kills. Yet, here he was, wounded, stricken down, and helpless but otherwise free of the wolf's savagery.

Had someone chased the wolf away? Ana? The stranger in the barn?

A scream shattered the thick fog of his consciousness.

The wolf. Ana.

Thoughts came rushing through his mind in a torrent. He lifted his head, and thick rivulets of blood ran from his face and pooled on the ground. Pain surged up his shoulder and neck, threatening to jolt him back into unconsciousness. A burning sensation coursed through his body, and his limbs felt leaden as he willed them to move.

There was another scream, terrified and woeful in its despair, and he let out an anguished cry for Ana. He looked toward the house, where the thick wooden door of their home stood ajar.

Where was the man in the barn? He must have heard the wolf's attack.

The sounds of a struggle from within the house reached his ears, and he reached out with his right hand and pulled his body toward the open door. His left arm and shoulder hung uselessly at his side as he pushed with what strength remained in his legs. The burning feeling increased in intensity as if his blood was boiling in his veins. His eyeballs felt like they were cooking inside his head, and he gritted his teeth against the pain, pushing himself onward.

The farmer wept openly at the sound of his wife's violent struggle against the beast as he dragged himself across the ground. Thick smears of blood trailed behind his ruined body. He blew droplets of blood and spit from his mouth as he edged closer to the house, thankful only that a fresh wave of coughing did not waylay him.

I'm coming, Ana. The thought seared his brain and drove his body forward.

The farmer reached his hand across the stone entranceway to the house, a threshold that always marked being home safe, and pulled himself up. His eyes opened wide in disbelief and terror as he beheld the wolf, standing on its hind legs like a man. Ana lay sprawled across the wooden table; her eyes rolled back in her head, white and sightless like two chicken eggs.

The wolf clutched her in its two large front paws and raised her to a sitting position, her head lolled forward lifelessly, exposing the pale white skin of her neck to the beast. The farmer had always laid gentle kisses and caresses on that spot, eliciting his wife's mischievous smiles in happier times.

As black as night, the wolf's eyes stared at the farmer. Blood rimmed its lips and matted the fur of its muzzle. His blood, the farmer realized, as he glimpsed his terrified face reflected in the creature's dark eyes.

"Don't you hurt her," the farmer meant to scream the words with enough force to shake the heavens, however, they came out as a weak, pitiful rasp.

The wolf's nostrils flared as it opened its jaws, blood and saliva hanging down from the jagged points of its teeth. The hearth fire glinted off the creature's four long canines, teeth designed to rip and rend prey, already crimson with blood. Its eyes locked with the farmer's as it closed its jaws down upon the crook of Ana's neck, its muzzle awash in a sudden spray of blood.

Chapter 2

Galina's pale blue eyes watched the smooth white skin of Mali's back disappear beneath the soft, red fabric of the dress. She pouted her full lips as she leaned on her elbow, sitting up in bed just far enough for the sheet to slide down to reveal the complete circle of her pink nipple.

"Mal," Galina tried to make her voice soft and seductive as she slid her hair over her shoulder so that the view of her breast was unobstructed by the dark strands.

Mali turned as her fingers nimbly fastened the ornate gold buttons on the front of the dress, mouth poised to speak when she caught sight of Galina's nakedness. Her eyes opened so wide Galina could see her dark pupils surrounded by white. Galina flashed the woman a mischievous smile.

"Galina, you are a villain," Mali grabbed one of the pillows from the bed and tossed it at Galina. "You know I have to go."

"Why do you have to go so soon?" Galina snatched the pillow from the air and held it close against her chest. "Stay, and we will get drunk and make love under the stars like we used to."

"Because I have responsibilities, Galina," Mali sighed and sat down on the edge of the bed, resting her hand on Galina's thigh with a gentle squeeze. "We're not sixteen-year-old girls in the court of the Tsar anymore. Those carefree days are gone. We're twenty years old and..."

"And now you are the Countess of Kalinin. Yes, I know," Galina pressed her back against the wooden headboard and clutched the pillow tightly, giving Mali a sideways glance. "You need to go running home to him."

"Don't you start with that; you know there is no affection between Gennady and I," Mali's eyebrows furrowed with annoyance, and then her face softened. "Ours is a marriage of convenience, joining our two families to stand stronger in the eyes of the Tsar."

"Now you even sound like him," Galina shook her head.

"Galina, you know that you are my love. My only love," Mali slowly rubbed her hand over Galina's leg, feeling the delicate contours through the soft sheet.

"And you do not share a bed with him?" the pout returned to Galina's lips.

"I've told you a thousand times, my love, we do not share a bed," Mali stared into Galina's blue eyes and smiled.

Galina reluctantly felt a smile cross her lips; she could never resist Mali's smile. Not since the first time she saw it as they sat, almost half a decade ago, listening to the Grand Duchess instruct the young ladies of the court on the proper etiquette when asked to dance at a royal function. Their eyes had met, and Galina detected a mischievous longing there that she had only seen when she looked at her own reflection.

They had become fast friends that day and quickly inseparable. Both women were young, beautiful daughters of wealthy boyars; however, where Galina was shy and introverted, Mali was outgoing and gregarious. Galina often felt like a weed growing in the shadow of Mali's blooming rose bush as the young men of the Tsar's court vied for the girl's attention.

She would watch as Mali effortlessly navigated her way through the petty social politics of the court, living for those moments when Mali would cast her a long glance or a secret smile. Galina's heart swelled with love and desire for her best friend and buried deep the fear of losing her if she made her feelings known.

In the evenings, they would sneak into each other's room to trade gossip and laugh at the happenings of the day. The proximity of Mali's body as they talked well into the night excited Galina in a way none of the courtships by the sons of boyars and nobles ever did. She hung upon every word that Mali spoke, memorized every movement of her face and look of her eyes.

Their friendship was the source of the greatest joy and pain Galina had ever known.

Sometimes, the longing for Mali would overcome her, and Galina would break, crying in her room. Mali would find her and wipe away her tears, as Galina lied and blamed the sorrow on a heartbreak caused by one of the boys in court.

Until that night, when they had lain in bed and Galina relayed a particular salacious story she had heard about the Grand Duchess' seamstress and one the cooks. Mali leaned over and stroked Galina's face gently as she pressed her thin lips against the fullness of Galina's mouth.

Galina stared at Mali in utter surprise, registering the fear of a line overstepped in her friend's eyes. Mali tried to slip out of bed in embarrassment; however, Galina stopped her and pulled her close. She kissed Mali on the lips, infusing the kiss with every pent-up wanting and desire she had hidden since they met. Galina's heart leaped at the reciprocity of Mali's kiss, and her body echoed the sentiment.

The two friends crossed the threshold into lovers as they enjoyed the unbridled intimacy of each other's bodies. After that night, every glance and smile from Mali took on new meaning for Galina, hints of the forbidden love and desire they shared only for each other. Galina would smirk as noblemen courted Mali, desperate to have what Mali only gave to her in the warmth of their nightly embrace, until Gennady.

Galina's smile faded, and her blue eyes clouded with sadness, "Bring me back to Kalinin; I can come live with you. You can tell Gennady that you are a patron of the arts, and your old artist friend Galina will come stay with you and paint."

"Galina," Mali's shoulders sagged, and she looked down at the bed.

"Mali, I can sneak into your room at night." Galina grasped her friend's hand and dipped her head to stare into Mali's face. "Things will be just the way they were."

"Galina, Gennady may hold no affection for me," Mali looked at Galina with dark, melancholy eyes, "but he is a proud man. If he discovered I had taken a lover under his roof..." Her words trailed off as she shook her head.

"So, you'll keep me locked away in this prison in the woods," Galina released Mali's hand and let a coldness creep into her voice.

"Prison?" Mali stood and looked around the room. "This cottage is lovely. I make sure you have the finest things, food, and money. You want for nothing."

"I want for you," tears streamed down Galina's cheeks.

"You have me," Mali shook her head. "All those nights we sat up talking, you dreamed of living away from court. A place where you can paint all day. Look at how your talent has flourished out here." Mali crossed the room to look at the painting on the easel: a lifelike owl perched upon a branch in the moonlight, the feathers so realistic they appeared to flutter in the evening breeze.

"Those were dreams of us. Together," Galina wiped away the tears with shaking hands. "I appreciate everything you have done for me, and this cottage is beautiful, but its guest room is forever unused. I have no friends; the villagers in Obrechen despise me. They see your carriage come and go and think that I am the concubine of some nobleman."

"You are no concubine, Galina," Mali sat on the bed, her hand gently wiping away the trail of Galina's tears. "You are a wonderful artist and my best friend."

"You are the love of my life," Galina struggled to hold back another wave of emotion. "I am so lonely out here. Every day, I live to hear word from you or see your carriage coming down the road."

"And you are mine," Mali smiled, then leaned forward and kissed Galina softly. Her lips were soft and salty from the tears. "I will ask Gennady if my artist friend can stay with us."

"Really?" Galina's heart swelled with joy at the prospect.

"Really," Mali smiled so broadly the corners of her eyes creased. "Now, come see me off. I must return to Kalinin before nightfall."

***

Jacob ran gnarled fingers through his beard; the flowing gray hairs now easily reached the top button of his coachman's uniform. He was aware that stroking the coarse hairs through his fingers had become a nervous habit over the years, and his wife often chided him that if he continued, his chin would become as bald as the top of his head.

The coachman squinted at the sun, deepening the lines around the eyes in his weathered face, and shifted his weight on the riding board of the Countess' carriage. The sun was getting low in the sky, and unless they left soon, they would be hard-pressed to return to Kalinin by suppertime. The Countess' absence would raise questions, and Count Gennady Guriev was not a man to leave questions unanswered.

Jacob looked questioningly toward the cottage. The wooden door with its ornately carved birds, hummingbirds if his old, gray eyes did not betray him, sat closed and still. The Countess was always excited about her secret trips into the countryside, and the coachman was loathe to knock on the door to usher her home. He knew full well the joys and heartbreaks of forbidden love; his mind often strayed to those stolen nights with that young blacksmith a lifetime ago.

The Countess had told him the trips were to see an artist friend from childhood that Count Guriev disapproved of because of the revolutionary nature of her paintings. However, Jacob recognized the smile on the Countess' face and the look of fond memories replaying in her mind when they journeyed home from the cottage. He often made the trip alone to deliver missives or packages from the Countess to Galina, and when he did, the young lady would invite him in for tea and sweet bread. Jacob never claimed to be a consignor of the arts, but even he could see nothing revolutionary about the woman's paintings of birds and flowers. Both women were always kind to him, which was no small thing, and Galina gave him delicacies and fine gifts to bring home to his wife. The feeling of walking into his home and seeing the look on his wife's face when he handed her these things made him feel like a Tsar more than a coachman. For that, Jacob would keep the women's secret.

The white mare harnessed to the carriage blew a fierce snort of air from its nose and stomped its front hoof agitatedly, drawing Jacob's attention as the four large wheels of the carriage lurched forward.

"Whoah, girl. Easy. Easy," Jacob held firmly on the reigns and spoke soothingly to the horse.

The horse flared its dark nostrils and opened its jaws to expose a mouthful of large square teeth. Jacob noticed she held her tail high over her back and her ears pinned flat against her back. As the coachman struggled to calm the horse, he could see her eyes opening wide, showing the whites completely around the dark pools of her pupils. The horse's behavior alarmed him; Jacob had only seen this reaction in all his years around horses when danger was close at hand.

Jacob scanned the surrounding woods as the carriage jostled back and forth, mirroring the horse's movements.

Was there a faint musk in the air? Some predator straying close to the cottage, perhaps a wolf or a bear?

The coachman began to feel the horse's unease sinking deep into his bones. His steel gray eyes searched the forest for any movement as his ears strained to detect the slightest sound out of place. Something moved in the woods beyond the little clearing that surrounded the cottage; he felt certain. Yet his ears heard nothing; the forest had gone deathly quiet except for the heaving breaths of the mare. The birds had ceased their songs, and even the air suddenly felt still.

Jacob's eyes darted to a space between a tall green spruce tree and a tangle of thorny brambles as something large and black quickly passed the opening. He blinked rapidly, uncertain of what he had seen or if he had seen anything at all. The coachman knew that if you stared at the woods too long, your mind played tricks on you, seeing things that were not there.

Holding the reigns tightly with one hand and his eyes never straying from the forest, Jacob slowly reached behind the riding board. His fingers slipped inside a long folded blanket and searched until they closed around the smooth wooden stock of the shotgun. It was a precaution he kept to protect the Countess against brigands and highwaymen, though this was the first time he had ever had to take it out.

The coachman rested the shotgun in the cruck of the arm holding the reigns, his other hand running a finger over the cold steel of the trigger guard, ready to fire a shot at any approaching threat. The mare's snorting was coming rapidly, and Jacob had to hold the reigns fast to keep the horse from bolting. An innate sense within him told him the beast was watching him from behind a thick patch of brush directly in front of the carriage, and his body tensed for the confrontation.

"Jacob?" the woman's voice was a low gasp.

As the coachman turned toward the sound of the voice, the mare gave an abrupt snort and seemed to settle, her tail falling back down and her ears pricking up. The tension on the reigns slackened, and Jacob felt a light breeze brush the top of his bald head, which he only now realized was covered with beads of sweat.

The two women stood outside the cottage, the Countess in her red dress, her hair and makeup refreshed to mask her afternoon frolic. Beside her, Galina stood, holding a basket filled with bread and baked goods, in a delicate dark green dress that hinted at the shapely body beneath. Both women stared with bewilderment at the coachman, eyes wide and mouths questioning.

"Jacob, is everything alright?" the Countess placed a hand over her heart as if concern could stop it from beating.

The coachman glanced furtively around the clearing but sensed none of the impending danger of moments ago. He suddenly felt very self-conscious of the shotgun in his hands and quickly stowed it back behind the riding board.

"Jacob?" the Countess watched the coachman's behavior with increasing alarm.

"I'm sorry, ma'am," Jacob smiled and dipped his head in apology. "I seem to have spooked myself."

"That's quite alright, Jacob," Galina's smile was warm and welcoming. "I think I hear and see things out here all the time, especially when it gets dark."

"Are you sure it's safe?" the Countess glanced nervously toward the woods.

"Yes, Countess," Jacob nodded, stepping down from the carriage and unfolding the steps to the plush dark leather bench seat. He extended his hand, and the Countess stepped carefully up into the carriage, folding the hem of her dress underneath her as she sat.

"Jacob, I would like to ride home with the top up, please," the Countess still looked flustered as she gave Galina a weak smile. "Thank you for showing me your wonderful paintings, Galina. I do so look forward to joining you for lunch again soon."

"Of course, Countess. It was a very... delightful afternoon." Galina raised an eyebrow, a subtle hint of mischief, as she smiled and bowed her head. "You are welcome in my home anytime. Perhaps I will come to visit you next time."

"Yes, perhaps," the Countess smiled weakly at Galina, her face disappearing behind the dark, heavy fabric as Jacob unfolded the carriage's canopy.

"This is for your wife, Jacob," Galina passed the wicker basket handle to the coachman. "I added honey into the bread's dough just like she likes."

"Oh, thank you, Miss Galina," Jacob smiled as his eyes ran over the baked goods, then his face grew somber. "You be careful out here all alone in the woods."

"Thank you, Jacob," she tried to give the coachman her best reassuring smile as he placed the basket behind the riding board and climbed onto the seat. "I will be just fine."

Jacob nodded to her with grim resignation, then spurred the mare into a light trot toward the road. He looked back at Galina one last time, and she raised a hand to give a slight wave goodbye. The coachman knew she was hoping for a final glance back from the Countess, however, he could see the woman remained deep in the shadows of the carriage.

Once they got onto the open road, Jacob quickened the mare's pace, looking to quickly put distance between himself and the dark woods around the cottage. The Countess complained that the increased speed made for an uncomfortably bumpy ride; however, Jacob assured her he was trying to make up for lost time and would slow the carriage once he felt sure they would arrive home in time. The answer seemed to placate her, and he continued driving the carriage onward.

As they passed the village of Obrechen, a large man clad in a coat of thick wolf fur stepped onto the road from the forest's shadows. At first sight, the man appeared as a giant beast and nearly frightened Jacob enough to stop his heart. Only his years of experience as a coachman gave him the skills to navigate around the man instead of reigning the horse to a sudden stop, which, at this speed, would likely have overturned the carriage and killed them all.

The man had long black hair and a thick beard, making his head look nearly indiscernible from the wolf coat. He carried a large sack on his back, adding to the appearance of immense size as he stepped onto the road. Jacob scowled at the man as they rode past, then recoiled back on the riding board as the man stared impassively back with one dark eye. A thick scar ran down the left side of the man's face, leaving that eye pale and milky as it stared unseeingly at the coachman. Jacob flicked the reigns, encouraging the mare onward, eager to return to Kalinin and away from this dreadful place.

***

The wolf slowly stepped, careful not to crack a telltale twig or rustle some fallen leaves. The barn obscured him from the man with the gun. He stopped, raising his dark nose skyward and breathing in deeply. Two more scents were in the air.

Human. Female.

His nose detected the basket of food and twitched at the odor of fear pouring off the mare and the old man. The scent of an animal came from the barn, seeped through the cracks of the wood, and rolled out the side window.

Donkey.

The wolf paused, listening for the movements of the donkey inside its wooden stable. Donkeys were less predictable than horses, who were fearful, skittish creatures. Falsely maligned as slow-witted and stubborn, donkeys were thinkers and survivors. Their minds ran through permutations of fight or flight, picking through scenarios that best allowed them to live another day. They could just as quickly charge the wolf, biting with their hard, flat bites and kicking with bone-shattering force, as they could flee to safety. Unsurprisingly, shepherds often pastured donkeys with their sheep, natural guardians against wolves and other predators.

The wolf moved past the shelter of the barn, however, remaining concealed within the dense foliage of the forest. He swung his head toward the open window of the barn, knowing that at this distance, the donkey likely smelled him as well. The wolf detected the sound of shod hooves moving about inside the barn and tried to crouch low among the bushes and brambles.

The black carriage, its top pulled up, moved quickly out of the clearing, leaving only the dark-haired woman, her eyes trailing after the departing vehicle. She could not sense him, feel his presence, so deadly close. The woman did not even cast a glance in his direction.

The wolf sniffed; there was a new scent, faint but pungent. It bore the sickly, sweet odor of rot and decay. He was trying to pinpoint the source of the scent when a long, equine face appeared in the barn window.

The muscles in his shoulders tensed as the fur along his spine bristled, and he resisted the urge to growl menacingly at the donkey.

The donkey stood staring at him stoically, its eyes two large, brown, glassy orbs protruding from a coated face. An unruly tussle of sandy brown hair sprouted between the creature's ears. It studied him with such a quiet intensity the wolf felt as if it could hear his heart beating within the depths of those pointed ears.

The wolf slinked backward, deeper into the forest, closer to safety. His black eyes locked with the brown eyes of the donkey. He cast a split-second glance toward the woman. The look lasted no more than a fraction of a second, however, that was long enough to break the connection between wolf and donkey.

The donkey extended its head out the window, pulling its lips back from its immense equine teeth and opening its mouth wide. The donkey's braying felt ear-shattering to the delicate auditory system of the wolf, and he quickly retreated into the forest.

The woman's head turned quickly toward the sound as the donkey brayed a second time, even louder than the first. The wolf knew her eyes were likely scanning the woods for signs of danger, but he was already gone. Lupine legs propelled him through the forest as he snorted out sharp breaths, trying to clear the rotting smell from his nostrils.

Chapter 3

Dimitri's one good eye stared at the sign above the tavern door. Weathered letters, likely a decade old, spelled out the words "Kanti Gans" in the wooden plank crudely nailed into place.

"Stupid fucking name for a kabak," the hunter's voice was deep and gravelly as he shook his head and pushed the wooden door open.

The woodsman wrinkled his nose in distaste as the dank smell of the dimly lit tavern assailed his senses. The open door created a corridor of late afternoon daylight that sliced a path to the bar, where an overweight red-haired woman eyed the stranger with mild interest as she filled two fingerprint-covered glasses with vodka. Her dark eyes followed Dimitri as the hulking woodsman deposited his large sack beside a table in the rear of the room, and he seated himself with his back to the wall.

The tavern's main room was larger than Dimitri expected for a village as small as Obrechen. He suspected only the village's church was larger. Dimitri traveled throughout the Russian empire's western reaches as a wolf hunter and drank in hundreds of village kabaks like the Kanti Gans. The taverns were where the locals gathered to gossip, make business deals with traveling merchants, or escape the drear of their dull lives awash in cheap vodka.

Dimitri was surprised to find the tavern's rows of wooden tables primarily empty, except for a few quiet conversations in the darkened corners of the room. A blonde man sat in one of the dark corners of the tavern. The gloom failed to mask the man's well-groomed hair and mustache, and glimpses of expensive clothing beneath his riding coat. The man's eyes took note of the hunter's arrival, quick and appraising, then casually moved on. The practiced, predatory gaze of man accustomed to assessing threats.

Not one of the village rabble.

An officer in a faded light blue uniform of the Separate Corps of Gendarme sat quietly sipping from a large mug at a table in the center of the room, trying to discretely eye Dimitri without drawing the hunter's attention and failing. The gray epaulets on the gendarme's shoulder bore a single blue stripe and three golden stars, the lowly rank of poruchik, lieutenant.

"What are you drinking, friend?" Dimitri spoke in a quiet growl, the tone he liked to use to let someone know he was not intimidated.

"Oh," the officer did a poor job of pretending only now to notice the man, clad in dark wolf fur, seated by the wall. "Did you say something?"

He turned casually toward Dimitri, then stopped short at seeing the hunter's scarred face and milky white eye.

"I said, what are you drinking?" Dimitri grinned at the officer, more a feral flashing of teeth than an expression of pleasure.

The officer had dull, nervous, beady eyes and a face that reminded the hunter of a ferret. Dimitri had met men like this before, men who thought the uniform would provide them the courage and respect that life had denied them. He was willing to bet the policeman had yet to draw his pistol from his holster since leaving whatever passed for training by the local gendarme in Kalinin.

The policeman took a moment to regain his composure after looking at Dimitri's grizzled countenance. "The Kanti Gans is known for its exceptional *Medovukha*." The gendarme nodded politely and returned to his drink.

Dimitri's eyebrows rose in genuine surprise at the mention of the sweet honey mead. The vodka in these village shitholes may taste like piss, but Dimitri was damned if he would ever be seen drinking mead.

"I'm sure all the ladies in the village flock in for a sip," Dimitri smiled as the officer's shoulders visibly stiffened at the insult but offered no further response.

Dimitri saw the woman behind the bar nod toward him, sending a gaunt man in a greasy apron shuffling over to the hunter.

"Vodka. Bring the bottle," the hunter's voice boomed across the room, halting the man mid-shuffle. The man bobbed his head in acknowledgment and hurried back to where the red-haired barmaid was already placing the bottle on the bar.

Dimitri glanced sidelong at the village gendarme and smirked, sure the man heard him request the more potent drink. "Poruchik, I have another question."

The officer barely glanced back. "What can I help you with?"

"Who is the Land Captain in Obrechen?" Dimitri faced the officer's back, his eyes watching the man slowly shuffling toward him with the bottle of vodka.

"That would be Andrei Morozov," the gendarme turned in his seat, running a hand through thinning blonde hair. "Do you have business with the Land Captain?"

The man placed the bottle of vodka on Dimitri's table, averting his eyes to avoid looking at the hunter's ruined face, and quickly turned back toward the bar. Dimitri took the bottle and grabbed the man's wrist with his other hand. The man stared in alarm as the hunter's thick fingers closed around his thin wrist.

"Sir, is something wrong?" the man did not even attempt to hide the tremble in his voice. He cast an anxious glance toward the gendarme and appeared crestfallen to see the man slowly return to his mug of mead.

"Your tavern, why is it called Kanti Gans?" Dimitri pulled the cork from the vodka bottle with his teeth and spat it onto the floor.

"Sir?" the man looked from Dimitri's face to the tabletop.

"This place," the hunter took a swig from the bottle, letting the strong drink slide down his throat before continuing, "why do you call it the Kanti Gans? What does it mean? Why not the Slaughtered Lamb, the Farting Goat, or some shit like that?"

"I... I don't know what it means," the man shook his head. "It's always been the Kanti Gans."

"What he means," the red-haired woman walked over to stare down Dimitri, her hands resting on her wide hips, "is that when Morozov bought this place, it was already the Kanti Gans. The old owner had named it that, a man from Livonia. He's dead or gone now; I couldn't tell you which. Everyone knew the place as the Kanti Gans, and there was no reason to change it."

"Morozov?" Dimitri's eyes ran up and down the woman's full figure, and he gave her a leering smile. "The Land Captain owns this place?"

"That's what I said." She had caught sight of his gaze and tilted her head slightly as if intrigued. "Anton needs to get back to work."

Dimitri released the man's hand and smiled at the woman as he took another swig from the vodka bottle. "And who might you be?"

"I'm the one who'll take your other eye if you don't tread lightly around here. Drink your drink and pay your tab at the bar." she pointed at his one good eye, nodded once, and returned to the bar.

The hunter smiled at her back, sure she had added some extra swaying into the hips as she walked away. He caught her glance briefly his way as she returned to her place behind the bar, the slightest hint of a smirk on her lips.

The tavern door opened, momentarily flooding bright daylight into the room. A tall man in the long dark frock of an orthodox priest, stormed more than walked into the room, catching his toe on Dimitri's sack and stumbling. The priest turned to address Dimitri, an angry retort forming on the man's lips beneath his dark beard, and then he stopped, his dark eyes registering surprise at the sight of the burly hunter.

Dimitri slowly turned to look at the priest, running his tongue over his front teeth. The hunter winked his good eye and gave a slight nod, watching the holy man's gaze move down from Dimitri's pale ruin of an eye to the large knife belted at his waist. The priest's thin lips formed a tight scowl as he gave a curt nod in reply, then turned and walked purposefully over to the seated gendarme.

"Good afternoon, Father Grigori," the policeman dipped his head in greeting, his index finger absently circling the rim of his mug.

"Pavel Verenich, are you not the Separate Corps of Gendarme representative in Obrechen? Charged with enforcing the laws of Imperial Russia?" The priest placed both hands on the gendarme's table and leaned toward the officer.

"Father Grigori," Pavel leaned back in his chair. "You know that I am."

"Then why do you not enforce the Tsar's laws in our village?" Father Grigori slapped one palm down hard on the table. "Count Guriev's carriage has visited his harlot's home again this afternoon."

"Aye, Father, I saw that same carriage myself," Dimitri pointed his bottle of vodka toward the priest. "The coachman nearly ran me down on the road to Obrechen."

The priest looked up, startled at the interruption, and then turned his ire back on the gendarme. "There is only one reason a married man visits a woman's home like that," the priest leaned closer to Pavel, his eyes opening wide and teeth barring in a feral sneer, and let the disgust sound in his voice. "Fornication."

The gendarme sighed, rubbed his hand across his face, and looked up at the priest. "What would you have me do? Arrest Gennady Guriev on charges of adultery?"

"No," Father Grigori shook his head. "Count Guriev is a good and honorable man. I would have you arrest the harlot that has led him astray, that whore Galina Sekova."

"We all see how she flaunts her lover's gifts," the red-haired woman called from the bar, "walking around the village in her fine clothes."

"It is the Tsar's penal code and God's law. But among you, there must not be even a hint of sexual immorality, Ephesians five-three," the priest stood upright and folded his arms across his chest. "What are you going to do about this, Lieutenant Verenich?"

The gendarme's shoulders sagged, and he stared up at the priest with defeat in his pale blue eyes. Dimitri watched the exchange with no small degree of pleasure. He bore no love for the gendarme, and to see one of its officers so belittled in public warmed his insides almost as much as the half of a bottle of vodka he had already consumed. Not that he possessed any love of the church either; and he certainly did not agree with the priest's views on fucking. The thought made his eye drift toward the red-haired woman behind the bar, who appeared to raise her eyebrow in just the slightest way at his attention. A smile spread across his face, best not to drink too much tonight.

Light flooded the room once again as nearly a score of men filed into the room, taking seats at the tables around the priest and gendarme. Dimitri identified them as local farmers and foresters by their thick, homespun clothing, worn and dirty from hard work. They were lean, rough-looking men, weathered by working in the woods and fields of Obrechen. A few cast the hunter disinterested gazes as they entered and took their seats. A tall man with a nose crooked from a long ago break looked at Dimitri and muttered, "ugly fucker", intentionally loud enough for the hunter to hear, then smirked wickedly at the hunter as some of the other newcomers laughed amongst themselves. Dimitri pursed his lips and blew the man a kiss, eliciting a sour look in return.

One man stood out to Dimitri; he was heavy set and dressed in what would pass in Obrechen as finer clothes, though he would be easily spotted as peasant-rich by the nobles in Kalinin. The man's body may have once been muscular from hard work but had grown soft and flabby from easier living. His reddish brown hair and beard were long by city standards but neatly trimmed. A boy of perhaps fifteen trailed behind the man and, by the similarities of their faces, Dimitri thought him likely the man's son. Someone had given the boy a good thrashing in the past few days, his right eye bearing the telltale purple discoloration and swelling of a solid punch to the face. The boy gawked openly at Dimitri's scarred face; however, to his credit, the older man quickly masked his surprise at the stranger's appearance and nodded in greeting. The hunter returned the nod impassively.

Father Grigori and the gendarme turned to face the man as he approached them. Dimitri noticed the priest mustered a fair facsimile of a smile, however, the officer was visibly displeased by the new arrivals.

"Father Grigori," the man greeted the priest warmly, "it is my good fortune to find you here. My wife accompanied me into the village this afternoon. She is at the church and had hoped to discuss some matter she was seeking penance for with you. Likely, scolded one of the house girls too harshly."

"Of course, Andrei Morozov," the priest bowed his head in acquiescence. "I will see to your wife's needs immediately."

"Thank you, Grigori," Morozov gave the priest a friendly pat on the back. "Your devotion to my family is a source of great comfort to us."

"Of course, Andrei," Father Grigori made the sign of the cross in the air above Morozov's head. "May the Lord bless you in all your endeavors."

As Father Grigori quickly moved to the door, Dimitri detected a slight eagerness on the priest's face, though whether it was an eagerness to get to one Morozov or away from the other, the hunter could not tell.

Hearing Morozov's name piqued Dimitri's attention. To his good fortune, he would not have to go far to track the Land Captain down.

Tsar Alexander the Second freed the serfs from the nobility with the emancipation reform of 1861; however, few of his reforms survived his assassination by members of the Narodnaya Volya, the People's Will, twenty years later. His son and successor, Tsar Alexander the Third, created the office of Land Captain to exert control over the increasingly rebellious Russian countryside. The imperial state selected men from what passed for nobility in the villages and towns; often, they were little more than wealthy landowners or men capable of purchasing the office from local officials. The Land Captains had unlimited powers over the peasantry and their communities, essentially restoring the feudal order.

Morozov pulled out a chair and sat across from the gendarme, one hand resting on his ample stomach and the other stroking his beard as he leaned back.

"Pavel, what progress have you made in resolving our wolf issue?" Morozov cocked his head slightly.

The gendarme sighed deeply and folded his hands on the table before him. "I have advised my superiors in Kalinin of the issue and requested they send me additional men to handle it."

"Your superiors?" the man with the crooked nose snorted loudly. "Who's not superior to you, Pavel Verenich?"

Several men snickered as the gendarme shot the man an angry look.

"The wolves killed my sow; left nothing but bloody entrails behind," one of the newcomers shook a fist at the officer.

"They took all my chickens in one night," another man shouted from one of the far tables.

"And they killed my cow. Are you going to bring my children milk this winter, Pavel Verenich?" a third man pounded a table as others muttered angrily.

"Kalinin will send men," Pavel spoke through gritted teeth, trying to keep his frustration in check.

"They haven't sent us one yet," the crooked nose man sneered at the gendarme.

"You watch your mouth, Igor Balkov," Pavel pointed a finger at the man.

"And why's that, Pavel? You think you are more of a man than me?" Balkov licked his tongue over his dry, cracked lips. "Why, because you wear that gun?"

Morozov raised his hand for silence and then folded his arms across his chest. "What will these men do when they get here?"

"They'll hunt the wolves. Set traps," Pavel's voice lacked any conviction as he struggled to meet Morozov's gaze.

Dimitri shook his head in disgust at the man's lack of authority. He was an officer in the Separate Corps of Gendarme, the Tsar's Imperial police; all but the Land Captain should fear crossing him. As the hunter watched a roach, as long and thick as his thumb, crawl over the lip of his table, he contemplated that maybe this was the Land Captain's intent by this little show. Let all the peasants see there is only one authority in this village-Andrei Morozov.

"City policemen?" Morozov's voice was soft as if consoling a child awakened by a nightmare. "Hunting wolves in the forest? Setting traps?"

The gendarme just looked down into his glass of mead, and Dimitri saw Morozov smirk at the man's apparent defeat.

"I will offer a reward," Morozov turned to face the men seated around them, his voice loud and authoritative. "I will pay handsomely for every wolf pelt brought to me until this scourge is driven from Obrechen!"

The men cheered, pounding the tables with fists and stomping their feet on the wooden floorboards.

"A bottle of vodka for each table," Morozov yelled to the red-haired woman, and the din of cheering and pounding grew louder.

Thwack.

The noise rose above the cacophony of the tavern, silencing the men and drawing all eyes to Dimitri's table. The hunter released the grip on his knife and leaned back in his chair, pulling the cork from his bottle and tipping the bottle back against his lips. His throat made deep gulping noises, his Adam's apple bobbing beneath his unkempt beard, as he drained the remaining half bottle of vodka.

As the last drop slipped between his lips, Dimitri lowered the bottle to the table, placing it alongside his immense hunting knife. The point was buried several inches deep in the wooden tabletop, nearly cleaving the roach's body in half, its legs twitching and jerking. He smiled at the blank stares of the assembled men, then winked at the red-haired woman.

Morozov was studying him curiously; even the gendarme had looked over his shoulder at the hunter.

"I'm Dimitri Volkov, and I'll take your money," the hunter nodded to Morozov. "And I'll get rid of your wolves."

"Looks like one almost got rid of you," Balkov looked from the hunter to the men seated around him, narrowing his eyes when the men failed to offer the expected laughter.

"This ole boy got me good," Dimitri reached over, pulled his knife from the table, and tapped its tip against the scar on his face. "But now he keeps me warm in the winter," Dimitri lied. He had received the scar one drunken night in Moscow, but he did not think these simple-minded goatfuckers needed to know that. A tale was always better than the truth, and in this case, more effective.

Dimitri rolled his shoulders, making the dark wolf fur coat rise and fall.

"I may not be as pretty as your police officer there," Dimitri gestured for the man in the apron to bring him another bottle of vodka. "But I'll kill these wolves, sure as shit, faster than any city gendarme; and I'll do it without getting myself killed, like half the sheepfuckers in this room will."

The hunter saw a slight smile crease Morozov's face as the Land Captain nodded his head appreciably.

Dimitri took the offered bottle from the man in the apron and pulled the cork out, "Let me tell you something about wolves; you can't take down a pack by setting traps. If you're lucky and one's old or weak, you could get him with a trap. But once you do, you educate the whole pack to avoid the traps."

He took a long drink from the bottle and exhaled deeply, feeling like he could blow flames out his mouth like a dragon after the drink. The redhead had sent over the good stuff. She nodded when she saw his reaction, and he grinned in return.

"You can't fool a wolf's nose," he tapped the side of his nose with the knife edge. "They can smell your sweat and your piss."

"Not a man in this village will sell you a goat or sheep to bait the wolves," one of the men called from the other side of the room.

Dimitri laughed out loud and shook his head. "Only a fool tries to lure a wolf with livestock."

"In case you haven't heard, they seem to like the livestock in Obrechen just fine," Balkov cocked his head and tapped a finger to an ear.

"Oh, they'll come down and take the food right off your dinner plate if they choose to," Dimitri nodded, "but that's not how you lure them in; a pack is too smart to try for a goat tied to a tree unless they're starving. And the ones around here have been eating well enough."

"So, what do you use? Your charming disposition?" the gendarme chimed in, a weak attempt to extricate himself from his predicament by aligning himself with the other men in the room.

"Dog shit," Dimitri spat and then took another sip of vodka.

"What?" Pavel's face registered confusion and then disdain as some of the men in the room laughed wickedly at his dismissal by the hunter.

"I use dog shit and piss. Wolves can't help themselves; it drives them crazy with rage," Dimitri ran his tongue over his teeth. "They see it as an insult, a rival trespassing on their land. The whole pack will run snarling and howling out of the woods, looking for a fight."

"And you're there to give it to them," Morozov nodded appreciatively.

"Damn straight I am," Dimitri nodded.

***

The sound of Galina's paintbrush gently stroking the canvas filled the kitchen with a soft swooshing sound that reminded Oksana of a hummingbird's wings. Galina had positioned her easel by the window to take advantage of the afternoon light and was putting the finishing touches on a butterfly painting. The exquisite creature had bright yellow wings with two large blue oval spots and flitted above a red flower with a drop of dew dripping from one petal. The dewdrop looked so real that Oksana truly believed if she touched it, her hand would come away wet.

They had settled into their afternoon routine: Oksana cooking, and Galina painting. The water boiled in the large, brass barrel-shaped samovar for their late-day tea. Ornate etchings of galloping horses decorated the samovar; in such detail, Oksana could see their nostrils flared from the exertion of the run. A leather-bound copy of Alexander Pushkin's play Boris Goduov lay half opened on the dark polished tabletop, Oksana's afternoon reading lesson.

"Is that painting for the Countess?" Oksana cocked her head to get a better look at the canvas.

"It is," a warmth entered Galina's voice that Oksana noticed only happened when she spoke about the Countess. "Even when we were young girls in the Tsar's court, she loved butterflies."

"She's very special to you," Oksana had not intended to say it out loud, and her mind raced to change the topic quickly, but Galina glanced back at her with cheeks tinted red with a blush and smiled.

"She is. She is very special to me," Galina let out a little sigh that sounded like longing, and Oksana felt a pang of jealousy that no one made her feel that way. "But what about you? I see the way Alexei looks at you."

"Alexei is a good friend. I know he likes me more than that, but he feels more like a brother to me," Oksana said, looking down at her hands, pausing to hold back her emotions before looking back at Galina. "When my parents died, he begged me not to let my uncle move into their house. Alexei said he would marry me instead, and we could work the farm together, have children."

Galina gave the younger girl a sympathetic nod. Though the social status that divided her from Oksana was a chasm, she understood well that, rich or poor, the options afforded women in Imperial Russia were limited and unfair. Whether one married a count or farmer, it was a life of servitude.

"I hate Igor, but I couldn't marry Alexei," Oksana shook her head. "I know he would treat me well, and maybe we would even be happy, but the thought of spending my life in Obrechen sucks the air from my lungs. I want to be like you, Galina, free as a bird; free to go where you want, love who you want."

Galina looked around the cottage and gave a joyless laugh, "I am as free as a bird in a cage, Oksana."

"You've been to the Tsar's court and are best friends with a countess. She must invite you to all those spectacular balls. Even Leo and Alexei have been to Saint Petersburg," Oksana sighed. "Your cottage is the farthest I have ever been from my home."

"I understand, Oksana, I truly do," she gave Oksana a sad smile.

"I am sorry, Galina," Oksana brushed a stray strand of dark hair from her face. "I forget myself."

Galina walked to Oksana and grabbed her hands, squeezing them reassuringly. "No, it's quite alright. We're friends, Oksana. I always want you to feel comfortable talking to me about anything."

Oksana blushed at the feel of Galina's warm, soft hands in her own as a wave of embarrassment washed over her. Her hands were rough from working outside and not smooth and ladylike like the boyar's daughter. She chided herself for ever dreaming of dancing with counts and princes at grand affairs. The men of such a station would shrink away in horror at the leathery touch of a peasant girl's hands.

Galina winced at a sudden pang of lancing pain in her right side. She placed her right hand over the area beneath her ribs, bending slightly to relieve the sudden discomfort. It dissipated as quickly as the pain came, and Galina exhaled deeply.

"Galina, what's wrong?" Oksana rushed toward the woman, but Galina waved her off.

"I'm okay. I get a little pain sometimes when I stand too long," Galina turned to her painting and frowned. "I don't think that shade of yellow is right for the butterfly's wings."

Oksana studied the woman for a moment but, Galina had once again immersed herself in painting, so she checked on the soup, inhaling the sweet, briny smell of the solonina, a corned beef, cooked in cabbage soup. A smile crossed her face, reaching her hazel eyes as she stirred the pot with a long wooden spoon.

"Oksana Nostrova, I believe you are the happiest cook I have ever seen," Galina laughed, a pleasant, melodic sound that bore no mockery. "All the cooks I ever met before you looked like they had permanent frowns etched onto their faces."

Oksana turned from the cooking pot and wiped her hands down the red apron tied around her waist. "That's because they found no joy in cooking; I love cooking for you, Galina. You are teaching me to read. All you ask in return is something I love to do, so I am happy."

"I can bake a little," Galina shrugged, "but if I had to cook for myself, I would surely starve. As my mother always said, it was not a skill the daughter of a boyar needs to learn."

Oksana smiled. A small yellow dot of paint had found its way onto Galina's cheek. "At home, I mostly cook porridge, or salamata if it's a holiday, like Christmas."

"Salamata?" Galina rubbed at her cheek, unknowingly smearing the yellow in a thin arc across her cheek.

"It's a gruel," Oksana shrugged.

"Oh," Galina looked contemplative as if she was working out a problem in her head. "Then where did you learn to cook so wonderfully?"

"My mother," the memory of her mother made Oksana smile, but the sadness of the loss still stung her deeply. "She was an incredible cook, and she let me help in the kitchen. You would have loved her cooking, Galina."

Galina walked over and touched Oksana's arm, remorse etched across her face. "Oksana, I am so sorry; I did not mean to bring up your parents."

"It's okay," Oksana gave her a weak smile. "I think about them all the time. Sometimes, talking about them is nice, especially the good times."

"Your Uncle Igor must miss his sister too; I am sure he loves that you cook like her," Galina's pale eyes gleamed with a warmth and sincerity that accompanied the smile she gave the younger girl.

"Igor loves nothing but drink," Oksana shook her head. The thought of her uncle brought a sour taste to her mouth. "He hated my parents, and he hates me. The only reason Igor took me in when they died is that he believes he'll get a dowry for me when he marries me off. 'You'll bring a nice fat sow one day', he always says."

When Oksana saw the look of shock and grief on Galina's face, she regretted the venom in her words."

"Oksana," Galina's voice was soft, barely above a whisper.

"I'm sorry, Galina, I should check the soup; I don't want to overcook the beef." Oksana turned away and peered into the soup pot, blinking back tears.

"Oksana," Galina wrung her hands nervously. "I know we have only known each other for a few months, but I meant what I said, we are friends. I think of you as my little sister."

Oksana turned, feigning seriousness but unable to contain her smile, "We are friends, Galina. And I do think of you as if you were my sister, too. My much, much older sister."

Galina's eyes opened wide in surprise at the girl's jest, mouth dropping open in a shocked 'O' as Oksana covered her mouth with her hands to hide her laughter.

"You're a beast! I am only five years older than you," Galina could not suppress her laughter as she slapped Oksana's arm playfully. "I am going to check the samovar; I believe the water is ready for our tea."

The window rattled as Galina passed, causing her to jump in mild surprise. She peered out the window, staring at the darkening sky as storm clouds rolled in. The treetops swayed in the wind, heralding the storm to come, strong gusts billowing against the little cottage in its clearing.

"Oksana, it looks like a bad storm is rolling down from the mountains," concern laced Galina's voice as she looked back to Oksana. "Even if you leave now, you won't make it home before it pours. I think you should stay the night."

Oksana walked to the window and stood beside her, looking at the ominous clouds filling the sky. The window rattled from another strong gust, and they both jumped back. Galina covered her mouth with one hand as she let out a squeak-like cry of surprise. The two girls looked at each other and broke into a fit of giggles and laughter.

"Oh, please stay the night, Oksana; I am such a scaredy cat when it comes to storms," Galina clapped her hands together in a mock begging gesture. "We can hitch the donkey to the wagon, and I'll take you home in the morning. I need to go into town anyway."

"Ok," Oksana nodded tentatively and then more enthusiastically as her face broadened into a wide grin. "I'll stay the night."

Another gust battered against the window, and they both jumped and cried out in surprise before descending into another fit of laughter.

"It's going to be great fun," Galina beamed. "I'll make us some tea."

Oksana watched as Galina moved excitedly to the brass samovar, then stopped. Her head cocked to the side as if she was looking at something curious, then she peered closer at the samovar. The younger girl could see that Galina was studying her reflection in the brass barrel of the samovar. Oksana tried to hide her laughter as she watched Galina rub at the smear of yellow paint on her cheek. The reflection of Galina's face in the samovar suddenly registered a look of surprise, and she whirled on Oksana.

"You are the worst," Galina pointed a paint-smudged finger at Oksana as she tried to contain her laughter. "You knew this was here the whole time and didn't say anything!"

A loud crack of thunder echoed outside as the two girls cried out in surprise and laughed even harder.

***

A flash of lightning lit the sky, bathing the forest in sudden bright light as rain beat down from the night sky. The wolf crouched low, blinking away the rainwater that soaked his dark coat, as he scanned the cottage's clearing for signs of movement.

The lantern lights of the cottage lay darkened behind heavy curtains as the young women slumbered inside. It had watched the cottage all day and knew the younger girl had not left as it expected her to.

Its eyes, adept at seeing at night, studied the barn, its doors, and windows shuttered against the rain. It could sense the presence of the donkey inside, disquieted by the storm but otherwise unaware of the predator that lurked outside.

The wolf scanned the clearing one last time, then, sure there was no chance of detection, sprinted from the safety of the woods. It ran on all fours, building up speed as it traversed the clearing, the barn looming as a large shadow before it. Dark, wet earth flew from beneath its paws, making deep ruts in the ground that quickly filled with rain.

Lightning flashed as the wolf launched itself upward toward the barn, its fur standing on end from the electrically charged air. The clawed fingers of the wolf's forepaws dug into the edge of the barn's roof as its hind legs scratched frantically at the slick, wet wood of the barn's wall as they sought purchase. Inside the barn, the wolf could

hear the sudden pacing and snorting of the donkey, alarmed at the
sound of the intruder.

The wolf pulled itself further onto the curved roof of the barn, the
muscles in its shoulders tensing and exerting against the strain. The
claws on the paw of one of its hind legs dug into a wooden plank of
the wall, enabling the wolf to pull itself entirely onto the roof.

The donkey brayed in alarm; a sound that was lost in the storm's din
as the wolf rose on its hind legs. Rain soaked the fur around its face as
it raised its head to look into the stormy night. The wolf beast snarled
in defiance of the storm as the gusting wind and rain threatened to
dislodge it from the roof.

In a sudden burst of movement, the wolf reached down and began
tearing at the roof boards. Its claws sank deep into the wood, and
its arms shook as its muscles forced the long, thick nails securing the
board to yield to its primal strength. The nails screeched in protest as
the wolf tore the board free and tossed the wood plank out into the
night.

A second and then a third plank splintered and were pulled from
their moorings. The donkey's bray turned from alarm to terror as the
wolf tore gaping holes into the roof. The terrified creature backed
away from the rain that poured through the openings in the roof, the
whites of its eyes clearly showed as it stared upward.

The large black head of the wolf poked through one of the
openings, its black, coal-like eyes narrowed as it snarled ferociously at
the donkey, its teeth bared in a feral grin.

Chapter 4

Pavel's boots crunched rhythmically in the rocky dirt of the road as he stalked home. The humiliation he suffered in the tavern stung him and fueled a burning hatred inside him. The Land Captain had made a point of demeaning him every chance he could since the gendarme officer and his family arrived in Obrechen. Men like Igor Balkov thrived in the shadows of men like Morozov, undermining him with jabs and criticism at every turn.

This was not how Pavel's life was supposed to be when he joined the Separate Corps of Gendarme. Everything should have changed. People should have respected him—feared him. He represented the full power of Imperial Russia in Obrechen, and the Tsar's prisons awaited those who believed otherwise.

Pavel slammed his fist into his palm in frustration, gritting his teeth against the pain of his knuckles bruising the soft flesh of his hand. This plague of wolves had confounded him for weeks. Now, this stranger Volkov shows up to swing his dick around the Kanti Gans.

A fury roiled within his gut, blackening his thoughts at every turn. However, it was not the wolves or Morozov that fueled his ire; it was his son, Leo. Pavel Verenich knew without a shadow of a doubt that the boy was the cause of all the misfortune in his life.

Pavel had a good life, a young wife, and a promising job at the Muir and Mirrielees furniture factory. Then, the boy was born, with his frail body and twisted legs. So many times, he had wanted to smother the sickly baby in the night but stayed his hand because the child had his wife, Anya's, heart; how he regretted it now.

The child had become a source of ridicule for him among the factory workers at Muir and Mirrielees. He knew they laughed behind his back, thought him less than a man for having such a feeble offspring. After Leo's birth, the managers at the factory looked at him differently, and he knew it was what cost him his promotion.

He prayed the child would die every night, but the boy would not give him that dignity. Leo grew like a misshapen tree, thin and frail, confined to his small wooden wheelchair—never to walk or run.

Pavel joined the Separate Corps of Gendarme and forbade Anya to visit him during the weeks of training. The other officers did not know about the boy, and Pavel intended to keep it that way. People would see only a gendarme in his blue uniform and shiny black boots, and they would make way for him when he walked down the street.

However, after graduation, when Pavel stepped into his home and saw the child seated in the wheelchair, the ever-present book in his hand, and a wide gapped-tooth grin at the sight of his father's return, he knew the boy would ruin everything.

Pavel went to his superiors and requested an assignment to one of the gendarme's rural posts. They were happy to accommodate him; such posts were loathsome to most gendarme officers. However, Pavel believed that in a village like Obrechen, he would be like a

Tsar, and the villagers would seek his favor, maybe even pay for special privileges—especially the women. More importantly, life in the countryside was harsh, with brutal winters and few comforts. He doubted that the boy, with his frail health and weak constitution, would survive long in Obrechen. Then, once the boy was gone, Pavel would seek a transfer to Kalinin or St Petersburg to live the life he was destined to live.

However, after three winters in Obrechen, Leo was now fourteen and proving surprisingly resilient. Pavel felt sure it was his wife's doting care of the boy that kept him alive all of these years. Leo spent his days sitting in his wheelchair on the porch, reading his books, and watching the world go by. His only friends were Igor Balkov's ward, Oksana Nostrova, and that troublesome Jewish orphan boy, Alexei Kaminer. Pavel knew that to the rest of Obrechen, Leo was an object of pity and scorn, and by association, so was he. Men like Morozov and Balkov looked at Leo and saw him as evidence of Pavel's weakness and lack of virility. It was because of Leo that these men felt they could challenge Pavel's authority; of this, the gendarme was certain.

The boy had no life or future; his existence was an anchor around Pavel's neck. The gendarme believed that for as long as the boy lived, there would be more days like today, more humiliations as he experienced at Kanti Gans. Pavel lowered his head and walked toward his house on the outskirts of town, thankful his shame was not prominently displayed in a more central part of the village for all to see.

***

"Think about it," Leo grinned a gap-toothed grin at Alexei. "It is entirely possible."

"You're crazy," Alexei laughed, leaning against one of the posts supporting the porch roof.

The two boys sat on the porch of Leo's home in the midst of one of their epic debates about the mysteries of the world. Leo sat in his wooden wheelchair, a thick wool blanket spread over his legs and a well-worn book in his hands. While Alexei, nearly three years older than his friend, sat on the edge of the porch, one hand running through the gray-brown fur of the dog sprawled lazily alongside him. At the sound of his owner's loud laughter, Ivan the Terrible twitched a pointed ear and cracked his eyelids open only slightly before closing them again.

"Look, Leo," Alexei leaned forward, "everyone in Russia knows the fairy tale: the evil wizard Koschei steals the princess Marya Morevna, and the Tsar sends his three sons to rescue her. The two older boys cannot find the wizard's castle, but the youngest son, Petr, gets a magic horse from the witch Baba Yaga and finds the castle. He kills the wizard and saves the princess."

"The victors write history," Leo tapped the book cover with one slim finger. "Prince Petr defeated Koschei the Deathless, so the tale is that Koschei was an evil wizard. What if the real story was that Koschei and the princess were in love, and evil Prince Petr killed the wizard and stole her away?"

"Leo, it's a fairy tale," Alexei shook his head, wiping a palm across his dark eyes in mock frustration and then up through his unruly brown hair. "The story is what it is."

"No, I don't believe it," Leo shook his head. "Nobody would invoke the name of Baba Yaga in a made-up story."

"True," Alexei nodded. "But would they risk Baba Yaga's wrath in a story that was not true?"

Leo rubbed his chin, contemplating the issue. The lore of Baba Yaga was a sacred topic among the two boys and one they often debated for many long afternoons.

Baba Yaga was said to be a powerful, old witch who lived in the wilds of Russia, a ferocious eater of children. She lived in a house that walked on four giant chicken legs, so Baba Yaga never resided in the same place twice, making her nearly impossible to find—except through misfortune. They had once discussed whether it would be possible to capture the walking house in a snare trap, how large the trap would have to be, and how strong the trap's components would need to be.

"You have a good point there," Leo looked at the worn book of fairy tales in his lap.

Alexei looked at his friend; Leo stared down the road toward the village and stroked his chin thoughtfully. Leo had large brown eyes; they were the most prominent feature of his face, aside from his ever-present smile. The large dark pools from which Leo studied the world stood out from his gaunt face, skin that always looked pale to ashen, and short-cropped dark hair.

"What is it, Leo?" Alexei leaned to look down the road but saw only a figure walking in the distance.

"I was just wondering, how many people in the village do you think could read the stories in this book?" Leo turned his dark eyes toward Alexei.

It was one of those moments where Alexei knew his friend was contemplating things about the world that he had never thought about. Alexei shrugged, "I don't know. A few, I suppose."

"My parents can read, and my mother taught me," Leo raised three fingers on one hand. "You can read. Galina Sekova can read, and she's teaching Oksana. The Land Captain and Father Grigori..."

"Guess we can't count my parents," Alexei looked down and stroked a hand along the fur of Ivan's back.

"I'm sorry, Alexei, I didn't mean..." Leo's eyes grew even wider with concern as he stared at his friend.

"It's okay, Leo," Alexei smiled at him. "I just miss them. Sometimes, I forget they're gone, and then I catch myself. Last month, I walked in the woods and thought, 'Papa's birthday is soon; I have to think about what to make him.' Then I remembered."

"Alexei, what happened to your parents was horrible," Leo's voice dropped to a whisper, and his voice cracked with emotion. Alexei smiled and forced back his urge to let his parents' death boil to the surface. He was always amazed at the degree of empathy Leo felt for other people, their hurts and pains, when the world showed him so little of it in return. Leo just had a better heart than everyone else, he guessed.

"What's the count at?" Alexei asked to change the topic.

"Eight," Leo looked down at the number of fingers he had raised. "Maybe a few others that we missed."

"Let's call it twelve then," Alexei scratched a spot behind Ivan's ear as the dog yawned and stretched its legs.

"Only twelve," Leo shook his head as he ran his thin fingers over the book and gave Alexei a remorseful look. "Only twelve people in Obrechen can experience these incredible stories without someone else telling them about them."

"It's Obrechen, Leo, what do you expect? No one travels to the school in Kalinin," Alexei squinted at a figure heading toward the house from town. The man was too far off to see clearly, but from the familiar gait, Alexei suspected it was Leo's father. "Oksana is lucky Galina is willing to teach her. However, I suspect she enjoys the company, being all alone in that cottage."

"I wish you could bring her by to meet me," Leo smiled so widely it reached his eyes, a warm, genuine smile. "I would love to thank her for all the books she lets me borrow. I've read the few Mother brought with us from Saint Petersburg so often I have them practically memorized."

"I think she said she will have a new one for you this week," Alexei could see Leo's father approaching more quickly now. Ivan, too, had lifted his head, his ears pricked upward and eyes staring down the road. "Leo, your Father is coming; I am going to head home."

A look of disappointment crossed Leo's face, "My Father is a great man, Alexei; he has a lot of responsibility in Obrechen. If you would get to know him, I am sure you would both become fast friends."

"Your father and I know each other well enough, Leo," Alexei stepped off the porch, and Ivan leaped down beside him, staying close to his owner's side. Alexei thought of all the times he had seen bruises on Leo's arms where someone had grabbed him firmly; he knew his friend's mother would never handle Leo like that. However, mentioning such things would hurt Leo more than the physical injuries; he loved his father too much. "I'll come by later this week and bring you that book and some of Galina's pastries."

"Okay, Alexei," the smile returned to Leo's face. "I'll be here, working on my theory on Koschei the Deathless."

"Unless Baba Yaga gets you first," Alexei winked and smiled at his friend. It was a variant of their usual parting salutation: Don't let Baba Yaga get you!

"She won't eat me," Leo's grin widened. "I'm all skin and bones, but you'd make a fine meal for her!"

Pavel Verenich was close enough that Alexei could see the deep scowl on the man's face, his eyes locked on the boy and his dog.

"Ivan, go home, boy. Now," Alexei spoke firmly to the gray dog, who stared back with defiant brown eyes. "Ivan, go!"

The dog turned reluctantly away from Alexei and padded off into the woods, quickly disappearing into the forest's dense undergrowth. The dog often roamed alone in the woods but always found his way home before nightfall. Alexei headed down the road out of town, his back to Leo's father. The dirt path that led to his parent's home was close down the road; if he ran, he would easily reach the path before the gendarme could catch up to him. However, Alexei refused to run from this man or any man. He guessed he was like his father in that way, quick to anger and never one to turn from a fight. Alexei briefly wondered, as he did on many occasions, if that's what had gotten his parents killed that day in Kalinin.

Behind him, he heard Leo call a cheerful greeting to his father, a greeting that went unacknowledged. The man's booted feet were closing the distance between them. Alexei could tell by the rapid footfalls that the man was coming straight at him.

"Alexei Kaminer," Pavel Verenich's voice boomed with authority; a trick of the gendarme school, Alexei supposed, "I would like a word with you."

Alexei ignored the man and continued on his way down the road. The footsteps were louder now, and Alexei knew the man was close behind him. The thought of turning around and giving the man a thrashing within an inch of his life danced through his head. However, he could never do such a thing in front of Leo. The boy idolized his father for some godforsaken reason.

A hand closed firmly around Alexei's arm and roughly spun him around. The forest quickly passed Alexei's vision as he stopped before Pavel Verenich's ferret-like features. The man's pale, beady eyes narrowed into an angry squint, and his nostrils flared with anger and the exertion of catching up to Alexei.

"Boy, when I call you, you stop," Pavel seethed.

Alexei looked down at the hand grasping his arm, the fingers pressed in brutally tight through the woven fabric of his shirt. He imagined the man grabbing Leo, his kind, defenseless friend, in such a grip, bruising the younger boy's arm. When Alexei looked up into the gendarme's face, his dark eyes were hard and cold. Alexei noticed a slight widening of Pavel's eyes, an inadvertent show of surprise in the man's expression at Alexei's defiance.

Alexei was happy he had sent Ivan home; he knew the dog would respond protectively to the man grabbing him. The gendarme officer, he had little doubt, would shoot the dog in return.

"What do you want?" Alexei barely contained the wellspring of rage against this man, this bully, which threatened to erupt from deep inside him.

"You work for that whore, Galina Sekova?" Pavel's eyes roamed Alexei's face, a function of the man's inability to hold anyone's gaze for too long.

"I work in her barn and fix things around the house a few days a week," Alexei refused to be goaded by the man's slur of Galina.

"Who else have you seen there?" Pavel tugged at Alexei's arm.

"No one," Alexei stared back at the gendarme with an impassionate gaze.

Pavel's eyes narrowed suspiciously, "A boy like you could use friends in Obrechen. I saw the Morozov boy's eye. His father said you and your friends beat behind the blacksmith's barn—three on one."

"Me and my friends?" Alexei gave a short, sharp laugh. "Who did he say was with me? Leo? He pulled Oksana behind the blacksmith's barn and tried to make her kiss him. The only kiss that horse's ass got was my fist in his face, and he deserved it."

"If the boy is bothering Oksana, that is her uncle, Igor Balkov's, problem to fix, not yours," Pavel loosed his grip on Alexei's arm and gave the boy a disingenuous smile. "The Land Captain was quite angry about the incident, but I can protect you from him. All I need is some information about who visits Galina Sekova. Maybe you can keep your eyes open for me?"

"You know what I see?" Alexei sneered at the gendarme. "I see you every day down by the train tracks, hoping the train will stop and more gendarme will come to help you stop these wolf attacks. And every day, I see the train speed pass and never stop."

Pavel's eyebrows raised in surprise, then his face screwed tight, like a man sucking on a lemon. When he finally spoke, it was through gritted teeth, "If something happened to a Jewish orphan boy like you, one with radical parents killed for treason, nobody would question what happened. Nobody would come looking for you. Your body could dry up and blow away like a leaf in the wind, and nobody would care."

Pavel turned his back on Alexei and walked toward his house. Alexei stared at the man's blue-uniformed back as he strode away; a vision of charging up behind the man and dashing his brains out with a rock swam through his mind. He wanted to scream in rage to let the pressure building inside him escape as he watched the gendarme walk up the steps of his home, passing Leo without so much as a glance and disappearing inside.

Leo smiled at Alexei and gave a little wave of his hand. Alexei forced a smile and waved back, then turned for home.

***

Alexei smiled at the sight of Ivan waiting on the house's porch as he walked up the dirt path. The dog's gray head rose from its resting place on the porch, its dark eyes watching Alexei's approach as its long tail thudded happily against the old floorboards.

Shortly after his parents died, Oksana found the small gray pup wandering in one of the fields on the outskirts of town. She knew that, more than likely, the village youths would mistreat the poor dog unto death and instead brought it to her grieving friend. Alexei and the pup had immediately taken to each other, two orphans alone in the world, and quickly became inseparable.

The smile quickly slipped from Alexei's face. The door to the house was slightly ajar. He was sure that's not how he left it. The wooden planks he had nailed up over the broken windows now felt like they concealed eyes watching him ominously from the darkness inside. Alexei knelt as Ivan came padding down the steps, and he petted the dog playfully.

"Good boy, Ivan," Alexei plastered a grin to his face and tussled the fur between the dog's ears as he discretely eyed the porch for anything amiss.

Everything looks like I left it, and I am sure Ivan would be barking if someone was inside.

With Ivan, his tail still wagging, following by his side, Alexei walked up the few steps to the old house and gently pushed the door open. The fading sunlight cast a dim glow into the darkened house as Alexei peered inside. The main room, with its wooden table, chairs, and stove, sat quiet and undisturbed. He stepped cautiously into the room, listening for the telltale floorboard creaking or shuffling of feet.

Ivan walked past him and circled the pile of old rags in the corner three times before finding the right spot to curl up. Nothing alarmed the dog, so Alexei lit the oil lamp hanging by the door, casting the room into a warm glow once the fire sprang to life.

Then he smelled it: a dank, musk smell, like an unwashed man or animal. He peered into his bedroom; the bed and nightstand seemed untouched. Next, he checked his parents' bedroom, its solitary bed the only furnishing, with one wooden leg broken off at the foot of the bed.

Looking at his parents' bedroom, stripped of the furnishings and personal mementos they had collected over the years, broke his heart. For a moment, he pictured the room as it was, with the wooden nightstands his father had brought from Saint Petersburg, the artwork his mother had collected, and the big black steamer trunk that Alexei would sit on and laugh as his parents told funny stories of their youth.

They had had a good life in the little house tucked away in the woods outside Obrechen. Then there was that fateful day in March of eighty-one when the Narodnaya Volya assassinated Tsar Alexander the Second. The Tsar's court was quick to blame the deed on agents of foreign influence, a coy euphemism to imply the Jews had been behind the act.

The insinuation ignited a wave of violence against Jews in the southwestern corner of Imperial Russia, resulting in the deaths of hundreds of Jews and the widespread destruction of Jewish businesses. Alexei's father believed that much of the violence stemmed from opportunistic business competitors and merchants in debt to Jewish moneylenders; the riots were an easy way to resolve their problems.

Alexei's parents never hid their Jewish ancestry, though both were avowed and vocal atheists. The rioting that consumed Kalinin and other cities in the oblast left Obrechen relatively untouched, and aside from some heated words with Igor Balkov and his friends at times, Alexei's parents were left alone.

Alexei always attributed his family's relatively peaceful existence in Obrechen to two factors. First, Alexei's father was a big man, quick to anger and no stranger to fighting. As a college student in Saint Petersburg, Nicolai Kaminer regularly participated in workers' protests for better wages and conditions, which often ended in violent altercations with factory guards and the gendarme. Men like Igor Balkov talked a good game but, like all bullies, were cowards at heart. The thought of having his ears boxed in the middle of the Kanti Gans, in front of his friends and by a Jew, limited Balkov to puffing his chest and uttering snide comments from a distance, of course.

The other factor was that their little house sat on land that Andrei Morozov had no interest in. Alexei was confident that if the Land Captain desired their land, he would not have hesitated to use the pogroms as a pretense for seizing it for himself.

His parents avoided Kalinin for over a year after the assassination of Tsar Alexander until the waves of violence appeared to have died down. When they boarded the train for Kalinin to meet with old friends, they assured Alexei it was safe, and they would be home in a few days. They were wrong on both counts.

Alexei learned only scant details of what happened that afternoon from one of his parents' friends. She was an older woman, small in stature, with nervous eyes and thick glasses. A riot had broken out targeting a Jewish-owned factory; the mob stormed the building. Whether Alexei's parents were in the factory at the time of the assault or rushed in to help the people inside, the woman did not know. All she knew was that the mob had killed Alexei's parents and several other Jews, hanging their battered, naked bodies from lampposts. She heard city officials had burned the bodies, and the ashes were discarded with refuse.

The woman offered for Alexei to live with her in Kalinin, but he chose to stay in his parents' home. When word reached Obrechen that the Kaminers were dead, a group of villagers came with torches and ransacked the house. They wore burlap sacks over their heads with eyeholes cut out. Still, as he hid in the forest, Alexei recognized them by their clothes and voices: Igor Balkov, Olga Putina, and several other men and women from the village.

They stole everything of value in the house and destroyed anything they did not take. The ransackers did not leave so much as a spoon in the home; however, Alexei was thankful they did not set the house ablaze. Borrowing tools from Georgi Nostrov, Oksana's father, Alexei, made what repairs he could to the house. It was livable, though, without his parents' possessions, the house felt like a ghost of his home.

Alexei had taken his case to Pavel Verenich; however, the gendarme told him there was no proof against any of those the boy accused and sent him on his way. For several weeks, Alexei lurked through the village, confronting anyone he saw wearing clothes that had once belonged to his parents. He got into several fights, and the gendarme warned him that he would have him placed in jail if this continued.

After that, Alexei steered clear of the village except when necessary or to visit Leo. He took work with Galina Sekova, assisting her with work around the remote cottage for which she paid him a better than fair wage out of kindness.

Alexei could not shake the feeling that someone had been in the house, and that strange, musky smell lingered in the air. Suddenly, a feeling of alarm swept over Alexei, and he rushed to ensure the door was securely locked. Ivan raised his head and watched the boy run from the front door back into his parent's room.

His heart thudded in his chest, and he felt a panicked sweat on his forehead as he slid his parents' bed aside. Dropping to his knees, he searched for the notched floorboard. When his fingers found the small groove his father had meticulously carved into the wood plank, he paused, trying to quell the rising fear inside him, then lifted the board and moved it aside.

Ivan came padding into the room to stand beside him as Alexei removed the second board and stared down at the dark cloth covering the items in the secret compartment his father had crafted beneath the floor. Alexei pulled the heavy woolen cloth aside with shaky hands and exhaled deeply, unaware he had been holding his breath until this moment.

Everything is there.

Relief washed over Alexei like a heavy rainstorm as he sat back and reached into the compartment. He withdrew the small leather sack, the coins inside clinking as he jostled it. After the ransacking of his home, Alexei hid what few possessions he had remaining to him in the compartment.

He placed the purse of coins on the floor beside him, his saved wages from working for Galina. Reaching back into the compartment, he lifted out a small bundle wrapped in an oiled cloth that he placed in his lap. Ivan sniffed curiously at the cloth, and Alexei ran a hand along the fur of the dog's neck as he unwrapped the bundle.

The black steel of his father's revolver caught some of the lantern light and gleamed slightly. Alexei turned the pistol over in his hands, thinking how satisfying it would be to fire the weapon into Igor Balkov's smug face for what he had done to Alexei's home, for how he treated Oksana, for the beatings he gave her.

Alexei wondered if the weapon would have made a difference if his father had it with him in Kalinin as he wrapped it in the oilcloth and laid it alongside the purse of coins.

Would the gun have held the mob at bay? Would firing into the mob have dispersed them, sent them fleeing when they realized this Jew had teeth to bite back?

With great reverence, Alexei lifted the torn halves of a picture from the compartment. It was his most prized possession. In one half of the picture, his father stood stoically in a dark jacket and trousers, his dark hair combed to the side, his shoulders broad and square. He was holding a hand, barely visible along the tear that separated the photo into two pieces. Alexei had found the picture half discarded outside his home the night the village mob came.

The other half bore the image of his mother in a dark skirt and white blouse that came down to her elbows. Her dark hair was braided and placed in a bun behind her head, which only drew attention to the radiant smile she exhibited. She was a beautiful woman; his father had always said so, but Alexei never realized how beautiful she was until she was gone, and all that remained of her was the picture. Even in the faded picture, Alexei could see the twinkle in her eye, the ever-present kindness in her face.

Oksana had discovered the torn half of the picture among her uncle's things one afternoon; Alexei shuddered to speculate why Balkov had taken the photograph. She brought it to him one afternoon, and it was the only time he had let his friend see him cry.

Alexei placed the two halves of the picture next to each other on the floor, moving them until the tear that divided them was barely a seam. He smiled at the photo of his parents. They deserved a better life, and they certainly deserved a better death. A tear slipped from his eye and ran down his cheek.

With a deep sigh, he turned away from the picture and, putting one arm around Ivan, nuzzled his face against the soft fur of the dog's neck. He felt the fur dampen with his tears as the warmth of the dog's body comforted him.

Alexei sat up straight and wiped a hand across his eyes, blinking away the blurriness. Looking down at the last item in the compartment, he felt a slight smile cross his face. The large burlap-wrapped bundle was the reason his father built the compartment. He reached down and moved aside a corner of the burlap and surveyed the contents.

After college, Nicolai and Vera Kaminer joined Khozhdeniye v Narod, Going to the People, a group dedicated to inspiring the peasantry to overthrow Russia's ruling class. They took their young son and moved to Obrechen to live among the peasants, merge with them, and fight for their interests. However, like many others in Going to the People, they found the villagers unreceptive and disinterested in the movement. Nonetheless, the Kaminers believed that one day, the revolution would come. When that day came, Nicolai would blow the rail bridge over the Tvertsa River to prevent troops stationed in Kalinin from getting into the countryside.

Long, reddish cylindrical sticks of explosives, bound tightly together, poked out from beneath the burlap. Alexei knew the bundle contained the necessary components to set and detonate the explosives. When Alexei turned fourteen, his father instructed him in the proper handling and detonation techniques of the explosives as he laid them out on the wooden table. They would usher in the new age of Russia together.

His parents would never see the revolution, and in truth, Alexei did not share their concern for the peasants and factory workers. However,

Alexei would see that Russia and Obrechen paid for what they took
from him and atoned for the murder of his parents.

***

The light of Dimitri's fire barely held the darkness of the forest's night
at bay as he roasted the skinned rabbit over the flame. A brisk fall wind
blew through the woods, and the hunter pulled his heavy wolf fur coat
closer around him as he rotated the skewered rabbit over the fire; a
storm was coming. The smell of roasted meat filled the little clearing
as the rabbit's fat sizzled over the fire.

Dimitri leaned back on the log and smiled appreciatively at his first
night's haul of wolf skins. The gray-black hide of the she-wolf hung,
drying next to the small pelts of her four young pups. He had used
an old wolf hunter's trick. Dimitri had tracked the female wolf to her
den and killed the pups with cruel blows from a heavy branch. He
left one injured pup still alive and then hid with his rifle, shooting
the mother when she returned at the sound of her pup's cries. This
hunt had been good. The pelts and the others Dimitri would take in
the coming weeks would fetch him a considerable price; though not
in Obrechen, that beggar's hovel of a village he passed through. He
would have to take them to Kalinin, where wealthy merchants would
pay him top dollar.

"Sheepfuckers," Dimitri laughed and shook his head, thinking how
easily cowed the villagers had been. "If you're afraid of wolves, don't
go into the forest."

These wolves were nothing special, little more than hungry dogs.

The hunter rubbed a gnarled finger the full length of the scar that
bisected the left side of his face. The skin was rough and twisted, a

lasting remnant of the ragged wound, as the firelight reflected off the milky whiteness of his dead eye.

No, these wolves were nothing special.

He turned the spitted rabbit again, letting the meat cook thoroughly. Dimitri ran his fingers through his thick black beard as his belly rumbled at the smell of the savory meat. Just a little longer, and it would be ready. If it were earlier in the year, he would have gathered some lingonberries and mushrooms and cooked the fatted rabbit into a stew, but fall came early in this part of Russia, and there would be no berries or mushrooms to forage.

Dimitri stared up at the clear night sky. In his youth, he had hunted wolves with his older brother Arkady; they would spend weeks in the woods and ride out of their native Valdai Hills laden with wolf furs. Those were good times. But Arkady was a different kind of hunter. Dimitri loved the coin from selling the pelts, money he would spend on drink and whores all winter. Arkady loved the hunt and the thrill of the kill with a primal desire that Dimitri never possessed.

Eventually, the wolves bored his older brother, and Arkady left their village searching for more extraordinary prey, traveling to the great wilds of Russia to hunt bears and tigers. He had made quite the name for himself in the Kalinin oblast. Eventually, word spread of his hunting prowess even to St Petersburg, and now Arkady was Tsar Alexander's huntsman. He implored Dimitri to join him, but the city was no place for him. Dimitri loved the quiet of the woods. No, he would hunt his wolves, bed his village whores, and leave life in the Tsar's court to Arkady.

A branch cracked loudly behind him, causing the wolf hunter to bolt upright and turn to scan the woods. The crack was too loud to be a snapping twig underfoot. It had the sound of a thick tree limb breaking in half, but where was the telltale crash of the branch striking the ground?

As Dimitri's eyes scanned the impenetrable darkness of the wooded night, he slid his hand along the log to where he leaned his rifle but found only empty air. His eyes darted down to the log; he was sure he had left his rifle there.

Another loud crack echoed through the woods behind him on the other side of the camp. He spun to face the noise, drawing his long bone-handled hunting knife. Dimitri walked towards the sound, eyes desperately trying to pierce the darkness.

"Hey now, who's out there? Some whelp from that shit pile, Obrechen, come to try and steal my furs, eh?" A charring smell filled his nose, and he looked down in disgust to see that he had failed to turn the rabbit in his distraction, and now, one side had begun to blacken and burn.

"You little maggot, you've ruined my dinner." Dimitri lifted the spit holding the smoking rabbit. "Maybe I put you on my spit instead!"

To his right, Dimitri saw something immense and fur-covered charge from the darkness and run across the clearing. The beast ran crouched over on two legs like a man but covered in dark fur. Coal-black eyes stared hatefully at the hunter from the creature's lupine head, lips peeled back in a feral snarl that revealed a mouthful of jagged teeth that gleamed in the firelight. It ran straight at Dimitri at an incredible speed, and the hunter barely had time to raise one arm to protect his neck and face as he swung the knife in a wide arc with the other.

The creature ducked beneath the swinging blade, veering off from its collision course with Dimitri at the last moment. The hunter heard a sickening crack and popping sound as the wolf beast lashed out with a forepaw, striking his right knee with the force of a cannonball as it ran past and back into the darkness. Dimitri screamed in pain and clutched his knee as he crumpled to the ground, the knife tumbling from his hand.

He took a moment to try and control his breathing; the pain in his knee was nearly unbearable. Dimitri looked down, expecting to see a tattered bloody mess where his knee had once been, and was surprised to see no blood. His knee lay bent at the wrong angle, but there was no blood.

He could hear the animal breathing deeply in the woods and knew he could not lie vulnerable like this. Dimitri tried bracing himself with his right arm while getting back up on his uninjured left leg. The creature darted from the woods, springing out of the darkness first on two legs, then dropping down on all four as it charged him. The hunter's eyes desperately searched the clearing for his missing rifle and lost knife as the wolf beast bore down upon him.

Once again, at the last minute, the creature veered off, striking his left knee as it ran past, then back into the cover of the woods. Dimitri's screams echoed through the forest night as his left leg collapsed under him.

Despite the coolness of the night air, sweat poured from his brow and stung his eyes. He ground his teeth so hard he thought they would shatter as he looked down at his legs. His knees, destroyed by the wolf beast's blows, left the lower half of his legs pointed outwards from his body. They reminded him of a marionette doll lying on the ground, waiting for the puppet master to jerk life into its limbs.

His eye caught movement, and he turned to see the source of his torment stalk out of the darkness. The giant black wolf beast was as dark as night and larger than any wolf he had ever seen as it stepped forth on its hind legs. Its forepaws hung at its side, long black-clawed fingers clenching and unclenching into fists. The wolf reared its lips back in a ferocious snarl, revealing razor-like teeth in a horrific caricature of a human smile, as its dark eyes blazed malevolence at him.

"What the fuck are you?" Dimitri felt disgusted at the fear he heard in his voice.

The wolf beast moved towards him slowly, crouching so that the claws of its forepaws could scratch long streaks in the dirt. The scraping of the claws against the earth reminded Dimitri of the sound of a skinning knife slicing through flesh, separating skin from carcass.

Where had his rifle gone?

The thought felt distant and detached as he watched the wolf slowly circle him. The beast was a thing of nightmares, neither man nor wolf, yet some terrifying amalgamation of the two. Its hind legs were lupine yet capable of allowing the creature to walk upright like a man, and its forepaws ended in fingers reminiscent of a raccoon's, except with the addition of a very thumb-like appendage. The creature's head was indistinguishable from a wolf's, except more immense, and as it stepped between Dimitri and the firelight.

Was this Obrechen's own Beast of Gévaudan, a creature stepping out of myth and lore into Imperial Russia? A werewolf?

Dimitri's hand clawed through the dirt, fingers desperately searching until they closed around the deer bone handle of his knife; firelight reflected off its sharp edge as he raised it threateningly to the circling wolf beast.

The wolf leaped forward incredibly fast for such a large creature and grasped Dimitri's forearm, the long, black fingers closed like a vice grip just below the hand wielding the knife. The beast's hold on his arm was so tight the hunter feared his hand would burst like an overfilled wineskin. He beat at the creature with his free hand, his fist striking the soft fur of its massive head. The wolf jerked its forepaw to the side, snapping Dimitri's forearm so forcefully that the bone tore through the skin, sending an arc of rose-hued blood across the hunter's face and splattering the wolf's black fur.

Dimitri screamed in pain and beat at the creature with one good hand, hoping to catch the soft flesh of its eye. The wolf grabbed his arm mid-strike and wrenched his arm so hard that it dislocated Dimitri's elbow. Tears of pain and fear streamed down Dimitri's face as he lay there, his limbs shattered and useless. Through his pain-addled brain, he wondered what kind of beast attacks in such a manner. He had only known wolves to go for the soft spots like the neck, their jaws ripping and tearing. This creature had barely drawn any blood.

The wolf moved away from Dimitri's immobilized body, the hunter's eyes following its every movement. Dimitri wanted to lash out at the beast, spit in its face, and curse its name with a bravado that would make his brother, Arkady, proud. Instead, the hunter trembled with fear, pants soaking with urine as his bladder vacated.

The wolf stopped and, raising its nose, smelled the air, acrid with the stench of warm urine. It let out a low guttural noise that Dimitri thought sounded hauntingly like laughter.

The beast crouched just above Dimitri's head, warm saliva dripped from the fur beneath the wolf's mouth and splashed onto the hunter's face. Dimitri had to blink the droplets from his eyes. He wanted to turn his face away, but that would only offer his neck to the wolf.

He felt the creature reach beneath his shoulder with its long, clawed fingers, grasping handfuls of his wolf-fur coat. A scream escaped Dimitri's lips, piercing the night and silencing a distant owl as the wolf shook him violently. The jostling of his shattered limbs sent a shockwave of pain through his body that felt as if it would tear his mind asunder. Blackness loomed at the corners of his eyes as the pain threatened to submerge him in unconsciousness. Dimitri screamed uncontrollably as the beast shook him violently, lifting his head and shoulders off the cold earth.

The coat pulled free of his body, and the hunter's head slammed hard against the ground. He tried to suck air into his lungs that had seized up with pain. Wracking sobs escaped the hunter's lips as tears streamed down his face. He called out for his mother, for his brother Arkady, and he pleaded with God for help in an unintelligible blubbering. His black beard was soaked with drool and spittle as his body shook with the aftershocks of the pain.

The wolf slowly placed one lupine paw beside each side of Dimitri's chest until it stood astride him. Dimitri weakly shook his head and whimpered as the beast leaned down. Its snarling maw was inches from his face, the creature's hot saliva dripping onto his cheeks and mixing with his tears. Dimitri could only muster infantile gurgles, too terrified even to form words. Through his tears, he saw the malice in the wolf's dark, intelligent eyes as it extended one clawed finger and traced the scar down the side of his face.

The wolf shifted, and Dimitri felt the weight of the wolf's other forepaw on his chest, the beast's sharp claws piercing his woolen shirt and digging into the soft flesh of his chest, causing rivulets of blood to run down his torso.

Dimitri's lips trembled as his eyes watched in abject terror as the beast ran its claw slowly across the soft skin of his cheek and up the bridge of his nose to hover above his eye. The black claw was so close to the smooth, glass orb of his eye that it was impossible to focus clearly. It appeared to him as a dark blur, framed by the vicious countenance of the wolf's snarling maw.

Time slowed, like sands slipping from an hourglass, as the two figures poised motionless in the clearing. Then the wolf slowly pressed its claw into Dimitri's eye, fluid spraying onto the hunter's face as the orb burst. Dimitri's scream was primordial, mindless in the depth of his pain and suffering. It was a noise utterly absent of anything that resembled the sound a human vocal cord could make as the wolf pressed deeper into his eye socket, twisting its finger from left to right.

The wolf threw its head back and let out a long primal howl, mixing with Dimitri's anguished cries. It looked down into Dimitri's ruined face with immense satisfaction, its breath hot against his skin.

In a sudden frenzy of hatred and bloodlust, the wolf began tearing at the hunter's flesh, cutting deep into his face, neck, and chest. Gore coated the wolf's black fur, and tattered scraps of skin fluttered from its claws as it ripped and tore. Dimitri's body spasmed and jerked violently as his screams turned into wet gurgles.

The wolf howled in rage, sending the creatures of the forest fleeing from the sound of his fury. Animals crouched deep in the furthest recesses of their burrows as panicked deer ran terrified from the sound, and owls took flight into the night sky, seeking the safety of far-off purchases. Even the bears and wolves of the forest gave the area a wide berth, fearful of the terrible beast that fed there that night.

Chapter 5

Pavel lowered his spoonful of beef stew into the bowl and felt his jaw tighten with anger as he watched Leo spoon the stew into his mouth. He watched as the boy navigated the spoon around the chunks of meat, collecting only broth and vegetables onto the spoon. The gendarme officer laid his hands flat on the table to keep from balling them into fists as he felt his anger rising when Leo used one bony finger to push a piece of beef off his spoon and back into the bowl.

"Does the stew taste Okay, Pavel?" Anya Verenicha's brow furrowed with concern as she looked at her husband.

"The stew is fine," Pavel answered without breaking his stare at Leo as the boy slurped his stew, oblivious to the brewing storm across the table.

"Pavel," Anya's voice was soft, almost pleading, as she laid a hand on Pavel's arm.

He flinched his arm at her touch, and she quickly withdrew her hand, the hurt evident on her face. Pavel slowly turned his gaze from the boy to look at his wife, noting with some satisfaction how she withdrew slightly at the cold, loveless look in his eyes. Not that he had not loved her once. He had loved her deeply in those carefree days in Saint Petersburg before the boy was born, before caring for the sick child day and night sapped her of her youth and beauty. His eyes roamed her face, taking in the dark circles under her eyes, the wrinkles formed around her mouth, eyes, and across her forehead from the years of worry over the boy, and the paleness of her complexion. She was grotesque to him now, a sagging, wrinkled shell of the woman promised to him, and he took pleasure in the cruelty of letting it show on his face.

"I think the stew is just fine," Pavel made no effort to hide the contempt in his voice as he turned to Leo. "However, Leo seems to find it objectionable."

"What?" Leo was startled at being suddenly addressed by his usually aloof father. "No, the stew is delicious!"

Leo smiled broadly at his mother and sipped another mouthful of broth.

"Thank you, Leo," Anya cocked her head and beamed at her son. "I am happy you like it."

"I love it," Leo enthusiastically dipped his head for another spoonful.

"Is that so?" Pavel narrowed his eyes at the boy as he leaned forward in his chair. "Then why don't you eat the meat? Is the meat I bring home not good enough for you?"

Leo looked nervously from his mother to his father, "No, father, it's the best meat in Obrechen."

"Then why don't you have a piece?" Pavel watched the boy like a hawk preparing to pounce on a mouse.

"Pavel, Leo does not like to eat meat," Anya interjected as the boy stared at the chunks of beef sitting like dark icebergs in his bowl.

"Doesn't eat meat?" Pavel was genuinely surprised at this revelation as Leo slowly shook his head.

"No, Pavel, he hasn't for a very long time," Anya gave Leo a reassuring smile and patted his arm gently. "He loves animals and does not like the idea of eating them."

Pavel looked incredulously from his wife to his son, then threw his head back and laughed. It was the hardest Leo had ever seen his father laugh, and the boy grinned that he had so amused his father. However, Anya heard the mocking undertone to the laughter and eyed her husband warily.

The laughter died on the gendarme officer's lips, replaced by a cruel smile. The boy's wan face was a picture of resplendent joy as he smiled back at his father, enjoying the rarest moment of connection between them.

"Come now, Leo, don't you want to grow up to be big and strong?" Pavel picked up his spoon and, scooping a large chunk of meat from his bowl, leaned over the table and extended it toward Leo's face.

The smile slipped from Leo's face as he looked uncertainly from his mother to the offered piece of meat. Anya began to protest, but Pavel silenced her with a stern look.

"Go on," Pavel thrust the spoon closer to Leo's mouth.

Leo hesitantly leaned forward, opening his mouth as his mother brought her cloth napkin to her eye to dab away a silent tear.

"There you go," Pavel nodded as Leo's lips closed around the spoon.

He slid the spoon out of Leo's mouth, deposited the utensil on the table, and leaned back in his chair. Pavel watched as Leo chewed the meat slowly, a look of profound sadness on the boy's thin face. He glanced sidelong at his wife as she sniffled loudly, looking down at her hands in her lap.

Leo attempted to swallow the half-chewed chunk of meat, his eyes bulging in panic as the large piece slid into his throat. Anya sprang to her feet in alarm as Leo choked and coughed. However, Pavel remained seated, wincing in disgust at the retching sounds as the boy tried to dislodge the meat from his throat.

With his mouth opened wide like a fish gasping for air, Leo expelled the chunk of beef with a wet-sounding heave. The half-chewed lump of meat landed in the middle of the table with a sickening thwack. Anya hugged Leo comfortingly as the boy began to sob.

"Ugh, that is disgusting," Pavel shook his head as he pushed himself away from the table. A knock at the front door drew his attention. "What now?"

He walked past his sobbing wife and son without offering a glance in their direction and pulled open the door to their home. Two bearded men stood on his porch, dressed in dark tunics and trousers, which were common when the villagers who hunted in the woods. He recognized the men, two brothers, Alexander and Nicolai Chernyshevsky.

"What are you doing at my home?" Pavel's voice was sharp and authoritative. "I conduct business at the gendarme station, not here."

"We were setting wolf traps in the forest, and we found something we thought you should see," Nicolai, the taller and thinner of the brothers, answered the gendarme.

Pavel scowled as Alexander tried to look past him into the house. The gendarme officer stepped onto the porch, causing the two men to step backward as he pulled the door closed behind him.

"What is it you found?" Pavel folded his arms across his chest.

"We found a body," Alexander spoke slowly, his left eye drifting outward as his right eye focused on Pavel.

"It's that wolf hunter, Dimitri, the one from the Kanti Gans," Nicolai added.

Pavel was unable to hide his surprise, "Volkov? He's dead?"

"Torn to pieces." Nicolai nodded. "Unlike anything I have ever seen, and we have hunted these woods our whole lives."

"I guess Volkov is not so high and mighty now," Pavel smiled and shook his head. "Fetch the body and bring it to Father Grigori for burial."

The two brothers looked at each other and then back to Pavel. "I think you need to see the body where it is first," Nicolai said as his brother nodded.

"Why?" Pavel was growing tired of the conversation.

"There's something," Nicolai looked at his brother and then at Pavel, "irregular about the body."

"Yes, very strange," Alexander nodded.

"Wait by the road," Pavel sighed and pointed to where he would meet them, the two men following with their eyes. "I will get my gear."

***

Leo Verenich sat in his wooden wheelchair, his fingers absentmindedly caressing the worn leather cover of his copy of Romeo and Juliet as he watched his father walk off with the Chernyshevsky brothers. He had wished his father a good day, but the man had just walked past him as if he was not there. Leo knew that one day, his father would stop and sit on the step next to his chair, and the two would talk and laugh; maybe his father would even wheel his chair down the road into the woods and point things out to him. Nevertheless, today was not that day; perhaps tomorrow.

"Hey now, what's this?" Leo looked toward one of the shepherds' trails that wound out of the forest to the road leading to the village. A man, a stranger, was walking down the west path to the village. He was wearing a long brown coat and dark green trousers, and Leo could see he had dark black hair but no beard or mustache. A well-worn leather pack was slung across his back.

Where had this man come from? He certainly does not look like a shepherd, and there are no villages nearby, yet this man has no pack or even a hat. He walks with the step of a man full of energy, yet he must have walked a long way to get here.

The man caught sight of Leo sitting in his chair and waved. Leo waved back, and the man walked toward him.

"Well, hello. Friend, can you tell me what village lays ahead?" the black-haired man's accent was strange and foreign.

"It's Obrechen," answered Leo. "Where are you coming from?"

"Oh," the man looked back down the road he had traveled, then back to Leo and smiled, "I've travelled for a long time and come from many places, so I guess you could say I've come from the West."

"My name is Leo, Leo Verenich. Are you hungry?"

"It's nice to meet you, Leo Verenich. I am Bogdan Negrescu," the man dipped his head in greeting and gave Leo a warm, genuine smile. "And yes, I am quite hungry, so it would be very kind of you to spare some food."

"I have some bread here in the basket." Leo pointed to a basket beside his chair. "We could share it."

"That is very kind of you," Bogdan sat on the ground next to Leo's chair. "You would share your food with a total stranger?"

"Of course," nodded Leo. "Once you break bread with a stranger, you are no longer strangers!"

"Wise words indeed." The man reached into the basket and withdrew a fist-sized chunk of bread that he broke in half, handing the larger piece to Leo.

"This is delicious; thank you, Leo," Bogdan took a voracious bite of the bread.

"Were you out in that storm last night?" Leo asked.

"I would be a sorry sight if I was!" Bogdan grinned. "I was lucky enough to find shelter before the skies opened up."

"You have a strange accent," Leo managed between mouths full of bread. "Are you from Germany?"

"Germany? No, I am from Wallachia, in Romania," Bogdan eyed the boy curiously. "Have you ever heard of it?"

Leo shook his head, never having heard of either Wallachia or Romania. Then he saw the man's dark eyes looking intently at Leo's legs.

"What is wrong with your legs?" Bogdan's brows furrowed in genuine concern.

"There's nothing wrong with my legs; my mother says they are just how they are supposed to be." Leo gave a proud smile that crinkled the skin about his eyes.

"And she is right," Bogdan gave the boy a kind smile. "But you cannot walk or run?"

"I have nowhere to walk or run to, and my friends come to visit me here," Leo always felt uncomfortable when the topic of his legs came up. "All you carry with you is that pack?"

"The woods provide me everything I need," Bogdan finished the last bites of his bread and pointed to the book in Leo's lap. "What have you got there?"

"It's a play by an Englishman; my friend brought me the Russian translation," Leo offered the book to the stranger. "I can read it too. My mother taught me. I don't just look at the pictures like some people do."

"I'm sure you read very well, Leo," Bogdan chuckled and turned the book over. "Ahh, Romeo and Juliet. A fine play for a young man. Pretty women and swordfights."

"You've heard of Romeo and Juliet?" Leo's eyes blazed with interest in this strange traveler.

"Indeed, I have. I saw the play once in Paris, many years ago," Bogdan flipped through the pages, then stared curiously at the dozen rough edges poking from the binding where someone had torn pages out. "Leo, someone has deprived you of the story's ending."

"That was Petr Morozov," Leo smiled and shrugged. "It's Okay, though; I'll just make up the ending when I get to it."

Bogdan handed Leo the book, studying the boy curiously as Leo grinned back, "Leo, you are truly an interesting young man."

"Thank you, Bogdan," Leo nodded and placed the book back on his lap, folding his thin hands over the cover. "Are you a soldier?"

"Now, why do you ask that?" Bogdan cocked his head and looked at Leo with genuine interest.

"You have no tools, so you're not a woodsman or tradesman. I don't see any sheep, so you are no shepherd," Leo ran a hand through his close-cropped dark hair. "You're not a farmer; you don't look hungry. Farmers always look hungry. A soldier could live off the land, so I thought you could be a soldier."

"That's very perceptive thinking of you, Leo," Bogdan gave the boy a nod of approval. "I was a soldier once, long ago."

"Did you ever fight in a battle?" Leo leaned forward excitedly.

"Yes, they are terrible things, my young friend." Bogdan's eyes took on a far-off look. "But I was injured and am no longer a soldier."

"Oh, I'm sorry," Leo genuinely meant the sentiment and felt terrible that he had brought up bad memories for the man.

"It's Okay, Leo." Bogdan patted Leo on the shoulder and stood up. "Now I am just looking for a quiet place to live."

"Obrechen is very quiet!" Leo beamed with boyish excitement. "Nothing ever happens here. You should come live in Obrechen; you can sit with me and have bread again."

"I would much like to sit and talk with you again, Leo." Bogdan's laugh was rich and deep. "Next time I will bring the food. Is there anything you would like?"

"Apples! Apples are my favorite." Leo clapped his hands together, his eyes alighting with excitement.

"Well then, the next time I stop by, I will bring some apples," Bogdan smiled and extended his hand to Leo.

Leo shook Bogdan's hand; his hand looked small and fragile in the man's hand. It was a large, strong hand and very warm, as if he had been warming his hand by a fire, and his shoulders were broad and strong. Bogdan smiled down at Leo, and Leo smiled back, looking into the man's kind, dark eyes. It was rare that people showed him kindness. Aside from Alexei, Oksana, and his mother, most people in the village ignored him or tried to look away, even his father. However, this man, a soldier from a distant land, was nice to him, maybe even a friend.

"How do I get to Obrechen, Leo?" Bogdan stretched his neck, working out a kink.

"Just right down the road," Leo pointed toward the village. "You can't miss it."

"Thank you, Leo," Bogdan gave a warm smile that reached his eyes. "I very much look forward to seeing you again."

As Bogdan turned onto the road into the village, a thought occurred to Leo, "Bogdan?"

"Yes, Leo?" Bogdan turned back to the boy. His face bore none of the annoyance Leo often saw when he called out to people.

"Romeo and Juliet," Leo's eyes were large and filled with earnest curiosity, "does it have a happy ending?"

Bogdan's face clouded, and he shook his head solemnly, "No, Leo, the story does not have a happy ending."

"Oh," Leo looked down at the book, a little crestfallen before his smile returned. "Well, it is good that I can make my own ending then."

"That it is, Leo," Bogdan gave him a tight-lipped smile and nodded. "Have a good day."

"You too," Leo called back and gave a wave that Bogdan returned cheerily.

Leo felt a pang of guilt; he had lied to his new friend. He had told Bogdan that nothing exciting ever happened in Obrechen, which was not exactly true. The village was still all astir about the recent wolf attacks. However, that would not worry a soldier like Bogdan. Nothing really ever happens in Obrechen.

***

Pavel forced down the bile that rose in his throat, covering his nose and mouth with a handkerchief to block out the stench of the clearing. Volkov's body was in a horrific state. The man was sprawled spread eagle on the ground with his limbs twisted at an unnatural angle. His torso lay ripped open and crudely cleaned out like an autumn pumpkin, his innards strewn about the clearing. The jagged shards of ribs poked out from behind the skin, torn back, shredded, and darkening with the first signs of rot. Water pooled inside the cavity body from the night's rainfall, dark and wriggling with fly larvae. The man's one good eye was gouged out, the raw hole of his eye socket staring sightlessly toward the sky as a host of maggots squirmed in its depths.

The gendarme thought the ground had blackened around the man's body from the blood that drained from his carcass; however, as Pavel got closer, he saw that the blackness was a teaming mass of flies feeding upon the blood-soaked earth.

"Why does the body smell so awful?" Pavel's voice sounded muffled behind the handkerchief.

"Because he's dead," Nicolais' voice was deadpan as he gave a slack-jawed smile, and his brother snickered.

"I can see that, you dimwit," Pavel's retort was sharp enough to wipe the smiles from the brothers' faces. "I have seen dead bodies, and this one smells different."

"Piss," Alexander replied without emotion.

"Excuse me," Pavel stood before the man, his hand resting on the lead-cored wooden baton on his belt. "If you brought me out here to mock me, I will spread your brains around the clearing with Volkov's."

Alexander swallowed nervously, his good eye staring at Pavel's hand upon the baton. The man's other eye wandered to the far corner of his drooped eyelid.

"My brother means no disrespect," Nicolai came to stand beside his brother. "That smell is piss. Animal piss. It pissed all over the clearing to keep other animals away from its kill."

"It?" Pavel narrowed his eyes. "Surely, you don't mean only one animal did this?"

Nicolai nodded and walked closer to Volkov's body, causing the swarm of flies to take flight in a dark cloud above the carcass. He knelt and pointed to the dirt, "The rain washed away much of the tracks, but the ground is not disturbed enough for this to have been a wolf pack."

"So, what? A bear then?" Pavel tried to make sense of the mottled dirt, then glanced sideways at the younger Chernyshevsky brother, who began poking at a tubular length of intestine with a stick.

"No, a bear would have eaten much of the body and dragged it back to its cave," Nicolai shook his head.

"There are no chew marks," Alexander lifted the length of the intestine and examined it, his lazy eye appearing to peer at Pavel.

"Are you trying to tell me that a single wild animal took down an experienced and armed hunter for what? For what, sport?" Pavel felt his patience with the two men, whom he considered relative imbeciles, wearing very thin.

"Or revenge. The hunter had taken a lot of wolf skins," Alexander pointed to the rough-hewn racks where the wolf skins had lay but now sat empty. Nicolai shot his brother an angry look, and the younger man averted his eyes sheepishly.

Pavel looked to where Alexander gestured, then at the brothers. "Where are those skins now?"

Alexander glanced sidelong at his brother; however, Nicolai stared silently and impassively at Pavel.

"I think I have had enough of this," Pavel shook his head, frustrated at taking the long trek into the woods and irritated that he needed the brothers to guide him back. "We are going back to Obrechen. I will inform Father Grigori to prepare for the burial; you can gather what you need and return for the body."

"Show him, Alexander," Nicolai nodded toward the body.

"Show me what?" Pavel's eyes narrowed as he looked from brother to brother.

Alexander walked over to Volkov's body, stepping over what looked to be a lung discarded on the ground, sending the swarm of flies into renewed flight. He came to a stop beside Volkov's body and turned to face Pavel as he pointed down at the dead man's face.

Pavel sighed, exasperated, and replaced the handkerchief against his face as he walked over to join Alexander beside the body. He swatted at the flies with his free hand, disgusted at the feel of them landing on his skin and crawling about the collar of his shirt. Alexander nodded to the gendarme and gestured toward Volkov's head before returning to stand by his brother.

Volkov's face was a thing of ruin. His dead, milky eye was open wide and reminded Pavel of a frozen lake. He shivered as a fly landed and walked across Volkov's eyeball to worry its hands in the corner of his eyelid. Deep scratches had been torn into Volkov's scalp, revealing the white bone of his skull. The flesh covering it was decaying but alive with growing insect life. Sharp claws had shredded Volkov's cheeks, exposing the man's clenched teeth. A beetle dined on the blackened stub that had once contained Volkov's tongue as its thick black legs rubbing against the yellowing teeth as it.

Pavel felt his gorge rise, and he clenched the handkerchief to his mouth, unwilling to let the brothers see him sicken. That's when he saw it. The thin, straight edges were out of place in Volkov's mouth, and the beetle partially obscured it from sight. He reluctantly slid the handkerchief into his belt as he slipped on his black leather gloves.

Flies buzzed in his face as he knelt, causing nightmarish fears of the creatures crawling up his nostrils into his brain. Pavel fought back revulsion as he reached down, his gloves sinking into the rotting flesh of Volkov's lips as he pried the man's mouth open. The black beetle scurried out onto Pavel's gloved hand, and he quickly shook it away.

He reached a gloved hand into the ruined hollow of Volkov's mouth, disgusted by the feel of the man's teeth against his fingers. The gendarme withdrew his hand from Volkov's mouth and quickly backed away from the body and swirling mass of flies. In his haste, he stepped on a discarded organ that nauseatingly squished beneath his boot, causing him to slide and nearly lose his footing. Pavel glared at the brothers, irritated by the smirks on their faces.

Once he was safely away from the body, Pavel looked down into his hand at the neatly folded piece of parchment. It bore only the slightest blood staining, suggesting it entered Volkov's mouth after he was already dead.

He unfolded the parchment, his eyes scanning the note in neat, meticulous handwriting.

"Gendarme business," Pavel raised a hand to ward off the brothers as they approached. "Stay back."

As Pavel's eyes poured over the note, a thin smile spread across his lips. He saw the pathway to a new future, a better future, laid bare before him—a chance for recognition, promotion, and a life free of that twisted boy and the withered crone that shared his bed.

Pavel Verenich knew he was about to become a very important man.

Chapter 6

Galina breathed in deeply, filling her lungs with the cool autumn air. She rocked gently from side to side; beside her, Oksana guided the wagon down the dirt road to Obrechen.

"Poor donkey," Oksana stared at the animal's gray bobbing head as it pulled the cart. "It must have been terrifying when the storm damaged the roof."

"Seryy is a good soul. I feel terrible; he looked so miserable and wet this morning," Galina nodded at the donkey. "Would you please tell Alexei to come by and repair the barn roof?"

"Of course, Galina. He'll be glad for the work, and the saints know he needs something to keep him out of trouble," Oksana smiled at Galina, then noticed the woman's hand pressed against her side. "Are you in pain Galina?"

"I'm just nervous. Lately, it knots up my stomach," Galina gave her a weak smile. "I know the villagers don't care much for me; going to the market is not a very pleasant experience."

"Galina, we don't need to do this. I can go to the market for you and bring you whatever you need." Oksana pulled at the reigns, slowing the ambling donkey.

"Thank you, Oksana," Galina squeezed Oksana's hand. "You have already done so much, especially after the kindness of staying with me through the storm."

Galina watched a small brown rabbit stare at them, its small nose wriggling at the air as they approached before scurrying into the dense forest. The rhythmic footfalls of the donkey's hooves against the ground calmed Galina's nerves as she stared at the forest that slowly passed on either side.

Despite the storm battering loudly against her little cottage, Galina had had a wonderful night. She and Oksana had talked late into the evening as Galina recounted tales of her time in the Tsar's court, giggling and laughing like she used to with Mali in those days.

Oksana told her how Leo always had a happy word and a smile. She told her of the day one of the younger boys in the village had thrown an apple at Leo as he sat in his chair in front of his small house. The apple had struck him right in the head before landing in his lap. Galina laughed herself to tears as Oksana relayed how Leo had picked the apple up, thanked the boy for it, and taken a big bite as he told Oksana she should "Never turn down a gift, no matter how it's delivered."

Galina glanced sidelong at Oksana, a small smile of contentment on the girl's face as she lightly flicked the reigns to keep the donkey moving. The girl lived a difficult life in Obrechen, especially since her parents had passed away, but she had so much potential. Her mind was as quick as a whip, and Oksana was eager to learn from Galina. She had also been so welcoming to Galina, unlike the rest of Obrechen, and it went beyond her employment in the cottage; she had become a true friend. The thought that Galina would someday soon be going to live with Mali weighed heavily on her heart.

"Oksana," Galina spoke softly, her words almost drowned out by the crunching of the wagon wheels upon the road, "are you sure you will not be in trouble with your uncle for staying the night?"

"Even if Igor noticed I was gone last night, he would be well on his way to forgetting down at the *Kanti Gans* by now," Oksana shrugged and smiled.

"That's good," Galina looked down at her hands folded in her lap, then back to Oksana. "I may have to go to Kalinin soon to stay with the Countess."

"Oh, will you be gone long?" Oksana's forehead creased with concern.

"Yes, I think I will be staying for a very long time," Galina's eyes fell back to her hands.

"I see," Oksana's voice sounded disappointed, and Galina's heart broke for the sadness in the girl's tone.

"I don't think I will be coming back," Galina glanced sidelong at Oksana and could see the girl biting her lip to hold back her emotions.

"Galina Sekova, you have been very good to me," Oksana nodded curtly and then turned to stare down the road. "You have taught me to read and paid me very well. I could not have asked for a better Lady to work for, and I will serve you faithfully until the day you leave. If you should ever return, I would happily return to your service."

Galina turned to face Oksana, placing her hand on the young girl's arm, "Oksana, I meant it when I said you are like a sister to me."

"I did, too," Oksana's voice was low and somber.

"Come with me, Oksana; I am sure the Countess could find a place for you in her house," Galina said.

"Come with you?" Oksana turned to face Galina disbelief in her hazel eyes. "Leave Obrechen?"

"Yes," Galina nodded, feeling certain about her offer to Oksana. The girl deserved a better life than Obrechen.

"Live with you and the Countess in Kalinin?" Oksana's face was a mask of incredulity.

"The Countess is very charitable; she will be your patron. I am confident of it. You can travel with us to Saint Petersburg," Galina gripped the girl's arm more firmly, smiling now.

Oksana nodded, unable to speak.

"Yes?" Galina's pale eyes lit with excitement.

"Yes," Oksana smiled as she nodded again, this time more enthusiastically. "Yes, I will go with you."

The two women smiled at each other, laughing as they squeezed each other's hand.

They spent the rest of the short journey to Obrechen talking about people Galina would introduce to Oksana and the places they would visit together. However, as they approached Obrechen, their mood became more somber, the thatched roofs of the homes standing as a stark reminder that Kalinin would have to wait.

"The market looks busy today," Oksana said, reigning the wagon to a halt as she squinted at the number of people in the market. She thought she caught sight of Father Grigori's dark frock amid a group of villagers clustered in the market's center. Several other villagers walked among the vendor's stalls, examining the vegetables and cloth for sale.

"Wait here with the wagon," Galina feigned a good-natured smile that failed to hide her nervousness as she stepped down from the wagon. "I will grab a few things and we'll be on our way."

"Are you sure you don't want me to accompany you?" the concern was evident in Oksana's voice as she handed Galina an empty basket from the back of the wagon.

"I'll be fine," Galina winked as she turned toward the market.

Oksana smiled and exhaled deeply as she watched Galina walk toward the stalls, still disbelieving the unexpected possibilities unfolding before her. Then, a familiar shape caught her eye: the thin man, arms folded across his chest as he leaned against one of the posts outside the *Kanti Gans*, his dark cap pushed back on his head. Even from this distance, she could feel her uncle's disapproving gaze. He dipped his head forward, spitting on the ground, and disappeared into the tavern.

Galina strolled past the wooden tables filled with vegetables, homespun clothes, meats, and baked goods. She wore a plain brown dress and no jewelry to appear less like a wealthy boyar's daughter and to avoid drawing unnecessary attention and scorn from the villagers of Obrechen. However, as she passed each table, the villagers looked away or met her with cold, disapproving faces etched in deep frowns or tight-lipped stares.

The market held none of the charms of the markets she recalled visiting in St Petersburg with her father. Those markets bore the aromas of delectable foods, spices, and perfumes from the empire and beyond. There were richly detailed dresses and expensive baubles, sometimes even exotic animals, as she strode the cobblestone streets.

There were no cobblestone streets in Obrechen, only dark earthen roads muddied by the night's heavy rainfall. The market smelled of earth, sweat, and animal manure, and Galina wished she could cover her nose with a scented handkerchief but, that would only offend the villagers further.

The wares lay spread out on stained cloths with little regard to appearance. If you needed bread, you came to the market and purchased bread. Galina needed tomatoes, eggs, and milk, though she would prefer to buy some chickens and a cow to avoid these trips into the village. However, the recent deprivations of the wolf attacks on the livestock population in Obrechen made finding a cow for sale unlikely.

Standing alongside the *Kanti Gans*, a man across from the market caught her attention; he seemed misplaced in the village. The finery of his clothing set him apart from the villagers in their homespun tunics and trousers, as did his expensive leather boots. They reminded Galina of the boots the young cavalry officers wore in the Tsar's court. His neatly groomed blonde hair and mustache also appeared out of place in the wilds of Obrechen. Their eyes locked momentarily, and Galina had the distinct feeling that he was watching her. The sensation made her feel like a deer watched by a predator, and it unnerved her. She turned quickly from the man's gaze to peruse the table of a village merchant.

The merchant, a thin man with a bulbous nose and large eyes, ran his tongue over a mouth full of yellowing teeth as he stared at her. Nearly three dozen chicken eggs lay displayed on a soiled green blanket.

"The finest eggs in Obrechen," the man dipped his head slightly.

"I think I will take a dozen," Galina looked over the eggs, as much to break from his lascivious looks as to choose the one she wanted.

"If the lady prefers, I can deliver a fine selection to her home each week," he winked and gave her a smile that made her skin crawl. "Price negotiable."

"Thank you, but I prefer to choose the eggs myself," Galina gave the man a sour look, disgusted at the thoughts behind the man's smile, and began placing eggs into her basket.

"That one is rotten," a strangely accented voice commented behind her.

"Excuse me?" Galina was startled by the appearance of a man stepping beside her. He wore a woodsman's dark green and brown clothing with a well-worn leather pack on his back. The man was clean-shaven, a true novelty in Obrechen, and wore no hat covering his dark hair.

"The egg in your hand," the man pointed at the egg she was holding. "It's rotten."

"Rotten? How can you tell?" She looked from the egg to the newcomer.

The man shrugged and offered a smile that reached his dark eyes, "It just is."

"None of my eggs are rotten," the merchant stood, his eyes narrowing as he looked at the stranger. "They are the freshest in Obrechen."

"I have not been in Obrechen long," the man plucked the egg from Galina's fingers, "but if these are the freshest eggs in the village, perhaps I should keep walking."

The man let the egg fall from his fingers and crack upon the dark earth. A pungent stench of rot immediately permeated the air, causing Galina to gasp and cover her nose. The merchant glared at the stranger as the man looked over the eggs in Galina's basket, replacing three with fresh ones from the table and then selecting a half dozen more after carefully scrutinizing the lot.

"Thank you," Galina placed three coins on the table, nodding as she grimaced at the lingering smell of rotten egg.

The merchant scooped the coins into his hand as he slid a pile of dirt with his foot to cover the cracked egg. He gave her a baleful look but averted his eyes from the stranger's stern gaze.

"Thank you for that," Galina smiled at the stranger as he fell in beside her as she walked through the market. "I am Galina Sekova."

"You are quite welcome, though I fear I will not make many friends in Obrechen," the stranger smiled back. "I am Bogdan Negrescu."

"I have lived here for over a year and have made very few friends. I think it is safe to say that Obrechen is not very welcoming to strangers," Galina glanced at the man. "Are you a Transylvanian?"

"A Wallachian," Bogdan looked at her with surprise and respect. "You are familiar with Romania?"

"I met one of your countrymen in the Tsar's court when I was a girl," Galina said, eyes perusing a table of crusty loaves of bread. "He was quite dashing and made a point to tell all the girls of your country."

Bogdan laughed, a deep, hearty sound, "That certainly sounds like one of my countrymen."

"If you are as good at sniffing out tomatoes as you are eggs," Galina offered the basket of eggs to Bogdan, "then you can consider me your first friend in Obrechen."

"It is truly a gift," Bogdan dipped his head in acknowledgment as he took the basket. "Though I must admit, you are my second friend in Obrechen. I met a young boy in a wheelchair this morning. I came to the market looking to find him some apples."

"Leo and his apples," Galina laughed and shook her head.

"You know the boy?" Bogdan grinned. "I found him quite extraordinary."

"Oh, Leo is certainly exceptional," Galina cast a look toward the *Kanti Gans* and was relieved to see the blonde man was nowhere to be seen. "What brings you to Obrechen?"

"I am looking to find some farm work for the winter before journeying back to Romania in the spring," Bogdan glanced at the bread vendor, who scowled back at them, touching his forehead and chest, then his left and right shoulder, making the sign of the cross as they passed.

As they passed near the crowd of men gathered in the center of the market, Galina could hear Father Grigori's voice rising above the sounds of the market, "For the lips of a harlot are like a honeycomb dropping, and her throat is smoother than oil. But her end is bitter as wormwood and sharp as a two-edged sword. Her feet go down into death, and her steps go in as far as hell."

Between the heads and shoulders of the assembled men, Galina caught glimpses of Father Grigori's face, red and contorted in anger as he addressed the crowd. His hands gestured wildly and pointed a finger toward the heavens as he spoke.

"Tomatoes," Bogdan pointed toward a table covered in a host of root vegetables and a small pyramid of red, albeit slightly bruised, tomatoes.

A short woman, no more than a decade older than Galina, sat on a stool, watching them as they approached her table of vegetables. From beneath a faded blue scarf tied about her head, the woman stared at them with dark, heavy-lidded eyes. Galina could see a sneer cross the woman's face as she rubbed her palms against the homespun fabric of her gray dress.

"Keep walking, Galina Sekova," the woman stood and raised her hand to halt them. "I'll not be selling you any of my vegetables. Not today. Not ever."

"What?" Galina stopped in shock. "Olga Putina, what have I ever done to you?"

"I know all about you," Olga pointed at Galina. "That Englishman told me all about you. He told all of us all about you. You're sickening."

"I don't know what you are talking about," Galina said, her eyes wide in surprise at the woman's vitriol. "What Englishman?"

"Come, Galina," Bogdan whispered to Galina as he lightly grabbed her elbow. "Let's get away from this place."

"Whore," Father Grigori's screamed above the din of the market. "Harlot!"

Galina and Bogdan turned in unison to see Father Grigori stalking angrily toward them, the crowd of villagers now trailing behind him. The villagers shook their fists angrily toward the two, faces angry and menacing. Bogdan took a step forward, placing himself between Galina, the priest, and his small mob.

Father Grigori stopped and seemed to notice Bogdan for the first time; he stared at the man in surprise and then turned back to Galina.

"You're a deviant," Father Grigori spat on the ground. "You are the whore of Babylon, the mother of all harlots and abominations. We all know the depravity that takes place in your cottage—tucked away in the woods where the devil watches what you do."

"The Englander told us everything," one of the villagers shouted from the back of the crowd.

Galina felt her chest tighten and was finding it hard to breathe as the mob focused their anger on her. She felt like a trapped animal in the marketplace, and her eyes darted for an avenue of escape. Behind her, she saw villagers quickly moving out of the way as Oksana urged the donkey and wagon into the market, her expression a mix of fear and anger.

Bless that girl. Galina thought as she watched Oksana approach.

"Let this Englishman come forward," Bogdan's voice boomed loud enough that the villagers fell silent as he stepped toward them. "Let him waggle his tongue in my face so I can reveal him as the scoundrel he is."

The villagers looked about, suddenly unsure, and Galina began to suspect that the mysterious blonde stranger she spotted was the

Englishman in question. However, Galina had no idea who he was and what he had to do with her.

"Who are you?" Father Grigori looked confused as he stared at Bogdan.

"He is my farm hand," Galina tried to sound forceful, but her throat still felt tight, and her voice shook when she spoke.

"I am Bogdan Negrescu," Bogdan squared his shoulders and looked down at the priest, nearly a head shorter than the dark-haired stranger, "and I have witnessed no impropriety on the part of this woman in all the time I have known her. I call on any man who would challenge that assertion to step forward and say it to my face."

The villagers murmured amongst themselves, but none would meet Bogdan's unwavering gaze.

"I thought not," Bogdan shook his head in disgust.

"The Land Captain will hear about this," Father Grigori seethed, but he seemed to have deflated under Bogdan's gaze.

The priest turned and pushed his way through the crowd as the villagers began to disperse back into the market.

Oksana reigned the wagon alongside them, "Galina, are you ok?" Her voice bore a genuine concern.

"Yes, please, I just want to go home," Galina struggled to hold back tears as she climbed up alongside the girl.

"Okay, I'll get you home," Oksana glanced at Bogdan as he climbed into the back of the wagon. "Who's he?"

"That's Bogdan; he's a friend of Leo's," Galina laughed as the tears began rolling down her cheeks. "And apparently, my new farm hand."

"You mark my words, Galina," Olga spat onto the floor. "You are welcome in this market no more."

"I remember you, Olga Putina," Oksana held back none of her anger. "When my father had an apple tree, you and your brothers told everyone in the village that he thought he was a big man growing an orchard; that he thought he was better than everyone else."

Olga's brow furrowed in anger as she glared tight-lipped at Oksana.

"He knew it was your jealous brood that broke down his fence and tried to uproot the tree," Oksana shook her head in disgust. "Then, when the tree survived and bore fruit, you came back and stole every apple your greedy arms could reach.

"My father said you had been a pretty woman once, but your envy of others rotted you from the inside; made you an ugly, hateful thing," Oksana turned away from the woman and urged the donkey onward.

Olga spat onto the ground and glared at the wagon as someone walked up behind her. She saw the finely polished boots step into the mud beside her as the blonde man crossed his arms across his chest.

Chapter 7

"Are you sure you will be ok?" Galina held Oksana's hands in hers and searched the girl's face. "Everything seems wrong in the village, and then there are all the wolf attacks."

"Galina, I will be fine," Oksana tried to give a reassuring smile. The two girls stood beside the wagon; the pathway through the forest to Oksana's home lay just beyond the road. "I am supposed to meet Alexei at my house. If I don't show up soon, he'll wait for me, and I don't want him there when Igor gets home. There is bad blood between those two."

Galina sighed and nodded in resignation, letting go of Oksana's hands. "Please consider staying in my guest room until we leave for Kalinin. You don't have to give me an answer now; we can talk more during dinner tonight."

Both girls smiled at the mention of their escape from Obrechen, and Oksana nodded. Oksana glanced at Bogdan sitting atop the wagon, staring silently at the reigns in his hands.

"Are you sure about this?" Oksana nodded toward Bogdan and spoke in a hushed tone. "We don't know anything about him."

"He's a friend of Leo's," Galina said, looking back at Bogdan and smiling, "and he defended me in the market."

"Okay, just be careful,"

"I will," Galina turned and climbed up beside Bogdan in the wagon. She turned back suddenly, "Oksana, could you make that tomato and pepper soup tonight?"

"Of course, Galina," Oksana nodded, eliciting a broad smile from the other woman.

Bogdan nodded to Oksana, a friendly gesture as he flicked the reins and got the wagon moving. Oksana nodded back and waved to Galina, who enthusiastically returned the wave. She looked back at Oksana, smiling, several times before the wagon disappeared around a bend in the road, and Oksana stepped onto the path toward her uncle's house.

Bright sunlight showed through the forest's canopy as Oksana walked along the dirt path to the house she shared with her uncle—the house that had once been her parents and had once felt like a home. When they died, her Uncle Igor moved from his dilapidated shack on the Morozov's sprawling farm to take up residence in the house, oversee the small farm, and take care of his orphaned niece.

Igor proved more adept at drinking away her parents' savings than managing the farm, and most of the field lay overgrown. The once cheerful home became imbued with his boorishness. Her uncle took the wages that Galina paid her, as rent, to live in her own home, and Igor spent most of that at the Kanti Gans.

Oksana did not think Igor would take kindly to her leaving to live in Galina's home and would likely stir up even more trouble in the village for the woman. She sighed; as much as living in the cottage sounded like a dream come true, Oksana would have to turn down the offer. Igor was volatile and unpredictable; she did not want him to do anything that would jeopardize Galina taking her away to Kalinin. The thought made her smile. When the day came, she would leave with Galina, no goodbye for her uncle, no note. If he tried to go after her, Oksana was sure the Count's men were more than a match for the likes of Igor Balkov.

She looked up suddenly, feeling as if something was watching her. Oksana chided herself for daydreaming as she walked through the woods and tried to look sidelong into the forest, quickening her steps slightly. Although the sun shone brightly, the thick maze of branches in the forest cast deep shadows away from the path, shadows that could easily conceal a man or wolf.

Something moved in the shadows; Oksana was sure of it. Her home was not far now; she could see the faded wooden wall of the back of the house through the clearing ahead and increased her pace. A twig snapped loudly in the forest to her right, and Oksana broke into a run. She could hear movement in the forest; something or someone was moving quickly behind her in the woods.

Her heart thudded in her chest as her arms and legs pumped wildly, propelling her through the overgrown wheat field. Dried stalks and browning weeds bent over and crunched beneath her feet. The overgrowth slapped against her face, stinging her cheeks as she dashed through.

The bright afternoon sun stretched her dark shadow across the ground as she cleared the field and desperately sought to close the last few feet to the house. She glanced sideways at her shadow, a fear rising in her that she would see the dark silhouette of some ferocious beast rising behind her, but there was only sunlight on the ground between her shadow and the field.

Oksana was panting as she bounded onto the porch, and her hands touched her home's faded, wooden exterior. She stopped momentarily, trying to catch her breath. Her throat felt parched and sore from breathing so hard, but her mouth was dry with fear. The sound of rapidly crunching wheat stalks and brambles rose from the field as whatever pursued her closed the distance to the house.

Her legs were shaking from the exertion of the mad dash, and a knot of fear twisted in Oksana's stomach as she began to run toward the front of the house. The thudding of her feet on the porch mirrored the throbbing sound of her heartbeat in her ears. She almost cried with relief as she neared the corner of the house, the front door, and safety only feet away.

Would the door keep the wolf out?

She did not know. Oksana was desperate to get inside, to bolt the door and shutter the windows. Images flashed through her mind: arming herself with a kitchen knife, battering at the wolf with the skillet as it tried to force the door.

Where did her uncle keep his rifle?

As Oksana rounded the corner, a large, human-like shape stepped from the shadows and suddenly loomed before her. She stumbled sideways into the wall to avoid crashing into it. Her arms flailed to keep her balance as her knee slammed into the hardwood of the wall, causing her to cry out in pain. Something closed about Oksana's neck and thrust her backward, hitting her head against the wall with enough force that a bright light flashed before her eyes like a bolt of lightning.

Tears filled her eyes, and she tried to blink them away as the shape exhaled a breath of foul air into her face. It reeked of onions and vodka, a smell she knew all too well. As her vision cleared, the crooked nose of her uncle was the first thing that came into focus, then the rest of his face, twisted in anger. He clamped his hand tightly around her throat, pinning her to the wall. His eyes looked glassy and red-rimmed, as they usually did when he returned from the Kanti Gans.

"I saw you today with that whore, Galina Sekova," Igor's lip curled up into a snarl that revealed a mouth full of yellowed teeth, a blue-gray decay darkening the spaces between his front teeth. He pointed his gnarled finger in her face, poking her cheek with painful jabs.

She tried to tell him they were in the market to purchase vegetables, but his hand was so tight upon her throat that only a wheezy squeak escaped her lips.

"You better not fuck this up for me," spittle flew from his mouth and landed in wet globs on her face. "Where were you last night? The Englander, McMurrough, told everyone in the Kanti Gans how that deviant lies with women. Did you spend the night in her bed?"

Tears streamed down Oksana's face as she shook her head and tried to suck air into her pinched throat. Darkness was beginning to creep in around the corner of her eyes, and she feared she was about to pass out.

"If that woman ruins you, no man will have you. And then I will get nothing for marrying you off," Igor's eyes flared wide open, and he screamed in her face. "NOTHING!"

Oksana's lips trembled, and her body began to shake. A voice in the back of her head, her mother's voice, told her to bring her knee up hard between his legs. Crush his fruits like overripe tomatoes and then run. Run back to Galina. However, she felt immobilized with fear, too terrified to move.

Igor's eyes narrowed, and his voice got low and gravelly as he poked her in the stomach hard enough for her to give a cry that died in her constricted throat. "If you come home with that Jew boy's baby in your belly, I will cut it out of you and strangle you with your innards. I'll leave your bodies for the wolves."

A loud knocking noise, like two logs struck together, filled her ears, and the pressure on her throat suddenly disappeared. Igor's head rocked sideways, and he flew backward off the porch, sprawling in the dirt as Oksana sank to her knees, holding her throat as she coughed and gasped air into oxygen-starved lungs. Then Alexei was there, kneeling beside Oksana and helping her to her feet.

"Oksana, are you okay?" worry etched his face as he looked at her. She managed to nod, beginning to catch her breath finally.

"You bastard," Balkov spat the words as he struggled to sit up, his right eye already beginning to purple and swell shut.

"I'll fucking kill you," Alexei whirled to face him, his hands balled into fists.

"Alexei, no," Oksana's voice sounded hoarse as she grabbed his arm and held him back from charging off the porch to throttle her uncle.

"You don't think we're all on to you?" Balkov pointed at Alexei. "Everyone knows you have been setting off the wolf traps they set off in the forest. Your day is coming. You'll be burning with your parents in Jew hell soon enough."

Alexei shook free Oksana's arm and stepped to the edge of the porch, raising his fists and crouching in his fighting stance. He unballed a fist and gestured with his fingers for Igor to come to him, "Come Igor, try and send me to hell."

A wicked smile slowly crossed Balkov's face as he reached behind his back and drew the small blade he secreted in the belt beneath his woolen shirt. The blade was notched and not much longer than a man's palm. Alexei thought Balkov was likely too lazy to keep its edge sharp. However, the point would sink in deep, and a well-placed blow could still kill or seriously injure him.

"I'm going to carve the Holy Cross into your chest, little Jew," Balkov slowly sat up, trying to get to his feet, still a little unsteady after Alexei's punch.

The sounds of snarling and barking filled the air as Ivan darted from around the porch, a gray blur charging at Balkov with his teeth bared. The ferocity and suddenness of the dog's appearance startled Balkov badly enough that he fell backward onto his rear, frantically scrambling away from the dog and dropping the knife.

Ivan stopped short of the man, snapping at the air between them, a guttural growl rising from deep in the dog's chest. The need to defend his pack from danger had transformed Ivan's usually friendly and welcoming face into something feral and primal.

"Alexei, please, let's just go," Oksana tugged at Alexei's arm, a pleading tone to her voice.

Alexei looked from Balkov to Oksana, his expression softening as he stared at her. A thin smile spread across his lips, and he nodded in agreement. Oksana smiled in return and began running back toward the wheat field, Alexei following close behind her whooping victoriously.

"Come on, Ivan. Come, boy," Alexei called, following Oksana away from the house.

The dog immediately ceased barking and ran after them, his tail wagging cheerfully once again.

Igor Balkov collapsed back onto the soft ground and exhaled deeply. His head swooned from the afternoon's alcohol and the boy's punch. Only through force of will did he settle his rising gorge and not throw up. Staring up at the fall sky, Balkov poked one finger at his swelling eye and winced at the touch.

***

"Look at him," Alexei nodded his head toward the solitary figure of Pavel Verenich, standing impassively in his blue uniform and gendarme cap by the train tracks, "waiting for Kalinin to send men to help him."

They sat on the grassy hill overlooking the twin railroad tracks that ran to and from Kalinin. Ivan stretched out on the grass beside them, enjoying the warm sun on the thin white hair of his underside. He raised his head slightly, snapping at a fly that buzzed too close to his face, then rested his head back into the grass, one dark eye watching the fly buzzing around them.

Alexei shook his head as he looked down at the tracks. Obrechen is not even worthy of a train station.

A pole stood on either side of the tracks, and if a passenger wanted the train to stop, they unhooked a red flag and stuck the flagstaff into the side of the pole to hang down and alert the engineers to stop.

Just like his parents had done on that last trip to Kalinin.

Despite the warm fall day and the small victory over Igor Balkov, Alexei felt his mood darkening as a brooding melancholy began to take root in his mind. He glanced sidelong at Oksana; she had not said anything, just sat staring out over the tracks.

"Are you still mad at me for scaring you?" Alexei turned to her, baring his teeth and raising his hand like claws. "Did you think I was the big, bad wolf coming for you?"

"No," she turned to him, shaking her head. "But you're an asshole for doing it, especially with the wolf attacks that have been going on."

"You're right. I am sorry," Alexei leaned back onto his elbows. She could see by the look on his face that he meant it. She knew that he loved her and would never intentionally do anything to upset her. But Alexei was Alexei. He was reckless, foolhardy, and hot-tempered. She was as upset about the confrontation with her uncle as the scare in the woods. Moreover, the thought of the strange Romanian man alone with Galina troubled her.

"I'm worried about Galina," she said, leaning back on her elbows alongside him. "Are you sure Leo never mentioned this man, Bogdan? He said he was Leo's friend."

Alexei turned his face to feel the sun's warmth and chuckled, "Trust me, if Leo had made a friend like this man Bogdan, I would know; he would not stop talking about meeting a Romanov."

"He's Romanian, not a Romanov," Oksana rolled her eyes and shook her head.

"Romanian. Romanov. It doesn't matter; if Leo were friends with either, he would have talked about it until he was blue in the face." Alexei watched Ivan make a second attempt at the fly, catching it and chewing quickly.

"Then why would he say he knew Leo of all people?" Oksana shook her head. "It makes no sense."

Ivan looked lazily at Alexei, then leaned over to lick the boy's hand. Alexei spied little dark bits of fly still stuck to the dog's tongue, pulled his hand away from the long pink tongue, and rubbed the fur between Ivan's pointed ears. The dog's eyes narrowed in pleasure, delighted at the head scratch.

"Alexei, what if he knew WE were friends with Leo, and he said it to trick Galina?" She sat upright, a look of dire concern on her face.

"Then why help her in the market?"

"Ugh, I don't know," Oksana collapsed back onto the soft grass and rubbed her face. "I don't like it."

"What are you going to do about your uncle?" Alexei's tone turned suddenly serious. "It's too dangerous for you to live there. He could have really hurt you today if I hadn't come along."

"I don't know what I am going to do," Oksana stared at the blue sky, not wanting to make eye contact with Alexei. She sighed, knowing the direction this conversation would turn.

"You could come to live with me," Alexei started, and Oksana knew the proposal that would once again come next.

"Galina offered her guest room to me this morning," She glanced sidelong at Alexei, seeing the disappointment on his face. Oksana wanted to scream; it was unfair of Alexei to keep asking her, pressuring her. It was not that she did not love him; she did, and dearly, just not in the way he wanted and needed.

A train whistle sounded in the distance, and Alexei sat up excitedly. The chugging of the steam engine roared closer, coming from the north, the Kalinin bound train. Pavel Verenich placed the flagstaff in the groove on the poll, the red flag unfurling and fluttering in the breeze. He stepped back and stared down the tracks toward the approaching train.

"Hey now, what's this?" Alexei stood and watched the gendarme officer with great interest as Ivan sat up, ears perked at the sound of the train whistle.

"It looks like Leo's father is going to Kalinin," Oksana was relieved to move on to a new topic.

The train whistle blared again as the engineer spotted the flag and signaled the engine's brakemen to turn the brakes in each car. The squeal of metal on metal filled the air as the train slowed and stopped as it passed Pavel. The engine huffed and hissed steam as it sat on the tracks, reminding Oksana of a giant steel caterpillar catching its breath before running again.

"Pavel Verenich," Alexei cupped his hands and yelled just as the gendarme officer grabbed the railing along the door of one passenger car and stepped up. Oksana could see the man turn to look up the hill as Alexei stretched out his arm and extended his middle finger. "Those who are about to travel, we salute you!"

Pavel glared at the hill momentarily and then disappeared inside the train car. Alexei fell to the ground in a fit of laughter, and Ivan, mistaking it as a cue for playtime, leaped upon him, wagging his tail and trying to lick the boy's face.

Oksana jumped to her feet, furious, "Why did you have to do that, Alexei?"

"He deserves every insult," Alexei was trying and failing to keep Ivan's long pink tongue from repeatedly sliding up the side of his face. "You see the way he treats Leo and his mother."

"Pavel Verenich is still a gendarme officer," Oksana said, biting her lip in frustration. "Was what Igor said about the wolf traps true? Have you been setting off the traps the men are setting?"

"Yes, it's true," Alexei held up a hand in protest. "But only because I was worried Ivan would step into one of those traps and get hurt. They are using steel jaw traps; they will never catch wolves in those stupid things, but it would surely break Ivan's leg."

"Alexei, why must you be at war with everyone?" She shook her head as her eyes began to fill with tears.

"Wait, what?" Alexei sat up as Ivan became fixated, snapping at another fly.

"Pavel, Igor, Petr Morozov, and half the boys in the village," red hot tears rolled down Oksana's face. "You have such a rage in you, Alexei."

"If I have rage in me, it's because they put it in me. Obrechen, Kalinin, the fucking Tsar," Alexei's face flushed and he balled his hands into fists. "Anything I have had in this world, they've taken it all away. I am shit on the shoe of all of them, and they remind me of it every fucking day."

"Galina is going to leave. She is going to take me with her," Oksana did not mean to say it, did not mean to tell him this way.

Alexei opened his mouth to speak, then closed it. He looked stricken, as if someone had punched him in the stomach and taken all the air from his body. His fists unclenched, and his arms hung slack at his sides.

"What are you saying?" Alexei's voice cracked with emotion.

"Galina is planning to go back to Kalinin," Oksana could barely muster the words as she wiped away her tears. "She is going to bring me."

"For how long?" Alexei's face was a mask of pain as he searched Oksana's eyes.

"I don't think she plans on coming back," the words were a whisper as they escaped her lips.

Alexei sank to his knees; his eyes stared past Oksana into a future that did not include her. She ran to him, kneeling beside him and throwing her arms around his neck. She hated herself for blurting the news out in the middle of their argument.

"Come to her house. She needs you to fix the barn roof. We can talk to her about finding a place for you. I know she will let you come with us," Oksana sobbed.

Alexei gently pushed her away and stood; his eyes were cold and impassive. "I'm not leaving Leo. I don't leave my friends behind. Go live your life in Kalinin; we don't need you."

"Alexei," Oksana began. Then, she realized she had no words to make him feel better and fell silent.

"I am going to see Leo," Alexei's voice held no emotion. "I will find out if he knows this Bogdan Negrescu and come by to fix Galina's barn tomorrow."

Alexei turned away without saying anything more and walked off, Ivan following loyally behind him, tail wagging. Oksana watched him go, her heart breaking for Alexei, however, part of her felt a great relief. She had done it. She had torn the bandage from the wound; he knew she was leaving. Now, they both could move on with their lives.

She looked around the hilltop; this had always been a happy place for them, away from Obrechen. A place where they laughed and joked as they watched the trains pass and the sunset. They would lay on the grass on summer nights and stare at the stars. It was where she had first given Ivan, then a tiny gray ball of fur and wobbly legs, to Alexei.

Now, it was where she told him she was leaving Obrechen, and his dreams of spending their life together, of marrying her, were dead.

Oksana followed his footsteps in the grass down the hillside to the old dirt road. She could see Alexei walking in the distance, headed back toward Obrechen, his head hung low, and Ivan walking by his side. Her chest felt heavy, and no amount of deep breaths alleviated that feeling as she turned and walked in the opposite direction toward the woods and Galina's cottage.

***

Pavel watched the red flag flap in the breeze as the locomotive rolled to a stop. He dipped his head to shield himself from the dust the train's steel wheels kicked up as the engineer brought the train to a halt, his hand holding his uniform cap from blowing away.

He looked up at the train's passenger car before him; men and women bound for Kalinin or beyond to St Petersburg filled the window seats, talking or staring out at the countryside. The few who looked at the gendarme officer, curious at who waylaid their travels with a stop in this Russian backwater, eyed him with disinterest before turning away.

Someone called out his name, and he turned to see two people atop the hill by the tracks; one was standing with his arm outstretched and finger raised—the Kaminer boy. He yelled something else, a further insult, no doubt, but Pavel had already turned back to the train. Grabbing the handrail, he pulled himself up, bounding the three steps into the train car.

"Any others?" the train conductor leaned his head out of the car.

Pavel did not even bother to answer the man; he just walked past him into the passenger car. The air was a mix of cigar smoke and perfume as the gendarme surveyed the car and selected an empty seat by the door. There was only room for one person, and a wall section obstructed any view from the window, but Pavel did not care. He had no interest in watching the fields and villages pass by.

The gendarme patted his coat pocket for at least the hundredth time that morning, checking to ensure the note he had retrieved from Volkov's body was still there. As the train lurched and rolled forward, building up speed on its journey to Kalinin, Pavel leaned back against the wall and smiled.

He would present the note to his superiors in Kalinin. Pavel had little doubt that they would provide him with all the resources he required to bring the culprit to justice once they saw the note. His smile widened into a grin as he envisioned the favor and promotions that would follow once he handled the matter. The next time he boarded the train to Kalinin, it would be to leave his life in Obrechen behind. His family, and his humiliations—he would put it all behind him.

Chapter 8

"Oksana, the soup is delicious," Galina lifted another spoonful of the pepper soup to her lips.

"Thank you, Galina," Oksana smiled at the compliment. "I am sorry I did not get here sooner; I would have liked to cook the peppers more."

"Nonsense, it's perfect," Galina patted her on the arm and then looked at Bogdan, seated across from them. "Bogdan, do you like the soup?"

Bogdan gazed at a point behind Galina; his expression was studious and thoughtful. He appeared startled when he realized the two women were looking at him and smiled in embarrassment.

"I'm sorry. Yes, the soup is excellent. The finest I have had in a long time," Bogdan dipped his head toward Oksana. "My compliments to the chef."

"What has gotten you so enraptured that you are distracted from the finest meal in Obrechen?" Galina turned to look behind her.

"That painting of the butterfly," Bogdan gestured toward it with his spoon. "It is exquisite."

"Oh, I don't think it's very good at all," Galina turned back to the table, blushing.

"Butterflies are fascinating creatures. Do you know they are actually two different species inhabiting the same body?" Bogdan nodded. "It's true."

"Now you are just having fun at our expense," Galina narrowed her eyes, but the smile never left her lips. "Such a thing is not possible."

"Oh, I assure you it is possible and true," Bogdan placed his spoon on the table and leaned back in his chair.

"How can two different animals live in the same body?" Oksana looked from Galina to Bogdan. "This sounds like a story from one of Leo's fairy tale books."

"I did learn it in a book, but it was no fairy tale."

The girls exchanged questioning looks and then turned back to Bogdan. "How can this be true?" Galina asked.

"Look, everyone knows a butterfly starts as a caterpillar, and then it goes into its cocoon," Bogdan inched his index finger along the table like a caterpillar, then closed his hands together like a giant cocoon. "It transforms and emerges as a butterfly."

He opened his hands up in a flapping motion to mimic a butterfly soaring away. "But that is where people are wrong. When the caterpillar goes into its cocoon, it dies. But not completely. The butterfly forms from the caterpillar's dead body, repurposing the caterpillar's body and organs. Being neither wholly caterpillar nor butterfly, but some combination of both. Two creatures living in the same body."

"You said you read this in a book?" Galina shook her head, struggling with the disturbing thought of a butterfly growing from the dead body of a caterpillar.

"Yes, when I was in Paris, I read a book called *Metamorphosis Insectorum Surinamensium* by a German naturalist named Maria Merian," Bogdan placed his elbow on the table and rested his chin on his hand. "She wrote a whole chapter on the metamorphosis of the butterfly."

"This was all written by a woman?" Oksana was equal parts fascinated and amazed.

"She was quite an incredible woman, and she wrote the book in seventeen hundred and five, almost two hundred years ago."

"Incredible," Oksana shook her head.

"Quite," Bogdan agreed, picking up his spoon and sipping more of the soup.

"How did you come across this book?" Galina studied Bogdan, still trying to decide whether the man was jesting with them.

"It was the reason we went to Paris," Bogdan stared at his soup. "I had learned a copy of the book was in a private collection there and made arrangements to view it. We were very interested in Merian's research on metamorphosis, and original copies of her work were hard to locate. Naturalists altered later copies produced after her death to discredit her work because they did not believe her theories or were displeased that a woman had made such discoveries."

"So, you traveled to Paris to read a book," Oksana could not contain her shock, which showed on her face.

"We did," Bogdan gave a small, mirthless smile and nodded.

"We?" Galina looked sidelong at Bogdan as she spread butter across a piece of bread.

"My wife and I," the smile slipped from Bogdan's face. "The work was a passion of ours."

"Were you naturalists, too?" Oksana asked.

"No, I was a soldier, and she was a soldier's wife," Bogdan looked as if he was about to say more, then fell silent.

"Where is your wife now?" Oksana saw the pained look on Bogdan's face and regretted the words once they left her mouth.

"My beautiful wife is no longer with us. Taken too soon from this world, I'm afraid. By selfish, ignorant men," Bogdan wiped the cloth napkin across his lips and stood. "I will go chop some firewood; it feels like it will be a cold night. Thank you again for such a delicious meal."

"Thank you," Oksana averted her eyes to avoid meeting his gaze. "I am pleased you liked it."

Bogdan nodded to them both, slipping on his jacket as he walked out the door.

"Galina, I am sorry; I did not mean to upset him," Oksana's brows furrowed in worry.

"It's okay, Oksana," Galina stared at the closed door. "I am sure it will not be our only awkward conversation with our interesting guest."

***

"He said he was at the market buying apples for you," Alexei threw a stick, and Ivan leaped off the porch after it.

"Yep, that sounds like Bogdan," Leo gave a gap-toothed grin and shrugged. "What can I say? I am a man of the world."

Alexei shook his head and smiled at his friend, then frowned as Ivan trotted past him and deposited the stick in Leo's lap. The dog nuzzled his head against the blanket in Leo's lap as the boy ran his fingers against the dog's gray coat. Leo tossed the stick, and Ivan sprinted after it; however, when the dog retrieved it this time, he lay down and chewed on it with the vigor of a wolf gnawing on a bone.

The smile slipped from Leo's face, replaced by a serious expression as he looked at Alexei. "I am sorry that Oksana is leaving; I always thought you two would marry and build a big house here in Obrechen, and I would come live with you."

Alexei laughed, "And who would you marry if you lived with us?"

"Me?" Leo pointed to himself and grinned, "I could never settle for just one woman; that would not be fair to all the rest."

The boys laughed, and then Alexei caught sight of a rider on horseback galloping down the road toward them. Alexei nodded toward the rider, and Leo turned, watching curiously as the man approached. The man was blonde and finely dressed in a red coat, adorned with a gold-colored braid that circled his shoulder. Alexei could see the sunlight gleaming off the highly polished sword scabbard at the man's side. The dark handle of a pistol rode on his other hip.

Ivan stood as the rider approached, abandoning the stick and backing away toward the edge of the woods. His dark eyes watched the horse and rider warily as the hackles rose along the ridge of his back. He lowered into a crouch, emitting a noise between a whimper and a growl.

"The man looks like a nobleman," Leo stared in wonder as the man approached. "Look at that black horse he's riding; that's no plow horse."

"He looks like trouble," Alexei narrowed his eyes as the rider reined his mount to a halt before the house.

"I am looking for the gendarme Pavel Verenich," the man nodded toward the house. "Is this his home?"

A look of distaste crossed the man's thin face as he looked over the humble porch of the Verenich house. Something in the sharp features of the man's face and the way his intense steel-gray eyes conveyed a sense of cunning and hunger reminded Alexei of a wolf.

"It is," Leo beamed with pride. "He is my father."

"Your accent. Are you an Englishman?" Alexei felt his unease about the man growing.

"An Irishman, actually," the man answered Alexei, his tone short and annoyed before turning back to Leo. "Is your father home?"

"No, Sir," Leo shook his head. "He's gone to Kalinin."

"When will he return?" the man appeared agitated at Pavel's absence.

"I don't know, Sir," Leo shrugged.

"Are you the one they call McMurrough?" Alexei's eyes narrowed as he remembered Balkov mentioning the name during the attack on Oksana.

"Good, you've heard of me," the man gave Alexei a thin-lipped smile and nodded. "Tell the gendarme that I expect to be back in this shithole soon and may require his services. He should be ready when I call."

Leo appeared delighted by the news; however, Alexei gave the man a sour look, "I'm not the Tsar's goddamn town crier. Leave your message with the Land Captain, or better yet, just don't fucking come back."

"Alexei," Leo's voice was barely above a whisper as he pleaded with his friend.

McMurrough appeared surprised by Alexei's sharp retort, the smile slipping from his lips and his blonde mustache arching upwards in a sneer as he slowly eased the horse toward the porch. Alexei rose to his feet and stood between the approaching rider and Leo. He unwaveringly returned the man's steady gaze while his mind frantically raced with how he would fight off the horse and rider if they attacked.

His father had told him stories of gendarme riding their horses into the midst of protestors, the horses biting people and stomping those unfortunate enough to fall to the ground as the officers beat men and women with lead-lined police clubs.

"My husband is away on important business," Anya Verenich stepped out onto the porch, wiping her hands on a dark-stained apron. "He is not expected back for several days."

McMurrough stopped advancing on the porch and appraised the woman. He watched as her eyes anxiously went from his face to the boy in the wheelchair. She gripped and released the hem of her apron, a nervous habit.

"Alexei," she gestured toward Leo. "Please take Leo inside; supper is ready. I have set a place for you as well."

Alexei nodded, grabbed the wooden handles at the back of Leo's chair, and turned him toward the door. Leo's mother gave him a weak smile and a nod of thanks as he rolled Leo past her.

"Is there a message you want me to give my husband?" Anya returned her gaze to McMurrough.

"I already gave the message to the boy," McMurrough wheeled his horse about to face back toward Obrechen.

Alexei looked back as he rolled Leo into the house, locking eyes with McMurrough, who stared past Anya at him. There was menace in the man's cold gray eyes, an unspoken threat.

McMurrough looked away and kicked the horse into a fast gallop, kicking up dust and dirt as it sped its rider away.

Alexei, you have certainly become adept at making new enemies.

Alexei watched McMurrough ride off, relieved that Oksana had not witnessed the exchange. He did not need to give her any more reasons to hate him.

***

"This vegetable soup is delicious," Alexei barely looked up from the steaming bowl as he spooned several mouthfuls.

"I'm glad you like it," Anya gave him a genuine smile of delight.

"It's my favorite," Leo grinned, and Alexei saw that made the boy's mother's smile grow wider.

"I saw your father get on the train for Kalinin today," Alexei looked at his friend. Out of the corner of his eye, he saw Leo's mother's countenance grow concerned, and she was about to say something, but Leo excitedly jumped in first.

"I think he went about the hunter the Chernyshevsky brothers found dead in the woods," Leo beamed with, in Alexei's opinion, the inexplicable excitement he always showed when talking about his father. "Mother, do you think the rider was here about that too?"

"Leo," his mother spoke in a gently scolding tone. "You know your father does not like when we discuss gendarme matters with anyone. This is your father's business alone."

"But he doesn't know that I know about the hunter. I overheard Nicolai Chernyshevsky telling him on the porch," Leo insisted.

"A hunter was killed?" Alexei looked from Leo to his mother. "Someone from the village?"

"No, someone from far away," Leo's eyes gleamed excitedly. "I think that's why Father went to Kalinin."

"Leo, that's enough," Anya's face still looked happy, even as she gently scolded Leo. Leo opened his mouth to speak, but his mother stared at him until he took another sip of soup.

"Alexei, will you see Bogdan when you go to Galina's house?" Leo leaned back and wiped a drop of soup from his lip.

"I don't know. I guess so," Alexei shrugged. "I am supposed to go there tomorrow to fix some damage the storm did to her barn."

"Great," Leo's eyes opened wide. "Can you ask him if he's seen any strange footprints in the woods?"

"Strange footprints?" Alexei put his spoon down and glanced sidelong at Leo, then a knowing smile crept across his face. "Footprints, like from a giant chicken?"

Leo grinned as he slowly nodded.

"A giant chicken?" Anya laughed, and both boys turned excitedly toward her.

"He's a woodsman. He's traveled all the way from Romania. He may have come across tracks," Leo explained.

"It's possible," Alexei nodded, rubbing his chin.

"Possible that he's come across a giant chicken?" Anya looked at the two boys as if they were crazy.

"Not a giant chicken," Leo shook his head. "Giant chicken footprints."

"Baba Yaga's hut travels on two giant chicken legs," Alexei used two fingers to walk his hand across the table.

"Gracious me," Anya shook her head as she stood up from the table, the smile never leaving her lips. "You boys are obsessed with that fairy tale witch!"

"There are too many tales about Baba Yaga for her to be a fairy tale," Leo counted off on each finger. "There's *The Frog Princess, Maria Morevna, Vasilissa the Beautiful,* and so many others. And those are just the ones I have read."

"*Vasilissa the Beautiful,*" Alexei sat up straight and stared at Leo as the boy nodded.

"Do you see it now?" Leo grinned at Alexei.

"I can't believe that did not occur to me before," Alexei said.

"What are you boys talking about?" Anya folded her arms across her chest and looked from one boy to the other, laughing at the manic direction of their conversation.

"Baba Yaga tried to trick Vasilissa," Leo explained. "She told her to go out and sheer the sheep."

"But the sheep were wolves in disguise," Alexei added.

"Don't you see Mother," Leo said excitedly. "Baba Yaga can control wolves. That's why no one has been able to kill the wolf attacking Obrechen; the witch controls it."

***

Galina stacked the two heavy blankets from the ornately carved chest in her arms. She had not used them since she and Mali took them to a spring picnic. Mali had laid the dark green blanket on the grass, but the gold-trimmed red blanket they had wrapped around their naked bodies as they shared a bottle of wine, then kisses and intimate caresses until they laid sprawled, their bodies intertwined. Mali laughed and said she felt like a forest nymph, making love under the open sky. Galina breathed deeply, fancying she could still smell Mali's perfume on the soft fabric. Sighing with longing for Mali, Galina closed the chest and carried the blankets to Bogdan, who awaited in her sitting room.

"I feel awful that you will need to sleep in the barn, but with Oksana staying here now, there is no room in the cottage," Galina carried the blankets into the sitting room and stopped. Bogdan was staring intensely at a painting she had done of Mali. He cocked his head and studied the painting with a slight smile on his face.

She had painted the portrait from memory over the last winter, during a particularly long period between Mali's visits. Mali sat naked before the fireplace in the painting, her back to the painter. Her hair hung about her shoulders and back as the black blanket from Galina's bed lay beneath her. The firelight illuminated the gentle contours of Mali's body, the curve of her breasts and buttocks. Galina blushed that Bogdan should see Mali in such an intimate pose, then chided herself for such thoughts since she had hung it in the sitting room for all to see.

Bogdan suddenly noticed Galina in the doorway and gave her a smile that reached his eyes. "This is really quite remarkable. She must be very special to you."

"It is just a fanciful painting, an imaginary friend to keep me company in the sitting room on long winter nights," Galina stood beside Bogdan and gave the painting a dismissive wave of her hand. "I'll have to think up a name for her one of these days."

Bogdan gave her a knowing smile and then leaned closer to study the painting, "Oh, I think she has a name already."

Galina gave a nervous laugh as her mind raced to find a way to direct the conversation away from the painting, but Bogdan continued speaking.

"When I was in France, I learned a lot about art. How to recognize what the artist saw when they painted their subject," his finger traced the air above her brush strokes, "the loving way an artist captures the gentlest curve of the body; the subtle ways the light falls upon the subject."

Galina found herself staring at the portrait, remembering the emotion she felt as she painted it. The love and longing she felt for Mali as she poured her heart into the work. Her eyes began to well with tears as the memories came rushing back.

Bogdan nodded as he looked at the portrait, "This is no work of fancy; this is a work of the heart—an expression of love through art. It's a masterpiece, and that woman is lucky to be loved so completely and powerfully."

Galina sniffled as she wiped away her tears, and Bogdan turned to her in surprise.

"I am sorry," Galina tried to turn away to hide her tears.

"You have nothing to be sorry for, Galina. The heart loves who it loves, and there is nothing purer and more beautiful than that in all the world. I loved my wife that way, and it is a joyous thing if you love this woman that way."

"Not in Obrechen," Galina forced a smile onto her face as she wiped away the last trails of her tears.

"Obrechen is not the world," Bogdan's voice was soft and warm as he took the blankets from her. "Thank you for these; it's very kind of you."

"I'm sorry, the barn is all I can offer you. The storm did not damage the forward hayloft, so it should be warm and dry, and there is some spare furniture I can provide you tomorrow to make it feel more homey."

"I have been sleeping in the forest for a long time; the barn will feel like a castle," he dipped his head in gratitude.

"Alexei should be by tomorrow to help you mend the roof."

"Seems like he has much more to mend than just a roof," Bogdan nodded in the direction of the guest room where Oksana slept.

"She is a brave girl," Galina said, shaking her head and staring at the closed door of the guest room. "Unrequited love can be as painful to the one loved as the one loving."

"Very true words," Bogdan said as he walked to the door to the outside. "I wish you both a good and peaceful night."

Galina watched Bogdan go, then called out to him, "Mali."

Bogdan's face appeared in the half-closed doorway, "Miss?"

"Mali," Galina smiled broadly and tilted her head toward the painting. "Her name is Mali."

Bogdan returned her broad grin, "A fine name and a lucky woman."

The door closed, and Galina looked at the painting, her eyes pouring over the curves of Mali's body. Her chest heaved as she breathed deeply. She missed her friend. She missed her lover. Raising a hand to her lips, she blew the painting a kiss.

"Goodnight, my love."

***

The wolf beast stalked his prey. He had been careful to approach from downwind so the foraging deer would not be alerted by his scent in the air. His dark eyes watched the sun's angle, keeping the deer between him and the sun so that his shadow would fall behind him. Hunger filled his belly, and his nose burned with the strong scent of the young deer.

With careful movements, he navigated through the trees. His paws, powerful and nimble, moved with meticulous precision not to snap a dry twig or knock loose a rock that could roll free and warn the deer of the impending danger. His mind walked the fine line between the ravenous desire to feed and the need to approach cautiously, soundlessly. When he was newly made, he had often made the mistake of giving in to the desperate hunger and charging at first sight of his prey. More often than not, fleet-footed prey would outdistance him to freedom or dart into the safety of a tree or burrow.

However, he was a more experienced hunter now. He was the master of his hunger. He had learned that patience brought down the best prey, and then he could feed, gorge himself on the soft flesh, the hot blood, the still warm heart. Part of him envied the deer as it grazed upon the patch of grass at the edge of the wooded clearing. The deer did not need to hunt, chase, or kill; it simply needed to find its patch of grass and eat at its leisure. Fill its belly and be on its way. The forest was full of food for the deer's taking; whenever it was hungry, it ate.

He was so close now that he could hear the beating of the deer's heart on the wind. A hawk cried out as it flew overhead, and the deer looked up with casual interest. In that moment of distraction, the wolf beast sprang, powerful legs and shoulders propelling him forward, running on all fours for added speed; though at this distance, he likely could have closed the distance to his prey on just two. He was nearly upon the deer when it registered danger; it turned to flee but was too late. The wolf was upon it, its legs buckling under the beast's weight.

He could feel the terror-fueled frantic beating of the deer's pulse as the fingers of his dark paws closed around its neck and head. He jerked his massive paws and swiftly snapped the deer's neck in one clean movement. Feeling the deer's body slacken, he lowered the dying creature to the ground. Almost tenderly, the wolf positioned the deer's head so that its eyes looked up at the afternoon's fading sunlight as the wind rustled gently through the treetops. A serene final sight as the light in the young deer's eyes slowly extinguished.

Panting with the exertion of the kill, the wolf stared down at the deer. Aside from the odd angle of the deer's neck, it looked untouched, not even a scratch where he had grabbed it. His coal-black eyes watched as the rise and fall of the deer's chest slowed. The wolf placed a forepaw on the deer's side; the massive, well-padded paw, with its complex series of mechanoreceptor cells, could sense delicate changes in pressure as the creature's heartbeat ceased. His long, tapered fingers, covered in black fur and tipped with sharp curved claws, caressed the rough brown fur of the deer's side and patted it lightly. He regretted the deer had to give up its life for his nourishment, but that was the way of the world, and he had eased its passing as best he could. Suffering did not need to accompany death unless it was warranted.

The black wolf beast rose to his full height on his two hind legs, human-like except for the long, canine-like slope of his tibia and the deep angle of his ankle hock. He threw his head back and howled, a deep guttural sound from the depths of his body, honoring the fallen creature and announcing the deer spirit's passage into the other world.

Then he fed.

Chapter 9

Father Grigori looked out over the villagers of Obrechen assembled in his church. Many stared blankly back, ready for the service to be over so they could return to their homes or, in the case of most of the men, retire to the Kanti Gans for an afternoon of drink. With the Litanies of Prayers and the communion of the faithful with the Body and Blood of Christ complete, most expected the service to end swiftly.

Grigori Makarevich was the third son of a parish priest who ministered to a flock less than ten miles from Saint Petersburg. His father was a member of the white clergy, those priests who were allowed to live in the world, marry, and have children. In return for such concessions, reaching the upper echelons of the Russian Orthodox Church was denied to members of the white clergy. Grigori's father lived and died as an impoverished parish priest, living off the meager donations of his congregation.

His older brother sought greater glory in the world than the life of a parish priest could offer. Nikita joined the Tsar's army and was killed less than a month into his service in a meaningless skirmish in the North Caucasus. Grigori believed his other brother, Josef, suffered an even worse fate. Following their father's footsteps, Josef became a member of the white clergy, assigned as a parish priest in Yakutsk in Russia's frozen Far East, destined to live out his days with his cow of a wife and their brood, cold and impoverished.

Far more ambitious than his father or brothers, Grigori chose the path of the black clergy, those clerics who devoted their lives to God and took a vow of celibacy. Only these celibate clergy could ascend to the role of Bishops, Archbishops, and other privileged positions within the church. It was to these heights that Grigori firmly set his sights. However, he quickly learned rising within the ranks of the black clergy required the favor of seniors willing and capable of appointing him to positions of greater responsibility. To gain that favor, Grigori needed money, and with no familial wealth to rely upon, he needed to become resourceful.

He lobbied and received assignments to large, wealthy dioceses in Saint Petersburg and Kalinin; however, Grigori discovered that despite the constant stream of donations, very little trickled down to the more junior clergymen. Thus, to his superiors' surprise, Grigori requested a posting to a village parish and accepted an assignment to Obrechen.

Here in Obrechen, Grigori found the possibility for personal enrichment substantial despite the relative poverty of the village. The village priest held significant sway over the villagers. Grigori found the people of Obrechen lacked genuine piety; however, they possessed a healthy fear of divine retribution, which he attributed to their superstitious pagan past. The Land Captain paid Grigori handsomely for sermons that kept the villagers in line or provided a divine push in a direction that favored Morozov.

He pocketed some coin from providing blessings at weddings, funerals, and other pastoral functions. However, Grigori's most significant source of wealth came from the traveling merchants who frequented Obrechen, and the priest took no small satisfaction in his ingenuity. Grigori preached that the ill spirits that caused sickness and misfortune hid within the wares of outsiders who came to the village. In one of his most fiery sermons, he warned that if outsiders and their goods were not adequately blessed, dire times could befall Obrechen.

Within days, merchants were arriving at Grigori's church, complaining that the villagers would not purchase their goods until they received a blessing from the village priest, a service Grigori was happy to provide—for a fee. It had become quite a profitable enterprise for Grigori, which would fund his appointment to a position of more significant potential in Kalinin.

His coffers had recently become substantially buoyed by the contributions of the Irishman McMurrough, who paid exceedingly well to ensure Obrechen became inhospitable to Galina Sekova. In truth, even before McMurrough filled his ears with tales of Sekova's torrid escapades, Grigori detested the woman. Once villagers spotted the carriage secreting its way to and from the old Kravchinsky hunting lodge after Sekova took up residence, a rumor spread that she was a concubine to a nobleman in Kalinin; and in Obrechen, a rumor was as good as truth.

The first time Grigori had seen Sekova in the village square, the woman greeted him with a warm smile. However, the priest read what was behind that smile, a mockery that laughed at his piety and flaunted the accoutrements of wealth that came to her by merely spreading her legs when he had to toil for all he had. McMurrough's information about the depth of debauchery that the woman committed at her den of iniquity in the woods boiled Grigori's blood to his core. The very existence of a woman like Sekova in his rural diocese was an affront to all that Grigori held holy. Though on those nights when Grigori lay awake imagining the wages of sin Sekova was committing at that very moment, he knew that part of him hated her for indulging in carnal pleasures denied him.

Grigori scanned the assembled faces and was surprised to see Anya Verenicha and her lame son in attendance; that was a first as far as he could recall. The smiling face of Vera Morozova, standing in the front row of worshippers, also caught his attention. The petite brunette woman was attractive by any man's standards and a far better, if naive, woman than the Land Captain deserved for a wife. The daughter of a wealthy merchant from Kalinin had been quite the catch for Andrei Morozov and remained so even after giving birth to their son. Yet, as all the village knew, that did not keep Andrei from his dalliances with the young girls in his employ.

Grigori looked to Andrei Morozov, and the man gave him a slightly perceptible nod—the Land Captain's signal for him to begin.

"My children," the priest began, all eyes watching him. "The village of Obrechen is under attack from forces of the Devil himself. For weeks, we have lived under the scourge of the wolf. It has taken our livestock, depriving our children of food this winter. Some of us will face hunger, starvation, or worse because of the deprivations of this beast."

Grigori looked over the sea of faces, many nodding solemnly in agreement.

"This is Imperial Russia, and we are used to the plague of wolves that often befall us. But as the Chernyshevsky brothers have discovered, it is not a pack of wolves that attack Obrechen; it is one wolf," Grigori held up a finger. "One wolf."

He could hear murmuring from the assembled villagers from where the Chernyshevsky brothers stood. "It's true," Grigori heard Alexander Chernyshevsky tell several villagers as his brother nodded enthusiastically to all who made eye contact.

"The Bible warns that wolves will come among you, not sparing the flock," Grigori's voice raised above the murmuring, and the room silenced. "And why does it come?"

Grigori paused to let the anticipation build as the villagers watched him intently; some even leaned toward him as if they were about to be told a secret.

"In the Book of Jeremiah, the Lord tells us that the wolf will come because of transgressions and apostasies," Grigori shouted the words loudly enough that several in the front row jumped.

The priest's eyes searched the sea of faces until he found Olga Putina's dark eyes. His eyes locked with hers and held her gaze as she stood flanked by her brothers. Grigori had to withstand the urge to smile as Olga's eyebrows raised slightly in surprise at the priest's attention.

"The wolf comes to punish Obrechen for our sins," Grigori held Olga's gaze as he spoke.

"We have done nothing to deserve this," a woman's voice called from the back of the room.

"Oh, but we have," Grigori stared at Olga with unwavering intensity. "Our sin is that we have not punished the great sinner among us. A woman, a fornicator of such debased depravity that the Devil's wolf smells her sins and comes running. The desire for the wolf to commit these atrocities against us comes from the same dark place as the urge of the fornicator to spread her legs; there can be no doubt that this is the instigation of the devil."

Olga Putina nodded knowingly as Grigori spoke the words with utter distaste, his face contorting as if he had eaten an unripe berry. "Galina Sekova."

"So, what is to be done? How can Obrechen be saved?" Grigori's eyes scanned the villagers, who looked at him with expectant faces. Only the Verenich boy seemed to frown and look away.

"My flock, I beseech you to be strong and courageous in the face of these assaults upon the body of Christ by the instruments of the Devil. The wolf must be destroyed," Grigori's face again turned toward Olga Putina. "And as the Apostle Paul wrote, I have already judged them who has so committed this, as though I were present. In the name of our Lord Jesus, when you are assembled, and I with you in spirit, with the power of the Lord Jesus, deliver such a one to Satan for the destruction of his flesh."

"Father Grigori, as Land Captain of Obrechen, I pledge to see this wolf destroyed," Andrei Morozov lifted a small leather purse stuffed with rubles, their round edges poking out against the soft leather. "And I will reward any hunters that join me with this purse."

"The Lord Bless you, Andrei Morozov," Grigori raised his hands in benediction. "Go with God, my children."

***

Father Grigori stood by the door as the villagers filed out of the small church, exchanging brief pleasantries and blessings as they passed.

"Anya Verenicha, this was a delightful surprise," Grigori dipped his head as Anya rolled Leo's wheelchair to the door.

"Thank you, Father Grigori," Anya smiled at the priest. "My husband is away dealing with a gendarme matter in Kalinin, so I thought it would be a good opportunity to bring Leo to hear the Lord's words."

"And how did you enjoy the service, young man?" Grigori looked at Leo, who did not meet his gaze.

"It was fine, Father Grigori, thank you." Leo looked down at his hands, fidgeting his thumbs.

"Was there something you found displeasing, Leo?" the smile slipped from Grigori's face.

"Oh, no, Father," Anya interjected. "It's just this business with the wolf. It has everyone frightened."

"I see," Grigori stared at Leo a moment longer, then looked to Anya, the smile returning. "I hope we will see you in church more often."

"I will try, Father," Anya said, shaking her head and looking down at Leo. "But there is very little time left in the day after being a wife and mother."

Grigori reached out and took her hand in his. Anya looked at the priest, surprised at the gesture, and Grigori stared into her eyes, "We must always make time for God. Perhaps... perhaps you could find time to come and see me. Caring for a sickly child and being married to such an important man in the village are weighty responsibilities and carry with them their own spiritual needs that need tending to."

"Thank you, I will have to see," Anya quickly withdrew her hand and resumed pushing Leo's wheelchair. "Good day, Father Grigori."

"Good day," Grigori watched her slowly maneuver the wheelchair down the stairs and roll the boy toward home. His eyes followed her until he realized someone had stopped before him.

"Father Grigori," Olga Putina was flanked by her brothers, tall, brutish boys who worked in the village stables. They nodded in greeting as their deep-set eyes peered at the priest from round faces pockmarked from a childhood illness. Grigori smelled the odor of dirt and manure strongly from the young men and wrinkled his nose in distaste.

"Olga, did you enjoy the service?" Grigori tried to speak without inhaling more of the odor through his nose.

"I did, Father," Olga bobbed her head. "It was almost as if you were talking to me."

"Sometimes Olga," Grigori made the sign of the cross, "that is because the Lord speaks directly to his children through his faithful servants."

"Yes, Father, thank you," Olga's eyes lit with fervor, and a smile crossed her face that the priest suspected concealed more than a bit of malice.

Grigori nodded to the trio as they turned away and departed the church. He took a deep breath once he felt the air was sufficiently clear of the aroma of manure. Olga was speaking animatedly to her brothers, and the men were nodding their heads and grinning wickedly. The priest let a self-satisfied smile cross his face. McMurrough had chosen wisely to seek the priest's assistance and paid handsomely for it.

"Father, what a wonderful service," Vera Morozova's voice was breathy with reverence as she stopped before the priest.

Grigori smiled so widely it reached the corners of his eyes as he placed his hand over his heart, "It does my heart wonders to hear such praise."

"Yes, Grigori, it was excellent," Andrei Morozov extended a hand and gave the priest a firm handshake.

"Thank you, Andrei," Grigori shook the man's offered hand and dipped his head.

"Father, we are so grateful to have a servant of the Lord defending us from this wickedness," Vera clasped her hands together as if in prayer. "You are true a warrior of God."

"I am just his humble servant," Grigori gestured to the Land Captain. "It is your husband who will undoubtedly deliver us from the dark specter of this wolf."

Vera sighed deeply, her ample breasts rising and falling with the motion, though Grigori tried hard not to appear to notice. "Father, I fear every night for the safety of our livestock," she shook her head as a worried look crossed her face. "Is there any way you can come and bless our barn? To keep it safe from the evils of the wolf?"

Andrei groaned and rolled his eyes, "Woman, must you ceaselessly trouble Father Grigori with your fears? You've had him come and bless our home, and the fields, and even that damn calf last month. The good priest spends more time at our home than I do!"

"Andrei, it is no trouble," Grigori assured him. "I am always glad to be in the service of the Land Captain's household. I can come the day after tomorrow."

"Oh, Father, thank you," Vera beamed.

"Now go, run along," Morozov patted his wife on the backside. "Go see what mischief our fool of a son has gotten himself into now."

"Wait a moment," Grigori put a hand up to stop her from leaving, then made the sign of the cross before her. "There, now you go with all the Lord's protection."

A look of sheer rapture crossed Vera's face, her smile spreading wide to show perfectly white teeth. Then she turned and hurried down the steps.

"Grigori, you should be made a saint for putting up with that woman. I swear I have cows smarter than her," the Land Captain shook his head as he watched Vera depart.

"I'd settle for bishop one day," Grigori shrugged and grinned broadly.

Morozov laughed so hard his sizeable belly bounced up and down in a way that reminded Grigori of the stories of Saint Nicholas, "I am sure you would, Grigori!"

"I trust my sermon was to the Land Captain's liking?" Grigori dipped his head in a deferential bow.

"It was indeed," Morozov produced a small purse of coins, handing it to the priest. "These peasants will build a statue in my honor once I rid them of this fucking wolf scourge. What was all of that business with the Sekova woman?"

"The Church is grateful for your donation," Grigori quickly palmed the purse and slipped it into the pocket of his black cassock. "That was at the request of a certain well-dressed visitor from Kalinin."

"McMurrough? What's his interest in her?" Morozov raised an eyebrow, then smiled with lascivious delight. "Is he a jilted lover? I must admit that is one pony I would not mind taking for a ride myself."

"Andrei, please. We are in the house of the Lord," Grigori extended his hands, gesturing to the now empty church.

"Apologies. I forget myself," the Land Captain shrugged and gave the priest an insincere smile as he began walking down the stairs. "You know, Grigori, you priests would be a lot more bearable if you did not take that damn vow of celibacy. Of all the things to give up for one's god, fucking seems the most unnatural one of all."

"I guess that is my cross to bear as His servant," Grigori dipped his head in farewell.

***

Alexei brought the hammer down repeatedly on the nail, driving it into the wooden plank until the head of the hammer created a round dent in the wood.

"I believe the idea is to hammer the nail into the plank, not through the plank," Bogdan said, sliding a plank of wood across the hole in the barn roof and throwing Alexei a half smile.

Alexei gave him a sour look and hammered a second nail into place beside the first. Bogdan straddled the peak of the barn roof and lined up two long planks over a gap toward the top of the roof. He had tried unsuccessfully to make small talk with Alexei several times as the boy fixed holes further down the roof.

Why could the man just not let him work in silence? Why must he comment on the sun's brightness, the day's clearness, and any other insanely annoying thing that popped into the man's head?

"I understand this was once the hunting lodge of a Polish noble," Bogdan looked out over the grounds of the small cottage. "Kravecek, I believe the man's name was."

"Kravchinsky," Alexei rolled his eyes and shook his head in annoyance at needing to correct the man. Even worse, Alexei suspected Bogdan had intentionally misstated the man's name to goad him into conversation.

"Kravchinsky, yes, that's right," Bogdan nodded as he sank a nail into the wood in two quick hammer strikes. "Must have cost Galina a few rubles to buy this place, eh?"

"I'm sure the Countess purchased it for her," Alexei responded without looking at the man as he slid along the roof to position another nail. The time-worn tread of his boot skidded along the roof, but he caught himself before he started to slip.

"Be careful there," Bogdan looked up from his hammering. "You'll hurt more than that stubborn pride if you fall off the roof."

"I'm fine," Alexei growled and hammered in the next nail.

A movement by the house caught Alexei's eye, and he saw Oksana crossing the courtyard with a basket of bread and meats. Her dark braid swayed from left to right as she walked, and Alexei noticed she intentionally kept her eyes averted from where he worked on the roof. Despite working in the close confines of Galina's cottage, they had barely spoken a word to each other since the outburst in the meadow. He pointedly arrived after breakfast to avoid an awkward meal together, and Oksana had mumbled a quick good morning as they passed each other in the courtyard.

Alexei pounded the nail with renewed vigor, cursing as an errant stroke caused it to bend against the wood. He hammered another nail alongside it, drowning out the faint sound of Oksana's voice as she called up to the men that lunch was ready. As Oksana walked back to the house, Alexei watched her with a sidelong glance, disappointed she did not look back at him to see if he stared after her.

"C'mon boy, let's grab some lunch," Bogdan tucked the hammer into his belt and stretched his back.

"I'll be down once I finish this board," Alexei responded as he cast about for another nail. With a sigh, he realized he had left the pouch of nails back where he had started.

Alexei was lost in his thoughts of Oksana as he walked across the roof, running through the many things he had wished he had done differently in the meadow that afternoon, in his life. Aside from Leo, Oksana was the one thing he truly cared about, and he had somehow lost her, likely forever, once she left for Kalinin. Their fight replayed in his mind, as it did every moment his thoughts were not otherwise occupied.

His boot slid on a moss-covered roof board, throwing him dangerously off balance. Alexei's arms pinwheeled in the air as he tried to regain his balance as he tumbled forward. There was a surreal second when his body hung suspended over the roof as he fell, and then his body slammed down onto the roof. The jarring impact expelled the air from his lungs in a sudden whoosh, and his vision went bright white before clearing. He was sliding head-first down the roof, his hands desperately clawing at the old planks and finding only the wet sheen of moss.

The lip of the roof and the unforgiving ground below loomed before his eyes as he slid forward. He could see Ivan on his feet, staring upward just below him, and Alexei said a silent prayer that he would not land on his friend. An image of Oksana crying over his broken body flashed through his mind, and he nearly smiled with satisfaction at the thought that she would regret her treatment of him.

He stopped sliding so abruptly that his chin smacked hard against the roof, causing him to bite his tongue. The iron taste of blood filled his mouth as he found himself sliding back up the roof; the motion sliding his shirt upward and painfully scrapping his chest against the roof. Alexei looked over his shoulder and glimpsed Bogdan, dragging him back up the roof, the man's two large hands closed about his ankle.

***

Alexei took a bite of the buttered bread as he sat in the shade of the barn. He tore a piece off and tossed it to Ivan, who snatched it out of the air and quickly downed the morsel. The bread was warm and fresh, though Alexei's tongue throbbed from its injury with every bite. As he leaned his head back against the barn wall, Alexei had to admit he was hard-pressed to think of a part of his body that did not hurt from his misadventure along the roof.

"I know I already said it, but thank you, Bogdan," Alexei turned his head to look at the man happily devouring his own loaf of fresh bread. "I don't know how you reached me so quickly."

"Don't look at the age of the tree; look at the magic in the branches," Bogdan slapped his hand against his leg and grinned. "You may be the most ornery person I have encountered in a long while, but that does not mean I'll let you fall off the barn and stick face first in the dirt like a misspent arrow. No, if you are going to come flying off that roof, it's because I will have tossed your stubborn ass off."

Alexei gave him a sidelong glance, unsure if Bogdan was threatening him, then both men laughed. "Yeah, I guessed I deserved that."

"You sure did," Bogdan nodded as he took a mammoth-sized bite of the bread.

Alexei stared at the bread in his hand, then turned sheepishly toward Bogdan, "Hey, can I ask you something? It's something Leo wanted to know."

Bogdan turned and nodded, the mouthful of bread he had been chewing wadded up in the side of his mouth like a squirrel with an acorn.

"Have you ever seen any unusual footprints in the woods in your travels?"

"These forests are older than mankind," Bogdan gestured with the loaf of bread to the surrounding woods. "There's shit out there that would empty the bowels of the bravest men if they came across it."

"Have you ever seen a walking house or come across footprints that looked like a giant chicken?" Alexei winced at the sound of his question.

Bogdan's eyebrows rose in surprise, then narrowed in concern, "How hard did you hit your head on that roof?"

"I know it sounds crazy. Leo wanted to know if you had seen any trace of Baba Yaga's house. They say it moves around on two giant chicken legs, so she never sleeps in the same location twice."

Bogdan laughed, a deep, hearty sound, "Boy, Baba Yaga is an old wives' tale, used to scare little children."

"Leo believes she's real. He is compiling evidence."

Bogdan shook his head, "That boy may be the most interesting person in all of Imperial Russia. And what do you believe, Alexei?"

"I don't know," Alexei shrugged. "There are so many stories of her from all over; I find it hard to believe they are all made up."

"Stranger things have proven to be true." Bogdan stared at the forest, then looked back at Alexei. "It is safer to believe Baba Yaga is real and be wrong than to believe she is a fairy tale and be proven wrong."

Alexei thought about that as he bit off a piece of bread.

Sound reasoning.

"Now it's my turn," Bogdan grabbed the bottle of wine from the basket and took a drink.

"For?"

"To ask a question," Bogdan handed the bottle to Alexei.

"Okay, I guess that's fair," Alexei took a deep swig of the wine; it was sweet with hints of blackberry and sour cherries. "Wow, that is good."

"Galina seems to be that rare member of the nobility who does not hoard the finest things for herself," Bogdan leaned his head back against the barn wall. "So, what is the story with you and young Oksana?"

Alexei took another long drink of the wine and sighed, "What is there to tell? She is leaving with Galina to Kalinin."

"She obviously loves you."

"Well, she has a funny way of showing it," Alexei threw the last of his bread to Ivan, who happily trotted off with his prize. "Our fathers were friends when we were growing up, and we spent as many days at each other's homes as we did our own. When my parents died, Oksana's family took me in. I was there with Oksana when her mother fell ill and died, and then her father. The world took everyone away from us except each other. Now she is leaving."

Bogdan sat silently, choosing his words. His voice was gentle when he spoke, "Going with Galina gives Oksana a chance at a better life than she could ever have in Obrechen."

"Better than she could have with me, you mean," Alexei said, the rawness of the emotions roiling up within him.

"Yes, Alexei, better than she would have with you here," Bogdan put a comforting hand on Alexei's shoulder and sighed as the boy shrugged it off.

"So, love means nothing?" Alexei gritted his teeth as he attempted to push down his feelings of hurt and abandonment.

"No, love means everything," Bogdan pointed toward the cottage. "And that young woman loves you deeply, differently than you love her, but no less intensely. I had a younger brother, and I loved that boy fiercely. There has never been a day that I would not take a bullet in the heart for him. My love for my wife was no greater or lesser, but it was different."

Alexei laughed, a harsh sound imbued with bitterness, "So she loves me like a brother?"

Bogdan nodded slowly, his eyes sad for the boy's angst.

"And that's all there is to it? I am cursed to go through life with this emptiness? With this pain in my heart?" Alexei thudded a finger hard enough against his chest that it would likely bruise later.

"Alexei, look at me." The softness had retreated from Bogdan's eyes, replaced with an intense strength. "Oksana cannot help the way her heart loves any more than you can. She may go to Kalinin and come running home to you, or she may go to Kalinin and never look back. But if you love her, truly love her, you will support whatever she decides."

"The world takes everything from me," Alexei folded his arms across his chest.

Bogdan grabbed Alexei's shirt and shook the boy, "You're damn right it does, and it always will. The world is not your fucking friend, and it never will be. That's why you stand up and fight for you and yours—always. You shun that girl, and you've taken away the only person she loves in this world, and that's on you. If you love Oksana, tell her you will always be there for her, no matter where she goes. If someone pushes her, you knock them down. If someone makes her cry, you make them bleed. That kind of love will endure through all things, for all times."

"Then what do I do?" Alexei felt his cheeks flush red. "She'll still be gone."

"Then you fight for whatever you have left that you love. You fight for Leo, you fight for that dog, and you fight for the fucking clothes on your back."

Alexei nodded his head.

Bogdan let go of Alexei's shirt, a horrified look on his face, "Alexei, I am sorry, I forget myself." He sat back against the barn, running his hands through his black hair. "The world has not been kind to me either, my young friend. I, too, know what it is like to have loved and lost. Sometimes... Sometimes, my anger gets the best of me."

Alexei stood and brushed off his trousers; his scraped chest throbbed beneath his shirt, and his tongue felt swollen and awkward.

He walked to stand before Bogdan and offered his hand to the man. Bogdan took it and let Alexei pull him up to his feet.

"We should finish the roof before dinner; I'll stay and eat tonight if Galina has a place for me at the table." Alexei nodded to Bogdan.

"I am sure she will," Bogdan said, slapping Alexei on the shoulder and grinning. "If I don't throw your ass off the roof before we finish."

***

"I'm really surprised you asked me to come with you," Oksana said, then quickly added, "I am happy you did; I'm just surprised."

"Well, I am happy you decided to come with me," Alexei gave her a quick smile, flicking the reigns to keep Seryy moving down the road.

The two rode side by side in the wagon as the donkey plodded steadily toward Obrechen. The sun's rays poked tendrils of bright sunlight through the branches, offering hints of the clear sky above as they rode. They had sat in awkward silence for much of the trip from the cottage until Oksana could not take it anymore.

"I don't like it when we're not friends, Alexei," Oksana said, looking down at her hands and then at Alexei. "I'm sorry for what I said; it was unfair of me to say those things to you."

"Oksana, I will always be your friend," he looked at her, his brow creasing with the seriousness of his expression. "And the things you said, you were right. You spoke the truth, even if hearing it was hard for me. I was the one who was unfair to you. I should have reacted better.

"But you're right; my parents' death and the way Obrechen treats me has left me with an anger inside I don't know how to calm." Alexei shook his head, and when he looked at her, there were tears in his eyes.

"You deserve better than that, better than Obrechen has to offer. If you stayed here and married me, one day, there would be a knock at the door, and someone would tell you I got killed in a fight or arrested by the gendarme for killing someone else."

"It doesn't have to be that way, Alexei," Oksana felt her own tears beginning to well in her eyes. "Come with us to Kalinin; Galina will find you a good job. You could build a life for yourself, and we would always be close."

Alexei gave her a wistful smile, "Kalinin is the last place I need to go. I would walk the streets and wonder if the person walking next to me was part of the mob that killed my parents. No, Kalinin would kill me faster than Obrechen."

"So, what will you do?"

He genuinely smiled, giving Oksana the hope that the future would be okay, "I think I will go with Bogdan. He says when he leaves Obrechen, he is returning to Romania to build a house in the Carpathians. It sounds beautiful there."

"That sounds wonderful, Alexei," Oksana hooked her arm through Alexei's and rested her head on his shoulder. "What will you tell Leo?"

"I'm going to bring him if he wants to come."

"Take Leo to the Romania?" Oksana sat up and looked at him, and Alexei laughed at the look of shock on her face.

"That's right," Alexei grinned and nodded. "Pavel would dance an Irish jig if I took Leo with me."

"But Leo's mother, Alexei; she has not let Leo more than a few feet away from her since he was born."

"I know," Alexei's grin turned mischievous. "That's why we're getting him now. To show her how happy Leo would be if he got off the porch and away from that house."

***

"What?" Anya Verenicha looked from Oksana and Alexei to the bare wooden back of the wagon, then finally to Seryy, as his ears twitched away a buzzing fly.

"We want to take Leo to a birthday party," Alexei grinned as Leo bobbed up and down so excitedly in his wheelchair that his mother placed a restraining hand on it to prevent it from toppling off the porch.

"A birthday?" Anya looked at Oksana and Alexei in utter confusion. "Whose birthday?"

"Leo's," Alexei pointed at Leo, whose grin grew wider.

"Yes, Mrs. Verenich, with a cake and presents," Oksana added.

"Leo's birthday?" Anya looked at the two as if they had gone insane. "But it's not Leo's birthday. Not for another three months."

"Oh, Mother, please let me go," Leo grabbed the side of his mother's dress and looked up at her with pleading eyes.

"It's for all his birthdays we've missed," Alexei gave Anya his most sincere look. "Has Leo ever had a birthday party?"

"Well, his father does not like to entertain people at the house, you see," Anya's tone became defensive, almost apologetic.

"Exactly," Alexei raised a finger as if making a point. "With his father away for a few days, we can finally throw Leo a grand birthday party! You can come along if you like, too."

"I couldn't. Pavel may come home early, and I would not want him to find the house empty."

"We'll have Leo back by this evening and we'll be with him the whole time," Oksana saw a crack in Anya's argument and sought to exploit it. "I promise he will be okay."

"Mother, please," Leo looked at his mother, and the desperation in his eyes melted her heart.

"Okay," the word came out as a whisper as she nodded and wiped a tear from her eye. "But you must dress warm and keep a blanket around you."

"Thank you, Mother. Thank you! I promise I will," Leo's smile reached his eyes as Alexei gave a little shout of victory.

"Alexei, are you sure this thing is safe?" Anya eyed the wagon. "You won't go too fast?"

"It's perfectly safe," Alexei assured her. "And I will ride in back with Leo. We brought a ramp to wheel him right off the porch into the wagon bed. Oksana will guide Seryy, and believe me, that old donkey wouldn't go fast if his tail were on fire!"

"I'll be careful, I promise," Oksana tried to make her voice sound grown-up and responsible.

"This is going to be the best birthday ever," Leo raised both hands high, his face beaming with delight.

"Leo, you know it's not..." Anya began, then, seeing Leo's joy, sighed and smiled.

"Not what, Mother?" Leo's grin was infectious, and they were all smiling as he looked at her.

Anya patted him gently on the shoulder, "It's not polite to chew birthday cake with your mouth open, so mind your manners at Lady Sekova's house."

"Yeah, we already have one donkey chomping apples in the barn; we don't need another one at the table," Alexei teased, and Oksana slapped him playfully on the head.

"I will," Leo's good cheer made him look more vibrant and healthy than Anya had seen in years. The sight brought tears to her eyes, and she turned away so he could not see.

"That's good, Leo," Anya nodded, fighting back the tears. They were tears of worry, fearing all that could befall her little boy while he was out of her sight. However, they were also tears of joy that he could know such happiness in a life that had deprived him of so much.

She looked at Oksana and Alexei as they laughed and joked with Leo. Her baby boy was born into a world that despised him for no doing of his own and to a father too ashamed to acknowledge him. Yet here were two children, misfits in their own right, who brought so much joy into his life. Many nights, Anya lay awake wondering what would become of Leo if something happened to her. She knew that with Leo's poor health, the prognosis for a long life was not optimistic; still, village life had shown her that illness and misfortune often robbed children of their parents while still young. Oksana and Alexei were two examples of that. Although it hurt her to her core to admit it, if Anya died prematurely, she had little doubt Pavel would abandon the boy on the steps of a church before she was cold in her grave. However, with friends like these, Leo could find a place in this world, or at least be surrounded by people who loved him.

Leo turned to her, his gap-toothed grin spread wide across his face, "Thank you for letting me go, Mother. I love you!"

"I love you too, Leo," Anya hugged her boy and pressed a cheek wet with tears against his head.

***

With his wheelchair facing out the back of the wagon, Leo waved one last time as the figure of his mother standing on the porch waving receded behind them. She returned the wave and blew him a kiss as the wagon wound down the curve in the road, and the little house disappeared from view.

"Hold on, Leo. This part of the road is a bit bumpy," Alexei held on tight to the wheelchair and leaned down to pat Leo on the shoulder.

"I love it!" Leo shouted as the wagon shook and rattled on the bumpy road. "Oksana, go faster!"

"I will not," Oksana protested with a smile as she looked back at the boys. "You'll bounce right out of this cart, and your mom will string me up by my ears!"

"You're no fun," Alexei teased.

"Yeah, you're no fun," Leo added between bouts of laughter as he extended his arms. "I feel like a bird!"

Alexei and Oksana exchanged smiles as their friend reveled in the ride. Leo threw his head back, breathing deeply of the fresh forest air as he watched the canopy of branches pass overhead.

"Enjoy it, buddy," Alexei patted Leo's shoulder again. "It's your day!"

"Look there," Oksana pointed off to the right as a large buck ran through the brush a few yards to their right.

"Wow," Leo gasped in wide-eyed amazement. "It's beautiful!"

"Look at those antlers, Leo," Alexei pointed after the buck. "I count eight points on his rack."

"He's so fast," Leo was riveted to the deer as it outpaced them. "Maybe he's fleeing from a wolf."

"Maybe," Alexei leaned down to whisper in his ear. "Or Baba Yaga."

Leo's head snapped up to look at his friend, a broad grin splitting his face as he nodded, "Or Baba Yaga."

Oksana shook her head and smiled as the boys laughed incessantly behind her, and she guided the donkey onward.

Bogdan and Galina waited on the porch as Seryy ambled the wagon to the cottage, smiles lighting up their faces at the sight of the three friends.

Alexei opened the back of the wagon and slid down the wooden planks he and Bogdan had fashioned into a ramp as Oksana jumped down from the running board to stand beside him. Once the boards were in place, Alexei hopped back into the wagon bed and slowly eased Leo's wheelchair forward.

"Hold on, Leo," Alexei dipped the front end of the wheelchair down the ramp. Bogdan had chosen long wooden boards for the ramp, so the angle of the decline out of the wagon would not be so great. The forethought paid off, and Alexei rolled Leo down without any peril.

"Leo, it is good to see you, my friend," Bogdan's voice boomed, and he waved a greeting.

"Bogdan!" Leo waved as Alexei guided the wheelchair onto firm ground. "It is good to see you too!"

Ivan came racing out of the barn, tail wagging happily. He raced past Alexei, who had bent down, outstretching his arms in greeting, and ran up to Leo's wheelchair. The dog hopped up, placed his front paws on Leo's lap, and licked the boy's face and neck, eliciting giggles of delight from Leo.

"No loyalty," Alexei shook his head in mock disappointment.

"Maybe Leo just tastes better," Oksana elbowed Alexei playfully in the ribs. "He certainly smells better!"

"Hey! I bathed yesterday. Or was it the other day?"

"Exactly," Oksana pursed her lips and gave Alexei a disapproving shake of her head.

"Leo," Galina stepped forward, "Welcome to my home; it is so good to finally meet you!"

"Thank you so much, Galina," Leo extended a frail hand in greeting. "I have loved all the books you have given me."

"Oh no, sir, a handshake will simply not do for such an auspicious occasion," Galina leaned over and kissed Leo on the cheek, careful to avoid the gleaming streaks left on the boy's face by Ivan.

Leo's face visibly reddened at the kiss, and he smiled sheepishly. He turned to Alexei and waggled his eyebrows, "I told you, women cannot resist me."

Bogdan let out a deep, hearty laugh, and the others soon joined in as Alexei rolled his eyes.

"Galina, you have created a monster! I will not hear the end of this until my hair is as gray as Ivan's."

***

"Bogdan, this is delicious," Galina sipped the vegetable stew and nodded with approval.

The Romanian woodsman beamed with pride as everyone at the table echoed the praise of the savory bowls of broth.

"Thank you. It is a traditional dish in Romania. I made it since I know the guest of honor does not eat meat," Bogdan dipped his head toward Leo. "It is made with only herbs and vegetables."

"That's right, nothing with a face," Leo smiled and loudly slurped another spoonful. "It's so good."

"Everyone in Obrechen better learn to live off vegetables if the wolf keeps eating all the livestock," Alexei laughed as he tore off a piece of bread from the warm loaf on the table. "Even the Land Captain will have to tighten his belt by the end of winter."

"Please, that man would just fill his belly with all the potatoes in Obrechen before he goes hungry for a night," Oksana looked as if the mention of Morozov brought a sour taste to her mouth.

"I heard some hunters walking past my house say that Morozov was offering a bounty for hunters to kill the wolf, but none of them wanted to go into the woods after that Volkov man got killed," Leo leaned in toward the table, excited to share the gossip.

"Hunters afraid to hunt," Alexei shook his as he chewed a mouthful of bread. "Sounds about right for Obrechen."

"Maybe Igor will take Morozov up on his offer and get himself eaten," Oksana added with a slight smile.

"The wolf would probably spit out that rotten piece of meat," Alexei winked and smiled back at her.

"The hunters said they thought the wolf was a forest devil and couldn't be killed," Leo's eyes lit up with the prospect of the conversation turning toward the supernatural.

"Oh, all this wolf business is just dreadful," Galina dabbed at a bit of soup on her lip with a white cloth napkin.

"I wouldn't worry too much about it," Bogdan sopped up the last of his stew with a handful of bread, circling the inside of the bowl to capture every drop. "Word will spread of the wolf, and hunters will come from Kalinin or St Petersburg to kill the beast."

"Why? The wolf is just doing what's in his nature," Leo shook his head.

"Because it is in man's nature to kill what it cannot tame," Bogdan said, his tone turning somber as he pushed his empty bowl away. "If a beast has an indomitable will to be free and can defend that will with teeth or claws, some men will hunt it just for the power they feel at killing such a creature. Those are the kind of men who will come to kill this wolf."

"There was a book in the Tsar's library that contained a Native American legend from a tribe called the Pawnee that said that at one time, every living creature in the world was immortal until men killed a wolf and brought death into this world," Galina added as she rose from the table.

"The Tsar's library must be a wondrous place," Leo's eyes took on a faraway look as he tried to imagine the shelves of priceless tomes in the St Petersburg palace.

Alexei stood, collecting the finished bowls from the table, "Well, from what I have seen of this world, I am rooting for the wolf."

As Galina carried the cake to the table, Leo's face lit up as he mouthed a silent "wow." Two candles rose from the cake's white creamy top, flames flickering as Galina approached the table. Leo looked questioningly at the candles, searching the faces around the table for an answer.

Seeing his confusion, Galina smiled at Leo as she placed the cake on the table and nodded toward Bogdan, "The candles were Bogdan's idea."

"Ahh yes, Leo. The candles are a tradition that pre-dates even Christ himself," Bogdan pointed to each candle as he explained. "The first candle represents your life until this point, and the second represents your future. If you make a wish in your heart and blow the candles out, the smoke of the two candles brings your wish to the heavens for the ancient gods to hear."

"Will they grant my wish?" Leo stared at the flickering flames.

"They may, Leo," Bogdan nodded.

"Bogdan, are Romanians not Christians?" Galina cocked her head and looked at Bogdan. "I remember the Romanian emissary in court wearing a large cross."

"Oh, they are most certainly Christians, and I was once, too," Bogdan smiled and gave her a knowing look. "However, once you have seen enough of the world, you realize that our world lies upon the ruins of a much more ancient story. The pagan world has existed since our species' dawning, yet the church tells us that it is all myth and fancy and that we should only believe the events of the last nineteen centuries."

"So, you are a pagan then?" Galina was genuinely intrigued by this revelation.

Bogdan shrugged, "I have no word for it. I believe in the earth, the sky, the rivers of the mountain, and the beasts in the forest. In my travels, I have seen enough fallacies of the church and truths of the old ways to believe what I believe."

"Why is the cake round?" Oksana looked suddenly embarrassed at blurting out the question, then quickly added. "It looks delicious; I have never seen a round cake before."

Bogdan twirled a circle over the cake with his finger, "It is round to represent the moon; the lunar cycle was essential to our ancestors' way of life. I figure this was probably how Baba Yaga celebrated the passing of each year."

Leo's eyes grew wide at the mention of the forest witch, and he looked from the candles to Bogdan, "Can I blow out the candles now?"

"Make your wish, then blow them out," the corners of Bogdan's mouth curled up in a smile as he nodded to Leo.

Leo took a deep breath and blew on the candles; the flames bent sideways and extinguished, thin entrails of smoke twining upwards. His eyes watched the smoke trail toward the ceiling and dissipate.

"What did you wish for?" Oksana leaned in and asked in a hushed tone. "For Alexei to grow long ears like a donkey?"

"Hey, I heard that," protested Alexei.

"You can't tell anyone your wish, Leo, or it won't come true," Bogdan warned in a serious tone, and Leo nodded in understanding. "It must be for the gods' ears only."

Galina cut pieces of cake for everyone, giving Leo the biggest piece. Oksana shook her head in mock disappointment as Alexei and Leo displayed how much frosting they could get stuck to their upper lip with each bite.

"You are both children," she scolded them as Alexei tried to pretend he did not have a dot of frosting on the tip of his nose, which caused Leo to laugh so hard that tears streamed down his face.

Galina laughed along with them, then saw Bogdan was not laughing. He sat back in his chair, his cake untouched, with his lips pursed as if biting back emotion.

"Bogdan, is there something wrong? Did you not like the cake?" she asked.

Bogdan seemed to snap out of his reverence at her words, picking up his fork and leaning back into the table, "The cake is delicious, Galina. It's just that sitting here with all of you, it feels like a family, and I have not felt that in a long time."

Alexei wiped the frosting from his nose and nodded solemnly, "It does."

Bogdan placed his forearms on the table and looked at each of them in turn, "My wife and I dreamed of having a family one day, of filling the house with children. It never came to pass, but sitting here with all of you, I think she would have loved this, loved all of you. I have been on the road for a long time, since her death, and this place, here with all of you, this is the first place that has ever felt like home. So, thank you."

Galina found herself choking back tears at his words, and she thought she saw Alexei and Oksana struggling with their own emotions. Only Leo appeared unmoved as he studied Bogdan with a degree of reverence. She knew some of the boy's home life from what Oksana had told her, and Galina wondered if Leo was contemplating what it would be like to have a man like Bogdan as his father instead of the cold Pavel Verenich.

Bogdan looked up at all the serious faces and blanched, "I did not mean to cast such a pall over so joyous an occasion."

With a flick of his wrist, he sliced his fork through the thick, creamy frosting and sent a large white droplet sailing across the table to land on Alexei's cheek. Alexei sat up in shock as everyone stared, from the white glob on his cheek to Bogdan in stunned silence.

"Alexei, I believe you got some cream on your cheek," a smile spread across Bogdan's face as he gestured to his cheek.

Leo was the first to laugh, almost choking on the bite of cake he had just placed in his mouth. Soon, Oksana and Galina joined in, and even Alexei flashed a wide, embarrassed grin as he wiped the offending cream from his cheek.

***

Alexei slowly rolled Leo's wheelchair up the ramp into the back of the wagon as the sun began to dip on the horizon. Leo clutched a small stack of books, gifts from Galina, in his lap. His fingers caressed a leather-bound volume of German fairy tales, dyed a deep forest green with beautiful hand-painted pictures inside. It was the most fantastic book he had ever seen, and Galina had said it once belonged to a Swiss noble who gifted it to her when she was in the Tsar's court.

Bogdan placed a basket with a bushel of apples on the boards beside Leo, who had marveled at such bright-red, unbruised fruit so late in the season.

"Thank you again, Bogdan," Leo gave the huntsman a grateful nod of his head.

"No thanks necessary, Leo," Bogdan said, placing a hand on Leo's forearm. "And remember, when I am done carving your birthday gift, I will bring it to you as well."

"I won't forget, Bogdan," Leo smiled and placed his thin fingers atop the man's large hand.

"Leo, it was wonderful having you here; you are welcome in my home anytime," Galina smiled but felt a well of sadness at the parting.

"A guy only gets one birthday a year," Leo shrugged, though he, too, could not hide the sadness in his voice.

"Be safe; stay on the road," Bogdan advised Oksana as she climbed onto the wagon running board.

"I will," Oksana nodded.

Seryy ambled forward at Oksana's urging, and Leo gave a last wave to Bogdan and Galina. The two waved back, watching the wagon roll away before Galina returned to the house, and Bogdan crossed to the barn to settle in for the night.

The three rode in silence as Leo appeared to be taking in the sounds of the coming night in the forest. Owls, awaking from their daytime slumber, hooted as a murder of crows roosted for the night, their cackles signaling the coming dying of the light. Frogs began to croak, and the forest bustled with creatures settling down in burrows or rising to hunt and forage. Leo listened to it all with a serene smile on his face.

Oksana looked back at Alexei, who shrugged in a way she knew meant to let Leo enjoy the moment. She slowed the pace of Seryy's progression, stretching the short journey home a bit longer.

"I think Bogdan was right," Leo said, breaking the silence.

"About what?" Alexei settled down beside Leo's wheelchair, keeping one hand on the frame to prevent it from jostling on the bumpy road.

"About the old world and the things that lived in it," Leo looked out into the night.

"I guess. I haven't thought much about it."

"I think Baba Yaga is a remnant of creatures that walked the earth in the ancient days. She is probably the last of her kind." Leo looked over at Alexei. "She's crafty, so she has lasted longer than all the others."

A ghostly wail pierced the night, and both boys jumped, their eyes searching the darkness until they heard Oksana's giggling.

"Very funny," Alexei playfully poked her in the back.

"You boys and that Baba Yaga," Oksana shook her head as she struggled to control her laughter. "If that witch showed herself, you two would wet your trousers."

"I'd marry her," Leo announced with a wide grin as all three descended into a fit of laughter.

Seryy gave an indignant snort and flick of his head. "It sounds like Seryy objects to the marriage," added Oksana, which elicited a new round of laughter.

"Thank you," Leo only barely managed to get the words out between bouts of laughter that brought tears to his eyes.

"For what?" Alexei had laughed so hard he was nearly winded.

"For the best day of my life."

***

Galina shifted the heavy woolen blanket in her arm as she stared at the new wooden planks that now covered the holes the storm had wrought in the barn roof.

"You should stay nice and dry now, Seryy," Galina smiled at the donkey and withdrew an apple from the folds of her dress. "I brought you a treat."

The donkey stared at her from the far corner of the sizable stall. Seryy's head followed the track of her hand holding the bright red treat, but he uncustomarily did not come forward to retrieve it. Galina frowned and extended her arm, but the donkey still did not advance.

"Are you not hungry tonight?" Galina puffed her lip out in a mock pout as the glassy brown orbs of the donkey's eyes stared at her impassively.

"Okay, well then, you eat it when you get hungry later," Galina gave the apple an underarm toss into the stall and watched as it bounced once and rolled across the straw and dirt floor before stopping against the donkey's hoof.

She smiled, proud of herself for such an excellent throw of the apple and watched as Seryy dipped his head to take the apple between his teeth. "Hungry after all I see!"

Galina crossed to the other side of the barn, to the previously empty stall that Bogdan had now taken up residence. A light glowed inside the stall as she knocked lightly on the door frame.

"Come in," Bogdan's voice called from inside.

As she stepped into the stall, Galina looked around in surprise. Bogdan had crafted a small table with two chairs, a small bedside stand on which the lantern burned, and a square bed with a crude straw-filled mattress. His weather-beaten leather backpack, packed full of whatever possessions Bogdan traveled with, hung on a peg beside the bed. The man sat on the bed, whittling long slivers of wood from a hand-size length of timber. He looked up and smiled at her, placing the piece of wood and knife on the bed stand as he stood.

"You have been busy," Galina looked at the roughly crafted furniture with sheer amazement.

Bogdan laughed as he put a hand on one of the chairs and rocked it back and forth, "I know it's not much to look at, but it's sturdy enough."

"How did you do all of this so quickly?"

"It wasn't just me; Alexei helped," Bogdan continued, appraising the chair. "The boy can do some fine work when you can get him to stop being angry for a few moments."

"Well, he certainly seemed in good spirits tonight," Galina extended the blankets toward Bogdan. "I wanted to bring you some extra blankets; it may get chilly tonight."

"Thank you, Galina," Bogdan nodded in thanks as he took the folded blankets and set them on the bed. He gestured toward the table and chairs. "If today is any indication, I think Oksana and the boy will be just fine. Would you like to have a seat?"

"Thank you. It has been a long day. It was good to see them all laughing together though," Galina said as she sat in the chair closest to her and looked over at the piece of wood on the bedside table. "What are you making there?"

"Oh, that," Bogdan shrugged. "That's something I am making for Leo. I should probably be working on making a door for this room before someone sees me walking around in my breeches!"

Galina laughed, "It seems you've already gotten Seryy too frightened to look; he's hanging back in his stable. I couldn't even draw him out with an apple; he usually can't resist those. He plucked one out of my hand the other day; leaned over my shoulder and grabbed it."

Bogdan laughed and nodded, "Donkeys are strange creatures and a lot more complex than we give them credit for. He's probably just thrown off by having such a close neighbor after having the place all to himself for so long."

"The poor thing suffered a terrible fright during the storm," Galina craned to look out the doorway toward the donkey's stall, then turned back to Bogdan, concern etched across her face. "He was still terrified the next morning and nearly bolted when we were hooking him up to the cart."

"Well, donkeys are resilient animals," Bogdan sat on the edge of the bed. "I'm sure he'll settle down in a few days."

"What will it be when you are finished?" Galina nodded toward the block of wood.

"With my paltry woodcarving skills," Bogdan picked up the wood block from the bedside table and turned it several times before reaching for the knife and carving a fresh sliver off, "probably a piece of firewood."

Galina laughed pleasantly, carefree, "I doubt that very much!"

She sat momentarily, watching him alternately studying the wood and slicing off thin slivers until she thought she could make out the beginning of a peaked roof on one end of the block.

"Bogdan, I wanted to thank you for last night," her voice sounded low and uncertain. He stopped carving and looked at her curiously. "I have never talked about Mali like I did with you last night, not even to Oksana."

"Do you mean as your lover?" He set the wood and knife aside as she nodded.

"Not everyone would understand that two women could love each other that way," she said. She looked down at her hands, fidgeting before meeting his gaze. "Thank you for making me not feel like a two-headed goat."

"Galina, the world is a harsh and terrible place," Bogdan gave her a gentle smile. "If someone is lucky enough to find true love somewhere in it, that is a rare and wondrous thing. All that matters is that one heart loves another and is loved the same in return."

"Did you love your wife that way?"

"I did," Bogdan looked down at the floor and exhaled gently. "I found my one true love and lost her too soon. It would not have been enough if we had ten lifetimes together."

"I'm so sorry, Bogdan," Galina felt her heart break for his loss. "May I ask how she died?"

When Bogdan met her gaze, she saw a momentary fury flash in his eyes, then, his look softened back to a subtle melancholy. "She was killed by men who thought they had the right to do as they pleased back in my native land."

"That's terrible," Galina gasped in horror. "Were they ever punished for their crime?"

"Some were," Bogdan nodded and swallowed hard, choking back the pain of the memories. "Others have escaped retribution to this day."

A silence fell between them as Bogdan glanced over at the shadow of the lantern flame on the wall, lost in his thoughts.

"I should head back to the house. Could you walk with me? All of this wolf talk lately has me a bit spooked."

"Of course," the sadness melted from Bogdan's face as his smile returned.

Galina gasped as she rose from the chair, her hand reflexively going to her side as her face contorted in pain. Bogdan was suddenly there by her side, steadying her with sure hands.

"Galina, are you okay?" Bogdan's voice mirrored the look of concern on his face.

"Yes, I just need a moment," Galina felt prickles of cold sweat on her forehead as the pain in her side pulsed.

"May I?" Bogdan gestured toward the pain in her side. "I have some medical experience."

"Were you a doctor once too?"

"No," Bogdan looked suddenly embarrassed. "I grew up on a farm with cattle and often helped my father when they fell ill."

"Oh, cows," Galina feigned a look of indignation as she winced in pain. "Isn't that just the comparison a woman loves to hear?"

Bogdan shrugged apologetically, then gestured toward her side again. Galina bit her lip against the pain and gave a curt nod of approval. He reached out with three fingers and lightly touched her side, eliciting a gasp of pain from her. Bogdan quickly withdrew his fingers and gazed thoughtfully at her.

"How long has this been going on?"

"It's just some indigestion," Galina pushed aside a lock of hair matted by the sweat on her forehead. "Mali gave me a tincture from her physician, Doctor Artyom, that takes care of the pain."

"Galina, how long?" Bogdan stared at her with a severe gaze.

"A year, maybe more," Galina shrugged.

"Maybe we should take you to see a doctor," Bogdan's voice softened.

"Bogdan, I am fine," Galina straightened, though she could not hide a slight grimace of pain. "Now, if you see me back at the house, I will take my medicine and get some sleep."

Bogdan opened his mouth to protest further, but she cocked her head and stared at him in a silent warning that she was not in the mood to argue as she gingerly began walking. He gave her a defeated nod and fell in alongside her.

Seryy stopped chewing the apple and watched the two figures slowly walk across the barn and into the night. He let out a long bray of warning as they stepped into the darkness, spewing apple chunks across the stall. The man and woman turned to face the donkey, momentarily startled, before they continued on their way.

***

"Why are we out here setting traps while Pisarev and others are back at the cabin drinking vodka and playing cards?" Yuri watched his brother pound the wooden stake into the ground with a small mallet.

The four torches illuminating the clearing kept the forest's darkness at bay. As Anton Sleptsov hammered the stake, he cast a shadow upon the ground that reminded Yuri of the dwarves of folklore working at their fire forges, hammering out weapons for the gods.

A short length of rope was attached to the stake; the other end was tied around the neck of a small brown goat happily chewing a mouthful of forest grass. The bait to lure the wolf in close, so maddened with hunger for the taste of goat that it would stumble into the hunter's traps.

"Stop complaining, Yuri; think of the night this stupid beast will have." Anton pointed the mallet at the goat. "Where is Frolenko?"

Anton turned to peer back into the woods; he could see the bright flame of Frolenko's torch a few dozen yards away. The flame moved several paces to the left and stopped, indicating the hunter had identified a good place to set the next trap.

The traps utilized a pressure plate between two metal arms with jagged teeth-like protrusions. When a wolf stepped on the plate, the arms would close rapidly on the creature's foot, trapping it and holding it until the hunters arrived to finish it off. Yuri was old enough to remember when nobles used the same traps to keep peasants off their lands. He had seen the scars on his uncle's leg from such a trap that had snapped the bone in his leg like a dried twig; and the man walked with a limp for the rest of his days.

"Looks about done," Yuri turned back to his brother. "Our traps will catch the wolf, and then Pisarev and the rest of those piss pots will come out here and shoot it; take all the credit."

"So, what would you rather do?" satisfied the stake was deep enough in the ground, Anton stood and leaned back, stretching his back. "Sit out here all night with the fucking goat until the wolf comes?"

"Why not? We both have rifles. We can split Morozov's reward between us." Yuri tucked a thumb under the shoulder strap of his rifle.

"I saw that fellow Volkov in the Kanti Gans; he was no dandelion, and that wolf tore him to pieces," Anton shook his head. "Besides, you think Frolenko will let us just sit out here and collect the reward/"

"Fuck Frolenko," Yuri turned back to watch the progress Frolenko's torch was making through the woods. The flame had stopped moving again, then suddenly disappeared. Yuri shook his head, annoyed that Frolenko would let the flame extinguish before lighting another. He watched for several moments longer, but a new flame failed to blaze to life. "What is that horse's ass doing?"

"What is it?" Anton stepped up beside his brother and peered out into the darkness.

"Frolenko's torch went out," Yuri squinted, trying to discern any movement in the last place he had seen the flame.

"He had at least two spare torches with him," Anton looked from his brother back into the darkness.

A loud metallic clang rang out, shattering the silence of the night. The brothers jumped at the unexpected sound, and the goat looked up from its grassy feast and turned its head toward the woods.

"The damn fool must have stepped in his own damn trap," Anton shook his head.

"Then why isn't he screaming?" Yuri looked at his brother, but Anton just shrugged.

Another metallic clang rang out, closer than the first, and the goat began to bleat a loud, shrill, fearful sound. The brothers took a step back and unslung their rifles. Yuri's rifle nearly slipped out of his hand, and he barely caught it before it hit the ground.

"My fucking hands are sweating," Yuri dismissed his brother's questioning look.

Two more clangs echoed through the forest as a pair of traps set off in quick succession, each getting closer to the clearing. The goat continued bleating and began pacing a circle around the stake.

The sound of something large crashing through the brush accompanied the clang of another trap just outside the perimeter of the clearing. The brothers looked at each other, nervously adjusting their rifles in their hands.

"That's not Frolenko," Anton's eyes were wide with fear, the torchlight dancing off his dark pupils.

"Fuck this," Yuri turned and ran. He crashed through the forest, ignoring the branches that scratched his face as he passed. The light dimmed as soon as Yuri left the glow of the clearing, but the hunter felt sure he could navigate his way to the cabin by moonlight. Yuri could hear the labored breathing of Anton following close behind him.

Another metallic clang rang out, dulled by a meaty thud and punctuated by a scream of pain. Yuri turned back as Anton sprawled to the ground, clutching at the metal jaws clamped tight around his left leg.

"Oh fuck, it hurts," Anton was crying as his sweaty face looked to Yuri in desperation, reaching out a bloody hand. "Yuri, help me, please."

Yuri stepped back toward his brother, and something immense pounced on Anton from the darkness. His brother disappeared beneath the dark mass as a terrible rending sound filled the forest, followed by a wet gurgling sound from where Anton had laid only moments earlier. The rifle slipped from Yuri's fingers as his bladder released a wave of hot piss into his trousers. Yuri knew he should have fired into the beast to rescue his brother or, at the very least, offered a prayer to God for his brother's swift ascension to heaven. His dearly departed mother would have expected no less. Instead, unarmed and soaked in his own urine, Yuri Sleptsov fled into the night.

***

"Go easy on that," Pisarev gave the hunter a disapproving look as the man pressed the bottle of vodka to his lips, upending it as his throat bobbed with each swallow.

Kolotkevitch removed the bottle from his lips and wiped his sleeve against his mouth as he lowered the half-empty bottle to the table. He looked at Pisarev with half-glazed eyes and gave him a half grin, revealing a mouthful of dark-stained teeth. "Don't worry, Serge. I'll be able to shoot straight enough to kill your trapped wolf."

The other two hunters seated around the old wooden table laughed and looked sidelong at Pisarev as they played cards.

"The Land Captain wants this done right; no mistakes," Pisarev leaned back in his chair, which creaked dangerously under his sizable weight.

"Then Morozov should not have sent you with us," Kolotkevitch leaned forward and leered at Pisarev, swaying in a way that confirmed he was no longer sober.

Kolotkevitch pointed a gnarled, dirty finger at Pisarev, "You are a farmer." He then pointed at himself and the two other men seated at the table. "We are hunters. Killing is a hunter's business.

"Now, if we wanted someone to come and pick plants out of the ground," Kolotkevitch raised his hands and made plucking gestures, "then we would have asked for a farmer."

"I'm no farmer. I'm the fucking foreman, which means I tell people what to do." Pisarev stood and grabbed the bottle of vodka from the table in his meaty hand. He threw it against the wall, the bottle exploding into shards of glass, leaving a wet splash of vodka that ran in rivulets down the wall. "And I'm telling you, no more drinking until the fucking wolf is dead. Do you understand me?"

Kolotkevitch glared at Pisarev before looking away and nodding his head slightly.

"Good," Pisarev pointed to the stove. "Now throw another log in the stove before we all freeze our asses off waiting for your shit for brains friends to finish setting their traps."

Kolotkevitch stood on wobbly legs and grabbed a log; he was near the stove when a frantic knock began at the door. He jumped at the sound, and the two hunters looked up from their card game to look warily at the door as the beating continued unabated.

"For fucks sake," Pisarev shook his head as he stomped to the door. "What is it now?"

The burly foreman swung the door open, letting in a cold gust of wind that bore an overwhelming iron-like stench of blood and the putrid odor of feces. He had halfway raised his hand to cover his nose when he stopped, staring agape out the door.

Yuri Sleptsov hung suspended from a beam over the door by a wire snare that looped over his neck, his eyes rolled back in his head as the snare cut into the skin of his neck. Sleptsov was sliced open in four ragged lines from neck to crotch with the shredded remains of his stomach and intestines dangled from his ravaged body and blood and shit pooling beneath him in a dark circle. The man's legs kicked out frantically in his death throes, and Pisarev had to duck to avoid the man's booted foot.

From behind Sleptsov, something immense moved in the darkness, batting the hanging man's body aside and storming into the room. Pisarev's mind barely processed what he saw before the dark-furred beast barreled past him, knocking him sideways. The massive wolf-like creature stormed into the cabin on two legs like a man, its black fur slick with blood and gore. It smashed a clawed hand into Pisarev's mouth as it moved past the man, dislodging his front teeth and then wrenching its arm downward and tearing Pisarev's jaw from his head. Pisarev slid down the wall in a gurgling heap, the upper portion of his mouth suspended over a gaping maw of blood and torn flesh.

The hunters overturned their chairs as they scrambled backward and the beast leaped onto the tabletop, the wooden legs collapsing under its weight in an explosion of splinted wood. It lashed out with one arm, its black claws slashing through the bone and cartilage of one hunter's neck so deeply his head flopped backward, attached by only a slim remnant of skin.

The other hunter turned to run for the rifles leaning against the cabin wall, but the wolf beast sank a clawed hand into the man's lower back. The room filled with a sound like a man pulling his boot from thick muck as the creature yanked upward and tore the man's spine from his back as effortlessly as lifting the handle on a water pump. The hunter was dead before his body hit the floor.

Kolotkevitch screamed, half mad with terror, and threw the log he held at the creature. It glanced off the creature's wolf-like head, knocking it sideways and drawing a thin trickle of blood from its black ear.

"Come on, you fucking monster," Kolotkevitch screamed the words as he drew his hunting knife, then reached down with his free hand and picked up another log. "I'm going to piss in your dead mouth."

The beast rose to its full height, its head nearly touching the cabin's roof. It stood on two long, powerful lupine legs with a long dark tail. However, its torso was more human-like, broad in the chest like a man with wide shoulders and muscular arms that ended in claw-tipped appendages. The head was unmistakably wolf-like, yet much larger than a regular wolf's.

"What the fuck are you?" Kolotkevitch shook his head, disbelieving his eyes.

The two hunters lay dead at the creature's feet as Pisarev lay gurgling by the opened door. Kolotkevitch noticed that Sleptsov had stopped kicking and swung lifelessly in the doorway, blood oozing from his gaping innards.

"Just you and me then," Kolotkevitch stared at the wolf beast, its night black eyes watching him as he dipped the end of the log into the fire, the flames greedily catching on the wood. He swung the flaming torch before him, his knife hand pulled back and ready to strike. "I'm going to let you burn for a while. Let your skin pop and sizzle before I kill you."

The wolf snarled, showing gleaming white teeth that seemed to glow in contrast to its dark, blood-matted fur. The beast sprang forward, roaring with fury as it charged, and Kolotkevitch held the burning torch before him, inadvertently obscuring his vision with the smoke and flame.

Blinking through blurred vision, Kolotkevitch did not see the beast sidestep the torch and bring its balled fist down on his forearm, splintering the bone as the compound fracture tore through the skin and poked upward inside his sleeve. Kolotkevitch howled in pain, dropping the knife and clutching at his wounded arm, the pain overriding all other thoughts. He vaguely registered the beast coming alongside him until its massive paws closed around his neck and pushed his head downward.

The last thing Kolotkevitch saw was the red hot top of the stove as his face made contact with the scorching metal. The acrid smell of burning flesh filled the room as the skin on Kolotkevitch's face sizzled and blistered, his eyeballs superheating and exploding as he screamed.

Pisarev lay sprawled on the floor, his mind numbed by pain, as he watched the monster release Kolotkevitch's body and let it fall to the ground like discarded refuse. The screaming had stopped, and the only sounds that reached Pisarev's ears were the choking sounds coming from his own throat. His eyes looked at the small furry creature lying still on the floor amidst the shattered ruin of the table, his mind failing to comprehend that he stared at the beard-covered remnant of his jaw.

The coal-black eyes of the creature fell upon Pisarev as it stalked toward him, crouched low with its claws outstretched toward him.

His head lolled to the side as the beast approached, and Pisarev found he could only track the creature with his eyes now.

It was very close to him; he could smell the stench of blood and burned flesh in its fur. The beast's hot breath beat against his face. The room spun suddenly, and Pisarev heard a loud crack that he only vaguely recognized as the sound of his neck breaking.

As the world grew distant and darkened, the last thing Pisarev heard was the loud howl of a wolf.

***

The night was dark as the cloudy sky blocked the moon's rays behind a blanket of impenetrable gray. A mist hung about the city, remnants of the rain that soaked the cobblestone streets.

Alexei ran through the streets, his footsteps splashing through the puddles and echoing loudly through the deserted streets. Ivan ran alongside him. He did not recognize this place, this strange city. So, he ran onward, the night-darkened streets illuminated by the glow of streetlights on the moonless night.

On either side of him, houses, separated by alleys of impenetrable darkness, lined the streets—their doors closed and windows dark.

Alexei tried to call out, but his throat could produce no sound.

The streetlights stretched their shadows up onto the facades of the shuttered buildings and shops like macabre wraiths following beside them.

A growl emanated from one of the darkened alleyways, and he stopped, afraid to cross its path. The alley absorbed the glow of the streetlights, consuming the light within its darkness. Ivan growled back, raising his hackles and showing his teeth. The darkness growled again, and Ivan charged forward.

Alexei tried to grab the dog, but it advanced too quickly toward the darkness. He gave chase, trying to call the dog back but unable to muster any sound. Ivan charged into the alleyway, snarling and growling, as Alexei stopped at the corner of the house at the mouth of the alley, beneath a darkened window. He feared to stray from the glow of the streetlights.

He heard Ivan growl ferociously. However, a louder growl drowned out the sound of the dog. Alexei heard Ivan yelp in pain, then fall silent.

His mouth opened in a silent scream as he stared into the darkness, grief clutching at his heart for the loyal dog.

Alexei blinked as bright light from the room above filled his vision. Behind the window shade, he could see the shadow of someone approaching. He stepped back to get a better look at the window as the figure raised the shade.

He shielded his eyes with his hand as they adjusted to the brightness pouring out from the room. When he looked back at the window, Leo stood in a white nightshirt, his eyes so wide and terrified that Alexei could see the whites all around his pupils.

"Don't let the Baba Yaga get you," Leo said, his voice breathy and harsh.

"Is it a wolf, or is it a witch?" Leo's body trembled.

"Is it a wolf, or is it a witch?"

"Is it a wolf, or is it a witch?"

"Is it a wolf, or is it a witch?"

Leo spoke the words faster each time he repeated them, his lips moving impossibly quickly. His eyes darkened into blackened ruins as he spoke until they were hollow sockets.

"Is it a wolf, or is it a witch?"

"Is it a wolf, or is it a witch?"

"Is it a wolf, or is it a witch?"

Alexei backed away from the window, fear knotting his innards, as Leo continued his manic mantra.

"Is it a wolf, or is it a witch?"

"Is it a wolf, or is it a witch?"

"Is it a wolf, or is it a witch?"

Something tapped Alexei's shoulder, and he jumped and turned, holding his hands up before his face to fend off any attack. A mud-crusted, booted foot dangled before his face, swinging from side to side in the breeze. Alexei backpedaled and tripped, his backside landing hard against the cobblestones as he splashed into a puddle, the cold water rapidly soaking his trousers. He looked up and saw a man dangling from the streetlight, suspended from a rope around his neck. The man's bearded head lay at an unnatural angle, his eyes bulged from a pale face, and his tongue, blue and swollen, protruded from purpled lips. He wore a white shirt with a black jacket and pants, a blood-soaked prayer shawl extending from beneath the coat. The man was a Jew.

Alexei tried to look away from the hanged man and saw now that men and women hung lifeless and broken from all of the streetlamps. He shook his head, trying to clear the image from his mind. He was sure that they had not been there only moments before.

"Is it a wolf, or is it a witch?"

"Is it a wolf, or is it a witch?"

"Is it a wolf, or is it a witch?"

Leo's voice faded into the distance as Alexei leaped to his feet and began to run down the corpse-lined street. He refused to look at their battered faces, their final expressions of shock, sadness, and horror as the nooses tightened around their necks, splintering bone and crushing cartilage.

A light flickered on in a house as Alexei ran; looking sidelong at the window, he saw Leo's shadowy form appear.

"Is it a wolf, or is it a witch?"

"Is it a wolf, or is it a witch?"

"Is it a wolf, or is it a witch?"

A few blocks further, the light in a butcher shop window sprang to life, and there in the window, beside the slabs of hanging meat, stood Leo, his hands pressed against the window glass, head trembling as his coal-black eye sockets followed Alexei.

"Is it a wolf, or is it a witch?"

"Is it a wolf, or is it a witch?"

"Is it a wolf, or is it a witch?"

House after house, windows alighted with Leo's ghostly image ceaselessly chanting. Alexei felt tears streaming down his face as he held his hands against his ears, desperate to drown out the boy's voice. Still, he ran, forcing his legs onward.

As he ran, the street began to narrow, drawing the streetlights and their menagerie of corpses closer. Alexei stumbled and fell, the unforgiving cobblestones cutting his palms and painfully scraping his knees. His knees throbbed from the impact, and he pulled them up close to his body. He sobbed silently, still unable to will any sound from his throat, as Leo appeared in the upstairs window of a house.

"Is it a wolf, or is it a witch?"

"Is it a wolf, or is it a witch?"

"Is it a wolf, or is it a witch?"

Alexei watched in horror as the street behind him narrowed and closed like a zipper. Bodies swung wildly from the streetlamps as both sides of the street came together, swallowing the street between them.

The closing street was rapidly approaching, and Alexei returned to his feet and began running. Behind him, he could hear the arms and legs of the swinging corpses bumping and thudding together as they swayed.

The corpses closed about him as the zippering street overtook him, the feet of the dead knocking against his head and shoulders as he pushed his way forward. A woman's legs swung before his face, one foot bare and smashed so badly that the bones of the toes poked through the torn and mangled flesh of what once had been a petite foot. A finely crafted green shoe hung precariously from the other foot, a luxury diligently saved for and lovingly given as a birthday gift. Alexei remembered the morning his mother unwrapped the gift and the tears she shed, knowing all his father had sacrificed to save for the pair of shoes.

Alexei silently groaned and shook his head as he looked at the corpse. They had torn his mother's dress and undergarments, revealing cruelly scratched and bruised flesh. The noose was pulled tight around her neck, leaving a ring of raw flesh that circled her throat and disappeared behind her head. Her once beautiful face appeared brutally battered; the lips that once smiled so sweetly at Alexei were split wide and crusted with blood. The left side of her face was a ruin. A deflated eyeball hung by a long strand of flesh and muscle from his mother's shattered left eye socket, bumping against the ruin of her cheek. Someone had struck her repeatedly with something hard and round, like the butt of a pole or the head of a hammer.

Coin-shaped indentations pockmarked the skin and bone around an area of her forehead that cratered inward where her skull had collapsed beneath the rain of blows. Drying blood and fluids seeped from the wound and glistened in the glow of the streetlights.

The right side of her face looked untouched, almost serene, aside from the purplish swelling around her eye, which mercifully closed in death. Alexei felt an unfathomable sorrow at the pain and horror his mother must have felt in those dying moments. Had she witnessed a similar mauling of his father, or had she died with a false glimmer of hope that he had survived? Did she know those who had done this to her? Had some once been acquaintances, or was she ravaged at the hands of strangers? Her pain and terror was unimaginable.

Tears streamed down Alexei's face as he reached up to touch her hand. Someone had stomped the hand cruelly and repeatedly, leaving the hand a purpled mess of shattered bones. The once delicate fingers were broken and bent at impossible angles. The skin of his mother's hand was ice cold to the touch and jagged where the skin had torn.

The instant the pads of his fingers brushed her skin, her right eye flew open. The bloodshot orb fixed on Alexei's face as he stifled a scream. *She opened her mouth to reveal teeth chipped and broken by the assault.*

"Alexei," his mother's voice was a hoarse gurgle. "Alexei, something terrible is coming."

Alexei began to scream.

Alexei was still screaming as he sat up in bed, covered in sweat. His eyes were open wide and swept the darkened room as his breath came in a heaving gasp. Ivan was there, on his feet, pawing at Alexei. He reached down and pressed his face against the dog's soft, furry ear as Ivan nuzzled against him.

"It's okay, boy," Ivan's fur felt wet, and Alexei realized his cheeks were wet with tears. "I just had a bad dream."

Ivan's ears suddenly perked up as a wolf's long, mournful howl sounded in the distance.

Chapter 10

Arkady Volkov, Imperial Huntsman to Tsar Alexander III, stared out the upper window of the Imperial Byelovvyezh Hunting Lodge at the sprawling forest of pines, firs, and oak trees. He yearned to be out there, hunting amongst the trees instead of cooped up inside the lodge by the endless bureaucracy of the newly formed Administration of Forestry and Hunting. There were still areas of the forest said to be impenetrable, where Volkov believed it possible for a herd of aurochs to still roam. The immense wild ancestors of cattle had been extinct for over two hundred and fifty years. Rogue aurochs were highly aggressive and known to attack humans with great ferocity. Volkov had hunted predators across the empire but relished the notion of being the first man in nearly three centuries to stare down a charging auroch. It would take nerves of steel to place his gunsights between the eyes of the auroch as all fifteen hundred pounds of the beast barreled toward him, with its three-foot-long horns lowered to gore him. The thrill would be exhilarating, and he would have the horns carved and polished into hunting horns, one for himself and the other as a gift for Tsar Alexander.

"Did you know that this forest was once held as sacred by the Yatvyags?" Volkov peered over his shoulder, his dark, piercing eyes falling upon Kirill Vladimirovich Romanov, second cousin to the Grand Duke, who sat at the polished oak desk reviewing papers.

"Is that some kind of wild stag?" Kirill's disinterested tone, exacerbated by his failure to look up from the papers, annoyed Volkov.

Volkov bristled at Kirill's response; he despised the young nobleman and his pompous titles. To the huntsman, it was further evidence of Kirill's lack of personal achievement and substance. The man was sixty-eighth in line to be the Tsar of Russia; it would require a cataclysm within the royal family for him to ever be of relevance. Volkov earned everything he had in this life. He took it with two hands, even when that meant dipping his hands to the elbows in blood.

"They were a tribe of Western Balts, exterminated by the Teutonic knights nearly five hundred years ago." Volkov turned back to stare out the window. His reflection stared back at him. He had a rough look about his tanned face that belied a life of less than gentile living despite his fastidiously trimmed beard and expensive black hunting attire.

"Fascinating," Kirill responded as he scanned the paper in his hand. "Listen to this."

Volkov turned to look at Kirill, the young blonde-haired, blue-eyed man, tall and clean-shaven and dressed in the finery of the Russian aristocracy, the polar opposite of the swarthy Volkov in appearance and demeanor.

"Andreyevski intends to restock the game in the forest; he proposes to transport Siberian stags and deer from Bohemia at an astronomical cost," Kirill stared from the paper to Volkov.

"Andreyevski is the Estate Manager," Volkov shrugged and shook his head, "though the fool does not realize that elk despise the smell of stags. He will drive the Tsar's prized elks from the forest by bringing in so many stags."

"That's good. That's very good," Kirill pointed at Volkov as he sat back at the desk, smiling. "I will point that out to the head of Forestry and Hunting. Golenko will be very pleased we prevented Andreyevski from making such a grievous error and displeasing the Tsar."

A knock at the door drew both men's attention as Sergeant Semyon Razin, a Cossack guard who accompanied Kirill to Byelovvyezh, escorted a young gendarme officer into the room. Razin was a short, stocky, heavily bearded man with a face scarred by burns and shrapnel from one of the empire's many conflicts. He was a seasoned soldier who eschewed the traditional Cossack attire, dressing in the simple uniform of a Russian non-commissioned officer. In contrast, the gendarme officer was a youth, barely old enough to shave, his blue gendarme uniform too large for his slight frame. With his blonde hair and blue eyes, the boy could have passed for Kirill's younger brother.

"Sir, I have an urgent message from the Separate Corps of Gendarme headquarters in Saint Petersburg," the young officer stopped before Kirill's desk.

"Very well, what is it?" Kirill leaned back in his chair, folding his arms across his chest.

Razin tapped the officer's elbow and gestured toward Volkov with his head.

"Sir, Colonel Magnitsky directed that I relay the message directly to the Imperial Huntsman." the officer faced Kirill but glanced nervously toward Volkov.

Kirill made little effort to hide his surprise as he glanced at Volkov.

Volkov shrugged, "Magnitsky is a friend."

Kirill turned to the officer and gestured toward Volkov, "Very well then, give the Imperial Huntsman your report."

"Sir," the officer turned to Volkov, "there have been a series of wolf attacks in the village of Obrechen with multiple fatalities."

"I see," Volkov placed his hand beneath his chin and ran a thumb across his jawline, a childhood habit he exhibited while thinking. The matter seemed hardly worthy of the attention of the Tsar's Imperial Huntsman. He suspected hunters trapped and killed the wolves in the time it took for word to reach Byelovvyezh.

"Gendarme Headquarters in Kalinin recovered this from one of the bodies," the officer reached into the inner pocket of his jacket and handed Volkov the message from Colonel Magnitsky attached to a heavily creased and bloodstained piece of paper.

Volkov took the message, his curiosity piqued, and scanned the note before carefully unfolding the attached paper. He blanched as he recognized the handwriting and then the letter. The Imperial Huntsman folded the paper and placed it in his pocket, taking a moment to compose himself before addressing the officer.

"Thank you," Volkov nodded to the officer. "Please extend my regards to Colonel Magnitsky; it is deeply appreciated."

"What is it, Arkady?" Kirill asked as Razin escorted the officer from the room.

"It would seem that my brother has been killed," Volkov tapped the breast pocket where he had slid the paper. "This is a letter I sent him two months ago asking him to join us here and hunt with me in the Byelovvyezh forest."

"I'm very sorry for your loss, Arkady," Kirill looked genuinely sorry, and Volkov admitted that empathy was one of the young Romanov's better qualities. "Do you need to make arrangements for his funeral?"

"No, my brother is long buried by now," Volkov shook his head, his eyes intense and focused. "But I will go to Obrechen and kill the wolf that took him if it still lives. I owe him that."

"And if they've already killed it?"

"Then I will kill every fucking wolf I find."

***

Batu was a short, thickly built man with the Asiatic eyes and long, thin beard of the men of the Mongolian steppe. He wore a *deel*, the long, dark coat of the Mongols that crossed in front to attach at the side and shoulder with white buttons made from polished animal bone. Two large knives sat in leather sheaths at his waist, and the curved bow that typically lay across his back sat safely nestled in the oilskin against the wall alongside a quiver of black arrows.

He had served as Volkov's tracker and hunting companion in the eight years since his exile from the Qing Imperial court and the Forbidden City in the heart of Beijing. Batu was summarily dismissed from service in the Mongolian Imperial Guard following the death of his charge, Empress Dowager Ci'an, poisoned by her rival and co-regent, Empress Dowager Cixi. For his failure, Batu, a warrior his entire life, left the Forbidden City disgraced and outcast.

He took work as a tracker for wealthy Russian nobles seeking to hunt Siberia's red deer and wild boar. However, the hunts bored him, providing little sport or challenge, and the arrogant, pampered Russian aristocrats rankled him. Then he met the Tsar's Imperial Huntsman. Volkov was a hard man, accustomed to living off the land and forsaking the comforts of the aristocracy. The Imperial Huntsman was not interested in deer or boar; he only wanted to hunt the most deadly predators. Unlike the Russian nobles who waited in warm tents for the trackers to flush the herds into the open, Volkov desired only to track his prey and kill it at close range. They hunted the Siberian plains together when lesser men would have succumbed to the cold and hunger of the harsh environment, taking lynx, bear, and Amur leopards as prizes.

However, it was the day the two men took down a female Siberian tiger that marked and bonded them for life. The cunning tigress had caught their scent and circled back, attacking the hunters' flank by surprise. They grappled and fought the four-hundred-pound predator with their knives as she raked them with her claws in a ferocious attempt to close her jaws on Batu's head. Volkov managed to separate himself from the melee and brought the tiger down with a hard thrust to the beast's chest that ruptured her heart. They were victorious but, Batu would forever bear the scars of the tiger's claws on his chest and back. Volkov, too, suffered deep gashes down his left arm and leg.

In the month that it took them to reach Nerchinsk, surviving their wounds in the unforgiving Siberian steppe was as desperate a struggle as the fight with the tiger. The battle against infection, blood loss, starvation, and subfreezing temperatures bonded the two men for life and made them more than friends and closer than comrades. To commemorate their survival, Volkov commissioned a coat of the tiger's hide, and Batu fashioned buttons from the animal's bones which he wore on his *deel*.

"I will understand if you wish to remain in Byelovvyezh," Volkov placed a spare pair of boots into his leather travel bag, along with several changes of hunting attire.

"I am your tracker," Batu's tone was, as usual, flat and emotionless as he leaned against the wall observing Volkov.

"I know that wolves are sacred to your people," Volkov tied the bag closed. "I will not ask you to do something against your conscience."

"Yes, to be Mongolian is to have the blood of the *tengerinokoi* in your veins. It has been that way since Chinggis Khan was born of a wolf and a deer," Batu countered. "However, there is also a saying among Mongols: if you see a wolf, you are its equal, but if you kill a wolf, you are its master."

"Your point, Batu?"

"There are no more than one or two hunters in the world who could debatably even claim to be your equal. You will kill the wolf who slew your brother and become its master; that is a fact. It is also a fact that I will track this wolf for you." Batu's face displayed no emotion, like an experienced poker player studying his opponents.

"And I suppose you are one of the one or two hunters who claim to be my equal?" Volkov folded his arms across his chest.

"No," Batu's tone was deathly serious. "I am the one hunter who is your greater."

Volkov laughed, then his eyes narrowed as Batu's expression remained unchanged. Batu met his gaze, his Asiatic eyes unwavering. This was a constant topic of debate between the two, however, none would challenge the notion that no two hunters made a more lethal pair.

A knock at the door averted the conversation from spiraling into their usual argument. Volkov shrugged and nodded for Batu to open the door; both men were surprised to see Semyon Razin standing in the doorway, a look of pure misery on his scarred face.

"Sir, I am sorry for disturbing you," Razin looked from Volkov to the floor. "I was hoping to discuss a matter with you."

"Of course, Sergeant, come in." Volkov was genuinely curious about what could cause the seasoned soldier to look so ill at ease.

"I was hoping to speak to the Imperial Huntsman privately," Razin glanced from Batu to Volkov.

"Whatever you wish to say to me, you may say in front of Batu," Volkov felt his patience with the man instantly evaporate, "or you may cease with this interruption."

Razin blanched at Volkov's rebuke and nodded, "Yes, Sir, I meant no offense."

"Well then, you have failed in your intent," Volkov's eyes narrowed, and he let a tone of menace drift into his voice.

"What is it you wish to discuss, Sergeant?" Batu's voice was more measured, having often witnessed Volkov's ability to verbally eviscerate those who angered or annoyed him.

"It's the Romanov. I understand he is to accompany you to Obrechen," the Cossack sergeant said. His discomfort only increased as he spoke. "I would like to ask you not to allow this."

A look of amused shock crossed Volkov's face, and even Batu raised his eyebrows in surprise, a rare display of emotion cracking the Mongolian tracker's usually stoic demeanor.

"Sergeant Razin, perhaps you live in a different world than I," a condescending smile spread across Volkov's lips. "However, in my world, in Imperial Russia, the Tsar's Huntsman takes orders from the Romanovs, not gives orders to them."

Batu's lips curled downward in a slight frown as he stared at Volkov, and then he addressed Razin in his heavily accented Russian, "Why is it you wish the Romanov to remain here?"

Razin's discomfort visibly increased, and he shifted his feet nervously. When he spoke, he glanced at Volkov and lowered his eyes, "I have a bad feeling about this trip."

"Oh, well, why didn't you say so," Volkov exclaimed, moving his hands with great flourishing sweeps. "Batu, Sergeant Razin has a bad feeling; bar the doors and lock the fucking windows."

Batu's frown deepened as Volkov walked to stand before Razin, who hung his head. Volkov's tendency to bully was in full bloom before the hapless sergeant.

"Instead of ordering the Romanov and the Imperial Huntsman to stay sequestered in their beds," Volkov poked Razin hard in the chest, "why don't you go take a shit and see if your bad feeling goes away?"

When Razin raised his head to look at Volkov, his face was flush, and his eyes blazed with anger. Batu could see that a proud Cossack and veteran soldier stirred beneath the sergeant's deference to Volkov's superior station. A sneer crossed Razin's scarred face as he restrained himself from responding to Volkov's insult.

Volkov narrowed his eyes, smiling cruelly, "Do you have something you wish to say, Sergeant Razin?"

"I would like to hear why this feeling bothers the sergeant so greatly," Batu's calm voice defused some of the rising tension in the room.

"It is an overwhelming feeling of dread; I have only had it once before in my life," Razin glanced at Batu, then back to Volkov, who glared menacingly at the sergeant, less than a hands breadth away from the man's face. "On the morning of Tsar Alexander the Second's assassination."

The Imperial Huntsman raised one eyebrow in curiosity but otherwise remained unmoving.

"I was one of the Cossack guards assigned to protect the Tsar's carriage on his visit to the Mikhailovsky Manège when the *Narodnaya Volya* struck with their bombs and killed the Tsar." Razin winced at the memory. "The first blast incapacitated me, and I could not protect the Tsar. I had a feeling like this that morning but said nothing. I will not make that mistake again."

"So now you fear you may lose another Romanov?" Volkov cocked his head and gave Razin a condescending smile.

"The Tsar's death was a stain upon my family and my honor," Razin's voice was a low growl. "I lost everything. If Kirill's father did not request my services, I would be begging in the streets."

"Is that why you dress like a common soldier, not a Cossack?" Batu's intelligent eyes studied the man.

Razin curtly nodded, "I disgraced my clan; I am not worthy of representing my people."

Batu nodded thoughtfully, stroking his chin.

Razin opened his mouth to speak, however, Volkov raised a hand, cutting him off, as he crossed the room to remove a pair of leather gloves from his wardrobe, "Regardless, with a Romanov traveling with us, we will face fewer delays in reaching Obrechen, and that is paramount."

The sergeant nodded in defeat, "Yes, Sir. I apologize for disturbing you this evening."

Volkov and Batu shared a look, a wordless moment of understanding passing between them as the sergeant exited the room.

The Imperial Huntsman nodded slightly in understanding, and the tracker followed the sergeant from the room.

"Sergeant Razin," Batu's voice echoed through the empty hall, and the man stopped and turned, clearly surprised to see the tracker. "May I have a word with you?"

"Yes, of course," Razin nodded, staring at Batu curiously as the tracker approached him.

"I believe I understand your concerns a little better than the Imperial Huntsman," Batu's face was impassive as he addressed the Cossack. "I was once a guard in the service of the Chinese Qing Emperor Tongzhi. On his deathbed, he charged me with the protection of the Empress Dowager Ci'an, but I failed in my duties, and her rival slew her. They stripped me of my position and cast me out of the Forbidden City."

"How was she killed?" Razin appraised him with a sympathetic gaze.

"They say her co-regent, Empress Dowager Cixi, slipped poison into her tea," Batu's left eyelid twitched slightly.

"That would have been very difficult for a guard to protect her against," Razin suggested.

"Perhaps," Batu nodded, "however, my greatest regret is outliving the people the Emperor charged me with protecting."

"You would have drunk the poison as well and followed her into death?" the notion shocked the sergeant.

"No," Batu shook his head, then stared at Razin with eyes as cold and emotionless as a shark, "I regret not returning to the Forbidden City and killing the Empress Dowager Cixi, even though it would have meant my life. There is a Chinese proverb, 'He who seeks revenge digs two graves.' It is meant as a warning, though I would gladly lay down in that grave if it meant I avenged the Empress Dowager Ci'an."

Razin appeared to contemplate Batu's words, his gnarled hand stroking this thick beard in thought.

"Sergeant, you could no better have protected the Tsar against bombs than I could the Dowager Empress against poison," Batu pursed his lips slightly. "I have sworn myself to protect the Imperial Huntsman with my life, and if he falls, I will see his killer laid at his feet, even if it means my death. That is what it means to guard someone. Do you understand?"

Razin squinted, studying the stoic tracker, and then nodded.

"So do not worry about the dangers that face the Romanov," Batu placed a hand on the sergeant's shoulder. "Be the danger for all that threaten him."

***

Pavel stood rigidly at attention before his direct superior's desk in the Kalinin Headquarters of the Separate Corps of Gendarme, the note he recovered from Volkov's body secreted in his uniform pocket.

"You can make your report to me, and I will see that Colonel Zelyabov is properly informed of your findings," Major Sazhin leaned back in his chair and regarded Pavel with unmasked disdain.

"Sir, I believe the gravity of my findings necessitate I communicate them directly to the Colonel," Pavel saw the Major's shoulders stiffen slightly at his response.

"Lieutenant Verenich, I understand that the Corps has stationed you in one of our more rural posts since graduating from the Academy," Major Sazhin narrowed his eyes as he leaned forward and placed his hands on his desk, "so I will forgive your impertinence. However, this is Kalinin, and we have a way of doing things here. There is a hierarchy. Every officer has their place and acts accordingly."

"Sir, with all due respect, Article 27 of the Separate Corps of Gendarmes code states that any officer of the gendarme may request a meeting with his regional commander if the matter is critical to maintaining the good order of the Empire."

"And this matter you have uncovered in..." Major Sazhin paused and looked at Pavel. "What is the name of the village again?"

"Obrechen, Sir"

"Ahh, yes, Obrechen. You believe this matter you have uncovered in Obrechen is essential to maintaining the good order of the Russian Empire," Major Sazhin did not attempt to hide his smirk.

"Yes, Sir, I do."

"Very well then, Verenich," Major Sazhin sighed, opening a side drawer in his desk and withdrawing a form. He dipped the tip of his fountain pen into the ink well on the corner of his desk, wrote three quick sentences that Pavel could not make out, and then signed the document with a flamboyantly large signature. The Major blew on the page to dry the ink, then folded it into thirds and handed it to Pavel. "Bring this to Captain Velasev, Colonel Zelyabov's adjunct; he will arrange an appointment."

"Thank you, Sir," Pavel saluted the Major sharply, a gesture Sazhin did not return. Pavel kept his face impassive; inside, he rejoiced at how he had outmaneuvered the Major. He was certain Sazhin had intended to steal the glory for himself and doubted the Major would even have mentioned his name in his report to Colonel Zelyabov.

After delivering the document to Captain Velasev, Pavel spent the next three days sitting on the bench in the Kalinin headquarters of the Separate Corps of Gendarmes as his fellow officers walked past him. At first, they looked at him with curiosity; however, as his vigil stretched from hours to days, the looks turned mocking with thinly veiled smiles, and then, most humiliating of all, the looks changed to pity. Pavel could weather their taunting gazes but could not abide by their pity.

On the morning of the fourth day, Pavel marched to Captain Velasev's desk and demanded the Colonel see him. "Sir, I am here on a matter of urgent importance to Tsar Alexander. Every day we delay allows a violent fugitive to roam free and threaten the empire."

Captain Velasev raised an eyebrow at the grandiose claim, then gestured to a chair directly beside the ornately carved wooden doors of the Colonel's private office, "Have a seat; I will advise the Colonel of the urgency of your request."

"Thank you, Sir," Pavel sat in the stiff-backed wooden chair as the Captain opened the wooden doors and disappeared inside. Behind the closed doors, Pavel could hear voices talking but could not discern any of the words.

"Lieutenant Verenich," Captain Velasev opened the door, the corners of his mouth slightly upturned as if he found something privately humorous. "Colonel Zelyabov will see you now."

Pavel stood and smoothed out his uniform before nodding curtly to the adjunct and entering the room. The Colonel's office was far more spacious than Major Sazhin's and richly decorated with artwork depicting military victories of the Imperial Russian Army. A stern-looking portrait of Tsar Alexander III hung on the wall behind an immense, dark wood desk emblazed with a carving of the Imperial Ministry of the Interior's coat of arms; a double-headed eagle with its wings outstretched beneath the imperial crown. A shield covered the eagle's body, emblazoned with the image of St. George on horseback, slaying a dragon with a spear. The eagle gripped a ribbon of the Order of St. Andrew in its talons alongside a torch and two crossed lightning bolts.

Although Pavel only glanced at it, he could see the carving was exquisite workmanship.

Seated behind the desk, Colonel Zelyabov's thinning white hair and close-cropped beard starkly contrasted his blue uniform, adorned with so many rows of medals that barely any uniform was visible on the left side of his chest. The man intently read a small stack of documents as Pavel stopped before his desk, brought himself to attention, and saluted.

"Lieutenant Pavel Verenich, reporting," Pavel stood rigidly at attention before the desk.

"Yes, the officer from Obrechen with information dire to the empire," Zelyabov's tone conveyed his disinterest as he continued reading the document before him without looking at Pavel.

"I was investigating a murder in the forest surrounding Obrechen," Pavel had rehearsed the report in his head hundreds of times over the past several days.

"Was a government official murdered?" Zelyabov interrupted him without looking up.

"A government official? No, Sir, it was a hunter," Pavel frowned at the interruption.

"Was he killed with an explosive device, such as the kind the revolutionaries employ?"

"No, Sir, he was mutilated," Pavel withdrew the note from his uniform pocket, unfolding it and placing it upon the Colonel's desk. "I discovered this in the man's mouth."

Zelyabov set aside his document and glanced down at the blood-stained note. Pavel watched as the man's eyes followed the lines of handwritten script and suppressed a self-satisfied smirk that the Colonel would shortly regret his disinterest.

"Yes, well, thank you for bringing this matter to my attention," Zelyabov glanced at Pavel for the merest of seconds before returning to his document. When he realized Pavel was still standing before his desk, the Colonel glanced up again. "Was there anything else, Lieutenant Verenich?"

Pavel was dumbstruck. He blinked several times, then opened his mouth to speak but could not find any words.

"Lieutenant Verenich, was there anything more?" Zelyabov's voice now held a tone of growing annoyance.

"Sir, I will need resources to investigate and hunt down the perpetrator," Pavel stammered and stumbled upon the words.

"I will take it under advisement. Leave word with Captain Velasev where he can reach you if I require any more information. Dismissed Lieutenant," Zelyabov returned to his document.

Pavel turned and strode from the room, defeated and humiliated. He left his hotel information with the adjunct and felt the man's mocking gaze bore a hole into the back of his head as he departed the headquarters without another word.

For three more days, Pavel sat in his hotel room waiting for a further summons to return to the headquarters. He had nearly given up hope and prepared to return to Obrechen when the desk clerk advised him that there was a message from Major Sazhin requesting his presence.

Pavel chided himself for losing faith so quickly as he strode through the headquarters doors, his face fixed into a mask of smugness for all those who had laughed at him only days earlier. He hoped some of those officers would be under his command during the investigation, and Pavel would make them regret their mockery. First, he would accept Major Sazhin's contrite apology for dismissing him so casually.

"Lieutenant Verenich," Major Sazhin stood, his hand outstretched in greeting as Pavel entered the office. "May I call you Pavel?"

"Yes, of course, Sir," Pavel nodded, a Cheshire cat grin crossing his face as he shook the Major's hand.

"Pavel, the Colonel was very grateful for you traveling such a distance to report your finds to us," Major Sazhin grinned back at Pavel and pointed a finger at him. "The Empire needs more officers like you!"

"Why, thank you, Sir. I am but a humble servant of the Tsar," Pavel said, feeling anything but humble.

"The Colonel has asked me to reward you for your faithful service," Major Sazhin crossed to his desk and withdrew a slip of paper and a red

and gold box from his desk drawer. A medal? Pavel felt his heart rate quicken and stiffened his back to stand straighter.

"Sir, it is my honor," Pavel began to speak, but Sazhin interrupted him.

"He instructed me to provide you with a return ticket purchased by the Corps and this box of chocolates, compliments of the Colonel. I understand they are excellent," Sazhin grinned as he extended the ticket and the box of chocolates to Pavel.

Pavel stared in disbelief as Major Sazhin handed the items to him.

"Have a safe trip back to Obrechen, Pavel, and do come see us again soon," Sazhin's grin broadened as he slapped Pavel on the shoulder.

Pavel threw the unopened box of chocolates into the trash outside of the headquarters. He hoped Major Sazhin and Colonel Zelyabov saw the brightly colored box in the refuse and understood what he thought of their hollow praise and reward. However, the train ticket he would use, as the personal cost of this fruitless endeavor, turned his stomach and left a sour bile taste in his mouth.

Pavel was still ruminating on the ignominy of the trip as he waved for the conductor to signal the engineer to stop the train in the field outside Obrechen. A week after Pavel boarded the train to Kalinin with high hopes of advancement and notoriety, he stepped off the steps of the second-class train car and immediately felt his boots sink into the muck of the rain-soaked field. He closed his eyes and suppressed the urge to scream in frustration as the rain quickly drenched his uniform.

"Hope it's not a long walk into town," the conductor peered up at the sky, barely poking his head from the safety of the stairways overhang, then back to Pavel.

He turned and gave the conductor a withering look, but the man's interest had migrated to a group of men exiting the third-class carriage further back on the train. Eight men filed out of the train car; seven were thickly bearded and clad in sheepskin hats, high-necked black woolen coats, and baggy trousers tucked into military-style leather boots. The gendarme noticed each man wore a long dagger belted at his waist and bore a rifle slung across his backs. To Pavel's surprise, he saw a row of diagonal pockets on the breast of each man's jacket, precisely sewn to hold ten rifle cartridges in place.

Cossacks. The arrival of the group certainly piqued Pavel's interest. The Tsar's enemies, foreign and domestic, feared them, and with good cause; the military prowess of the semi-nomadic Cossack people from the steppe of Ukraine was legendary throughout the Russian Empire.

Pavel watched as five of the Cossacks broke away from the group and slid open the doors of one of the cargo cars toward the rear of the train. They pulled down a long wooden ramp and disappeared into the car. He noticed the remaining two Cossacks stood talking to the final member of their group, a stocky man with a bald head and short, pointed beard. The man wore the long green coat of an Imperial Army veteran, worn and weather-beaten with age, with a pistol holstered on one hip and what appeared to be a hammer in a makeshift holster on the other.

Two Cossacks reappeared from the cargo car, leading three saddled horses down the wooden ramp. Behind him, Pavel could hear the conductor loudly clear his throat in an unsuccessful attempt to get the bald man's attention.

"Excuse me, Sir, we have a schedule to keep," the conductor called out and pointed to his pocket watch.

The bald man looked up with a sudden fury rising in his dark, beady eyes. He took three steps toward the conductor and pointed at the man, "You shut your fucking mouth. You can have your fucking train back after we unload. Until then, just shut your mouth and go inside."

Pavel could see the spittle flying from the man's mouth, even with the rain pouring down. The conductor looked from the man to Pavel, eyes imploring the gendarme's intervention. The bald man fixed his gaze upon Pavel, ready to unleash a fresh round of vitriol.

"I've already reached my stop," Pavel gave the conductor a disinterested shrug. "Your train can sit here all night for all I care."

Visibly defeated, the conductor retreated into the carriage to placate the first-class passengers over the delay. The bald man appeared to relax and gave Pavel a curt nod of greeting.

"You stationed in Obrechen?" the man cocked his head.

Pavel nodded and walked toward the man, "I am the gendarme for the village." He extended his hand, the cold rain slapping against the skin of his palm. "Pavel Verenich."

"Valerian Rostov," the man exchanged a firm, calloused handshake. "How do I get to this shithole of a village?"

"That way," Pavel pointed to his left. He looked over Rostov's shoulder as three Cossacks rolled a giant steel cage down the ramp. The cage was nine feet long and about half as high, with thick steel bars. They had seated it atop a wagon platform, its large wooden wheels moving slowly under the weight of the cage. Rostov turned to see what had caught the gendarme's attention, then yelled instructions to the Cossacks.

"Set it up in the field and pitch the tents alongside it," Rostov pointed into the field beside the tracks. The Cossacks nodded in acknowledgment as the wagon cleared the ramp, its wheels digging deep into the wet earth. The Cossacks guiding the three horses approached, and Rostov barked instructions at the men. "Leave the horses with Ilia and Petro and help the others set up camp."

"What is the cage for?" Pavel nodded toward the men struggling to push the heavy wagon through the muck.

Rostov turned and grinned, "I understand Obrechen has a very troublesome wolf hunting in these woods. We intend to capture it."

Pavel felt his shoulders stiffen at the mention of the wolf but quickly recovered, "Capture? Why not just kill it?"

"Have you ever heard of Albert Salamonsky?" Rostov asked as he grabbed the saddle of one of the horses and hoisted himself into the saddle.

"There was a Salamonsky Circus in Moscow," Pavel watched as the two Cossacks mounted their horses behind Rostov.

"The same," Rostov nodded. "You're pretty fucking worldly for a gendarme from Obrechen."

"I'm not from Obrechen; headquarters in Kalinin stationed me here."

"Well, my fucking condolences to you," Rostov lifted himself in his saddle to survey the road ahead before turning to Pavel. "Salamonsky wants the wolf captured for his circus. He's going to let people pay to stare at the Beast of Obrechen or some shit."

"The Beast of Obrechen?" Pavel raised an eyebrow in surprise.

"That's what they are calling it back in Kalinin. The Frenchies had their Beast of Gévaudan; now Russia has the Beast of Obrechen." Rostov gave him a look of disdain. "It's killed at least a dozen villagers. How piss poor a gendarme do you have to be to not know about the wolf in your own fucking village?"

Pavel seethed at the insult as the two Cossacks laughed at Rostov's gest. He opened his mouth to speak, a hot retort on the tip of his tongue, but Rostov cut him off.

"You say Obrechen is that way?" Rostov pointed toward the road to town, and Pavel only nodded. "Come on, men."

Rostov kicked his horse into a trot, and the two mounted Cossacks fell in behind him. The horses kicked up large drops of mud that splattered Pavel's rain-soaked uniform and smacked against his cheek. He stepped back, angrily wiping the mud from his cheek as the conductor reappeared on the carriage stairs.

"Sir, is it ok for the train to leave now?" the man's voice was shrill and questioning.

Pavel gave the man a sneer of derision and began walking toward Obrechen.

***

The rain continued unabated as Pavel's feet slogged through the muddy road. The indignity of Rostov's dismissal of him at the train served to fuel the anger brewing inside him after the already infuriating and fruitless trip to Kalinin. His woolen blue uniform coat had soaked through, and the visor on his cap did little to keep the rain from streaking down his face as he approached his home.

Leo sat on the porch with a broad smile as he leaned back in the wheelchair and watched his father approach. Pavel glared at the boy, a green blanket covering his withered legs to keep the chill of the rainy day from him, and wondered if the boy had even moved from the spot in the seven days he had been gone.

"Father," Leo waved vigorously, a green leather book clutched in his lap. "Welcome home; how was your trip?"

"What have you got there?" Pavel frowned as he stared from the book to the boy. "Did your mother buy that for you?"

"No," Leo grinned and held up the book. "It was a gift. It's a book of German fairy tales."

"Fairy tales," Pavel spat the words out and shook his head. "The world is not a fairy tale, Leo. The world is a harsh, unforgiving place. It may not seem that way, all snug in your chair, but that is the truth of things."

Leo stared at him, his lower lip trembling, and he shrank back in his chair as if his father's words were physical blows. Pavel's eyes narrowed, and his anger rose as he saw the first hint of tears welling in the boy's eyes. Somewhere deep inside Pavel, a volcano of rage erupted. The disrespect shown to him by the gendarme in Kalinin, then Rostov and his Cossack thugs, churned inside him.

Pavel grabbed the handles of Leo's wheelchair and roughly rolled the chair down the stairs into the street. The boy's body jolted as the wheels thudded down each step, and Leo curled forward to protect the leather-bound book from the pouring rain. He let out a mewling cry of despair as he desperately tried to shield the book from the rain that quickly soaked his clothes and ran down his face.

The wheels of Leo's chair sank into the mud, and Pavel had to strain to push it into the middle of the road. He let go of the chair and stood before Leo, who only raised his eyes to look at his father as he hunched over the book. The rain mixed with Leo's tears and ran down his face in rivers as he sobbed.

"Leo, the world is a cruel place." Pavel leaned down to place his face close to the boy's. "The sooner you learn that, the better."

"Verenich," an approaching voice called over the din of the rain.

Pavel looked up to see Igor Balkov approaching on horseback; he wore a wide-brimmed hat and hunter's cloak to ward off the worst of the rain. Balkov clutched a second horse's bridle, and a brown mare trailed him.

"I just returned from Kalinin," Pavel shouted to Balkov. "I'm tired; come see me tomorrow at the gendarme station."

"The Land Captain wants to see you now," Balkov sneered at Pavel. "It's not a request."

"Morozov sent you? Where's Pisarev?"

"Pisarev's dead," Balkov pulled the mare up alongside him. "Get on; the Land Captain is waiting."

Balkov eyed Leo curiously as Pavel swung into the mare's saddle; the leather was wet and slippery against his drenched trousers.

"Boy needed a bath, eh?" Balkov looked at Leo and flashed Pavel a cruel smile.

"Let's go," Pavel turned the horse toward town. Behind him, Pavel heard an anguished cry as his wife came running out of the house to Leo's side. Her footsteps splashed loudly through the rain and mud as she ran.

"Leo. Leo, are you ok?" her voice sounded shrill and frantic as Pavel kicked the horse into a steady trot. "Pavel, how could you do this to him?"

***

Pavel's horse followed closely behind Balkov's black mare as they passed through the iron-barred gate of the Land Captain's sprawling estate. The rain had finally ceased, replaced by a thick fog that hung just above the eight-foot-high stone and mortar wall that surrounded the land held by countless generations of Morozovs. Pavel had once heard that Andrei Morozov's great-grandfather commissioned the wall's construction during a years-long famine to keep the peasantry of Obrechen from stealing his livestock and pillaging his fields. As Pavel entered the gate, he could understand why the Morozovs needed the wall.

Fields stretched wide on both sides of the dirt road that led to Morozov's manor house and though they were now cut low after the fall harvests, Pavel could imagine the bounty of vegetables they would produce come the following year. They passed two large barns and a long stable as they approached the main house, then a series of tiny houses that served as quarters for the farm's male workers and servants. The female servants all resided in quarters inside the manor house. If the rumors Pavel heard were true, Morozov paid regular nightly visits to several of the female servant's quarters.

The Land Captain's manor house reflected the continuing good fortune of generations of Morozovs. The home's two lower floors were constructed of stone at least a century earlier, an imposing structure for the estate's peasant workers who dwelled in drafty thatched huts. The lower floor contained the great hall, several smaller living rooms for entertaining, a kitchen, and food storage areas. The second story originally housed the Morozov family's bedrooms and dressing rooms, with the servant quarters relegated to the basement. However, Andrei's father had a more spacious upper story built of timber and moved the family and guest quarters to the new third floor. He moved the male servants to the outer building and graciously allowed the female servants to reside in the old rooms on the second floor. The female quarters, lavish by Obrechen's standards, made finding employment in the Morozov's manor house highly desirable for young women from the surrounding villages—a fact the Morozov men exploited to the fullest.

Pavel and Balkov dismounted their horses and passed the reigns to grooms, who came running out of the stable to meet them. The smell of warm food and burning firewood greeted the men as they pushed open the manor house's thick oak door and entered the entry hall. Pavel's stomach grumbled hungrily at the scent, and the sound of crackling and popping wood made him look forward to an opportunity to chase the chill from his bones by the fire.

Morozov sat with his wife and son at the great hall's long table, feasting on a large roasted turkey surrounded by several savory side plates. Pavel felt his mouth watering at the lavish meal and wondered how long it had been since he dined on that bland bowl of borsch at the railway station in Kalinin. The Land Captain looked up as they entered and gestured for Balkov to come to him. Pavel returned a polite nod of greeting from the Land Captain's wife and observed that the boy never turned his attention away from the turkey leg. He continued to tear large pieces off with his teeth, chewing noisily.

"Land Captain, I brought the gendarme," Balkov thumbed a finger back toward Pavel.

"Thank you, Igor, excellent work on this stormy afternoon," Morozov reached into his purse and flipped a shiny coin in the air toward Balkov. "You were a fine choice to replace Pisarev. Why don't you get yourself down to the *Kanti Gans*? Get some spirits to chase the cold away."

Balkov grinned as he snatched the coin from the air and quickly slipped it into his pocket, "I think I will at that. A drink sounds just perfect right now." He turned and gave Pavel a wink and a cruel smile. "Have a good day, Verenich."

"Lieutenant Verenich," Pavel corrected the man and gave him a withering look, bristling at the disrespect shown him in front of Morozov.

"Yeah, right," Balkov gave a snort that turned into a mocking laugh.

"Pavel, where have you been?" Morozov did not even look at the officer as he reached for more bread.

"I have been in Kalinin on gendarme business," Pavel straightened his back and squared his shoulders to present more authoritatively.

"Gendarme business," Morozov's voice was a low growl as he raised his eyes to meet Pavel's gaze. "Are you not the gendarme of Obrechen?"

"Yes, of course..." Pavel began, but Morozov slammed his hand hard on the table, cutting him off.

"Then where were you when that wolf killed six of my men?" Morozov hurled the handful of half-eaten bread at Pavel. The gendarme officer tried to dodge the projectile, but the bread bounced off his shoulder and into his face, causing him to blink crumbs from his eyes.

Morozov's wife quietly looked down at her hands, but her son looked sidelong at Pavel, trying to contain his snickering laughter with his mouth full of chewed turkey. Pavel looked up, stunned into silence by the sudden, unexpected attack.

"I had to keep those men's bodies in my ice house for six days while you got your dick wet in Kalinin," Morozov rose and pointed toward where the ice house stood beyond the manor house. "I had to tell Pisarev's wife she had to wait to give him a Christian burial until our auspicious gendarme returned from his gallivanting. Thirteen years that man served me, now he lays like a side of meat, waiting on you."

Pavel wanted to protest. He wanted to yell back that he alone went to Kalinin to seek help hunting the killer, that this was more than the mere case of a wolf attack. However, all he could muster was a question, "Why did you not bury them?"

"Because I needed you to see the bodies," Morozov sank back into his seat, his rage dissipating.

"I will examine them immediately," Pavel straightened and nodded, eager to withdraw from the Land Captain's presence.

"No, you will wait," Morozov gazed at Pavel as he tore free a new piece of bread and sopped it around his plate. "I will take you to the ice house when I finish eating."

"Very well," Pavel dipped his head in acknowledgment and walked to stand by the fire.

"Verenich!" Morozov barked, his voice filled with indignation.

Pavel nearly jumped at the Land Captain's raised voice. He heard the boy snicker again and felt his face flush with anger and humiliation. As Pavel turned to look at the man, it took all his willpower to mask his distaste for the Land Captain's conduct.

"Are you going to walk across my grandfather's Turkish rug with those wet boots?" Morozov pointed at Pavel's feet.

Pavel looked down at his feet, his boot planted on the faded red carpet. Then he stepped back, placing both feet on the stone floor.

"Wait in the entry hall," Morozov dropped the remaining bread onto his plate in disgust. "You've cost me my appetite."

***

Pavel walked behind Morozov as the man led him behind the manor to the ice house. Each man held a lantern to fend off the encroaching dark of evening, and Pavel noticed Morozov continuously scanning the darkness.

Coward. Safe behind his stone walls, the Land Captain still fears the wolf.

An owl hooted in the night, and Pavel gave a tight-lipped smile as Morozov stopped and lifted his lantern to peer into the darkness, eyes searching, before continuing on his way.

The man was all bellows and bluster until the cards were on the table. If he were not a Morozov, he would be just another peasant drinking in the Kanti Gans.

Pavel's eyes narrowed as he stared at Morozov's back, thinking how perfect it would be if the wolf did leap out of the darkness. His hand absently strayed to the pistol he had holstered at his side. He would put a bullet right through the beast's head and end all this wolf nonsense, be the hero Obrechen so desperately craved. A cruel smile twisted Pavel's lips as his mind wandered; of course, he would stay his hand at first, just long enough for the wolf to rid Obrechen of the Land Captain. He pictured Morozov sprawled on the ground, broken, and choking on his own blood, his throat shredded by the wolf's jaws. Morozov would reach out for Pavel to help and save him, his eyes pleading, and Pavel would kick the man's fat hand away.

"Verenich!" Morozov's harsh whisper snapped Pavel's thoughts back to the moment, the Land Captain raising his lantern and bathing the gendarme's face in bright light. "This is no game; men are dead; I need you to pay attention."

Pavel raised his hand to shield his eyes from the light and nodded curtly. They had reached the old wooden door of the ice house. Morozov opened the door and ushered Pavel inside. The cold air instantly brought goosebumps to the skin beneath Pavel's damp clothing.

Large blocks of ice, insulated with straw and stacked a full head higher than Pavel, filled the windowless ice house. The walls of ice blocks filled nearly a third of the room, much of the stores having been used during the year and awaiting winter replenishment. Seven long lumps lay on the floor, covered in horse blankets that had soaked through with dark blood and froze in the frigid air. Five lay packed close together, and two man-shaped lumps lay side-by-side a few feet away."

"Who else was killed aside from Pisarev?"

"Frolenko, the Sleptsov brothers, Kolotkevitch, and two of his cousins from another village," Morozov held his lantern out over the five covered corpses. "Torn to shreds."

"Just like Volkov. Where did this happen?" Pavel was eager to conclude this business and get somewhere warm.

"East of the village, not far from here. My father kept a hunting cabin in the woods," Morozov leaned down by the two frozen bodies separated from the others.

"But why keep them here? Why not bury them?"

"I wanted you to see this," Morozov grabbed the corner of the horse blanket and pulled it back, wincing as the blanket made a sickening ripping sound as it tore free of the frozen blood.

"Oh, good God," Pavel gasped and turned away at the sight of the two horribly disfigured corpses. He felt his gorge rise in his throat and had to force down the urge to vomit. Morozov snorted with disgust at the gendarme's squeamishness, and Pavel forced himself to look at the two men.

It was Pisarev and Yuri Sleptsov. Both men were now blueish with dark blood-spattered speckles on their faces. Pisarev's jaw was missing, and ragged curtains of skin hung from his top teeth, forming a ledge above his gaping maw. His eyes were closed, and he looked otherwise like he was sleeping serenely. In contrast, Sleptsov's eyes were open wide in terror and bulged from their sockets. Yellowed teeth showed from a mouth opened wide in an eternal silent scream, lips pulled back toward the gums. The man's torso was in utter ruins, gutted like a slaughterhouse cow; Morozov's men appeared to have haphazardly piled his innards back inside him before they froze into an amalgamation of gore.

"This is what I wanted you to see," Morozov lowered the lantern close to Pisarev's mangled face and pointed to the unusual angle of the man's neck. "There's something wrong here; Pisarev's neck is broken."

"Andrei, I am sure the loss of your man is very upsetting," Pavel relished using a placating tone with Morozov as if speaking to someone overcome by hysterics. "The wolf must have wrenched his face with incredible force to tear his jaw free; I would be more surprised if Pisarev's neck was not broken."

"Then how do you explain this?" Morozov moved the lantern alongside Sleptsov's ghostly face and pointed to a thin gash that traversed the circumference of the man's neck.

Pavel leaned over and squinted at the unusual wound. Dark bruising on the man's neck nearly masked the fine line, however, he could see that the wound cut deep into Sleptsov's throat and suspected it would have been fatal even without his evisceration. "What is that?"

"The men found Sleptsov gutted and hanging in front of the cabin by a wire snare," Morozov looked sidelong up at Pavel, his face grim and severe.

"Caught in his own trap?"

"The men used steel traps, not wire snares, and they set them around the goat, not by the cabin," Morozov said, looking at the gendarme with mild irritation. "Regardless, no one sets a snare trap nine feet off the ground."

"Goat?" Pavel wished the Land Captain would explain what had happened from the beginning rather than force him to piece the incident together.

"The goat was the bait," Morozov explained, though his expression indicated that Pavel should have understood that without further explanation. "These men were experienced hunters; they set the traps along avenues a wolf should have taken to get the bait."

"It avoided all the traps?"

Morozov shook his head, "Every trap was sprung."

"What?" Pavel was annoyed he could not hide the surprise in his voice. "Are you saying this wolf set off every trap, stole the bait, and then killed all the hunters?"

Morozov shook his head, "The fucking goat is the only one that survived the whole mess. The wolf didn't even touch it. We found the terrified thing still tethered to the ground."

Pavel debated telling the Land Captain about the note he found in Volkov's mouth, then decided to keep that detail to himself. However, he could see by the look on Morozov's face that the man was already arriving at the same conclusion.

"It set off thirteen steel traps unscathed, leaving not so much as a wisp of hair in the jaws, then strolled past a fatted goat to kill seven armed hunters and string one up by his neck," Morozov stood and stared into the gendarme's face, the flickering lantern light dancing against the man's dark eyes. "Does that sound like a wolf to you?"

Pavel stared back at Morozov, unblinking. "You think a man did this to these men?"

"I think that someone very clever set off those traps and strung up Sleptsov to attract the wolf," Morozov's eyes were cold and hard. "A wild animal tore these men apart, of that I am certain. I believe someone is making sure this wolf doesn't get caught, using the wolf to cover up killings."

Pavel nodded, mulling over the Land Captain's theory, closely mirroring his own since discovering Volkov's body and the note. "We have a murderer in Obrechen."

"I believe we do indeed, Officer Verenich," Morozov nodded.

"Who would target these men? And Volkov was not even from Obrechen," Pavel looked down at the two frozen corpses.

"I think my men and your hunter were a threat to the wolf, so the killer eliminated them and led the wolf to the bodies to mask his crimes."

"But why go through all that trouble?"

"Because the killer has yet to strike his true target."

Pavel's mind raced with the implications, "So you're saying these deaths are just a decoy?"

Morozov nodded, his tone grave, "The killer needs everyone to believe a wolf is responsible for these killings so that when he takes his intended victim, no one will suspect his hand in the deed."

Pavel shook his head slowly, contemplating the implications.

"Pavel, who in Obrechen would require such a ruse to avoid inquiry into their death?" Morozov's voice was low and conspiratorial.

The gendarme looked up with sudden understanding, "The Land Captain."

Morozov nodded, "Or the local gendarme. Have you ever heard the tale of Prince Vseslav of Polotsk?"

Pavel shook his head.

"There is a tale; everyone who grew up in these parts has heard it as a warning at one time or another as a child.'Be good or Vseslav will get you.' That sort of thing. According to legend, Prince Vseslav was capable of transforming into a wolf. By day, he would rule as a prince but, by night, he would hunt in the guise of a wolf, killing those who had done ill or wronged him. Obrechen is a superstitious village. Before long, those childhood tales of Vseslav will have people believing a werewolf is stalking Obrechen and punishing the wicked. People will begin questioning the order of things, and then we will have anarchy. Which is just what our killer would want."

"You believe the killer is a revolutionary? Like those who killed Tsar Alexander?" Pavel narrowed his eyes. "Someone like the Kaminer boy?"

Morozov nodded, "The boy's parents were suspected radicals, were they not? And according to Balkov, he has interfered with traps in the past."

"Yes," Pavel agreed. "And he has certainly not hidden his dislike for either of us."

"Lieutenant Verenich," Morozov leaned in close, placing a hand on Pavel's shoulder, his white puffs of vaporous breath warm against Pavel's cold cheek. "We must eliminate this wolf and the Kaminer boy before he can strike again."

"There's a man, Rostov; he arrived on the train with several Cossacks to hunt the wolf," Pavel let a tight smile cross his lips. "Perhaps he could be of some use to us."

"Cossacks," Morozov smiled and nodded knowingly. "Yes, they could be very useful."

"I will see to it right away, Land Captain," Pavel straightened his back and nodded curtly.

"Lieutenant Verenich, I believe I have underestimated you," Morozov gave him an approving look. "I think we may prove very useful to each other."

"I could not agree more," Pavel grinned and, for the first time in several days, felt that things were finally going his way.

Chapter 11

Pavel dismounted the horse and tied the reigns to the hitching post outside the *Kanti Gans*. Morozov had provided the horse as a gesture of goodwill to assist the local gendarme in carrying out his duties for the Tsar and empire. The Land Captain sent word to the Obrechen stable to arrange a place for the horse and promised to send several hay bales for its upkeep.

Four other horses lined the hitching rail, Balkov's black mare, and the three ridden by Rostov and the Cossacks. Pavel smiled; all the toys were in the toy box. He had just become the most important ally of the most powerful man in Obrechen. It was not the end goal he sought, not by a long shot but, it was the first stepping stone in the right direction.

He pushed through the bar's faded wooden door; the hearth fire's smell mingled with the stale aroma of alcohol and musty wood that defined the *Kanti Gans*. Pavel walked into the bar with an authoritative air he had not felt since his early days as an officer. He fixed his eyes forward and walked decisively toward the bar, intent on sending the message that none inside was worth his notice. Using only his peripheral vision, Pavel noted Balkov and several other local men clustered in the corner around a table where Rostov and his Cossacks sat. As he crossed the room, he heard Balkov's voice rise above the others, followed by laughter and knew the man made a jest at his expense.

Laugh now. That is all about to change.

Pavel placed his hands on the edge of the bar as the red-haired bartender nodded in acknowledgment and reached for the jug of *medouvukha*. She raised an eyebrow questioningly when he waved her off from the jug of mead.

"Vodka," Pavel gave her a slight smile.

She looked genuinely surprised as she grabbed a smudged glass of questionable cleanliness and placed it before him, pouring a shot of vodka into the glass. Pavel gestured for her to make it a double, and the woman shook her head in disbelief.

"Bad day, Officer Verenich?" the woman's face was a mix of surprise and amusement.

"Not at all," Pavel smiled, tipped the glass toward her in a silent toast, and downed the contents in one motion.

The cheap vodka burned his throat going down and felt like fire in his belly, but Pavel delighted in the sensation. He slammed the glass down hard on the wooden top of the bar; the sound resonated through the bar like a gunshot. Pavel gestured for her to fill it again and heard the conversation behind him dwindling to hush. He knew that if he turned at that moment, all eyes would be on him.

Again, Pavel downed the contents of the glass and slammed it down on the bar. His movement was the authoritative strike of a judge slamming his gavel against the bench. The bartender's auburn eyebrows shut up in surprise, and she quickly refilled the glass when he gestured. The room was now silent behind Pavel, and he winked mischievously at the bartender, eliciting a sly smile in return. *What was the woman's name? Yulia. That was it.*

Pavel turned to face the room, leaning back against the bar. As he suspected, all eyes were on him. Balkov glowered at him and rubbed a finger alongside his crooked nose while Rostov studied him with genuine curiosity.

"I have examined your friends' bodies, men you often sat with here in the *Kanti Gans* and shared a drink," Pavel paused and looked over the men in the room. He downed his drink, starting to feel the alcohol warming his face, and placed the glass behind him on the bar. "And it is the opinion of the Separate Corps of Gendarme that an individual disabled the traps, enabling the wolf to catch the men in the forest at unaware and then let the wolf into the cabin to attack your friends while they slept."

An uproar swept the room as angry voices rose at the thought that somebody had betrayed their friends to the wolf. Pavel had taken great liberty with the details, however, he did not think that would matter. He caught sight of Rostov, who watched him closely, calculating what Pavel was up to.

"Further," Pavel raised his voice above the din, "the Separate Corps of Gendarme now holds the Jew, Alexei Kaminer, as its prime suspect."

Outrage swept the room again, and even Rostov appeared to register shock and intense interest at the proclamation.

"There's a Jew?" Rostov leaned toward Balkov, who nodded and responded with something Pavel could not hear.

"The Jew may control the wolf," Rostov appeared excited and animated now.

"The boy is always followed by a dog, a vicious thing," one of the other men added.

One of the Cossacks leaned in close and said something to Rostov, who agreed enthusiastically, "You're right; it could be some manner of Talmudic demon. Jews are known to command hell spawn."

Pavel was not sure that Morozov would be pleased with that interpretation, but as the vodka began working in his system, he cared more about the ends of his plan than the means.

"I can get you the Jew," Pavel heard Balkov assure Rostov as the gendarme turned back toward the bar.

Yulia stared at him with interest as if reassessing him; then, a look crept into her eyes that Pavel had not seen from a woman in a very long time. He smiled at her, a sloppy grin fueled by the vodka coursing through his system, and felt slightly unsteady on his feet. Her eyes lit up at his smile, and she returned it with a mischievous leering grin as she motioned with her head toward the back room.

Today is turning into an unexpectedly good day. Pavel left Rostov and the others to discuss the finer points of Jews and wolves and followed Yulia into the back room.

***

Oksana tied Seryy's reigns to the hitching post on the Obrechen market's outskirts. She patted the donkey's long neck as it dipped its head to drink deeply from the water trough. *The poor thing must build up quite a thirst, pulling the cart from Galina's cottage to the market.*

"I'll be back soon, Seryy," The donkey looked up at her, his eyes two large brown pools, and she scratched her fingers from his snout to between his eyes, a spot she knew he loved itched. "I'll bring you a nice apple for the trip back."

Pickles, eggs, carrots, potatoes, and an apple for Seryy; Oksana ran through her mental list of items Galina had asked her to pick up as she strolled through the market. She adjusted the large, empty basket on her arm. Galina had told her to wait until Bogdan and Alexei had finished constructing and hanging the door in the barn, however, Oksana feigned indignation and insisted she did not need a boy to steer the cart and carry her basket. Saturday was always a busy day at the market, and Oksana wanted to get there before the villagers could pick over all the choice vegetables.

Oksana scanned the usual stalls at the market, smiling and nodding in greeting to some. However, she pretended to study something interesting in her basket when she passed Olga Putina's vegetable stall. Out of the corner of her eye, Oksana could see Olga glaring at her, and from the expressions of two women passing her in the opposite direction, Oksana was sure Olga made a vulgar gesture behind her back. Father Grigori was making his rounds of the market, and Oksana saw Nadia Ponomareva seated before her three large tubs of pickles and sauerkraut, waving for the priest to come to her stall.

Nadia was very animated, and Father Grigori appeared to be trying to calm her, but they were too far away for Oksana to hear the conversation. Oksana casually attempted to get a little closer to see what Nadia's distress was about. She watched as the woman fished around in her tub of pickles and withdrew the limp form of a tiny mouse. Nadia flung the tiny body into the shadows behind her stall, the mouse landing unmoving with a dull thump.

Oksana felt heartbroken for the unfortunate creature; the poor creature must have smelled the pickles and thought it had discovered a feast, only to drown in the brine. She watched as Father Grigori raised his hands, saying a prayer and making the sign of the cross over the tub three times. When he finished, Nadia looked visibly relieved and handed the priest a coin, which he quickly secreted into his black frock. With a nod, Father Grigori bid Nadia a good day, though he politely refused her offer of a pickle before moving on to the other stalls.

Obrechen's version of sanitizing. Oksana knew this was long the way of the village, but the thought of how much despoiled produce she had consumed in her young life that had its contamination blessed away made her stomach turn.

Nadia turned to see Oksana, her face lighting up in the welcoming expression that vendors like to use to draw customers to wares. Oksana returned the smile but crossed pickles off Galina's list in her head.

There was a moment when Oksana caught a movement out of the corner of her eye, but her mind registered it too late to avoid the blow. Something struck her on the side of her face with such force that the world went entirely white as if someone had encased her in a snow drift. Oksana reeled from the blow, her head spinning as she fell to the ground. Her body felt limp as it crumpled, her head again rocked by the jarring contact with the hard earth. Oksana could hear voices, but they felt far away, and she struggled to will her eyes to focus. The sun was bright overhead, and the light rays felt like needles piercing her brain. She just wanted to close her eyes and make the pain stop, but doing so brought on a wave of nausea that threatened to bring her breakfast up.

A dark shadow stood over her, mercifully blocking the sunlight. She tried to murmur a thank you, but as her vision cleared, the words caught in her throat. The visage of her uncle, Igor Balkov, stared down at her. Even in her current stupor, there was no mistaking the crooked nose, leering grin, and rancid smell of his breath.

"Where's your Jew boy now?" Igor ran his tongue over his chapped lips as he stared at her.

"Why? You looking for another beating?" Oksana struggled to get the words out and even managed a mocking smile, or what she hoped looked like a mocking smile.

Balkov's eyes registered the shock of her words, but then he shook his head and smiled a cruel, twisted smile, "Oh, no. It's not me getting a beating today."

The last thing Oksana saw before she passed out was Balkov rearing back to strike her.

***

"There," Bogdan gave a last twist of the Mahogany-handled screwdriver and stood back to survey his work. "What do you think?"

Alexei eyed the two cast iron hinges Bogdan had affixed to the doorway leading to his room in the barn. Three screws held the metal plate to the door frame, and an iron pin as thick as his finger extended upwards from each hinge. They had attached the other half of the hinges to the thick wooden door they had constructed; now, they only needed to lift the door and slide the hinges over the iron pins. Alexei tugged at the hinges attached to the door frame and nodded approvingly when they did not budge, "That should hold the door."

"Come give me a hand," Bogdan bent over and lifted the door. "Just guide the top hinge over the pin."

Alexei nodded and adjusted the door so the two parts of the hinge lined up. "They're lined up. Wait a moment."

"Why, what's wrong?"

"Ivan, move, boy. Move," Alexei shooed away the dog, which had laid in the hay and lazily watched them construct the door all afternoon. Ivan slowly stood and stretched one back leg and then the other before relocating to a sunny spot in the barn's doorway.

"Just in case the door falls," Alexei shrugged at the man's questioning look.

Bogdan eased the door into place, smiling as he heard the top hinge slide over the metal pin. He flashed Alexei a broad grin of success before noticing the boy's furrowed brow.

"What is it?"

Alexei pointed to the bottom hinge, and Bogdan groaned when he looked. They had somehow measured in error and placed the hinge too far up the door; it sat a good two inches above the iron pin.

"How did we do that?" Bogdan shook his head in disbelief.

"Hold the door still," Alexei knelt to retrieve the screwdriver. "I'll move the hinge down the door."

Just as Alexei's fingers closed around the worn wooden handle, an anguished scream shattered the afternoon's quiet. Alexei looked up in alarm and saw Bogdan's face echoing his concern.

"That's Galina," Bogdan lifted the door off its one hinge and let it fall to the floor. It struck with a loud *thud* and a whoosh of air that sent a small cloud of dirt into the air as the two men rushed out into the bright daylight with Ivan trailing closely behind them.

Galina appeared to have been bringing them lunch, though the basket now lay on the ground, a bottle of wine rolling in the dirt alongside a wedge of cheese and loaf of bread. She stared transfixed toward the road, hands covering her mouth. As one, Bogdan and Alexei followed the line of her gaze to the wagon ambling up toward the cottage. Seryy, his reigns trailing along the ground, appeared to have found his way back to the cottage by sheer memory. Oksana sat on the riding board of the wagon, her arms hanging limply by her side. Her body swayed heavily, and her head lolled from side to side as the wagon slowly rolled over the rough ground, every bump threatening to topple her from the seat. Alexei broke into a dead run for the wagon, Ivan chasing closely behind.

"Oh, no," Bogdan groaned as Oksana managed to raise her head weakly, her face blood-streaked and swollen from a terrible beating.

Seryy came to a stop, and the lurching motion of the wagon caused Oksana to topple from the running board. She would have crashed to the ground, further aggravating her injuries, had Alexei not reached the side of the wagon in time to catch her and gently lower her to the ground.

"Oksana, Oksana," tears streaked down Alexei's face as he gently brushed the hair from her blood-encrusted face. "You'll be okay. Galina will fix you up."

Oksana managed to open her eyes halfway, a sea of burst blood vessels surrounding her hazel irises. She tried to speak, but the effort caused a split on her swollen lower lip to re-open and streak her chin with fresh pink blood.

"I'll get some rags and water," Galina rushed into the house as Bogdan came to kneel alongside the injured girl.

"Shh, don't try and talk," Bogdan's voice was soft and soothing. "You're going to be okay. I'm just going to check you out."

Alexei stood and moved back to give Bogdan some room as he felt along the back of her neck. Distraught, Alexei ran his hands through his hair as Oksana groaned when Bogdan examined the back of her head with his fingers.

"Who did this?" Alexei's voice came out a strangled cry as he tried to contain his emotions.

"Let her save her strength, Alexei," Bogdan said as he gently raised one of Oksana's eyelids and then the other.

"I promise you, I'll make them pay for hurting you," Alexei's voice was suddenly bitter.

"Now is not the time for this," Bogdan gave him a stern look. "First, we see to Oksana, then we find out who did this."

"I know who did this," a sneer twisted Alexei's face into a mask of anger, and his eyes grew cold.

"Bring her inside," Galina waved from the porch. "I have warm water and towels ready."

Bogdan gently scooped Oksana up in his arms; she let out a low groan as he lifted her, and her head came to rest against his shoulder. He looked down at her, concern etched over his face, then glanced up at Alexei. The boy stood there trembling with rage as he looked at the limp form of Oksana in Bogdan's arms.

"Alexei, let's go inside," Bogdan spoke softly, trying to keep the boy calm.

Alexei looked from Oksana to Bogdan; his eyes seethed with anger as his fists clenched and unclenched. Then, as if a dam burst inside him, Alexei turned and ran down the road toward Obrechen, Ivan running at his heels.

"Alexei," Bogdan called after him, but Alexei was already running hard.

"Bogdan, let him go," Galina yelled from the porch. "We need to get Oksana inside quickly."

Bogdan watched Alexei and Ivan run around the bend in the road and out of sight before turning to carry Oksana into the house. He was concerned for the girl's injuries and even more fearful of what danger Alexei would get himself into. Bogdan could do nothing now but help Galina tend to Oksana and hope Alexei came to his senses before things got too out of hand. He had little doubt that, in this state of mind, the boy was capable of killing someone or getting himself killed. Oksana groaned in his arms, and his heart broke for the peril his little surrogate family was facing this dark day.

***

Alexei lowered his shoulder and struck the door of Igor Balkov's house at a dead run. The iron hinges, brittle with age and weathering, broke under the force of Alexei's blow, sending him and the door tumbling inside. He staggered from the impact with the door but quickly recovered his footing as he entered the house.

Alexei's eyes darted around the disheveled room, his chest heaving from running and his fists clenched, ready for confrontation. Feeding off Alexei's emotions, Ivan followed through the open doorway, hackles raised along his gray back and teeth bared. Adrenaline coursed through Alexei's body as he forced his rage-fueled mind to focus. Nobody was home, and it appeared Balkov had not lived there for some time.

After several deep breaths, Alexei could finally control his breathing and think. Balkov must have relocated to Morozov's estate after the death of Pisarev and the others. He shook his head; of course, Balkov would benefit from the misfortune of others. The man probably felt safe enough behind Morozov's manor walls and surrounded by workers, to seek revenge on Oksana without fear of reprisal.

He slid over a faded wooded chair and sat down as Ivan walked over and rested his head on Alexei's leg. Alexei smiled as the dog wagged its tail, clearly happy the tension of the last few moments had passed. He went to run his hand along the dog's head, then noticed the dried blood smeared on his hand—Oksana's blood.

Alexei leaned back in the chair, scratched the dog's furry head, and exhaled deeply. Ivan always calmed him; something about the shaggy dog, always so happy and loyal, set him at ease. He loved the dog as much as he loved anyone or anything, even as much as he did Oksana.

The thought of her hurt at Balkov's hands, no doubt with his drinking buddies goading him on, infuriated Alexei anew. Balkov was an envious and cruel man; his black heart would rather see her dead on the ground than happy. The man would hurt Oksana again; Alexei was sure of it. Balkov would kill Oksana before she escaped Obrechen unless Alexei stopped him.

Drinking buddies.

The thought shot through Alexei's mind like a lightning bolt. Alexei stood and laughed out loud, which caused Ivan to jump up and place his front paws on Alexei's chest, his tail wagging excitedly. Still laughing, Alexei rubbed his hands through Ivan's coat. Alexei knew exactly where Balkov and his drinking buddies would be, and he knew what he needed to do.

Chapter 12

Alexei stayed concealed within the forest's shadows as he watched the rear door of the *Kanti Gans*. The back of the bar faced the forest, with the only window belonging to a darkened storage room. His father had told him that the original owner of the *Kanti Gans* used the storage room as sleeping quarters and installed a hidden trap door to slip beneath the bar. More importantly to Alexei, the man also installed a removable panel along the wood skirting of the bar to move unseen from beneath the building and out into the woods. Alexei's father had no idea why the man needed to be able to move about with such secrecy but suspected it was for some illicit activity or another. After hearing the story, Alexei located the removable panel in the rear of the building. However, notions of what could live inside the darkened space beneath the bar prevented him from exploring further. Tonight would be different.

He adjusted the heavy burlap sack on his back, shifting the corners of the explosive charges that poked hard against his ribs. Alexei knew his father intended to use the device against the Tsar's forces, but he believed he would approve of his work that night. Alexei ensured his father's pistol sat securely tucked into his belt against the small of his back and then scanned the surroundings one last time to ensure no one was around.

"You stay here, boy," Alexei looked down at Ivan, seated on his haunches. The dog whined in disapproval until Alexei reiterated the command more forcefully. "Stay."

The dog lowered his ears and dipped his head slightly at the command but stayed where he sat as Alexei ran out of the woods. The heavy sack made the short run awkward and unbalanced as he hunched low and quickly closed the distance from the forest to the back of the building. Alexei was already sweating hard, equal parts exertion and stress, making the wooden board feel slippery to the touch as he felt for the hidden door. His fingertips brushed a mark, three small lines carved into the corner of the panel, the mark Alexei had left when he first discovered the secret panel.

Alexei pushed against the panels; they resisted at first and then easily fell away as a tiny dark spider quickly scurried for cover. An odor of dampness and old drink exuded from the space, and Alexei wrinkled his nose at the sour smell. He peered into the space, no taller than three feet high, at the networks of spider webs that hung down among dark patches of mold and rot. Something scampered in the distant dark of the space as Alexei slid his body inside, pulling the heavy sack behind him. He placed the board back in place to avoid detection, leaving it only slightly ajar to identify his exit quickly.

Narrow bands of light shone through the cracks between floorboards, preventing the space from enshrouding him in total darkness. Alexei let his eyes adjust to the low light, then slid across the dank earthen floor. Cobwebs brushed against his face and head, tangling into his hair. He had to stymie the feeling of revulsion as his hand slid through damp earth reeking of fresh urine, where one villager must have relieved himself beneath a table.

His shoulder ached under the weight of the sack as he dragged it through the muck. Before leaving his house, Alexei had prepared the explosives as his father had instructed. He affixed the detonators into the explosives and then ran the wire to the blasting machine. Alexei would deposit the explosives beneath the *Kanti Gans'* main room, then slip back into the woods and depress the t-shaped handle on the palm-sized blasting machine. He attached a long enough wire between the explosives and the blasting machine that he would be well away from the detonation.

A sudden pang of sadness washed over Alexei as he realized he would have to leave Obrechen forever after tonight, to get as far away as possible before the gendarme catches up with him. The thought of never seeing Leo and Oksana again weighed heavily upon his heart, but he steeled his will. Balkov needed to die; there was no other way.

When he was confident that he was beneath the main seating area, close to the corner where he knew Balkov liked to sit, Alexei listened intently to the voices above. He strained his ears to make out Balkov's voice but sounds below the floor were too muffled to distinguish individuals. Alexei tried peering up through the cracks in the floor, however, the spaces were too thin to see anything but light and shadow.

He lay his head down on the sack in frustration, the angles of the explosive charges pressing into his forehead. Blowing up the *Kanti Gans* would only be worthwhile if Balkov was present. Alexei would have to go inside and see for himself; it was the only way to be sure.

Leaving the explosives in place, Alexei gripped the blasting machine and slowly unwound the wire as he retraced his steps toward the hidden door. The trip proved much faster without the heavy sack to drag, and Alexei was thankful to fill his lungs with fresh night air as he slid the panel away. Alexei contemplated quickly running the blasting machine into the forest and readying it to detonate the explosives. Still, he decided that anyone coming across a wire from the woods to the *Kanti Gans* would arouse too much suspicion, so he stashed the blasting machine just inside the crawlspace and secured the panel back in place.

Standing, Alexei attempted to brush as much of the muck from his clothes as possible.

It's the Kanti Gans; who is going to notice?

Alexei smiled at the thought of Balkov and his drinking buddies laughing and mocking his dirty clothes, unaware that he was about to send them all to hell. He checked to ensure the back of his shirt covered his father's pistol then, he casually walked around the bar to the front door.

Gleb Andreev, the blacksmith's brother, watched Alexei approach from the *Kanti Gans'* one cloudy-paned window. His deep-set eyes stared at Alexei from beneath thick, dark eyebrows. From what Alexei knew of Andreev, the man had a reputation for being mean-spirited and crass; he would not have been surprised if it was he who relieved himself on the floorboards.

Better drink up quickly and get home, Gleb, Alexei thought as the man moved away from the window.

Alexei planned to head for the bar, turning and leaving once he spied Balkov and his friends. Balkov would no doubt take Alexei's sudden departure as a sign he feared a confrontation with the man and his friends and take great pleasure in pointing that out. He would likely hurl an insult or two at Alexei as he left. It would be the high point of Balkov's day until the fiery inferno Alexei unleashed engulfed him.

The thought of Balkov's skin melting and his bones charring was at the forefront of Alexei's mind as he stepped through the door of the *Kanti Gans.* The door had not closed fully behind him when the first punch struck his chin, surprising and staggering him. Rough hands grabbed his arms as a second attacker punched him in the stomach, causing the air to rush from his lungs in a sudden whoosh. He was aware of several men surrounding him, the stench of their sweat and breath assailing his nose as they attacked him with their fists. Stunned and gasping for breath, Alexei kicked out as the attackers tried to force him to the ground. He heard a man cry out in pain as Alexei's kick made contact with the man's knee. Blows began to rain down on him from all directions as the men pushed him to his knees. Alexei's right arm slipped free in the melee, and he quickly reached for the gun secreted behind his back, however, one of the attackers grabbed his arm and pinned it roughly behind his back. Alexei gritted his teeth in pain, but it was a cry of despair that slipped past his lips as he felt the pistol pulled from his waistband.

"What have we here?" Alexei heard Balkov's voice pronounce with no small measure of glee.

Alexei looked in the direction of Balkov's voice and saw the man holding his father's pistol, a cruel smile on his face. When Balkov saw Alexei glaring at him, recognizing the defiance and hatred in his eyes, he swung the gun downward at the beleaguered boy. The butt of the pistol struck Alexei in the middle of his forehead with a loud thud, and his limbs went limp. The room spun as the men's voices became suddenly distant in Alexei's head. His body slumped to the ground, his face striking the dank wood of the floor, and Alexei was vaguely aware of his warm blood pooling around his head. They held his arms and legs down, and one man placed a foot or knee on Alexei's back, making it difficult to breathe.

"Quickly. Stuff this in the Jew's mouth before he can summon the demon wolf," a man's voice that Alexei did not recognize ordered. Someone yanked Alexei's head up by the hair so hard he felt as if his scalp would tear free of his skull as a hand shoved a rag deep into his mouth. Alexei gagged as the rough fabric ran over his tongue and scraped against his teeth. Somewhere in his mind, he envisioned the rag wiping a spill off a table or the floor. It was gritty and tasted of grime and alcohol.

"Not in here," Alexei heard Yulia, the barmaid, yell. "Don't you do it in here."

"Ilia, Petro, grab his arms. We'll take him to the woods," the man's voice, which Alexei did not recognize, decided. The man said more, but the words were lost in the fogginess of Alexei's dazed mind.

Alexei felt his body lifted, a pair of hands roughly grabbing him under each arm and dragging him out into the night. The rush of cool night air against his face helped clear Alexei's mind, though his body was still sluggish to respond. Two bearded men he did not know, with rifles slung over their backs, dragged him, as Balkov, Gleb Andreev, and a third man, Anton Mezentsov, who Alexei recognized as one of Morozov's workers, followed along. A bald man walked in front of their procession; Alexei surmised he was their leader, the voice giving orders in the *Kanti Gans*.

His feet dragged behind him, leaving ruts in the dirt as they followed the road out of town. Alexei could lift his head now but let it hang limp, letting them think he was still semi-conscious. He could see the few people on the street or outside their homes quickly move inside, shutting doors and drawing the curtains. Balkov and the other village men laughed and joked, exuding a bully's bravado brought on by drink and outnumbering their prey. Alexei felt certain their courage would quickly melt if he could break free; however, he was not as sure of Ilia and Petro, the two men carrying him. They dragged him silently through Obrechen, forgoing the banter of the village men, their grip firm and their stride unwavering. He guessed they were likely veterans accustomed to carrying out commands. These men would not shrink from a fight, and from the glimpses Alexei managed, they carried rifles and knives.

Alexei spied a figure standing on a porch and recognized Pavel Verenich, a cup of tea in his hand. His stomach sank with the realization that Leo's house was the last house on the edge of Obrechen; the men were likely close to where they intended to deal with him. He glanced up at Pavel and made eye contact with the gendarme officer. A smile crept across Pavel's face, and he raised his teacup in a silent salute to Alexei as the men dragged him past the house.

The men dragged him around the bend in the road and out of sight of Obrechen when the leader signaled the men to stop.

"This is far enough; I want the villagers to hear his screams," The leader turned and grinned at Alexei. He gestured to the men, "Hold his arms and legs."

The two men laid Alexei down on the ground on his back, holding him by his arms as Gleb Andreev and Anton Mezentsov pinned down each of his legs. The bald man stroked his pointed beard and looked down thoughtfully at Alexei.

"My name is Valerian Rostov," the bald man glared at Alexei. "I only tell you my name, Jew, so that when you get to hell, you can tell all the other Jews who sent you there. You'll find I have made it quite crowded down there."

Ilia and Petro emitted low, rumbling laughter, the only reaction he had detected from the men. Balkov and the others laughed raucously in response, far more than the remark merited, and Alexei knew they were trying to garner the man's favor. Rostov saw through their charade and eyed them with unmasked scorn before returning his gaze to Alexei. Rostov's eyes blazed with fanaticism as he slid a hammer from his belt. He held it up in the moonlight as if appraising the battered iron tool with its worn and stained wooden handle.

"I want to make another introduction," Rostov held the hammer before Alexei's face. "This is my Jew hammer. The Bible says the word of God is like a mighty hammer that smashes a rock to pieces." Rostov hefted the hammer and made a striking motion in the air, "I use my Jew Hammer to smash Jews to pieces."

Alexei's eyes opened wide at the implication of the menace in Rostov's words. Images of his mother's shattered face from the dream flooded his mind, jarring Alexei like a dip in frigid water. Gleb Andreev laughed again as if Rostov was joking, then quieted when the man glared at him.

"Now, where should I start?" Rostov leaned over and lightly tapped the hammer against Alexei's knees, then, the man's face lit up like he had solved a complex riddle. "That's right, you like to set off traps. We can't have that, now, can we?"

Rostov suddenly swung the hammer in a wide arc, bringing the head down upon Alexei's right hand with crushing force. Alexei screamed into the rag stuffed in his mouth and flailed against the men restraining him. His body arched and bucked as Rostov brought the hammer down repeatedly on the hand, Alexei's bones shattered and his skin pulped under the blows. The jarring pain of the hammer destroying his hand overloaded Alexei's senses, and he lost consciousness.

Only after he saw the boy's body go limp did Rostov stop the assault. He stood and wiped the sweat from his brow, the iron head of the hammer covered in blood. Gleb glanced over at the mangled mess of Alexei's hand and began to wretch.

"Oh, come now," Rostov shook his head with disgust. "We've just started; it won't get messy until we get to his head."

A dark shape snarling in a fury leaped from the woods, landing on the man holding Alexei's injured appendage. The man cried out in surprise and pain as the creature's teeth sank into the man's neck.

"The Jew summoned the demon wolf," Anton cried out and let go of Alexei's leg as he backed away, tripping over the retching Gleb and sending both men tumbling to the ground in a tangle of limbs.

Rostov crouched defensively, holding the hammer before him, as his man cried out for someone to get the beast off him. Balkov drew the pistol he had taken from Alexei and pointed it at the beleaguered man.

"No, you'll hit Ilia," Rostov pushed Balkov's hand down.

Petro released Alexei's other arm and stepped back as he unslung his rifle, trying to get a clear shot at the beast. Alexei's eyes flew open as the pain of his hand surged him back to consciousness. He could see Ilia struggling to draw the knife on his belt as something gray and fur-covered bit at his face and neck. *Ivan.*

The sight spurred Alexei into action as he rolled onto his side and sprang to his feet. Cradling his damaged hand against his body, Alexei ran for the woods. From the corner of his eye, he saw Ilia struggling with Ivan. He finally dislodged the dog and heaved him several feet away. Ivan landed on his feet and looked ready to rejoin the battle with the man when a rifle shot rang out. Alexei echoed the dog's cry of pain when he saw Ivan's gray body fly several feet into the brush and disappear from sight.

"It's just a dog," Petro yelled as he lowered his smoking rifle and readied another shot should Ivan re-emerge from the forest. "It's not a wolf."

"The Jew is escaping," Rostov pointed as Alexei fled into the forest.

Balkov raised his pistol and fired all six shots in quick succession in the direction Alexei fled. "I got him!"

Balkov tucked the pistol into his belt, a smug triumph on his face that quickly faded into a scowl when he saw Rostov's skeptical gaze.

"My shot took him in the back of the head. I saw him fall," Balkov narrowed his eyes as he glared at Rostov. "I fixed our problem."

Petro pushed past Anton and Gleb, peering fearfully into the woods, his rifle gripped in both hands.

"How is Ilia?" Rostov asked as the man approached.

"Mostly flesh wounds, but I believe he will lose the eye," Petro gestured to Ilia, who was stoically wrapping a bandage around his head and the right side of his face. The white bandage was quickly staining red with blood. "Should we retrieve the body from the forest?"

"There's no need, Petro. Balkov assures us he has handled the problem," Rostov laced his words with a tone of mockery that visibly irritated Balkov. "Ilia, can you ride?"

Ilia nodded in acknowledgment as he tied off the bandage and stood.

"Good," Rostov turned to Petro. "We'll head back to camp and get Ilia's wounds tended to. Go back to the *Kanti Gans* and retrieve our horses."

"Yes, Valerian," Petro nodded curtly before heading back down the road to Obrechen, rifle at ready and eyes scanning the surrounding forest as he broke into a steady jog.

"I have a wolf to capture," Rostov looked from Balkov to the other villagers with visible scorn. "I don't believe I will need your assistance any further."

"A stray dog just mauled your man," Balkov sneered at Rostov. "I shudder to think what happens when they face a wolf that has already killed nearly a dozen armed men."

Rostov smiled a cruel, wicked grin as he tapped the bloody head of the hammer against Balkov's chest, "Let's just hope your little Jew stays dead. If he were to show himself again, I may have to ask myself if you lied about shooting him to aid his escape."

"The Kaminer boy is dead," Balkov's countenance darkened. "I am certain of it."

Chapter 13

The first shot from Balkov's gun struck Alexei between his neck and right shoulder. The impact of the bullet knocked him to the ground and likely saved his life as Balkov's remaining bullets whizzed harmlessly over his head, striking nearby trees or journeying further into the forest. He would have cried out in pain had the rag not been stuffed in his mouth.

The bullet severely damaged Alexei's brachial plexus, the bundle of nerves that carry signals between the spinal cord and the right shoulder, arm, and hand. While the wound itself was exceedingly painful, it had granted Alexei the inadvertent mercy of numbing all sensation from the shoulder down to his mangled right hand.

Alexei dragged himself beneath the cover of a bush, still lush with its yellowing fall foliage, and tried to lay as still as he could. He pulled the filthy rag from his mouth and fought to control his breathing as he panted heavily from the pain and exertion. As sweat poured down his face and his shirt continued to soak with blood from his wounded shoulder, Alexei knew he had to get somewhere safe to tend to his wounds before he slipped into shock.

He listened to the muffled voices along the road as Balkov and the village men departed, and then Rostov and his men left on horseback. Rostov rode off toward the train stop while Balkov and the locals headed back to Obrechen. Alexei contemplated trying to reach Galina's cottage. However, the severity of his wounds dictated he needed to be someplace much closer.

Leo's home was the closest, but Alexei was confident that Pavel would send him away, if not turn him back over to Rostov. That left only his house; Alexei thought if he cut through the woods to the footpath, and no one was waiting to ambush him, he could make it home before passing out from his injuries. Alexei's skin felt cold and clammy, and his heartbeat raced in his chest. He did not think there was much in the way of medical supplies in his home, but with any luck, the embers in the stove would still be warm enough to chase away the chill.

Alexei glanced down at his hand and blanched at the ruination Rostov's hammer had caused. His hand had swollen and turned bright purple; a crimson gash split the back of the hand where a thin, jagged white bone splinter pierced the skin. All his fingers appeared crooked and broken, while his thumb dangled perilously as if held to hand by skin alone. The hand was a ruin; he would never use it again, of that he was sure. He wrapped it in the folds of his blood-soaked shirt and began to run for home.

The sound of his heart pounding and his heavy breathing filled his ears, drowning out the night sounds of the forest. He cared little about the long hanging branches that brushed and scratched his face as he raced.

Alexei's thoughts turned to all he had lost on this fateful night. Was Oksana ok? Did she still live? He had no idea. However, he knew that Ivan was gone, bringing tears streaming down his face. Rostov and his men had ripped his most faithful friend and companion from the world. Ivan deserved better than to be shot down on the road and left to die in the brush. Once he bandaged his wounds, Alexei would look for his friend and give him a proper burial. He swore a silent promise to Ivan that he would do that. Alexei owed the dog that much for saving his life tonight.

He loathed that Balkov had taken his father's gun and used it against him. Even the precious explosives his father had so painstakingly hidden were lost now. Though perhaps not. Alexei had hidden them under the *Kanti Gans*; with some luck, they should still be there undetected. If they had not searched the forest for him, Rostov, Balkov, and the others likely thought him dead. Once he cared for his wounds, Alexei could sneak back to the *Kanti Gans* and get revenge on them all.

Alexei crouched beside a thick oak tree and peered into the gloom; the path that led to his house appeared quiet. He sat very still, hidden among the trees and brush, straining his ears to detect any movement or sound that would give away someone lying in wait for him along the path. Confident that he was alone, Alexei stepped onto the path and started to walk quickly toward his house. He breathed a sigh of relief; he would be safely inside his home in a few minutes. It would be too late once Alexei tended to his wounds to return to the *Kanti Gans*; Balkov and the others would have staggered home by then. However, he could lay low at Galina's for a few days to recover and check on Oksana.

The sound of something rustling in the woods to his left brought Alexei's mind back to the moment. He crouched low and stared into the darkness; the noise reminded him of a person shuffling their feet through dried leaves. It was too deliberate for anything trying to move stealthily through the forest, perhaps it was a raccoon foraging along the forest floor. The moonlight played tricks on his eyes, and the gnarled trunks of trees took on the visage of faces peering back at him, their branches reaching limbs.

His ears picked up the sound of movement now, this time closer, following along the path. Someone or something was moving out in the darkness. Alexei looked down at the tiny dark droplets of blood dripping from his wounded arm and silently cursed. The scent of his blood would carry on the wind, attracting nearby predators.

The Wolf.

The thought sent a chill of fear down Alexei's spine. He leaped up and began to run for the house; behind him, something broke from the forest and followed on the path. Alexei could hear its feet kicking up dirt and rocks as it raced toward him. Glancing over his shoulder, he spotted the black shape following quickly down the path. As the creature crossed through a ray of moonlight, Alexei saw the black lupine head, two dark eyes shining atop a muzzle that revealed razor-like teeth in the celestial light. The creature moved quickly but with a gait, unlike any animal he had ever seen.

As Alexei followed the path into the overgrown clearing where his parents' home stood, he felt his head swoon and his strength quickly ebb. He had pushed his wounded body to its limit, and now unconsciousness threatened to take him. He screamed in defiance of his body's betrayal and forced his legs to continue the last few feet to the house. Alexei dared not look back again at the beast; he could hear its heavy breathing and knew it was close.

Summoning the last of his energy, Alexei leaped over the porch steps and reached for the door but, something hard stuck his body from behind and pulled him from the air as he felt a searing pain in his right leg. Alexei crashed onto the porch so violently that he heard several weathered floorboards crack. His ravaged right side took the brunt of the impact, and the pain exploding from his wounded shoulder nearly caused him to pass out.

The wolf landed hard on the ground, just short of the porch, its jaws releasing their hold upon Alexei's leg as it crashed through the boards of the steps. At that moment, as they both lay sprawled, Alexei's gaze met that of the wolf's, and they locked eyes. The creature's eyes were dark and wild. However, Alexei saw no malice in the opaque orbs and thought he detected a hint of sadness.

Alexei gaped as the wolf rose, first onto all fours and then fully upright. He saw that the creature's front legs ended in something closer to a hand than a paw, with long, wicked claws. It stood watching Alexei but advanced no further.

"What the fuck are you?" Alexei breathed the words more than he spoke them.

The wolf's chest heaved with every breath as it appraised Alexei, and then it sniffed the air and turned its head sharply toward the surrounding brush. It dropped into a crouch and then all fours as something charged out of the undergrowth, snarling and snapping at the wolf. In the moonlight, Alexei saw the gray fur of the dog, matted dark with blood, as it advanced on the wolf. A gaping wound, glistening with fresh blood, marred Ivan's side where the bullet had pierced his flesh, and Alexei knew the dog was severely wounded, if not mortally.

A feral growl escaped Ivan's throat; the dog would have stood little chance against the beast even unwounded. Nonetheless, Ivan advanced on the wolf, hackles raised and teeth bared. The wolf turned its immense head to gaze once more at Alexei and then, to his surprise, began to retreat toward the safety of the forest.

Ivan's steps faltered; the journey to the house likely sapped much of the dog's remaining strength, and Alexei feared that the wolf would sense this weakness and attack. Instead, the wolf broke into a run, leaping into the cover of the forest and disappearing.

"I don't believe it," Alexei shook his head; he would have laughed had his body not hurt so badly.

Ivan walked gingerly up the ruined steps, whimpering as he nuzzled his head against Alexei's chest.

"I'm so happy to see you," Alexei felt fresh tears on his cheeks as he leaned his forehead against the dog's bloody head. "The two of us are a real mess, aren't we?"

Alexei slid over to the door, reached up, unlatched it, and swung it open. He dragged himself inside, with Ivan slowly following alongside him. Kicking the door closed with his good leg, Alexei pulled himself up by the door handle to slip the lock into place before sliding back to the ground. He could not put any weight on his injured leg. The wolf's bite felt icy cold, like an icicle thrust into his skin, and the sensation began spreading up and down the leg. Ivan collapsed into the pile of rags in the corner, his breathe ragged and labored.

"That looks like an excellent idea," Alexei nodded as he dragged himself to where the dog lay. He leaned against the wall beside Ivan, resting his head on the worn wood of the wall. "I'm just going to rest here for a bit, then I'll get us all fixed up." He patted Ivan lightly on the shoulder.

My leg is so cold. The thought crossed Alexei's mind as unconsciousness finally took him.

***

The cold brought Alexei back to consciousness. He awoke, shivering, the pain of his wounds numbed by the intense cold wracking his body. Alexei looked at Ivan; the dog lay deathly still by his side; absent was the gentle rise and fall of the dog's breathing. Trembling from the cold, Alexei rubbed his hand along Ivan's head and whispered a silent prayer for the dog's soul, thankful that the dog had passed peacefully in the night.

Alexei inspected his wounds and noticed the bleeding had stopped. *Maybe I have just run out of blood.*

Using the wall to brace himself, Alexei slowly rose to his feet and found he could put weight on his injured leg. He wrapped his arms around himself, unsure how it could have gotten so terribly cold. Alexei felt as if freezing ice water ran through his veins. The stove emitted a faint orange glow, and Alexei shuffled toward it and tossed a log onto the embers.

Shivering, Alexei placed his hands before the glowing embers but felt no warmth against his fingers despite the flames beginning to lick at the log. His breathing felt labored, though he wondered why he could not see his breath in the cold. Alexei tossed a second log into the stove as the fire roared to life.

"We'll get this place nice and toasty," Alexei told no one in particular through chattering teeth.

Alexei slowly entered his bedroom and collapsed onto the bed, his body trembling as he pulled all the blankets around him.

"I'm so cold."

***

Bogdan squinted against the morning light as he approached the house; the stillness surrounding the place troubled him. He detected faint trails of smoke spiraling into the sky from the home's stove pipe, lending hope that Alexei had spent the night inside. The stairs leading up to the house were splintered and broken, so the woodsman leaped onto the porch.

Kneeling, Bogdan inspected the dark stains on the wooden planks, scratching at them with his fingernail—bloodstains. A fair amount of blood had soaked into the wood, indicating someone with a severe wound had lain or sat by the door. He also spotted a partial bloody paw print near the door and upon closer examination, the woodsman determined it was canine in nature, likely Ivan's. Standing, Bogdan tried the door hand and found it locked.

Thump. Thump. Thump. Bogdan struck the door three resounding blows with his open palm. He leaned his ear against the door, hoping to hear movement inside in response.

"Alexei," Bogdan's voice was loud and deep. He followed it with three more bangs on the door. "Alexei, open the door. It's Bogdan. Oksana's awake. She's okay. She's concerned about you; we all are."

He listened again by the door but detected no sign of life. A deep frown creased his weathered face as he placed both hands on the doorframe and stared at the blood stains.

"Damn you, Alexei. Damn your reckless soul," Bogdan shook his head.

Bogdan took a deep breath and, in one powerful movement, kicked the door with such force that the iron latch snapped and the door swung open. He stepped inside, noting the sparseness of Alexei's home—a table and two chairs, a stove for warmth and cooking, but no pictures or decor. The open door cast a rectangular box of sunlight into the room, and in the farther corner, touched upon something gray and furry.

He walked over and knelt by the still form of Ivan; if not for the wound in his side, Bogdan would have thought the dog was sleeping. Bogdan stroked Ivan's fur, saddened by the death of the friendly creature. Touching the dog tenderly, he inspected the bullet wound, now crusted over with dried blood. The shot had struck Ivan low and just behind his front legs, piercing his liver—a fatal shot. It was a testament to the dog's force of will that he survived long enough to die here.

"Rest easy, boy," Bogdan patted the dog as he stood, the open bedroom door drawing his attention.

He walked slowly across the room to stand in the bedroom's doorway; a form lay huddled on the bed, covered in blankets.

"Alexei?" Bogdan hoped the boy would stir but detected no sound or movement.

The floorboards creaked as Bogdan walked into the room, and he craned his neck for a better look at the form on the bed. Alexei lay curled in a ball, with three well-worn and faded blankets pulled around his body. As Bogdan came alongside the bed, he could see Alexei's face poking from beneath the blankets. The boy's eyes stared sightless and unblinking.

Bogdan groaned and sank to the floor, his back coming to lean against the wall beside the bed. He ran his hands through his hair and sighed deeply.

"I am sorry, Alexei," Bogdan rested his head back against the wall, then willed himself to look at the boy's lifeless face. "I thought I could reach you in time before the wounds they inflicted on you could claim you. But I was too late. I will carry that regret with me always."

***

Bogdan found a shovel among scattered tools on the porch and buried Ivan on the forest's edge in a sunny spot. He dug a second grave alongside the faithful dog and solemnly returned to the house. Removing the blankets from Alexei's body, Bogdan was shocked at the severity of the boy's wounds.

"What the hell did you get yourself into?" Bogdan shook his head as his eyes moved from the massive bite wound on Alexei's leg to the gunshot through his shoulder and the devastated hand.

He wrapped Alexei's body in the bedsheet and carried him out into the sunlight. The boy's death touched a well of memories deep inside Bogdan, remembrances of loss and pain. Bogdan fought back the tears, except for a solitary one that escaped his eye and trailed down his cheek.

"I picked a good spot for you and Ivan," Bogdan told the boy softly as he walked. "You will have lots of sun during the day and a view of the stars at night. I will hide your resting place so your enemies will not disturb you."

Bogdan laid the body in the grave and covered it with earth. He would pull Magnolia vines over the graves to hide their location before he departed. When he finished smoothing the earth, Bogdan sat beside where he had laid Alexei to rest, quietly listening to the birds flittering amongst the trees.

"You would have grown into a fine man someday, and I would have been proud to show you my homeland," Bogdan spoke without looking at the graves. "I want you to know that Oksana is okay. She is a little sore and bruised, but she will be fine. I promise you I will watch over her until she leaves with Galina. Leo, as well. Though this will break their hearts."

***

Leo's father had come home early that afternoon and announced that Igor Balkov and some hunters discovered Alexei destroying wolf traps in the forest. They tried to apprehend the boy, but he fired on the hunters with a pistol he had acquired from somewhere. They had no choice but to return fire; Alexei was shot and killed. He died gurgling and choking on his blood. Leo's mother had been angry that Pavel had discussed the matter so cavalierly in front of Leo.

Pavel shrugged with marked indifference as he poured himself tea, "The boy was a common malcontent, and he died a troublemaker's death. Leo should never have associated with a boy like that."

"I think you're happy the boy is dead, and I think it's despicable that you revel in the sorrow it causes Leo," it was one of the few times Leo had ever seen his mother scold his father.

Pavel's initial shock was evident; however, he quickly recovered and slammed his hands down on the table, a look of sheer fury overtaking his countenance, "Woman, you forget yourself!"

Leo's mother fell silent, and Leo asked to go to his room. He showed no emotion as his mother wheeled his chair into his room and helped him into his bed. Once she had left the small room and closed the door behind her, Leo sank his face into his pillow and sobbed as memories of Alexei filled his thoughts and fueled his tears. Leo cried until his chest ached and his eyes burned; he cried until he felt like there was no more water left in his body to stream down his cheeks.

Leo skipped dinner that night, remaining curled in bed watching the sunset. He said unanswered prayers to God for word of Alexei's death to be a mistake, and then he whispered appeals to Baba Yaga for the witch to bring his friend back from the Netherworld. His mother checked on him before she turned in for the night; she brought the green leather-bound book Galina gave him for his birthday.

"Are you feeling any better, Leo?" his mother sat on the corner of his bed, concern lacing her eyes as she ran her hand across his forehead, brushing aside stray strands of hair. "You have barely eaten anything all day."

"I'm just feeling a little tired," Leo attempted to smile for her but could only muster a weak imitation. "I'll be better tomorrow."

Pulling the wool blanket higher on his neck, she sighed, "Leo, Alexei was your best friend. It's okay to be sad."

"I know, Mother, I'm just tired."

"I brought your book," she placed the tome on Leo's bed. "You can keep the lamp and read for as long as you like."

Leo glanced over at the oil lamp flickering on his bedside table, "Father does not like for me to keep the lamp on too long. He says it burns too much oil."

"Well, we can make an exception tonight," she smiled, though her eyes brimmed with pity. "You can burn it all night if you want. I will refill it in the morning."

"No, that's okay. You can turn it off," Leo said, shaking his head and turning over in the bed to face the window that shined bright moonlight down onto his bed.

"Okay, Leo," his mother leaned over and kissed him on the head. She extinguished the oil lamp and walked to his door; the floorboards creaked as she turned back to look at Leo. "Leo?"

"Yes, Mother?" He turned slightly to peer at her over his shoulder.

"When my mother died, I would dream that she would come to me at night. It made me feel better like she was not really gone, you know?"

Leo said nothing as he stared at the pale outline of his mother in the moonlight.

"Maybe Alexei will come to you in your dreams too," her voice was soft and filled with heartbreak.

Leo turned back toward the window and pulled the blanket around him. She stood there staring at his silent, still form for several heartbeats. Then he heard the floorboards creak again as she turned toward the door and left the room, the door closing softly behind her.

The tears came more quietly now as Leo stared at the moonlit sky, his eyes fixed on the darkened heavens until sleep slowly overtook him.

***

Leo's eyes fluttered open. He felt suddenly alert but was unsure what had disrupted his slumber. His eyes scanned his small room. A thin veil of clouds had dimmed the moonlight, but he could still make out the familiar shapes—the oil lamp on the table, the rectangular wardrobe against the wall, and his empty wheelchair.

Tick.

The sound was sharp and loud in the quiet of the room, causing Leo to jump. His eyes opened wide, searching and failing to detect the source of the noise.

Tick.

Something struck his window. On some nights, bats congregated beneath the overhang of the house's roof, but the only sound that caused was a slight fluttering noise and an occasion thump if one strayed too far and bounced off his window. This noise was different.

TICK.

Leo's window spider-webbed into a series of spindly cracks radiating from a small chip that appeared in the lower right of the pane. Grabbing the window ledge, Leo pulled himself up into a sitting position and peered closely at the cracks, bewildered by their sudden appearance. He ran the tip of his finger over the crack, wincing as a sliver sliced his finger. A tiny rivulet of blood dotted his finger and slightly smeared along the crack.

Leo pulled his hand from the window and pressed his thumb against the cut to stop the bleeding. A rustling in the bushes indicated something moved out in the darkness, and he peered into the night, squinting as his eyes adjusted to the darkness.

"Leo," a whispered voice called from the woods.

Leo's eyes opened wide in shock, and his lower lip began to tremble with fear as Alexei stood to reveal himself. Blood smeared his mouth and ran down his pale, shirtless torso in dark streaks.

"Leo, I think I'm dead," Alexei's ethereal body stepped from the forest into the moonlight, and Leo could see that he was completely naked.

Leo shrank down on his bed, pressing his body against the wall and pulling the blanket around him. He attempted to conceal his body in the shadows, away from the moonlight streaming in the window and hidden from sight.

"Leo. Leo, are you there?" Alexei's voice called to him.

A dark shadow appeared in the window, close to the glass, and peered inside. Leo covered his mouth to prevent an involuntary cry of fear from escaping his lips.

"Leo?"

Leo's body trembled with fear, and he chided himself.

This was Alexei. This was his friend. Was it not? Why should he fear Alexei? Or even Alexei's ghost?

Nevertheless, Leo held his breath, fearing that even the sound of his beating heart would give him away. The shadow receded from the window, and Leo finally exhaled, the tension draining from his body as he emptied his lungs. Then the shadow suddenly returned, pressing its hands and face against the windowpane, craning its neck to see inside the room. The windowpane cracked further under the pressure, and Leo feared it would shatter and rain glass down upon him. He imagined the rush of cold air entering the room, followed by the naked and bloody form of Alexei crawling through the window, the jagged shards of glass slicing his pale skin.

Leo felt the sudden urge to empty his bladder and pressed his hand against his groin, praying that the stream of urine would not come. The urge slowly subsided as the shadow moved away from the window again, followed by feet running from the house and bushes rustling as the ghostly form disappeared into the forest.

The night grew quiet as Leo huddled against the wall, too frightened to move as his ears strained to detect any sound outside. Sleep gradually overtook him, causing him to drift in and out of a dazed slumber. In his wakeful moments, Leo wondered if it had all been a terrible nightmare brought on by the day's events. When he fitfully slept, he dreamed of the bloody form of Alexei reaching to grab him from beneath the bed or sitting in Leo's wheelchair, watching him sleep.

As dawn's light streamed into the room, the thought of Alexei's visit seemed less and less plausible to Leo.
It was all a terrible dream.

Alexei was his friend, his best friend; he would never hurt Leo-not in life or death. Pulling himself into a sitting position on the bed, Leo glanced out the window and felt his blood run cold at the sight of the spider web crack in the pane. A tiny smear of dried blood along the crack drew his attention, and Leo grabbed the window ledge and pulled himself toward it to inspect the pane more closely. He scratched at the blood, and tiny pieces flaked off and stuck beneath his nail. Remembering cutting himself the night before, Leo looked at his index finger, a slight dark line marking where the broken glass had sliced it. He smiled and shook his head; his imagination was getting the best of him.

The smile slowly slipped from Leo's face as he looked again at the bloody smear on the window. He scratched at it more intently, chipping off the specks of blood, then licking his thumb; he rubbed at the smear until all traces of the blood were gone. However, a thin pink smear remained on the window despite his rubbing and scratching.

Leo leaned closer, peering at the smear. His eyes opened wide in realization as he sat back on his bed, frowning as his mind flooded with deeply troubling thoughts.

There was a smear of blood on the outside of the window.

Chapter 14

Leo sat on the porch in his wheelchair, and he stared at the title page of the green leather-bound book Galina had given him. The blanket his mother usually tucked over his lap lay bunched down by his feet, the late fall air chilling his legs. He did not want to sit all warm and cozy; nothing about the past few days made him want to feel that way. Leo wanted to feel the coldness of the world today.

He traced his finger over the letters on the page, spelling out *Children's and Household Tales*. A circle of flowers, ornately detailed in black ink, circled the words, mesmerizing Leo with the incredible detail evident in every stem and petal.

"I see you are enjoying your birthday gift," Bogdan's deep voice startled Leo enough to make him jump in his chair, the book tumbling from his fingers.

Leo was shocked to see Bogdan standing before him, holding a small burlap sack. He had been so engrossed in his thoughts he had not even seen the man approach.

"Leo. Leo, I'm sorry for startling you so," Bogdan looked apologetic, even as he chuckled and retrieved Leo's book, handing it to him as he sat on the porch beside the wheelchair. "I called to you several times, but you must not have heard me."

"It's ok, Bogdan, I was just lost in my thoughts," Leo tried to cover his embarrassment with a weak smile.

Bogdan looked grim as he nodded, understanding, "You have heard about Alexei. I had come here to tell you myself."

Leo nodded, biting his lip to control his emotions. He felt his eyes brim with wetness and did not trust his ability to speak without bringing on the tears.

"He was a good friend," Bogdan looked out into the forest.

"He was," Leo's voice was barely above a whisper as he nodded in agreement. "My father said Igor Balkov and his friends shot him."

"They shot Alexei, and Ivan too," Bogdan looked down at his hands. "I buried them side by side."

"You buried them?" Leo's head snapped up. "You saw him dead? His body is not somewhere out in the woods?"

"He died in his bed, Ivan beside him. I found them in his home yesterday morning."

"So then he is truly dead and gone," Leo hung his head, saddened by the fact of Alexei's death and even more perplexed by his nighttime visitor.

"I'm afraid so, Leo. I am truly sorry for your loss," Bogdan held genuine sadness in his eyes as he placed his hand on Leo's arm.

"Thank you, Bogdan," Leo nodded but did not look at the man.

"I brought you something," Bogdan placed the burlap sack in his lap and reached inside. "I had intended it to be a birthday gift, but it took me longer to carve than I expected."

Bogdan slid what looked like a carved wooden box from the sack, and then Leo's eyes lit with excitement when he realized what it was as the woodsman handed it to him. Leo turned the box in his hands, studying the incredible detail with which Bogdan had carved a house out of a solid wood block. The shutters, shingles, and doors were all carved with painstaking minute detail. However, what truly awed Leo were the two intricately carved chicken legs that protruded from the bottom of the house. It was as perfect a representation of Baba Yaga's hut as Leo had ever seen, as if the wooden house had leaped from the pages of one of his books.

"Here, let me show you something," Bogdan took the house from Leo and set it on the wood boards of the porch. The house balanced perfectly on the chicken legs, standing as steady as a tree. "It took me quite a while to get the proportions of the feet just right to stand upright."

"Bogdan, it's incredible," Leo grinned as he shook his head in disbelief.

"I'm happy you like it," Bogdan's smile was warm and genuine, but then his expression changed to excitement. "And look at this."

He picked up the house and returned it to Leo, pointing one thick finger at one of the two front windows. Leo peered at the window, spotting the head and shoulders of a figure peering out the window. He could see long, stringy hair, narrow eyes, and a long, pointed nose.

"Is that?" Leo looked from the house to Bogdan and then back to the figure in the window.

Bogdan laughed as he nodded, "It's the witch herself, Baba Yaga!"

Leo turned the house over in his hands, lovingly examining every detail, the smile never fading from his face, "It is the most wonderful thing I have ever seen; thank you, Bogdan!"

Bogdan watched Leo examine the present, pointing out little details he had added.

Leo's expression turned bittersweet, "Alexei would have thought this was amazing, too."

"He helped. I did the carving, but Alexei watched me like a shop steward, suggesting things to add and how the feet should look. Adding Baba Yaga inside was his idea."

Leo smiled again, his eyes brimming with emotion, "So it is a gift from him as well."

"That it is, Leo," Bogdan smiled, but his tone showed an unmistakable hint of sadness. He tapped his finger against the image of Baba Yaga in the widow. "I never understood you boys' fascination with that old crone."

Leo laughed, a soft, mirthless sound, "It was initially Alexei's idea. When we were younger, Alexei thought if we could find Baba Yaga's house, we could force the witch to fix my legs so I could run through the forest with him. I guess it sounds pretty stupid now, huh?"

"No, Leo," Bogdan shook his head. "It is a beautiful idea."

***

Wihu huw-huhuwo

The sound of an Ural owl immediately drew Galina's attention as she stepped out onto the porch with her afternoon cup of tea in hand. Excitedly, her eyes scanned the branches of the surrounding trees, searching for the white and brown-streaked feathers of the owl amidst the leafless oaks. Ever since she was a child, owls had fascinated and enchanted her.

A subtle movement on one of the branches caught her eye, and she watched as the owl swooped down from the tree, arced back toward the woods, and, with three effortless flaps of its wings, disappeared into the forest's folds. Galina stared after its retreating form, transfixed by the beauty and majesty of the creature.

"I knew a soldier who carried an owl's claws in his pocket. He believed the spirit of the bird would carry his soul to heaven if he should fall on the battlefield," Bogdan's deep voice startled Galina so severely she nearly dropped her tea.

She turned and was surprised to see Bogdan sitting in the old ladder-back rocking chair where she usually sat and drank her tea.

"Bogdan," Galina quickly recovered from her surprise. "I'm sorry I did not see you there. Have you been there long?"

"I just returned from visiting Leo a little while ago," Bogdan smiled faintly and nodded in greeting. "I did not mean to startle you; I just needed a few minutes alone with my thoughts. How is Oksana doing today?"

Galina sighed, "She is recovering quickly; I believe sadness over Alexei's death keeps her in bed now more than her injuries."

"Yes, the boy's death has plagued my thoughts," his face became dark and troubled. "I blame myself for not doing more."

"I was fond of Alexei too, but the boy could be wild and reckless in his anger," Galina began, then noticed Bogdan's attention drifting to something behind her. The lines of his jaw tightened with tension as his expression grew grim. "Bogdan?"

Galina turned to see a black carriage navigating the bend in the road and moving quickly toward the cottage. A smile spread across her face as she set the teacup on the porch and ran toward the stairs.

"Galina, wait," Bogdan leaped up and grabbed her arm.

"It's Mali," Galina's face radiated pure joy as she pulled her arm away from him and ran to meet the carriage.

As Galina watched the carriage approach, she touched her hair, fretting that she had not had time to make herself more presentable. Hopefully, Mali would be amenable to slipping into a warm bath together, and Galina could freshen up.

Maybe I should ask Bogdan to start heating some water.

Galina's smile faded as she noticed the blonde rider and two imperial soldiers on horseback trailing behind the carriage. She turned back to look at Bogdan for reassurance, but the man was grimly staring at the approaching carriage and rider.

"Has Mali ever come with an escort before?" Bogdan asked, not taking his eyes off the approaching riders.

A hollow tremor of fear pinched at her insides as she shook her head.

Maybe there is trouble on the road with brigands or revolutionaries, and Mali is taking extra precautions.

As the carriage reined to a halt, the blonde man and the soldiers rode past to stop in front of the cottage, facing Bogdan and Galina. She saw the wooden stocks of rifles poking from long leather holsters attached to the men's saddles, designed to give riders quick access to the weapon while riding.

The soldiers stared coldly at Bogdan while the blonde man seemed to appraise her with a slightly mocking smile. He wore a red coat cut in a military style and adorned with a gold-colored braid that circled his shoulder. Galina could see a highly polished sword scabbard at the man's side, and he rested a gloved hand on the dark handle of a pistol on his other hip.

She turned toward the carriage and spotted an unfamiliar face at the reins as the coachman spit a wad of mucus onto the earth. The coachman was many years younger than Jacob, with a dark shadow of stubble on his cheeks and neck. Like the soldiers, the man's eyes were cold and impassive.

"Where is Jacob?" Galina winced at how flustered her voice sounded.

"He works in the stables," the man raised the reins he gripped in his hand. "I'm the Countess' coachman now."

At the mention of Mali's title, Galina felt herself relax. If Mali was here, that meant everything would be okay. Behind Galina, Bogdan began to walk down the steps toward her, however, the blonde man reined his horse forward and drew his pistol.

"Let's just stay where we are now," the man said in a thick brogue as he pointed the pistol at Bogdan and cocked the hammer back. The two soldiers slid their rifles from the saddle holsters, holding them ready.

"Please, no," Galina held a hand toward the armed men. "Bogdan works in the stables; he's no threat to you."

"McMurrough?" Bogdan's eyes narrowed as he stared at the blonde man but proceeded no further down the steps.

"You've heard of me then?" McMurrough looked pleased with his notoriety.

"It wasn't hard to figure out. How many Englishmen do you think come to Obrechen?" Bogdan folded his arms across his chest.

McMurrough rolled his eyes in exasperation and thrust the barrel of his pistol toward Bogdan, "You fucking peasants are genuinely the most ignorant people on earth; you think the whole goddamn world is either Russian, French, or English. I'm a fucking Irishman."

"Galina," Mali's voice drew all attention back to the carriage.

Mali stood by the carriage's open door in a red long-sleeved velvet topped dress that opened in the front to reveal a white satin skirt, a bejeweled *kokoshnik* tiara holding her dark hair in place. The jewels in the tiara caught the sun's rays and sparkled, making Mali look even more radiant. Galina's heart leaped at the sight of her, and she had to restrain herself from running into Mali's arms. Then Galina froze as a man in highly polished boots stepped from the carriage behind her. The man wore black trousers and a bright blue, military-styled coat; gleaming gold buttons ran down the middle of the coat, and several rows of ornate medals adorned the left side. His piercing gray eyes starkly contrasted his midnight black hair and mustache, giving them an otherworldly intensity.

"Count Guriev," Galina bowed deeply. "Welcome to my home."

Galina prayed silently that the Count had traveled all this way at Mali's bequest to ask her artist friend to stay with them personally. Her relationship with Gennady Guriev had always been icy, in no small measure, due to Galina's jealousy over his courtship and eventual marriage to Mali. However, Guriev, too, had disliked his betrothed's ever-present unwed friend and deemed her a bad influence. Mali had begged Galina to marry one of the lesser nobles of Kalinin; she knew several older widowed noblemen who would jump at the chance to marry the beautiful young merchant's daughter. She would be wealthy, live in a beautiful home with servants and the finest clothes, and best of all, they could always spend time together and not raise suspicion. However, as much as Galina yearned to spend her days with Mali, the thought of spending her nights under the fat, sweating body of a Kalinin noble was too repulsive a thought. Her illusions about the Count's visit quickly dissipated as he spoke, replaced with a gut-wrenching fear.

"I think you mean my home," Count Guriev glanced at the small cottage, a derisive scowl on his face. "James, who did you say this shack belonged to before me?"

"Kravchinsky, a Polish nobleman," McMurrough responded without taking his eyes from Bogdan, who glared back at him.

"Ah yes, well, the Poles do have a fondness for the rustic," Guriev nodded, then looked at Galina, his eyes cold. "It has recently come to my attention that my lovely wife purchased this quaint little property and that you now reside here, Galina Sekova."

"Oh, yes," Galina gave a smile; however, the blank expression on Mali's face disquieted her deeply. "The Countess is a great patron of the arts; I have been able to..."

Count Guriev cut her off with a dismissive wave, "You have thirty days to vacate the premises."

"What?" the word slipped from Galina's mouth. She looked at Mali, but the Countess averted her eyes.

"My dear," Guriev turned to Mali, a slight smile creasing his face, "do you agree?"

When Mali hesitated to respond, the Count raised an eyebrow and cocked his head as he stared at her.

"Yes, it is for the best," Mali spit the words out quickly, never looking at Galina.

"Good, then it is agreed," Guriev turned back to Galina, a malicious grin on his face. "You have thirty days to depart the premises. We will, of course, provide you with the means to return to your father."

Guriev gestured to McMurrough, who slipped a leather pouch from his jacket and tossed it to the ground at Galina's feet. The pouch landed heavily on the earth, clinking loudly as the coins jostled and bounced.

"I don't understand," Galina shook her head as her eyes brimmed with tears. She looked past Guriev to Mali, who stood stoically and refused to meet her gaze, beseeching her friend and lover in a pleading tone. "Mali?"

Guriev stepped forward, towering menacingly over Galina and blocking her view of the Countess. Bogdan lurched forward, off the steps, determined to reach her side. However, McMurrough raised his pistol toward the man's chest and shook his head, a warning that Bogdan begrudgingly heeded.

"Listen to me, you little whore," Guriev hissed the words through clenched teeth, loud enough for only the two of them to hear. "I know how you tried to seduce Mali, how you used your friendship to mask your deviant desires for her. She confessed to me how you blackmailed her when she refused you. Mali would have kept your secret and supported your art out of the goodness of her heart. You did not need to extort it from her to keep you from spreading heinous lies about her. You sicken me. I would see you gutted like a fat sow, but Mali begged me to spare you. If you ever come near Mali or try to contact her, I'll kill you. If I ever see you again, I'll kill you. If I hear that your whore mouth is shaming my family name, I'll kill you."

The tears flowed down Galina's cheeks, and her body trembled. She wanted only to collapse to the ground and have the earth swallow her up. Galina felt like her heart, her whole world, was shattering like a Faberge egg dashed upon the cobblestone. His words struck her like physical blows, and Guriev's tongue ran over his teeth as he relished the moment.

"I will give you to my men until you are broken, and then I will let McMurrough kill you oh so very slowly. He has a unique talent for it," Guriev's eyes flickered toward McMurrough, then back to Galina as he smiled cruelly and tapped the bag of coins with his boot. "So take the money and disappear forever, or consider yourself warned of the consequences."

As Guriev turned away from her, Galina's eyes met Mali's gaze, and she felt no solace in her cold stare. The Count extended his arm as he walked to the carriage, and Mali took his arm and followed alongside him. They disappeared inside the carriage without another glance in her direction.

"If you need a warm bed, I've got one for you," the coachman grinned at Galina with a mouthful of yellowing teeth that broke into a cackling laugh as he flicked the reigns to get the horses moving.

Hoof beats drowned out his laughter as the soldiers thundered past, following the carriage and kicking up a small shower of dirt and rocks.

"I'll be back in thirty days with the gendarme to ensure you've complied," McMurrough sneered down at her as his horse trotted by.

Galina collapsed to the ground as the carriage and riders disappeared from view. Tears streamed down her face as heaving sobs wracked her slim body. Bogdan ran to Galina's side and wrapped his arms around her as she beat and clawed at the earth in despair.

"It'll be okay, Galina," Bogdan hugged her as she sobbed into his shoulder. "I promise you, everything will be okay."

***

"Are you happy now, my love?" Guriev patted his wife's hand as the carriage wound down the road to Kalinin.

"Yes, Gennady. Thank you for showing such kindness to Galina," Mali smiled back at him. "I cannot forgive her actions, but for the friend she was to me for many years before, it does my heart good to know she has the means to return to her father's house. I hope she can right her ways and make something of her life."

"As do I, my love," Guriev nodded as he smoothed down the hairs of his mustache with two fingers. Mali frowned; she recognized the gesture as a habit her husband exhibited when concerned over a matter.

"Is there something wrong, Gennady?" Mali placed her hand on his arm, concern etched on her face.

Guriev sighed, "It just galls me to know she would take advantage of your kind-heartedness and cause you so much pain. Where is our justice? Where is her punishment?"

"You are such a gallant man," Mali leaned over and kissed his cheek. "Her sad and lonely life will be punishment enough. I remember the young and innocent girl she was; it would pain my heart to know any harm had come to her on my account. It is enough to know I shall never have to see her again. Thank you for staying your vengeful hand, my love."

"Of course, my love,"

They lapsed into a pleasant silence as the carriage continued on its way. Count Guriev stared out the window at the blonde horseman riding alongside the carriage. McMurrough had proved very useful since coming into the Count's service several years ago.

Time and again, the man showed a keen ability to deal with the Count's rivals and personal indiscretions without hesitation or questions. The Irishman had become an invaluable member of the Count's household ever since he ensured that Pavel Zhukovsky, a younger and wealthier rival for Mali's hand, died suddenly and tragically without any suspicion falling upon Guriev. That was not to mention the numerous servant girls and young ladies of Kalinin who found themselves no longer a problem for Guriev, thanks to McMurrough.

Guriev surmised that McMurrough's moral turpitude was responsible for leaving the service of his native lands; the English, unlike Guriev, could be squeamish regarding bloodshed. However, in the Count of Kalinin's household, McMurrough discovered that his lack of moral boundaries were welcome and profitable.

When the English officer glanced toward the carriage, Guriev caught his eye and subtly nodded to the man. McMurrough gave an almost undetectable nod of acknowledgment, slowing his horse to let the carriage move past him.

As the carriage rolled out of sight, McMurrough turned back and headed for the road to Obrechen.

***

The loud snort of a horse sounded as Olga Putina opened the door of her house and peered outside. Her eyes lit with curiosity as she spied McMurrough sitting upon his horse at the end of her path.

"You come to trade that horse for something wilder between your legs, Englishman?" Olga gave McMurrough what she thought was her most alluring smile.

McMurrough did nothing to hide his distaste for her offer as he reached into his jacket and withdrew a small leather purse. The bag clinked as he deposited it atop her fencepost.

"There's a bag of coins five... six times that size in Galina Sekova's cottage," McMurrough pointed to the bag.

"Is that so?" Olga walked over and picked up the purse.

"Doesn't seem right that she should profit so from her debauchery," McMurrough stared down at her, his face emotionless. "Especially when that money could do so much good in honest Christian hands."

"No, it does not," Olga nodded as she edged closer to his horse and placed a hand on his leg. "The offer for that ride still stands."

"Olga," McMurrough reached down and placed two fingers under her chin, tilting her head upward. "Just think how beautiful you would look with a new dress."

McMurrough released her chin and kicked his horse into a steady trot without another word or look in her direction. Olga stood there watching him leave, her thumb running over the leather purse and rounded edges of the coins inside as she imagined what a purse five times that size could buy.

***

Volkov ran his hand along the horse's thick, muscular neck and into its long brown mane as it noisily munched on the apple in his other hand. He could feel the tension in the stallion's neck and knew it did not like the confines of the train's stable car.

"Easy, boy. It will be a quick trip, then you'll be under the sky again," Volkov patted the horse's neck as he reached into his pocket and produced another apple he offered to the jet-black stallion alongside it.

The horse's rough lips brushed his palm as the horse took the apple from him as gently as a baby. The two steeds, brothers, were Mongolian horses descended from the herds of Chinggis Khan, a bloodline that carried warriors across the Asian continent and into Europe. They were shorter and stockier than the typical horse with thick, powerful legs and long flowing manes and tails. Mongolians prized the horses for their hardiness and stamina.

After surviving their ordeal, Volkov purchased the pair for Batu and himself from a local merchant in Nerchinsk. The stallions were named Nar and Sar, the Mongolian words for sun and moon. Aside from Batu, there was nothing that Volkov cared about more than the brown stallion Nar. He had ridden the horse across the Russian empire; it had graced the Tsar's stables in Saint Petersburg and Moscow, and Volkov took pride in riding Nar through the streets in the rain and snow when the nobles huddled in their carriages. With significant cajoling, Batu convinced Volkov to sit in the passenger car with Kirill and the others during the trip to Obrechen rather than in the stable car with Nar. Even then, Volkov would not trust the loading and unloading of the horses to anyone but Batu and himself. He had insisted the two horses be housed separately from the other horses by a rope line that divided the car; Volkov did not want one of these skittish Russian horses to injure Nar or Sar by panicking during the trip and kicking frantically.

With great reluctance, Volkov patted each horse one last time and walked down the ramp to where the station hands waited. He waited and watched as the men slid closed the train car door and placed a large padlock on the latch. Inside, the horses had already started to snort and move around nervously. Not Nar and Sar; Volkov knew the two war horses would be standing stoically.

Volkov stepped before the train worker and blocked the man's path. The worker looked at him, surprised blue eyes peeking out from a face largely concealed by a cap and a white beard.

"Sir?" the man looked at Volkov, surprised to see the huntsman standing before him.

"The key," Volkov extended his hand, palm upward.

"Sir?" the man repeated, genuinely confused at being waylaid.

"The key to the horse car," Volkov pointed toward the car with his other hand.

"I'm sorry, Sir," the man shook his head. "I cannot..."

Volkov's arm shot up, his hand closing about the man's windpipe. The man's eyes bulged in shock and pain as Volkov squeezed the man's throat.

"You will give me the key, or I will crush your throat and take it from your body as you gasp for pinpricks of air," Volkov's voice was a menacing whisper.

The man fumbled in his pocket and produced the iron key, glinting in the morning light. Volkov took the key from the man's fingers; he released his hold, turning away as the man fell to his knees, clutching his throat and gasping.

***

Volkov watched as Kirill ran his hand over the green fabric of the sofa, then eyed the oilcloth-covered walls and ceilings with disapproval as the train lurched into motion. The huntsman pinched the bridge of his nose where it intersected his brow to relieve the tension that would manifest a headache before long. Traveling with the pampered Romanov had proved far more trying on his patience than he expected. However, Volkov had to admit they would be traveling in the yellow second-class or possibly even green third-class train cars if not for Kirill's Romanov name. Instead, they lounged on sofas in a first-class car with Sergeant Razin and Batu seated across from them as "aides" to such prestigious travelers. Only Herzen and Tyutchev, two soldiers Razin had brought along as extra security, rode back in third-class.

"Where is the steward?" Kirill craned his neck to look around the car. "The wait for a bottle of wine is insufferable."

Batu, who was carefully expecting each arrow in his quiver for cracks or defects, looked at Volkov with subtle amusement in his eyes. The Mongolian tracker knew Volkov's lack of patience for the Russian elite all too well.

"The Tsar has a seven-car imperial train," Kirill lamented. "He had the walls furnished with blue silk and leather; bronze sconces illuminate the cars, and all the woodwork is an exquisite Karelian birch. You feel like you are traveling in a world-class hotel instead of a train. "

"You didn't need to come on this trip," Volkov crossed his arms across his chest as he stared darkly at the Russian aristocrat. "You could have visited St Petersburg and enjoyed your winter balls and parties."

"Spend my nights chased by those plump Perovskaya sisters looking to catch themselves a Romanov and miss this hunt?" Kirill waved a hand dismissively at Volkov. "Never."

"This is more than a hunt," a fierce look crossed Volkov's scarred and weather-beaten face. "I have hunted every manner of beast across the face of Russia for sport. But this wolf killed my brother; this is personal."

"Such passion for a brother you called a drunkard and a whoremonger just last month," Kirill leaned back on his sofa and rolled his eyes.

"I have yet to meet a Romanov I would not also count as a drunkard and a whoremonger," Volkov's noticed Razin, who had been staring intently down the row of sofas, eye the huntsman and shift uncomfortably at the flagrant insult.

"Careful, Arkady, you forget yourself," Kirill's blue eyes looked icy cold. "I would hate for Tsar Alexander to find cause to find a new Imperial Huntsman."

"Sir," Razin leaned across the aisle, his voice hushed as he spoke to Volkov. "I think your tracker is drawing attention."

Razin gestured with his head toward a seating area several rows back. Three men sat on a pair of sofas; a table adorned with an unopened bottle of wine and three empty glasses sat between them. Two of the men sat with their backs to Volkov, however, a gaunt, hawkish-looking man with thinning hair and a dark mustache sat facing the front of the train car and talking loudly. Judging from the expression of disapproval and constant looks in Batu's direction, there was no question on the topic of conversation.

"My God, man, have you no sense of decorum?" Kirill rolled his eyes as Volkov turned to stare in the direction Razin indicated. "You gawk like a man accustomed to riding in a cattle car."

"Then you will like this even less," Volkov turned back to sneer at Kirill before sliding off the sofa and heading back toward the three men.

The Tsar's huntsman strolled to the men's table, catching the mustached man's eye and noticing the man lowering his voice as Volkov approached.

"Gentlemen, good afternoon," Volkov let a feral grin cross his face. "I could not help but notice your perturbance. Is there something I can help you with?"

The two younger men, whom Volkov took for the mustached man's sons or junior business associates, looked down at the table uncomfortably. The mustached man, however, met Volkov's gaze confidently and nodded.

"Is that," the man paused as if trying to get a bad taste from his mouth, "passenger traveling with you?"

"And which passenger would that be?" Volkov feigned ignorance as he looked from the man to where Batu and Razin sat.

"That man, the Chinaman," he pointed at Batu, "is he traveling with you?"

"Why, yes, he is! He's traveled with me for a great distance," Volkov grinned mirthlessly at the man. "From the court of the Chinese emperor, in fact."

"Well, this is the Russian Empire," the Mustache Man's expression was pure smugness as he folded his arms across his chest. "China is not a part of it yet."

"Sir, it's just that this is a first-class carriage," one of the men, a finely dressed blonde man in his early twenties, spoke, then hushed himself as the man next to him nudged him to be quiet.

Volkov looked about as if noticing the car for the first time, then back at the young man who averted his eyes, "Why, I believe you are right. This is undoubtedly the first-class carriage."

"Sir, I will have you know that I am in charge of the largest ore-smelting foundry in the Donets coalfields, and I paid good money not to travel with passengers who should be traveling in the greens," the mustached man gestured toward Batu. "For heaven's sake, the man has arrows, like an American savage."

"Greens?" Volkov cocked his head and stroked his chin.

"The color of the outside of the carriages, Sir," the blonde man offered. "First-class cars are painted blue, second-class yellow, and green for third-class."

"Ah, yes," Volkov turned back to the mustache man. "You think my companion should be riding in third-class."

"It is only right," the man nodded. "This carriage is for first-class passengers only."

"Well, there is only one problem with that," Volkov rolled up his sleeves and placed his hands on the table. The man's eyes widened at the thick lines of deep scars running the length of Volkov's arms. "You were right; my companion is quite the savage, especially when angered. He did this to me over the slightest insult."

The eyes of all three men poured over the deep scars. The two younger men exchanged disquieted glances while the mustached-man licked his lips nervously.

"I will relay to him your request to remove himself to third-class," Volkov rolled his sleeves down and stood. "Batu!"

The Mongolian tracker leaned over to look at Volkov, his eyes cold and his face expressionless.

"Now hold on, Sir," the mustache-man placed his hand on Volkov's arm and swallowed visibly. "That's not necessary; he does not seem to be bothering anyone. Let's just let sleeping dogs lie."

"Oh, no, Sir. You are quite right. You paid to travel with first-class passengers; he should accommodate your request and move back to the greens," Volkov turned back to the tracker. "No matter how foul his mood."

"That's really not necessary," the blonde man said, fear etched across his young face. "My associate spoke in error. He made a terrible mistake."

"But I have already called to him," Volkov gestured toward Batu. "He already knows we have been speaking about him. Whatever would I tell him?"

"Tell him we send our regards and welcome him to Russia," the blonde man's eyes darted to the table, and then he lit with excitement as he grabbed the wine bottle and offered it to Volkov. "Here, a gesture of our hospitality."

The mustache-man opened his mouth to protest but the third man cut him off, "You can order another bottle Mr. Zimin."

Zimin sank back on his sofa in defeat and reluctantly nodded his agreement as the blonde man extended the bottle to Volkov.

"Well, I think I can make this work," Volkov took the bottle from the man and then scooped the three glasses from the table. "Of course, if there is no placating him, moving forward into the next first-class carriage may be advisable."

"This is the only first-class carriage on this train," Zimin protested.

"That's fine; we'll move to second-class; it's not a long trip to Kalinin," the blonde man quickly interjected.

As Volkov headed back toward Kirill, he could hear the men getting up and moving to the next carriage. The whoosh of passing air and the sound of the train's wheels churning on the rails filled the room as the men opened the door and passed to the next train car. Kirill watched him approach, a slight appreciative smile on his face.

"Here's your fucking wine," Volkov handed the bottle to Kirill as he sat heavily on the sofa.

"Romanian Palugyay," Kirill appraised the bottle with great delight as he freed the cork and filled his glass. "I may not approve of your tactics, but I admire the results."

Volkov offered a glass to Batu, who shook his head.

"Arkady, you know I do not drink," the tracker's voice was soft and measured.

"Excellent," Kirill took a deep sip from his glass. "Batu, you deprive yourself of one of the finest joys in life."

"I thank you kindly, Sir," Razin nodded as the huntsman offered him the tracker's glass of wine. The sergeant tipped the glass back and finished the drink with one deep swallow.

"Sergeant Razin, it is a fine wine, not cheap vodka," Kirill shook his head with obvious disapproval.

"I'm going to check on Herzen and Tyutchev," the Cossack sergeant said, standing and nodding to Kirill.

"Go, see to your men," Kirill gave a dismissive wave, then looked at Volkov as he took another sip of wine. "Sergeant Razin still believes our trip is ill-fated. He would have brought a whole garrison with us if he could."

"Chinggis Khan taught my people that one arrow alone can be easily broken, but many arrows together are indestructible," Batu examined the tip of one of his arrows as he spoke. "So I think there is great wisdom in his actions."

"So, do you think this hunt is too dangerous, Batu?" Kirill eyed the tracker with mild amusement.

"The strength of walls depends on the courage of those who guard them," Batu continued his examination of the arrow without looking up. "Sergeant Razin has a warrior's heart, so with him guarding your wall, I believe you are in safe hands, Kirill Romanov."

"Are you guarding my wall, Batu?" Volkov raised an eyebrow as he looked at the tracker.

Batu placed the arrow in his lap and looked at Volkov, "Chinggis Khan also taught that you have no companions but your shadow. Arkady Volkov, I am your shadow."

"Well, then," Kirill refilled his glass of wine and raised it in a toast. "To killing the beast and to Dimitri Volkov."

Volkov nodded in approval and raised his glass before taking a sip. Batu frowned as he watched the two men drink; the rich dark-colored wine gave the men's lips a slightly rosy appearance, which the tracker thought looked too much like blood. His frown deepened; the tracker put little stock in signs and portents; however, his mother's superstitions concerning evil omens to start a journey echoed in his head.

Chapter 15

The nightmare returned. The jarring and disorienting sensation of his mind tearing its way back to consciousness as he awakes in darkness. He is gasping for air as his mouth fills with a thin fabric, his lungs pumping like a bellow, seeking oxygen. He tries to bring his hands up to his face to pull the fabric away, but a weight confines him from all sides. His heart is thudding widely in his chest, echoing in his ears, as he begins to panic, trapped in the confined space.

In the darkness, his eyes open wide as a burst of adrenaline courses through his body, accelerating his heartbeat and causing his limbs to tremble. He tries to scream, but he cannot dislodge the fabric sucked into his mouth by his attempts at breath. The edges of his teeth feel long and sharp against his lolling tongue, and he begins to bite and tear at the fabric, shredding the thin cloth. As the fabric tears, dirt pours into his mouth and face. He can now move his arms and legs as he tears at the fabric and claws at the dirt.

He's trapped, buried. The thought screams through his mind in desperate terror.

His back and shoulders push upwards against the smothering earth as his limbs savagely tear against it. He feels the weight against him giving way, and he strains with all his muscles to drive his body forward. One arm pushes through into open space, and he drives his head forward, pushing relentlessly against the yielding earth.

He bursts forth from his terrestrial confinement like a babe birthing from an earthen womb. His head pushes into the cold night air as he coughs the earth from his mouth and blinks it from his eyes. On all fours, he pulls himself from the hole and shakes the dirt from his body.

The fresh air fills his lungs in great heaving gasps as he crawls forward. The scents and sounds of the forest around overwhelm his senses as his eyes adjust to the moonlight. A ravenous hunger roils his insides with such severity he nearly cries out in pain.

He halts and raises his nose to the air; a musky odor rides on the night breeze. Without understanding why, he's suddenly running on all fours, a deeper primal subconscious driving him forward as he enters the forest. Trees and brush stream past him as he moves with a speed and adeptness he had never before possessed. The musky scent grows stronger as he hears rushing water from the nearby river. The forest is thinning, becoming less dense, and he realizes he is nearing the bank of the river. Something dark moves before him, and his legs propel him forward, leaping through the last of the brush.

As he clears the forest, he catches sight of the young buck drinking deeply from the cool river water. The deer senses his presence moments too late to escape as his jaws close about the doomed creature's neck. Cartilage and muscle snap and tear beneath his jaws, filling his mouth with the warm, salty taste of blood as he drives the deer to the ground.

He feeds ravenously on the deer, satiating the hunger inside him, then edges toward the river to quench his thirst. As his eyes clear the bank, he catchest sight of himself. His gray lupine reflection stares back at him, his long muzzle slick with the deer's blood and gore. The image jars him; the long fingerlike digits of his front paws dig into the earth as he peers closer at the reflection. His muscular shoulders appear in the reflection, broad and covered in gray fur.

He turns and sees the savaged form of the buck; its throat torn open, and its body cavity gaping and hollow from where he feasted upon the creature's heart, liver, and lungs. The deer's eye, a dark, sightless orb, is open, and he can see the bright shape of the moon's reflection above in its stare.

From deep within his body, a scream wells up and bursts forth from his open mouth, a long, mournful howl that shatters the quiet of the night and echoes through the trees.

Alexei awoke; the recurring memory of that first night haunted his dreams. He had passed out and awoke naked in the forest, the deer's blood still coating his mouth and neck. Terrified and uncomprehending, Alexei fled to Leo's house, seeking his friend's assistance. However, he accomplished little more than breaking Leo's window, likely scaring him half to death. Leo must have cut himself on the window because Alexei's nostrils picked up the strong scent of blood.

He returned to his house, though he was careful not to be seen. Alexei gathered from his grave that people thought him dead. Memories of his injuries at the hands of Rostov and Balkov flooded his mind, though as he examined his body, only a faint redness and scarring remained on the skin above his injuries. He ran his fingers over the pink scars that marked the wolf creature's bite on his leg. Tapping the healed bite wound with his finger, Alexei knew that was the key to all this.

The creature that bit him was neither wholly wolf nor man but something in between, much the way he had been when he awoke in what was undeniably his grave. The connection was unmistakable, and Alexei felt he was living one of Leo's fairy tales. He had died; Alexei was sure of it; yet somehow he had returned from beyond as a man-wolf? A wolf-man? Why? To seek revenge for what happened to him? To protect his friends? And how could this happen?

"Fucking Baba Yaga," Alexei shook his head. He did not know whether to laugh or cry.

Alexei sat in the pile of old rags where Ivan had slept in life, missing the loyal dog. Despite the insanity of his current circumstances, Alexei grieved the loss deeply. He always knew Ivan would wander into the woods one day and never return, the victim of a hunter's trap or predator, or at best, slowly fail as the frailties of age overtook the dog. Their lives were too short in even the best of circumstances. In Imperial Russia, to be a dog was not to live a happy existence. Villagers frequently treated the creatures with cruelty and abuse; however, Alexei took solace in knowing that was never the life Ivan had known.

He leaned against the wall and closed his eyes, welcoming the darkness. At the moment, everything felt overwhelming; Alexei wished he could sit down with Leo or Bogdan and talk through it all. Try to make some sense of things.

Alexei first detected it in the quiet darkness—a glimmer of something in his mind, akin to a thought but not his own. It brushed over his consciousness like the shadow of a cloud across a meadow. He recognized a presence in his mind distinct from his own, a bundle of primal instincts and senses pulsating in the corner of his head.

Was this the wolf?

The thought both thrilled and terrified him.

The feeling was like that of another sentient, conscious mind in his head; it accompanied a sensation like approaching the door of a burning home—the wood straining to contain the fire within. Alexei could feel the raw and feral power emanating from the presence, yearning for him to open the door and unleash it. He was unsure how the wolf emerged as he struggled to free himself from the grave or what called it back behind the door after he satiated himself upon the deer. Alexei speculated that perhaps his extreme distress while trapped beneath the earth unleashed the beast, transforming him, and then receded as he lapsed into sleep. He wondered if it was something he could control, summon upon demand, or was the beast the master of him? It might never happen again; or this was all in his imagination?

Perhaps his brain had been injured in the assault by Rostov and Balkov.

Voices approaching his house brought Alexei's thoughts back to the here and now. He could make out the sound of at least two men talking as he crawled across the floor to the front window. Alexei peered out the window, moving the edge of the faded gray curtain only slightly to avoid detection.

The brothers, Alexander and Nicolai Chernyshevsky, walked towards his house, hunting rifles slung over their shoulders. He could see tall, thin Nicolai carrying an axe in one hand while his shorter, stockier brother gripped a shovel. The men were nearly one hundred feet away, and Alexei was surprised at how clearly he could hear them speaking, even the sound of their footfalls upon the damp earth. He sniffed the air, sure he detected the sour scent of the men's body odor and the onions on their breath. He should not be able to hear or smell them at this distance, though a wolf would. The thought intrigued him, and Alexei filed the thought in the back of his mind to explore further.

Hopefully, they are just passing by. Even as the thought crossed Alexei's mind, his stomach knotted with fear as he listened to their conversation.

"But how do you know he had gold?" Alexander's speech sounded slow like he was struggling with the thought.

"He's a Jew," Nicolai snapped back, and Alexei suspected he had explained his reasoning to Alexander several times already. "Everyone knows that Jews hide a pot of gold in their house."

"But Alexei never looked like he had gold."

"Exactly. That's because Alexei never spent it; he kept it hidden away," responded Nicolai.

Alexander nodded, then looked around the clearing as they approached the house, "Where do we look for it?"

"In the house," Nicolai pointed toward Alexei's home. "My guess is he buried the gold under his bed, where he could sleep on top of it every night."

"That's why we brought the axe and shovel," Alexander smiled and nodded. "To chop through the floorboards and dig up the gold."

"That's right, brother," Nicolai slapped Alexander on the shoulder. "We'll be as rich as Morozov!"

"Richer!"

"Richer," Nicolai grinned and nodded his agreement.

Alexei let the curtain slip back into place as the brothers approached the house. The Chernyshevskys were coming in to search the home; his pulse quickened with fear as his eyes searched the room for anything he could use as a weapon. He had lost his father's gun and his knife, leaving him with only some dull kitchen utensils and an old pot. Escape seemed the better option. The house only had one door but, he could slip out the bedroom window and hide in the forest until they left.

Alexei ran into his bedroom, shutting and locking the door, just as the sound of an axe striking the front door echoed through the home. The brothers were chopping at the makeshift locking bolt he had worked to replace the snapped lock. He did not have much time before they were in the house. As quietly as he could, using the brothers' chopping to mask the sound, Alexei slid his bed up against the door. His heart thudded, and panic sweat dotted his forehead as he ran for the room's window.

Just as Alexei reached the window, a jolt of adrenaline so powerful it brought him to his knees coursed through his body. Alexei's vision went black, his head swooning, as his body began to shake. He felt the door burst open in his mind, unleashing a feral ferocity.

He was only vaguely aware of the sound of the front door giving way under the assault by the Chernyshevskys and the two men entering the house. Alexei stared in disbelief at his arms as they thickened with muscle and sprouted long gray hairs. His hands elongated into paws with fingerlike digits tipped with sharp, curled claws as his legs transformed from human to lupine appendages. As he felt his tailbone grow into a length of tail, Alexei opened his mouth to scream as his face extended into a wolf-like snout, but no sound emerged. He collapsed to the ground, curling into a fetal position as the rest of his body completed its transformation.

Alexei's hearing became even more acute, picking up the sound of the Chernyshevsky brothers ransacking the house in search of gold. He rose onto all four legs, the offensive smell of the brothers filling his nostrils, and then onto his hind legs. The soft skin of his tongue ran over the jagged points of his teeth—wolf teeth. As a feeling of strength and vitality surged through his limbs, Alexei turned toward the bedroom door, and the wolf's face contorted into a feral grin.

***

"This one's locked," Alexander pulled on the bedroom door, his lazy eye drifting toward the side of his face as he looked at his brother.

"I bet the gold is in there," Nicolai's eyes were alight with victory as he stepped beside his brother and hefted his axe.

Alexander licked his lips excitedly as Nicolai nodded to him. Nicolai swung the axe, striking the door and sending wood shards flying as his brother wedged the head of the shovel between the door and the doorframe.

Thwack. Thwack.

Nicolai's axe struck the door repeatedly as Alexander grunted and strained to pry the door open.

BUMP.

Something large struck the door from the other side. The brothers stepped back in surprise, the shovel tumbling from Alexander's hand to clang upon the floor. They exchanged uncertain glances, then looked at the door.

BUMP.

They both jumped at the sound, eyes opening wide in surprise. Nicolai threw down the axe and unslung his rifle as Alexander followed his lead, clumsily slipping his rifle off his shoulder and pointing it at the door.

"What was that? Is someone already here looking for the gold?" Alexander looked from the door to his brother, hands shifting nervously on his rifle.

"I don't know. Keep prying the door, and I'll cover you," Nicolai pointed at the door with his rifle.

Alexander shook his head, "No. Why don't we fire a couple of shots and see if they jump out the back window and run away?"

"You're going to let someone steal our gold? Keep prying the door," Nicolai pointed again at the door.

Alexander's shoulders sagged in defeat as he slowly walked toward the door, wincing with every creak of the floorboards. Placing his rifle against the wall, Alexander slowly picked up the shovel. The head of the shovel shook noticeably in Alexander's nervous hands as he eased it toward the door.

"Be quick about it," Nicolai hissed.

"Why don't I cover you, and you pry the d...?" As Alexander turned to look at his brother, his words caught in his throat. The immense form of a large gray wolf, standing on its hind legs, loomed directly behind Nicolai. Alexander's eyes opened wide with terror, his throat so constricted by fear that he could only produce a high-pitched keeling noise.

"What is wrong with you? Stop that awful noise," Nicolai's eyes narrowed in irritation, another sharp retort coming to his lips until he realized his brother's horror-filled gaze looked past him. He swallowed deeply and gripped his rifle tightly in now sweaty hands as he prepared to wheel on the intruder.

Before Nicolai could act, the wolf beast stepped forward and closed its arms around the man in a vice-like hug. Nicolai screamed as the wolf's snarling maw brushed against his face, the rifle dropping from his hands and discharging as it struck the floor. The loud crack of the gunshot in the small house mixed with the terrified screams of the brothers as the bright flash of the barrel illuminated the wolf in all its primal ferocity. Alexander screamed in terror, falling back against the door and sliding to the floor.

Nicolai screamed in pain and tried to break free of the wolf's grasp as it sunk its clawed fingers deep into his chest. Then, in one quick wrenching motion, the wolf tore open Nicolai's rib cage. The man's screams were inhuman as his skin tore with the ripping sound of a cotton cloth, and his ribs snapped like dried twigs. His eyes rolled in his head as his body convulsed violently and emptied his internal organs upon the wooden floor.

Alexander screamed, vacating his bladder, as the wolf released the dead husk of his brother to topple to the floor. Nicolai struck the floor, landing in a heap amidst the blood and gore of his innards. The wolf stared at the warm organs on the floor, licking the dripping saliva from its lips. Then it turned as if noticing Alexander for the first time.

The wolf stepped toward him, its gray paws splashing through the pooling blood on the floor. Alexander's eyes opened wide, and he shook his head vigorously, unable to believe what was happening, as the beast approached. In desperation, Alexander reached for his rifle, leaning against the wall. However, when his fingers were so close they could almost feel the wood of the weapon's stock, the wolf's massive paw slammed down on the rifle, splintering the stock and bending the barrel.

Alexander looked up at the beast, staring fearfully into the malicious glare of the wolf's eyes as his lousy eye drifted toward the corner of the room. He had hunted and killed animals in the forests around Obrechen with Nicolai since he was a small child. His favorite part was coming across a creature trapped in one of his traps; the look of fear that filled the animal's eyes always excited him. The feeling that he, Alexander, held the power of life and death over the creature made him feel almighty, like a god. Alexander liked to watch the animal's growing fear spiral into a terrified frenzy as it struggled to break free of the trap, tearing at its ensnared limb to escape; the unbridled look of terror in their eyes aroused him unlike anything else.

Alexander now bore that same look in his eyes as the wolf's claws tore into his body. He was no longer aware of the screams that passed his lips as his body rocked, blood spurting from his mouth as the creature tore free a dark reddish-brown, cone-shaped organ from his ravaged torso and gorged upon it.

***

"You were the best dog," Alexei said as he laid his hand on the small mound of earth that marked Ivan's resting place. "I'm sorry this happened to you."

Behind him, the sound of cracking and popping wood signaled the fire he had set in his house was beginning to catch. He could not stay here any longer, and the thought of villagers scavenging his house and defiling his parents' home appalled him. It was better to let the flames take it all and the corpses of the Chernyshevsky brothers along with it.

"You were my best friend and always loyal. I will never forget that. I will never forget you, Ivan." Alexei wiped a tear from his cheek. "I'll get the ones who did this to you; I promise you that."

Alexei kept his eyes averted from the disturbed earth and torn fabric of the empty grave beside Ivan; the memory was still too vivid.

"I hope that if there is a dog heaven, you're there chasing chickens," the thought made Alexei smile, then he laughed. "Who knows? Maybe I'll go to dog heaven now too."

Alexei grabbed a handful of dirt from the grave and slipped it into a small leather pouch, closing the drawstring. He would carry the dirt with him; in a way, keeping Ivan by his side always.

"Goodbye, Ivan," Alexei laid his hand on the grave, biting his lip to hold back the emotion. He imagined his hand resting upon the dog's head, fingers running through his fur, as Ivan sat by his side, and wished harder than he had for anything since his parents died that he could do that again.

Alexei stood, securing the small leather pouch on his belt and slinging a bag with his last few possessions over his shoulder. He slipped into the woods, leaving the clearing as the flames consumed his home.

Transforming into a wolf had a ravenous effect on his body, a hunger he had satiated with the brothers' hearts, livers, and lungs. He knew from his father's hunting lessons that these were the most vital parts of an animal, rich in nutrients. The thought of consuming human flesh repulsed him, yet it felt as natural as drinking water or breathing air when he was the wolf.

His second transformation into the wolf form had been less jarring than the first time, and he could assess the changes. Alexei's mind remained in complete control, though a feral instinct lurked beneath the surface of his thoughts, and he suspected that in a moment of surprise or duress, he might unwittingly respond as a wolf would. The most significant change Alexei detected was the heightening of his senses of hearing, sight, and smell to a level of acuity far beyond a human's ability. His strength, too, seemed magnified to many times greater than that of even a strong man. The most disturbing aspect of his transformation was the presence of a tail. Something about the wagging appendage just felt wrong to Alexei.

Alexei could feel the wolf's presence pulsing behind that door in his head. The stress of discovery by the Chernyshevskys had released the wolf, though he wondered if he reached out in his mind and opened that door if he could summon the wolf on demand. He would experiment once he found someplace safe to hide out.

Alexei felt no pain or discomfort during the transformation into the wolf or his body's return to its natural form. That shocked him, considering the drastic reconfiguration of his skin and bones. He surmised that whatever mystical force was responsible for his condition was not subject to the customary laws of science and the human body.

Once his appetite was satisfied and the adrenaline rush of the confrontation with the Chernyshevskys passed, Alexei rapidly transformed back into human form, leaving him curled naked on the floor amidst a full coat of shed gray fur. In addition to trying to summon the wolf on demand, Alexei wanted to see if he could learn to keep its form until he wished to shift back.

So much to learn and master.

As he walked deeper into the forest, keeping alert to steer clear of any roaming villagers, troubling thoughts crept into his mind.

Had the wolf that bit him been some magical beast, or was it a wolf-man like him?

Where was it now?

Would Alexei's bite spread this wolf power like a disease?

If it was another wolf-man, was it a stranger lurking in the woods or someone in Obrechen?

If so, who?

Chapter 16

Bogdan squinted as he stepped into the bright afternoon sunlight, allowing his eyes to adjust as he stepped from the barn. He clutched a bottle in one hand as he walked the short distance to the cottage. Galina sat on the porch, slumped in her chair and staring out into the forest, lost in thought. She had spent most of the past two days in that chair, leaving only to sleep and use the bathroom.

He did not blame Galina; Bogdan had lost his love and spent long days dwelling in darkness. She was entitled to her grief. However, Bogdan knew how easy it could be for someone to succumb to despair and slip from this world. He had nearly done so himself and feared Galina was quickly heading down that path.

Galina watched a hawk circling in the sky, her eyes red-rimmed from crying, oblivious to Bogdan's approach, even as he mounted the steps to the porch. As his shadow spread over her, Galina snapped out of her daze and turned her startled eyes toward him.

"Bogdan," Galina appeared confused by his sudden appearance. "I... I didn't notice you standing there."

"Hold this," Bogdan placed the bottle of pale-yellow liquid in her hands and walked into the cottage, leaving the door open. "Where is Oksana?"

"She went to place flowers on Alexei's grave," Galina's voice sounded distant and dreamy as she eyed the bottle.

Bogdan emerged from the house holding two glasses and sat down beside her. He took the bottle from her and placed one of the empty glasses in her hand. Tilting the bottle toward his mouth, Bogdan pulled the cork out with his teeth and sent it tumbling into the dirt with a puff of his lips. She looked from the cork to Bogdan in astonishment. He smiled and winked as he filled his glass half-full with the liquid, then leaned over and did the same for hers.

Galina sniffed the glass and wrinkled her nose in surprise at the pungent aroma of fruit and alcohol, "What is this?"

"It's called Țuică," Bogdan breathed deeply of the drink's aroma and smiled. "I brought a bottle from Romania. They ferment the finest plums and heat them in a copper still over a fire made of wood from the Hoia Forest. Strong Romanian trees, not these sickly Russian twigs."

Bogdan waved his hand to encompass the surrounding forest. A mischievous grin crossed his face, "Little lady, we're going to get drunk—blind fucking drunk."

Galina gave him a wistful smile, "Bogdan, that's very kind of you, but I don't think that will help. Besides, my stomach has been giving me fits." She rubbed a hand across her belly.

"Your stomach hurts because it is too empty, and your heart aches because it is too full," Bogdan leaned over and clinked his glass against her. "So, we drink to fill our stomachs and empty our hearts."

"If only I could speak to Mali. I'm sure I could fix this," Galina looked down into the glass of yellow liquid.

Bogdan took a sip and exhaled through his teeth as he swallowed the strong drink.

"Would you have just stood there like she did?" Bogdan held his glass of *Țuică* up to the sunlight and watched the rays dance through the yellow liquid.

Galina sighed and shook her head, "No, I would have fought tooth and nail for her."

"I believe you would have," Bogdan nodded and looked sidelong at her. "And I think you deserve someone that would do the same. Nothing less."

Galina fell silent, looking at her hands. When Galina looked up, she slowly nodded her agreement and gave Bogdan a small, sad smile.

Bogdan leaned back and held out his arm toward her, glass slightly tilted toward her. "Fuck them." He gave her a roguish grin.

Galina's smile widened, and she clinked her glass lightly against his. "Fuck them."

They both drank. Bogdan downed the remainder of his glass, and Galina sipped the strong drink. She immediately spit the drink out in a spray of water, eliciting an uproarious laugh from Bogdan.

"Oh, come now, Galina. I know Țuică is strong, but there's no reason to... " the words died on his lips as she bent over in pain, blood trailing from her bottom lip in a thick rivulet that splattered against the floorboards. He bolted up in alarm, "Galina, what is it? What's wrong?"

The glass slipped from Galina's fingers and shattered on the floor, the yellow drink mixing with droplets of blood. A cough wracked her body, and she doubled over in pain, grabbing her stomach; flecks of blood dotted her dress.

"Bogdan, it hurts; please get me to my bed," Galina gasped through gritted teeth.

The hunter scooped her up in his arms, lifting her as effortlessly as if she were a feather. Galina groaned in pain as she curled up in his arms, laying her head against his chest; a small red stain appeared where her mouth pressed against his shirt. Bogdan wasted no time; kicking the door open with a swift blow of his boot, he rushed her into the house.

"On my bedside table, there is an amber vial; please give it to me," Galina pointed toward the table as he lay her in bed.

Bogdan picked up the small vial and freed the silver stopper with his fingers. A frown creased his brow as he gave the vial a slight shake.

"It's empty," Bogdan sniffed the vial, detecting the smell of rose water with an additional floral undertone. "What is this?"

"It's my medicine; it's the only thing that helps the pain," Galina reached for Bogdan and grabbed his hand. Her skin was pale, her brow was sweaty, and her lips looked nearly colorless except for the dark specks of blood. "You must go to Kalinin, Mali's doctor; Doctor Artyom will give you more. His office is across from the central theater."

"Galina, you need a doctor," Bogdan squeezed her hand and gave her a pleading look.

"Please, Bogdan, please just go get the medicine," Galina grimaced as another wave of pain washed over her.

"Kalinin is too far to leave you alone," Bogdan shook his head in protest.

"Take Seryy and the wagon; if you hurry, you'll be back in a few hours. Oksana will return soon; she'll stay with me," Galina said, laying her head back against the pillow and taking a long, slow breath. "The pain is subsiding. I'll be Okay."

Bogdan studied her face, concern filling his eyes. Galina closed her eyes as if to rest, however, Bogdan knew she was only doing it to prevent further protests from him. She looked so small and frail lying there that he felt his throat tighten with emotion. He could not lose her, too.

"Okay," Bogdan whispered as he nodded his head. "Okay, I'll go to Doctor Artyom."

A wave of relief appeared to wash tension from Galina's features, but she did not open her eyes. The hunter went to the kitchen and brought her a pitcher of water and glass that he filled and left on her night table.

"I'll be back soon," Bogdan said, brushing sweat-matted hair from her face with his hand. "We'll talk more about getting you to a doctor when I return."

A slight smile crossed her lips, and she nodded slightly, "Okay, Bogdan, I promise."

Bogdan turned and ran for the door.

***

Galina heard the creaking of the front door opening and leaned up on her elbows. She had dozed off as the pain receded, however, her side still burned terribly, and she felt as if her stomach had twisted into tight knots.

Late afternoon sunlight streamed in the doorway, framing the dark silhouette of a woman entering from the porch.

"Oksana," Galina's voice sounded like a hoarse whisper in her parched throat. "I'm not feeling well; I am in the bedroom. Bogdan has gone to Kalinin for medicine."

"I know. We watched him go," Olga Putina said as she stepped further into the cottage.

"Olga? What are you doing here?" Galina's confusion turned to dread as she saw Olga's brothers follow her into the cottage and close the door.

"We've come for our due," Galina's dark eyes glittered with malice as she sneered at Galina. "Get her out of bed."

Olga's brothers rushed forward into the room, their deep-set eyes fixed on Galina as she tried to free herself of her blankets. Thick arms, muscled from farm work, reached for her, and she wanted to slap them away but could not muster the strength. Galina could smell the odor of dirt and manure on the two men as they pulled her from the bed and threw her down onto the floor.

Galina's hands and knees took the brunt of the impact with the hard wooden floor, however, it was the intense flash of pain in her midsection that caused her to cry out and nearly lose consciousness.

She felt a wave of bile rise in her throat mixed with the iron taste of blood.

"Olga, please," Galina gasped, spraying tiny droplets of blood onto the floor.

"Stand her up," Olga commanded as she prodded at Galina with the toe of her shoe.

Galina felt a hand grasp a handful of her hair and pull upward as the other brother did the same with her shoulder. She screamed as the hand wrenching her hair felt like it would tear the scalp from her head, and she felt a rush of warm tears run down her face.

As they brought her unsteadily to her feet, the brother holding Galina's hair let go and roughly grabbed her other arm as her head dipped forward, and she began to topple forward.

Olga's hand gripped Galina's chin and tilted her head upright, "Where is the gold the Count gave you?"

At that moment, Galina felt a surge of anger at her treatment by her father, Mali, Gennady, the whole village of Obrechen, and now these people. She wanted to spit a wad of bloody phlegm into Olga's spiteful face and tell her to go fuck off. Let them beat her. Let them kill her. Galina did not care anymore; she felt done with this world, and she was ready for the world to finish inflicting its pain on her.

Galina knew that if she did not tell them, they would search the house until they found it. It may take them long enough for Bogdan to get back and rescue her. He would deal brutally with the brothers for hurting her, of that she was sure. However, he was still likely hours away from the cottage; no, he would not return in time to save her. Then, a terrible thought crossed her mind.

What if they were still here when Oksana returned?

They could hurt her, possibly even kill her, and Galina could not let that happen.

Galina slowly raised an arm and pointed toward her wardrobe, "It's in there."

Olga's eyes lit with excitement, and a grin split her weather face, showing a mouthful of yellowing teeth. She rushed to the wardrobe like a raccoon chasing a fleeing meal and yanked open the wardrobe doors. Galina had felt no need to hide the purse of coins away, so Olga located the pouch quickly. The woman stepped back from the wardrobe with a triumphant shout as she felt the heft of the purse in her hands.

She reached into the purse, pulled out a handful of coins, and cackled joyfully, "Boys, we're rich!"

The brothers laughed, breathing foul breath down upon Galina, adding to their reek and making her nauseous.

"You got what you wanted; now go," Galina spat the words out as she fought against the pain in her abdomen.

"Go?" Olga's eyes narrowed as she walked to stand before Galina, her smile turning wicked. "The Tsarina is still giving orders to the peasants."

Galina held Olga's gaze; she would not give this vile woman the satisfaction of seeing the fear that coursed through her veins.

Olga moved her face close to Galina's, the woman's spittle dotting Galina's cheeks as she spoke. "Now it's your turn to kneel, whore." On either side of her, the brothers tightened their grip on Galina's arms, vice-like and painful.

Galina barely detected the movement of Olga's arm until she felt the blow in her midsection. Air escaped from Galina's body in a rush as she doubled over in pain, the brothers releasing their grip as she crumbled to the floor. She heard Olga curse in disgust as she wiped Galina's blood-flecked saliva from her face.

The pain in Galina's side was so excruciating she struggled to catch her breath. Galina stared in shock as her hand came away from her side covered in blood. Only then did she look at Olga and realize the woman clutched a knife in her hand, red and slick with Galina's blood. She was stabbed, not punched. *Stabbed.*

"Take anything we can use or sell and put it in the cart. We'll burn the rest," Olga told her brothers as she wiped the bloody knife on Galina's sheets.

One of the brothers thudded past Galina to search the kitchen while the other began to rifle through her nightstand. The man seemed to delight in throwing anything glass to the floor to shatter into glittering snowflakes of glass. Galina shielded her eyes to ward off a shower of glass from a perfume bottle thrown against the wall.

The other brother searched the kitchen, shoving silver dining utensils into his pocket. He halted only to take the butterfly picture from its easel and smash it over one of the kitchen chairs as he laughed. Meanwhile, Olga was pulling dresses from Galina's wardrobe, collecting ones she wished to keep and tossing the rest to the floor.

"I bet that Englishman would like me in this," Olga held the dress up against her body and turned to show her brother. It was a red dress, a favorite of Mali's that Galina had worn for her one spring afternoon; the defilement would have brought a tear to Galina's eye if she was not so overcome with pain.

Galina lay curled on the floor, futilely trying to staunch the flow of her lifeblood pooling in a dark puddle beside her. She felt cold and dizzy, as if in a fog. The searing pain seemed to dull slightly, and Galina knew that was likely her brain starting to respond sluggishly.

"Put this in the wagon," Olga held the dress out, and her brother reluctantly ceased his destruction and grabbed the dress. The man stepped toward the door but returned to the bed and snatched one of Galina's pillows.

"It's soft and smells nice," he said to Olga.

"Don't you put that dress where it will get dirty; I want it all nice and like," she told him before returning to search the wardrobe.

Galina laid her head on the floor; she could feel tiny shards of glass cold against her cheek but no longer cared. Darkness swam at the edges of her vision, and she curled into what her mother used to call her favorite sleeping position.

There are so many tufts of dust under here.

The thought felt distant in Galina's mind. Her world now consisted of what she could see in the foot of space between the floor and the bottom of the bed. Galina watched the brother's feet stomp off with the pillow and dress. She could see the legs of the brother noisily moving about the kitchen, stealing or destroying anything he found. Closest to her were the legs that belonged to Olga, surrounded by a mounting pile of discarded dresses on the floor.

A shadow fell across the door to the cottage, signaling the brother's return. However, it was not the brother; the legs were different. Instead of the thick, mud-crusted boots and homespun trousers of the Putina brother, Galina watched as two muscular, black fur-covered legs, dog or wolf-like, slowly crossed the floor. She could see large paws tipped with black claws and the shadow of the creature's tail on the ground, but her brain struggled to process what she saw.

Galina felt like she was watching one of the cinema films that traveling fairs showed in the Tsar's palace. The creature's legs stealthily approached the brother in the kitchen, who had his back to the newcomer. The creature's legs rushed forward in a sudden rush of movement, just as Galina saw the brother's feet turn toward it. The man's legs went stiff as a sound like someone sticking their finger in a fresh pie reached her ears. Then his body slowly lowered to the floor, his head lolled as it made contact with the wooden boards, and his face tilted toward Galina. Two gaping holes looked out from where his deep-set, beady eyes had sat, streams of blood running from them like rivers. The man's mouth appeared frozen in the silent rigor of a scream. Galina let out a squeal of pure terror as her mind rushed back into awareness.

"Shut up and die, whore," Galina heard Olga yell at her.

Galina tried to speak as she saw the creature's feet turn and approach the bedroom. However, she could produce no further sound from her trembling lips. As it crossed the threshold into the room, Galina tried to curl into a small ball and wished she could pull a blanket from the bed to hide beneath as she clamped a blood-slick hand across her mouth to prevent any sound. She could not slide a blanket from the bed without alerting the beast to her presence.

Beneath the bed.

Galina heard Olga scream in terror as the creature's paws rushed forward. Horrible cracking, tearing, and gurgling sounds filled the room as blood splashed down onto the discarded dresses in what seemed to Galina to look like a waterfall. She used the cacophony of death to mask the noise of her sliding beneath the bed.

There was a sound like a thick blanket torn asunder and then a sickeningly squishy thud as the room fell silent. Galina's eyes opened wide, and she had to bite her hand to keep from screaming as she turned her head and saw Olga's body. The woman's head and spine were torn backward like a de-boned fish. Olga's twitching hands made a slight tapping sound on the floor until they finally stilled.

Galina feared that the terrified shaking of her own body would make a similar sound on the floor and reveal her hiding place. One of the creature's legs disappeared, and then the other, as the bed above her, bulged downward until the mattress touched her face.

It's on the bed.

She could hear the creature sniffing the air, and then the weight above her shifted. Two large, hand-like paws slid off the bed toward a dark puddle on the floor, and Galina realized in horror that it was her pooled blood. The paws had long clawed fingers, like a giant raccoon, covered in gore from the slaughtered Putinas.

The weight on the bed eased further and then disappeared as the creature's two hind paws stepped off the bed. Galina held her breath, too terrified to breathe, as the beast lowered its massive, black, wolf-like head to sniff the pooled blood. She could see its black fur was slick with blood and glistened in the light.

The creature went deathly still and raised its head beyond where Galina could see from her hiding spot, and she feared that the beast had detected Oksana or Bogdan returning. She would cry out and warn them, even though it meant her life. Galina knew that she was dying; she had lost too much blood. However, if her death meant she could save them, then maybe that was worth something.

Suddenly, the beast's head reappeared; this time, it faced directly beneath the bed. It stared right into Galina's eyes, and she screamed. The creature lunged forward, trying to fit its massive frame beneath the bed as Galina scrambled to slide out the other side. Her illness and injury had made her limbs respond sluggishly, and she felt as if she was trying to flee through water. The bed bounced and jolted above her as the creature forced its massive bulk beneath it. She could hear its claws scratching at the floor and its hot breath upon her legs. Galina's hair and back were soaked with Olga's blood as she reached the far side of the bed and slid her head out, fingers clutching the bedframe.

"Run!" Galina screamed. "Flee! Get away from here."

Galina desperate scream turned to one of pain as she felt the beast's teeth sink into her calf. Her energy expended, Galina felt her body slacken as tears for all that was lost streamed down her cheeks.

"Run Bogdan. Run Oksana. Live," the words escaped her lips like a tear-filled whisper.

The room was deathly still. The beast's teeth held her fast, the heavy breaths of its exertion puffing onto her bloody leg.

Galina's fingers shook from the strain and then slid free of the bedframe. Her limp hands did not have time to strike the floor before her body was pulled along the rough wood of the floorboards.

Galina's fleeting view of the room slid away in a blur, replaced by darkness as she was pulled beneath the bed.

About the Author

Jack Finn is an award winning horror author and active Horror Writers Association member living in the wilds of the Pacific Northwest with his wife and two fiendishly clever dogs. He is a lifelong believer that the Tooth Fairy proves you can trade body parts for cold, hard cash. Jack is on Instagram, Threads, Bluesky ,and Twitter @TheRealJackFinn